REROUTE

THE NEW WORLD SERIES | BOOK FOUR

Stephen Llewelyn

FOSSIL ROCK PUBLISHING

Published by Fossil Rock Publishing 2021

ISBNs:
978-1-8382125-2-0 hardcover
978-1-8382125-0-6 paperback
978-1-8382125-1-3 ebook

For Sally
Thank you for your unwavering commitment to the cause.

The author also wishes to acknowledge:
Mum and Dad, Bill and Les for your extensive help through an immensely difficult time. Thanks to Sally-Marie and Melanie for all the reads, re-reads and support. Fossil Rock for making this book happen. To my long-suffering friends for your encouragement and help in spreading the word.

Special thanks to Allyson Coleman, who gave her name to a new character within the series. Also, to the experts who took time out of their frantic schedules to answer my emails and questions about our favourite subject. Cheers.

...And last but by no means least, to everyone who reads this book and enjoyed its predecessors, a sincere thank you.

The crew of the USS *New World* will return soon in
THE NEW WORLD SERIES | BOOK FIVE | REMAINS.

No dinosaurs were harmed during the making of this book.

Many of us have suffered loss during this most difficult time. I hope this story provides a little escapism for anyone who's hurting, as it did for me. We're all in this together, so please take care of yourselves and one another...

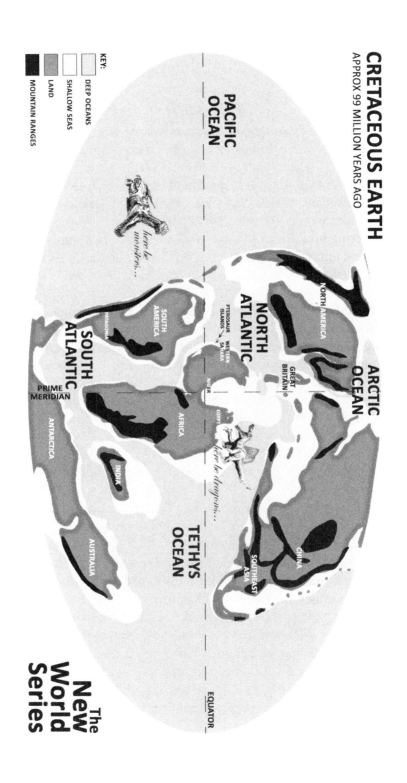

CRETACEOUS EARTH

APPROX 99 MILLION YEARS AGO

KEY:

- DEEP OCEANS
- SHALLOW SEAS
- LAND
- MOUNTAIN RANGES

PACIFIC OCEAN

NORTH AMERICA

ARCTIC OCEAN

NORTH ATLANTIC

PTEROSAUR ISLANDS

WESTERN SAHARA

GREAT BRITAIN

NIGER

EGYPT

here be monsters...

SOUTH AMERICA

PATAGONIA

SOUTH ATLANTIC

PRIME MERIDIAN

AFRICA

here be dragons...

ANTARCTICA

INDIA

TETHYS OCEAN

AUSTRALIA

CHINA

SOUTHEAST ASIA

EQUATOR

The New World Series

Prologue

He knelt in the grand audience chamber. His mission would lead to bloodshed, he knew, but he must have his way. The consequences otherwise would be catastrophic for their cause. The only potential stumbling block was the woman seated before him. Her weakness regarding her sister could spell doom for them all. Despite loathing the girl, still she would not act.

Considering how hopeful things had seemed in her grandfather's day, the lady's family had since brought nothing but darkness to their great land – at least during the last twenty years. He could see it no other way, and the clouds were certainly gathering once more.

He glanced up expectantly. She looked ill, worse than on his last visit, just a week ago. He so badly needed her to live, but whatever was wrong, it was serious. Should she also contract the influenza ravaging the land, her end might come even more quickly than feared. Either way, she could not be much longer for this world.

Of course, he would not dare utter that thought aloud, not in *any* company. Such words cost men their lives these days.

"Majesty?" he prompted.

She gave an almost imperceptible nod.

Pole smiled slyly as he rose. Bowing, he backed out of the chamber, glad to leave.

The sickness was so virulent, he had been anxious for his own safety at court, but at least he could now get to work, setting the gears in motion that would save them and, as a secondary concern, their nation. Gardiner would be delighted. They had cleared the first hurdle; the next must be approached with equal care and precision. Who knew how much time they had?

She remained seated, staring balefully at the huge, beautifully scrolled oak doors as Pole closed them behind him.

A lightning bolt of pain struck. She gasped, clutching at her lower belly. Her ladies seemed to appear from nowhere, but she waved them away crossly, ordering them from the chamber. The agony stabbed deep, wracking her whole. Concentrating with all her might, she willed it to recede and gradually it did so. One day soon, it would overwhelm her completely, she could not prevent that, but if her work were to be undone…

"*No!*" she cried out angrily. That, she would never allow.

Composed once more, she sat back, drinking in the glorious friezes painted upon the chamber's ceiling. They were scenes inspired by her beloved Bible. However, as she sat alone, pondering the full ramifications of her decision this day – for herself, for her country, for her sister – all inspiration drained away with the failing daylight. The last rays of gold lanced through grand and exquisitely stained mullioned windows, bathing the Queen of England in mocking afterglow.

Palace boys would begin the routine lighting of hundreds of candles soon, but for now, the encroaching darkness suited her mood.

"May God forgive me, and history remember me fairly," she said.

Chapter 1 | Der Reichsfarmer

A small, rectangular box lay half-buried in the sand. Slim, and no more than ten centimetres by six, it lit up with the words 'Bridge: *Heydrich*'.

Within seconds it came to life with a voice. "*Dr Schultz, this is* Heydrich*, come in. Dr Schultz?*"

A slender, female hand reached down to retrieve the comm and dusted it off.

"*Heydrich*, this is Sergeant Ally Coleman, receiving you."

"*Coleman, this is Lieutenant Devon. What's your status?*"

"Three confirmed dead, sir. Captain Nassaki is seriously injured. I've got someone checking on him now – not sure if he lives. Sir, we need a medical team here immediately."

"*Very good, Coleman. Do what you can for Nassaki. Help is already on the way – they'll arrive momentarily. Did Dr Schultz survive?*"

"We're just picking ourselves up, sir, but there's no sign of her so far. I was about to order a search when I heard this comm speaking from the sand."

"*OK, Sergeant. Begin your search and keep me posted. You should see our rescue team any second now.* Heydrich *out.*"

Pocketing the comm, Coleman approached the cave walls with care. There were many crags and crevasses, each easily large enough to hide an injured person. Unfortunately, they were large enough to hide any manner of vicious creature too, and she was unarmed.

One of the splits in the rock face turned out to be the mouth of a small cave. The light levels dropped dramatically after the first corner. Remembering the comm in her pocket, she activated the screen. She had been able to answer *Heydrich*'s call, but the device was otherwise locked, so she could not use its torch. However, in absolute blackness, even initialising the screen was helpful. Proceeding with extreme caution, she worked her way deeper.

She started at sudden movement within the shadows. Tremulously, she asked, "Dr Schultz? Is that you?"

The figure stirred once more. Eventually a voice, little more than a whisper, replied, "Leave me."

Breathing a sigh of relief, Coleman knelt before Dr Heidi Schultz. "Are you hurt, ma'am?"

"I said leave me."

"There's a med-team on the way. We'll soon have you out of here. Please, let me help you. Are you injured?"

Gradually, Coleman raised Heidi to her feet. It was too dark to be sure, but she did not appear injured. What was wrong with her? Shock, perhaps? Gently, she helped Heidi back out into the light.

"They are gone?"

"Yes, ma'am. The *New World* opened a wormhole and left. Our people scored a couple of direct hits on her, so I don't know what state she's in, but she's no longer here."

"And Tim? Has my cousin gone, too?"

"I believe so, Doctor. I'm sure he boarded the Pod, immediately before their departure."

"None of you tried to stop him?" Heidi's voice projected the first cadences of accusation.

Coleman stood her ground. "Impossible, ma'am. The dinosaur attack scattered us. It was vicious."

A medic ran over to them, flashing a penlight in Heidi's eyes and taking her pulse. She brushed him away, irritably. "Does Nassaki live?"

They watched a couple of stretcher-bearers carry an injured man to their vehicle at a jog, while a third ran alongside, working on him.

"He's in a bad way, ma'am, but he lives," answered the medic. "For now. He's suffered almost lethal exsanguination and lost his left hand. We can't find it."

"You won't," she replied, unemotionally.

A second vehicle arrived, a small four-wheel-drive, and Heidi strode towards it, shaking off any attempts to assist her.

Jumping into the passenger seat, and without greeting the driver, she ordered, "Take me back to my ship."

Shadows lengthened across the lake as a westering sun sank behind the mountains. The *Heydrich* sat motionless upon a beach, no more than half a kilometre from the vast cave mouth and former hiding place of the USS *New World*.

Heidi also sat motionless within her stateroom. She had not moved in many hours. Silent machinations, where plans for survival struggled hand-to-hand with thoughts of vengeance, had left her weary and confused. Twice she had tried to nap – no chance.

What should she do? On the plus side, she was in charge and still commanded significant resources. Her major opponents were all dead, it seemed, and the *New World* had at least left behind something vital to their continued existence – should she decide to stay here.

She stood, the better to shake off the apathy that threatened to smother her. It was time to plan their next move. Perhaps she would call a small meeting. That was how Douglas did it, and he always seemed to wriggle out from under whatever was thrown his way, *damn him!*

That decision led to a question: if she were to include others in the process, who could she trust? And of those, who *should* she trust? An ingenuous fool could be every bit as unreliable as a disingenuous genius.

She sighed. Reliance on anyone else was *hard*.

Three people had risked themselves before, coming to her rescue. In fact, Sergeant Ally Coleman, the pilot now fully recovered from her sprained ankle, had come for her twice.

When the woman had fallen behind some weeks ago after a dinosaur attack at the river in Patagonia, Heidi almost left her to fend for herself. Had Coleman died in those events, Heidi would have remained her grandfather's prisoner, or his victim.

Perhaps there was something to Douglas' philosophy, after all? Perhaps she *was* too willing to discard assets as soon as they became less useful – less useful did not necessarily mean *useless*, it seemed.

More confusion. Tim had really messed with her mind. Everything had always been so black and white until *he* came among them, spreading his poison like an indiscernible toxin in the water supply – a poison without taste or smell, but which pervaded long after the source was removed.

Heidi had held him prisoner, at least at first. Yet despite all the power being in her hands, she had fallen under attack without even realising it. Her early life had not been an upbringing, it had been a *design*. Finely tooled into a weapon, her enemies had always been clear – had been *made* clear. Her mission: to eradicate and begin anew. Now, she questioned. This was unforgivable in a soldier; could it be acceptable in a leader?

In a moment's weakness, she felt so agonisingly alone that she actually wished she were still aboard the *New World*. She despised those people, and yet she could *rely* on them. Conversely, she was in the belly of her new regime wondering who she could trust – it was a damned short list.

Coleman had two accomplices in Heidi's rescue from the Old Man's captivity. There was the soldier who carried her, unconscious, after the first unhappy reunion with Heinrich Schultz – where Tim Norris had shot her. She had not bothered to learn his name, but she would do so now. Coleman would know.

The second man who helped that night had also been a member of Captain Nassaki's team, taken captive aboard the *New World*. He had been killed by the dinosaur, earlier in the day. A waste.

Captain Aito Nassaki swam before her mind's eye. It would be good to have him back, assuming he lived through surgery. Even one-handed, he seemed a clever man, and a survivor – although perhaps it was too soon to speak of that.

The other member she had to consider was Lieutenant Devon. She knew little of him. Formerly Captain Emilia Franke's protégé – if that was all he was – he had been quick enough to swap his allegiance to Heidi. Obviously, he had seen which way the wind was blowing and played safe. She approved of that, in others. He could, after all, have taken the *Heydrich* for himself and stranded the survivors from the

Eisernes Kreuz along with the *Sabre*'s crew on that small island off the coast of Africa.

That is what she would have done in his place, but she was a Schultz. Who would have followed *him?* Clearly, that must have been his own conclusion, too. So, Devon was not a gambler, then. Of course, that could change if his odds began to look more favourable. Either way, it would be politic and much easier to win over the *Heydrich*'s crew if her most senior surviving officer was seen to be, at least nominally, part of her inner circle.

She was thinking like her enemy – like a politician. It was a weak stance, but what choice did she have? The old ways had failed her. Now she must do anything and everything possible to improve her odds.

During her afternoon of contemplation, the crew would have gathered every piece of evidence from the *New World*'s short-lived wormhole. She had heard Devon give the order across the ship's tannoy when she boarded, so perhaps he was not a complete fool.

The *New World* may have gone, but she too had a wormhole-capable ship, after all – a time machine, if you will. They could not – *would* not – escape her.

Yes, time was on her side; she would use it to bring all her assets together before hitting back. Her cousin had not only betrayed her, he had driven, no, had *been* the rift between her and her grandfather.

Strange, she mused. *All the time you were working to make me more like you, you were becoming more like me. You really are a Schultz, Cousin Timothy.*

The assembled group only lived through their meeting by virtue of diving for cover underneath the table.

Douglas' rule by committee was a running joke in the Schultz camp. Despite this, none of Heidi's people had ever actually attended one of his meetings. Nevertheless, they assumed, and fairly, that gunfire did not usually form part of the agenda. Hiding under the table, the lives of the new 'inner circle' could hardly be said to have been elevated – and they were certainly not charmed.

"*Idiots!*" their latest leader screamed.

Gradually, the bravest dared to raise their heads above the table once more.

"Dr Schultz?" asked Coleman, gingerly.

Heidi thrust the nine-millimetre pistol back into its holster. Leaning on her knuckles, she stood at the head of the table. "So, who amongst you geniuses wishes to tell me exactly *why* I was not informed of this before? You have had more than *three weeks!*"

Everyone looked at Devon, who swallowed nervously. Assuming any words made it past his Adam's apple, they might just be his last, so his inclination was to keep swallowing, if only to buy a little more life.

Heidi leaned still further forward. "*Well?*"

Clearing his throat nervously, Devon tried again. "When we fired upon the *Eisernes Kreuz*... Oh *Christ*..."

Heidi's colour was well and truly 'up' – had been before he began. Now, the vigour of youth seemed to be all that stood between her and a full-blown seizure. Tightly, she invited him to continue.

Devon swallowed for the *n*th time. "Sorry, Doctor. I mean when *Captain Franke* fired upon your ship, we took damage as the *Kreuz* came down. That was when Captain Nassaki brought his weapons to bear on us—"

"Yes, I know who my loyal followers are," she interrupted.

"Erm... yes, and Captain Franke ordered our retreat."

"What happened next?"

"We made orbit and began repairs immediately. When the top rocket motor in our engine cluster sustained damage, it back fed a massive power spike into the wormhole drive."

Heidi's rage was replaced by a calmness that made Devon quail. "Why was the wormhole drive not physically decoupled from the engines after use?"

"That's the way the wormhole drives work on the Mars Fleet ships, Doctor – the *New World* and the others," explained Devon. "However, your grandfather decreed that the WHDs on our ships should be permanently ready to jump."

Heidi's eyes narrowed. "This sounds foolish. Why would he order it so?"

"We suspect..." Devon's voice croaked with anxiety. He reached for his water, but it was no longer there. Seeing the broken glass spread across the carpet from Heidi's gun-toting tantrum, he cleared his throat and tried again. "We immediately attempted repairs using replacement parts, naturally. However, some of the replacements proved defective when fitted. Obviously, every item, every peripheral brought aboard before our launch, was checked thoroughly…"

"That is all very well, Lieutenant," Heidi led, "but you were about to tell me what you *suspect*, were you not?"

Devon looked around desperately for support. "Well, *we* suspected that the only way this could be possible was if it were a deliberate design of the Old— of your grandfath— *dein Großvater,* I mean…"

When Heidi did not answer, he produced his last card. "We thought that *dein Großvater* wanted to keep us here…"

His words tailed off into silence as Heidi considered, and everyone else held their breath.

Discomfited, Devon added, "We also assumed that you would have known, ma'am."

Heidi was even more prickly and unstable than usual, and his dogged explanation finally ground to a halt, awaiting her response.

The seconds dragged…

Slowly, she sat back down. "The old fool," she spat at last. "It looks like he got what he wanted, then, does it not? We are indeed trapped here. No way to follow Douglas or to travel back to our own time to replenish our resources."

Perhaps unwisely, Devon raised a hand to further add, "We are fortunate—"

"*Fortunate?*" snapped Heidi, not bothering to hear him out.

"Erm, yes, ma'am. We're fortunate that Douglas' rabble left us with a healthy crop in the fields off our starboard flank."

She fixed him with a glare, unwilling to accept that he might be right about anything, after his confession.

"Lieutenant Devon is correct, ma'am," agreed Coleman. "It's also lucky we didn't destroy it in our attack."

Heidi stared into space. With her plans utterly derailed, her anger towards her grandfather made it difficult to think straight. Although she believed *him* to be well beyond her reach now, at the moment, any target would do.

Despite the tension and threat, Coleman continued, "Doctor, I think the first thing we should do is secure the crop. It looks like we're going to need it, but if the animals get there first…"

Heidi spoke between clenched teeth. "I am *not* a farmer!"

"Of course not, ma'am, but we have people who know what to do," Devon chipped in helpfully.

The last person to speak was the soldier who had carried her to safety, all those weeks ago. "We should also strip everything of any use from the sites of the *Kreuz*, *Last Word* and *Newfoundland*."

Heidi evaluated him, clearly a man of few words; she preferred them that way. "What is your name?" she asked.

"Jansen, Benedictus Jansen, ma'am. Most call me Ben."

She remembered him as the man who showed 'puppy-dog excitement' when his loyalty was praised after her rescue. *Perhaps he will make an impressive guard dog, too?*

When she spoke, she was all business. "Jansen is correct. We leave tomorrow. Coleman, you will be in charge here. You will retain our fighter craft and small vehicle fleet. That should be plenty of firepower and resource to guard a few plants. Besides, we will need all of our hold space to bring back as much matériel as possible."

She stood suddenly, pushing her seat back. "Make preparations immediately, for a perimeter around our *farm!*" She sighed with annoyance. "It would not do for the animals to clear us out overnight, would it?"

"Of course, Doctor," Coleman acknowledged.

"Good. The rest of you, we have much to prepare for—"

Heidi was interrupted by a comm chime from the console mounted into the glass tabletop. She accepted the call irritably, "Yes?"

A female voice responded, *"Apologies for interrupting your meeting, Doctor, but we are picking up a distress call."*

They all glanced at one another in surprise. "Its source?" asked Heidi.

"It's one of ours, ma'am. An escape pod."

"Location?"

"Long distance. It's a way south and east of us, ma'am. If we were back home, I would say, erm... North Africa?"

"Very well. Understood." Heidi closed the channel and was about to clear the room when a thought struck her. A little uncomfortably, she asked, "Opinions? Ideas?"

The others eyed one another warily, obviously surprised by this sudden inclusivity. Heidi understood their surprise; she shared it. *Damn Tim Norris!* she thought.

Despite this, throwing it open to the floor proved advantageous, which yet again gave her pause.

"We don't really know what happened aboard the *Sabre*, Doctor," Devon sidled up to his point carefully, "but could this be a survivor, perhaps?"

Heidi's eyes narrowed. "That seems unlikely. The ship was utterly vaporised."

"Maybe someone aboard got warning?" he tried again.

"If you are hoping your dear Captain Franke is still alive, Lieutenant, think again! I *do* know what happened aboard the *Sabre*, and I can tell you—"

"Well, *someone* survived," interrupted Coleman.

Heidi shot her a frosty glare, but Coleman continued undeterred, "So who would be the most likely candidate? Perhaps, if you were to tell us what happened, Doctor?"

"Very well. Derek Bond was a double agent. Actually, that is an oversimplification. I am not really sure *who* he worked for. It certainly was not Douglas' people – at least, not directly. However, he *was* a walking bomb – of that, I *am* sure."

This drew a few sharp intakes of breath.

"I doubt that was his real name, either. You see, he was also Dutch. Jansen is a Dutch name, isn't it?" She stared searchingly at Benedictus Jansen. "Any relation, *Ben?*"

Up to that point the meeting had been most uncomfortable. It came as yet another surprise that anything could make it even more so. However, Ben merely shrugged mildly. "Not that I know of."

Heidi fixed him for a moment longer, before declaring, "The only way there could be a survivor from that ship, would be if Bond failed. And if Bond failed, the most likely survivor would certainly be…"

She could not finish the thought, but they all caught her implication.

LOOK AFTER MY TOMATOES !!

Chapter 2 | T.N.G.W.

When an object enters a wormhole, it steps outside normal space–time. Douglas' communication, stating that they were all back on board, had been frantic. Fortunately, Captain Baines, with everything already in hand, had launched immediately. Hers was the last voice they heard in Cretaceous Britain.

Wormholes provide no perception of time, nor even of existence, to the traveller. Baines simply was, and then she was not. In literally no time at all, give or take a hundred million years, she instantly found that she *was* again… and that was when the screams began.

The *Heydrich* left at dawn. Coleman watched it go with mixed feelings. Their new leader was a heavy presence to live with. A brief reprieve from her was welcome, even as their new status was worrisome. It was hard to deny that the nearest approximation they had to home or haven had just left and would soon be half a world away.

She shook her head sadly. Having shipped in aboard the *Last Word*, Coleman had worked with Heidi for a while, seeing her as a soldier – someone she could relate to. When Old Man Schultz arrived, he had shown himself to be an entirely different manner of creature.

Or so she believed then. Now, she was less sure.

We should have made peace with Douglas' people. This world is more than big enough for all of us, and now we've lost the very thing we came here for. Trouble is, at least half of our people still don't seem to see it.

The sun continued to rise from behind the peaks enclosing the eastern shore. It flooded the blackened surface of Crater Lake with bronze, before eventually submitting to the vibrance of clean Cretaceous blue.

No decorator's palette should be without it, she thought drily. Coleman had only heard tell of such beauty before, from her grandparents. Scottish expatriates, unable to stand it as their wonderful country fell under the steel tracks of progress, they had left for the Americas long ago, before her mother was born.

She had listened to the stories on her grandfather's knee, little more than faerie tales, to a little girl. Stuffed full of castles and heroes and heather. There may not have been any of the latter, but this landscape was an eye-opener, nevertheless. Worth fighting for, certainly.

But then, that was how we got into this mess in the first place, wasn't it?

She knew many of her people secretly believed a middle road would have been preferable, although few dared speak that opinion aloud.

The flutter of the wind seemed to create movement behind her, but her gaze was transfixed by the sunrise across the lake.

Maybe we should have spoken out? As the thought crossed her mind, an old military idiom followed almost immediately; something about 'dying and not reason *whying*'.

She sighed. *Too late now.*

A bone-jarring chop, immediately at Coleman's left ear, put her heart in her mouth. Instinctively, she dove into a forward roll. Springing back to her feet, three metres out and facing back towards the threat, she almost fell over again, in shock.

Standing on the sand was… what the hell *was* it? The bastard offspring of some type of *bird* and a *giraffe*?

It stood upright, if awkwardly on comparatively tiny hind legs, keeping its balance by folding its wings in half and touching them to the ground. Clawed hands, at the bend in each wing, seemed to support its weight easily, completing a most unwieldy looking quadruped.

Coleman began to recover from the shock of both the creature's appearance, and its *appearance*, but nothing could have prepared her for its size. When they wheeled through the air at distance, it was difficult to get a sense of scale, but as she looked up at the head, five or six metres above the ground, scale suddenly flung all sense aside – replacing it with disbelief and panic.

The animal's giant bill alone must have easily measured three metres, its end widening to an upright ridge – a bulge to both the lower, but especially the upper jaws. However, of more immediate concern to Coleman were the jagged, forward-facing teeth.

Logic suggested that these evolved to stick and hold slippery, violently struggling fish, prior to conveyance to either the gullet or the nest. However, on a strictly emotional level, they also looked like they would *really* hurt.

Coleman snapped her rifle to, ready to defend herself. The gun was on fully automatic, as was she, rational thought having temporarily deserted her. As she braced for the noise and the kick of the weapon, the giant bill snapped again, narrowly missing a *frenzy* of tiny – and quite possibly suicidal – birds.

Coleman relaxed, but only a little.

"So, I'm not your type then, eh, big fella?" Finding her voice brought some measure of relief, but it also brought attention.

The enormous pterosaur now appeared to be glaring, almost snootily, down its nose at her – *straight* at her, and this was a lot of nose to snoot.

Coleman unrelaxed, rather a lot.

The eyes were unemotional, utterly without warmth. Birds, reptiles, carnivorous dinosaurs, all divergences from the same stem; ruthlessness by design.

Suddenly feeling absurdly small, Coleman began to realise that, just maybe, this creature was interested in expanding its palate after all.

Great! Looks like Big Bird's a foodie!

'Big Bird' opened and closed its bill in a rapid, clattering succession. Coleman had no idea if this was threat behaviour or some weird avian greeting, but positive that it scared the hell out of her, she raised the rifle once more.

Many of her companions would have shot the beast by now, but she really wanted to understand this world if she was to be stuck here.

Besides, the grinding heel of the jackboot approach had not been working out too well for them recently.

The meaning of the pterosaur's behaviour became less abstruse when another pair of its kind alighted on the beach, directly behind her.

OK. Now *I'm afraid.*

Was this its family? Competition? Or just a panel of judges for some bizarre species of Mesozoic Masterchef?

Of the newcomers, the first was similarly huge, although its bill was less impressive and overall colouration blander. The second was smaller and most likely a subadult.

When they opened their mouths together, there was virtually nowhere for Coleman to go. It was like diving between the sails of erratically oscillating windmills, under a gust of knife-scraping, nails-down-the-blackboard bird call. Their shrieks alone pierced her to the bone. Covering her ears instinctively, she curled up to make herself small. Their agitation, nevertheless, seemed to increase, leaving her no choice but to fire into the air.

The rattle and rip of repetitive gunfire caused all three avians to run from the sound, throwing sand all over Coleman. Theirs was a peculiar, ungainly gambol; locomotion generated through a shifting of diagonal lines, like a man aided by skiing poles. She had visited a mining museum once, and the complexity of their mismatched limbs put Coleman in mind of the unfathomable piston and pushrod movements of early beam engines.

After the first several steps, their wings spread wide, instantly making sense of the whole mechanism, and when they leapt for the sky, it was with an elegance all their own.

Once airborne, they were nimble, almost elemental, as they turned thermal lift into choreography.

Coleman wiped her eyes and pulled sand from her mouth. Spitting and hacking, she celebrated the aerial display before her by shaking a fist at them.

The soft susurrus of running feet on sand sounded from behind. Coleman turned in alarm, but it was only the approach of her troops. Exhaling noisily, she sniped, "*Now* you come to check on me!"

They were probably travelling at around a hundred miles per hour when they entered the wormhole. Small change for a spaceship, but from a hundred to zero, in an instant, without the sympathy of deceleration, made it feel a whole lot more.

A 550-metre-long construct like the *New World* could *not* in fact decelerate instantly from a hundred to zero in normal space, and therein lay the problem. A problem augmented by the secondary fact that there was absolutely nowhere for her to go.

Something had to give…

The mountain gave. Unfortunately, at Sir Isaac Newton's insistence, the vehicle gave too – as is often the case when humans make a mess of things.

Crumple zones, inertial dampeners, multi-laminate materials technology and spaceframe rigidity all played their parts admirably, allowing the USS *New World* to save all the precious lives in her care, but sadly not her own.

Baines came round to a bridge where things she had never even seen before were lit up in red – a bridge that also appeared rather shorter than it used to be. Her very first thoughts were, *James is gonna freak. This is the second time I've crashed his ship!*

Electrical smoke choked her. She heard coughing from other quarters, too, and filed that under the 'good news' column of the two lists already forming in her mind.

She tried to uncouple her safety harness, but the clasp was misshapen. As if in recognition of this, her ribcage, for forty-one years pretty much taken for granted, suddenly made its presence felt. Were she to take an X-ray at that point, she would lay odds that her skeleton, too, would be covered in flashing red and amber lights.

Another coughing fit, from somewhere in the haze before her, refocused Baines' attention away from her personal woes. "Sandy? Is that you? Are you OK?"

More coughing, eventually followed by the pilot's dry-throated voice, "That's not gone well…"

The *Heydrich* was thousands of miles and millions of years away as she flew over western Gondwana. Leaving so early, she had left the sun behind at one point, crossing back into deep pre-dawn blue.

As they neared their destination, her crew were able to admire their second 'dawn of the day' *of the day*.

All except one. Locked away in her stateroom again, Heidi was as unmoved by the majesty of creation as she was by the needs of her crew.

Lieutenant Devon was beginning to wonder if he had made the right decision in committing their forces to this remaining Schultz. Emelia Franke had been fanatical to their cause, but so long as her crew performed their duties adequately, they were safe. He had never met Heinrich Schultz but knew that Franke had doted on the man. He must have been something. However, his granddaughter was as dangerous to her own side as the enemy, it seemed. He had simply not known.

There was a subdued air aboard the *Heydrich*. Glancing around, Devon suspected his crewmates were having similar doubts. Word about Heidi shooting up the meeting room had filled the ship like a bad case of gas – quiet, lingering and particularly unpleasant, given no way out.

They would be landing soon. He just hoped she would show more leadership going forward. *Otherwise, we'll have to see,* he mused. *After all, we may now have another candidate available in North Africa.*

Yes, it had been odd that Heidi should refuse point-blank to even contact the survivor. Devon knew, of course, that there had been a falling out with her grandfather.

But surely everything's different now, isn't it? I think I might do a little poking around on the satellite net when the dust settles. See if I can find some answers.

At least the *New World* still appeared to have power. Fire suppression was winning the war and the smoke was clearing.

Singh limped over to Baines and, with the assistance of a few hand tools, managed to unclasp her harness.

"What do we have that works?" she asked.

"Absolutely fu—" a rapid succession of electrical cracks and pops from the pilot's console behind him caused Singh to duck, wincing under a shower of sparks.

"Sorry I asked," Baines murmured quietly.

"—utile to guess at this stage, Captain," Singh continued, batting out burning metal fragments on his sleeves. "Captain?"

"Sorry, Sandy. I thought you were going somewhere else with that. Are the comms up? We need to know if…" She tailed off.

"If we're alone?" Singh completed.

Baines nodded.

"I'll see what I can do, Captain. Maybe one of these consoles will still answer. I think Dr Patel and Mother Sarah are stirring."

"Right, I'll see to them. Do what you can."

Engineering was in a state of almost complete devastation. However, Hiro had managed to get power to a terminal and set it to work, running as many checks as he could load.

Sitting back for a moment, he realised that, despite the lack of engine noise – he doubted he would ever hear that again here – there was also another unusual absence of sound.

"Georgio?"

A wheezy reply came from under a pile of component bins. "Are we dead?"

"Not sure," Hiro answered, honestly. "There's some power getting around, but…"

"I wasn't talking about the ship."

Hiro blinked. "Do you need help climbing from under all that?"

"No, I'm just taking it easy!"

"Oh, OK."

"HIRO!"

"Ahh, that was sarcasm, right?"

"*Yes.*"

Hiro mumbled under his breath as he climbed across the debris field that was once his squeaky-clean engineering deck. "If people only spoke with track-changes, they'd be so much easier to read."

Georgio thrust his one free arm out from under a pile of containers. "Hand signals any good to you?"

"That's sarcasm agai—"

"*No*, Hiro. That's *get me out of here! Please?*"

Hiro was about to pull his friend clear when, joy of joys, the comms came to life. Letting Georgio drop once more, he scrambled back over to his console and answered breathlessly, "Engineering – Hiro speaking."

"*Hiro, thank God! It's Sandy. What can you tell me?*"

After a pause, Hiro asked, "What do you wish to know?"

"*What state is the ship in, of course!*"

"Everything appears to be broken. Were *you* driving?"

"*Not exactly— well, alright, yes it was me. I would have opened the wormhole at altitude, but we were under heavy fire, remember?*"

"Hmm," Hiro acknowledged coolly.

"*What's that noise in the background? Is that shouting I can hear?*"

"No, it's just Georgio. Look, you're going to have to give me a little time to get a handle on things."

"*OK, Hiro. But first things first, can you get power to the doors? We can use the hand-winder to get off the bridge if we have to, but there are a hell of a lot of doors between us and, hopefully, everyone else.*"

"Right. I'll make it my top priority – engineering out."

"Could I ask you to make it your *second* from top?" shouted Georgio, angrily.

"Tim? Are you hurt, laddie?"

The young man stirred. "Captain?"

Douglas grinned. "Aye. Can you move?"

"Definitely. How the hell did I get all over here? OW! Ow, ow, ow, ow!"

"Friction burns?" asked Douglas, sagely. "We've all got them, son. Ah think we hit something and, well, Ah don't know what came next. Here, let's get you up on your feet."

"Thanks, Captain." Tim clutched Douglas' arm meaningfully. "I mean for everything."

"No. It should be us thanking you, Tim. You gave us a window we wouldnae have had otherwise. We only escaped because of you. Volunteering to stay with them, with *her*, was as brave an act as Ah've ever seen – Ah'm so very proud of you, son."

"Will I be able to see Mum now?"

Douglas sighed, scratching his head thoughtfully. "She's in the new medical bay just over there, on the opposite side of the hangar, but Ah dinnae know what kind of state they're in yet."

He saw Tim's look of disappointment, mixed with real fear for Patricia's well-being, and relented. "Tell you what, while people are picking themselves up around here, why don't we go and find out?"

Tim smiled, but it was a haunted smile, and Douglas wondered what other damage may lurk below his abrasions and bruises.

"Come on, laddie."

Captain Tobias Meritus woke up groggily in the quarters he shared with personnel from the ruined *Last Word*. He and his people had known the wormhole jump was coming; they also knew that no one had any idea what would be on the other side. All his fellow ship-crash survivors across the Pod had once again found themselves strapping in as best they could, tying themselves to anything with a reliable fixing. There were but a finite number of secure, belted seats aboard the *New World* and *Factory Pod 4*, so many of them simply had to make do.

Meritus had elected to stay with his people for several reasons. Firstly, it was entirely possible they would not survive the jump, and as their leader, the least he could do was join them in their fate. Secondly, he felt sure his presence at Douglas' prisoner exchange would only have stoked resentment, destabilising the situation further. Lastly, his invitation to join Captain Baines on the bridge had felt like merely good manners, and as such was by no means genuine.

His relationship with Captain Baines was best described as cool. Perhaps it was understandable, given their brief past, but he instinctively sensed that if he wished to build a new life for himself and his people with Douglas' crew – wherever they eventually ended up – it was Baines he would need to win over.

His mind was freewheeling, he knew. She may not even be alive. Come to that, he was not a hundred percent sure he was either. Whatever had befallen them was clearly serious. The shock of some sort of impact had knocked Meritus, and his five 'roomies', out cold.

Perhaps it's time to try opening my eyes, he thought blearily. He had a sense of 'coming home' as consciousness returned to his body, but with it came alarm – he could not move.

His thinking was woolly, he could feel it, but as the fog gradually cleared, realisation dawned that he was strapped in place. With the warmth of relief, he began testing his bonds, searching for a knot or clasp. There was pain too, but he chalked that up as a good thing, given their circumstances. His quarters looked as though they had been ransacked.

Finally, he gave up his ineffectual fumbling to breathe a heavy sigh. *Maybe I'll just give it a minute…*

Corporal Jones' first memory of their journey was a terrible shudder through the ship, followed almost immediately by another. The second had seemed worse, or perhaps merely closer. Either way, the explosions left him in no doubt that they had been hit, with both impacts sounding some distance aft of his location.

The Sarge had left with Douglas, leaving Jones in charge of embarkation and the *New World*'s passengers, and as many of Meritus' people as they could securely seat, too.

Despite the shock and juddering, the *New World* was clearly still moving – hundreds of thousands of tons could not so easily be stopped. The very next instant, from Jones' personal perspective, he was thrown against his crash webbing with such force that he blacked out.

In the millisecond before oblivion claimed him, he heard a groan of compressed metal. No. Heard was the wrong word – his *world* was the groan of compressed metal.

Now he was awake again.

Embarkation spanned the entire width of the Pod with portholes on either side. Looking left and then right, hoping for a view, Jones found only dismay.

Both ends of the embarkation lounge appeared to have been crushed. He could hardly imagine the force necessary to accomplish this. The portholes were all gone. Jones knew the multilaminate glass portholes were every bit as crucial to the overall integrity of the structure as the spaceframe and other components, but they had not failed – they had simply been popped out by the colossal distortion of the hull and bulkheads. The spaces left by the portholes must have then been torn open by... what was it?

Jones squinted. His head was still spinning. "What the hell?" he murmured under his breath. Finding the catch on his safety harness he released it and stood – too quickly – and crashed back into his seat, shaking his head to clear it. With a little more care, he tried again. Once on his feet, he walked, staggering slightly, towards the starboard end of embarkation.

His mind and vision were beginning to clear and he could now see what had happened.

"Well, at least we're not in space, boy. We'd all be dead now, isn'it."

The remains of torn and distorted bulkheads were mixed up with rocks and what looked like a heavy, peaty soil. The debris spilled into the chamber some metres. Jones surmised that the ingress stopped after some sort of equilibrium had been struck.

"What the hell has happened?"

Behind him, he heard the moaning of many people drifting back to consciousness. With shaking hands, he rubbed his eyes to refresh himself before returning to his duty. Better leave the big questions until later; he had over a hundred people to take care of.

The new medical bay was in turmoil. Nurses and drafted orderlies ran left and right, moving people and equipment.

Douglas managed to grab Nurse Smyth as he strode past. "Justin, where's Dr Flannigan?"

Smyth turned back the way he had come. "He's... er. Ah, there he is, coming out of Patricia's room."

"Thanks," replied Douglas. Moving along, with Tim in tow, he called, "Dave! How are we?"

Flannigan veered towards them, meeting them halfway. "It's a good job Major White gave us the heads-up, James. Would have been carnage otherwise, if we hadn't got everyone secured. That said, we're still in trouble. Some of these guys are very fragile. It's just a pity Ford didn't extend himself the courtesy he gave us."

A flash of concern crossed Douglas' face. "Is he hurt?"

"A little. That shockwave, or whatever hit us, sent him pinwheeling across the hangar. He slammed into a lorry, and needless to say, came off worse in the exchange, but he's OK. His shoulder's well out of joint. I've given him some happy time until I can get round to him – he's not in danger.

"By the way, talking of lives in danger, guess who came through without a scratch – didn't even wake up until a few minutes ago!"

Douglas looked blank, so Flannigan elaborated, "Our old friend, Geoff Lloyd."

Douglas smiled sardonically. "How many lives does the man have?"

"At least one more, it seems!" Flannigan glanced at Douglas' companion. "Mr Norris, how are you? Been quite an ordeal, I hear?"

"I'm OK, Doctor. Would it be possible to see my mum?"

"Soon. She made it through the shock without further complication. I think being only semi-conscious helped – made her more relaxed while we were all panicking!" He smiled at the young man. "She's been shaken around, but she's OK, kid. I just wanna check her one more time, to make sure she's strong enough for visitors. She's been desperate to see you all these weeks, but I don't want her to get too emotional just now – not even in a good way, yeah?"

"I understand," Tim replied, his disappointment obvious.

Douglas placed a fatherly hand on his shoulder. "You'll see her soon now, laddie. While we're waiting for Dave to do his rounds, why don't we go and see Geoff? Ah think Ah may just have some good – if a little sad – news for him."

Tim nodded and followed the captain, through a crowd of rushing people, into a second ward.

"Geoff? Are ye awake?"

Lloyd opened one eye. "Depends what you want."

Douglas laughed, pulling a seat up to Lloyd's bed for Tim, and then fetching another for himself. "Ah think you'll want to hear this, Geoff."

"Why's the boy here?" asked Lloyd, sitting up in bed.

"I heard what you did," Tim said, quietly. "Following that young Mapusaurus over a cliff to save Georgio Baccini. It was very brave."

"It was damned stupid!" Lloyd retorted, truculently. Studying his young visitor, he tempered slightly. "Still, I hear I'm in good company, if it's courage we're talking about. You're quite the talk of the town, Mr Norris."

"Just Tim will do fine, please."

Lloyd nodded, giving Tim a sideways look, but did not respond.

Douglas was keen that no one dwelt overly on Tim's possible identity crisis, so he gathered Lloyd's attention back to himself. "Ah've quite a tale to tell ye, Geoff."

"Another one. Will I need half a bottle of single malt to swallow it, this time?"

"The way Ah remember it, Ah had to swallow *your* story last time. You just kept swallowing my finest dram!"

Lloyd smiled at the memory. "You remember it, do you? Will you be working it into song this time?"

Douglas sighed. "No' exactly."

For the next fifteen minutes, Douglas explained the story of Del Bond. When he got to the part where the erstwhile philosopher was reintroduced as Lucas Jansen, Lloyd suddenly straightened.

Douglas' explanation of Bond's final demise was naturally rather sketchy – had he been there he would not be alive to tell the tale. Lloyd could also discern a certain whiff of romanticism – he put that down to being for the boy's benefit, more than his own.

"That's quite a story, Captain," Lloyd acknowledged. "And don't think I didn't get the reference to the name Jansen. Is there more you'd like to tell me?"

Douglas nodded slowly. "Aye. There is. Audrey Jansen – your Audrey, as was, that is – was Bond's niece. More than that, she joined the Order of the Silver Cross around ten years ago – our time, of course."

Lloyd leaned closer. "What are you saying?"

"Ah'm *saying*, she made a solemn undertaking to a cause she believed in – a commitment to the Order. Sadly, at the cost of her own life, in the end. Ah *suspect* she foresaw that to be the likely outcome, and gave ye the elbow to protect ye."

Lloyd's face fell, his expression tormented as he murmured, "I can't believe it."

"Ah know. Ah just assumed she dumped you because you were the worst boyfriend ever, but it turns out you weren't. That's a win for you, surely?"

Lloyd was no longer hearing him. "I had no idea…"

Douglas' expression softened. "Aye, laddie. Audrey was a good friend o' mine, but Ah never suspected, either. Arnold Bessel was one of the best friends a man could have. When we found they'd gone together, lost to violence… well, you remember."

He stood and nodded for Tim to do likewise. "Ah'm sorry, Geoff. But Ah thought ye should know. Glad you're on the mend."

As they turned to leave, Lloyd called after them, "Hey! What do you mean, 'worst boyfriend ever'?"

Douglas was about to answer when he was jostled, quite rudely, out of the way.

"This man should be resting. *Go,*" ordered Matron.

Douglas bristled, blurting, "Ah'm captain of this ship—"

"Really? I thought you'd be younger. Well, don't let me keep you, then. I'm sure you have plenty to keep you occupied, looking at the state we're in. Come on – off you go!"

Douglas and Tim were brusquely bustled from the ward, leaving Lloyd grinning like an ill-bred llama.

Jones' comm crackled to life. He reached for it instantly. "Jones here! Is that you, Sarge?"

"*Good to hear you're still with us, Jonesy!*"

"You're OK! That's champion, boy! Do you know what's happened to us?"

The Sarge explained that engineers were working on the interior hatches and the public address system at the moment, but there were indeed pockets of people all over the ship, labouring to come together.

Jones explained how soil and rocks had invaded embarkation. "People here will be made up to know you're all out there and coming for us, Sarge."

"That's right, lad. Don't keep it to yourself, now! By the time you're done explaining everything to them, we'll be with you – with a little bit o' luck! Sarge out."

"Hiro!" shouted the pilot, pulling his colleague and friend into a tight embrace.

Hiro, for his part, retorted, "Sandy! You crashed Sekai – *again!*"

Baines gave Georgio a warm hug and began to laugh. "We're glad to see you too, Hiro!"

Georgio moved on from Baines to slap Singh on the back.

"At least someone's glad I made it," Singh remarked, accusingly.

"Can we open the hatch between the ship and the Pod?" asked Baines.

Georgio shook his head. "Unfortunately, whatever hit us, or whatever we hit, has twisted her frame so badly that this hatch will never work again."

"What do you suggest then?" Baines prompted.

Hiro was still eyeing Singh, balefully. "I suppose we'll just have to cut our way through." The words seemed to pain him. "Trouble is, all of our cutting gear is still down in the Pod."

"So are you suggesting we wait until they cut their way in from the other side?" she asked.

"There's still the fore hatch leading to the Pod," suggested Georgio, hopefully. "Just because this one's mangled—"

Singh was already shaking his head. "No. We tried. We couldn't get to it. The front of the ship is in a hell of a…" Wilting under Hiro's glare, he changed tack, "Erm, she's looked better."

Hiro bent over, hands on his knees. "This is my worst nightmare. I think I'm hyperventilating!"

"If you think this is bad, I haven't asked the *big* question yet," remarked Baines, ominously.

They all looked in her direction, stolidly refusing to ask for clarification.

OK, she thought, *here goes.* "Did we make it?"

None of them wanted to take the lead on that point, and the silence was handed around like a game of pass-the-parcel. Unfortunately, without any music, they soon found themselves back to square one.

"*Anybody?*" asked Baines. "If it helps, I can remind you that I'm captain, and you have to answer me."

"I think—"

"It appears—"

Hiro and Sandy began together, and just as suddenly stopped together. Each unusually magnanimous about surrendering the floor to the other.

"*Come on,* guys—"

"I think we're inside a mountain," blurted Georgio.

The pilot and the chief refused to meet Baines' eye. "Is that possible?" she asked.

Singh sighed deeply. "It makes sense, Captain. Just because we were out in the clear over a lake a little while ago, the landscape might be very different here."

Baines nodded. "OK. That makes sense. The topography will have changed dramatically over the last hundred million years, I get it. So what's the answer to the other half of the question?"

"Other half?" asked Hiro, innocently.

"You mean, 'inside a mountain, *when*', don't you, Captain?" supplied Georgio once more.

Now the pilot and chief did look at one another, each hoping the other would have an answer – hopefully a correct one. Even more hopefully, a positive one.

Singh grasped the nettle. "We won't know that until we get out, Captain. There really is no way of telling from here. All our sensing instruments on the hull of the ship were destroyed in the crash. It's lucky we weren't travelling faster. None of us would have survived, if we had been. As it stands, the *New World* is…"

"Dead," murmured Hiro.

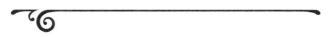

Heidi stood alone at the rim of the plateau, where her people had made camp all those weeks ago. The *Heydrich*'s crew had worked hard all day, stripping almost anything of use from the *Last Word*.

The battleship was so large, when compared with her final remaining capital ship, that it would take several flights to and fro, to completely strip her. Some items would be too large to move at all without disassembly. For the moment, she was content to focus on fuel, food, weapons and medical supplies. Whatever space they had left, they would stuff with spare parts.

The designers of the Dawn Fleet had specifically made the spares interchangeable. Unfortunately, Douglas' team had stolen the pieces her people would need to fix the *Heydrich*'s wormhole drive, and they lacked the manufacturing capability to produce anything that complex themselves.

It would have been far simpler to move her people back here, rather than travelling back and forth, wasting fuel on heavy cargo hauling. However, *there* was where the crops were planted. Douglas really had pulled a master stroke over her. No. Her cousin was the main architect of her downfall, and his treachery would not be forgotten, not by her.

Now it seemed there might be another traitor waiting in the wings, too. Could her grandfather really have survived? It seemed impossible.

There was no way he could have known Bond's intentions; he would never have allowed Franke to take him with them if he had. What *had* happened aboard that ship?

If Heinrich Schultz was alive and well, and sunning himself in – where was it? Egypt? What should she do with him? Leave him there? She had thought him dealt with twice already – the second time, in a most final manner. Yet still, it appeared that he lived.

There was always the chance it was someone else, of course, but Heidi flicked that thought aside immediately. It was him, she knew it… felt it.

After such a hot day, the evening breeze chilled her and she wrapped her arms close about her body, her blonde locks fluttering about her face as she stared west. It was a glorious sunset across the western foothills to the Pre-Andes, or *Petes* as her cousin had named them, but she did not see it. Her focus was on the past. Where had she gone wrong?

Tim would pay for his betrayal, but her grandfather was perhaps within reach, so he would have to pay first. However, he clearly still had secrets that were not hers; not yet. The failure of their ships proved that. She must learn more. Could she make peace with Heinrich one last time, for the sake of the mission and all that they had set out to achieve?

A memory snagged from her personal past – a memory from the old world lost in the future. A name surfaced, and that name was Ernst Stromer. The key was Egypt. There was a connection there with a German palaeontologist. Why would her mind flag those two facts as useful?

In the realm of imagination, there is no currency, nor even any form of barter. Ideas simply move and change, growing free and wild. Where any seed may grow into any *thing*, crossing whatever species or boundaries it cares to, along the way; the physical world is mocked. Location is no barrier. *Form* is no barrier. *Time* is no barrier.

"Time is no barrier," Heidi repeated the thought, whispering it on the wind; a wind that was growing stronger. The weather was changing.

Her people still worked the winches, dragging large crates up the embankment from the carcass of her lost battleship. She could hear them calling out to one another as they toiled.

Distracted, Heidi forced her mind back to Ernst Stromer. They had only a little background in their files about the man and his politics. He had apparently been staunchly anti-Nazi and had paid for it with the loss of two of his three sons during the Second World War, but that mattered little to her in the here and now. What *did* matter, was that he would make a discovery, so many years in the future, and that discovery would be critical to her plans.

This vital titbit had revealed itself within Tim's notes. She had been careful to steal everything the boy had written or uploaded before breaking cover to leave the *New World* collective, all those many weeks ago. They had helped her survive the Cretaceous alone. Moreover, the knowledge of Stromer's discovery would ultimately lead her to a man who certainly *could* help her.

She turned away from the view and walked briskly back to the *Heydrich*. She had a plan, and all would be well again…

"Sam? Is that you, hiding under that bruise?"

Sam Burton, chief of Pod operations, had to turn to see Douglas, his left eye so severely swollen that he was literally blindsided.

"I refuse to say 'aye, aye, Captain'." Burton grinned despite his discomfort.

"Have you been to see the doctor yet?"

"No. I'll get to it as soon as we get comms back up – we've only got hand comms working analogue at the moment. The coverage is lousy through so many bulkheads. Once we have the internal comm operational, I need to get the *damned* doors working!"

"How did you get to the hangar?" asked Douglas.

"Me team and me, we were on duty in ops when we made the jump. As you can see, I was a little slow to strap in. We used a battery pack to open the hatches between there and here. Much of our equipment is stored in these containers."

"Ye'll be heading to the power core next, Ah expect?"

"Yes, James." Burton leaned in close. "I just hope we can get main power back. I see no reason for the core to be down, but if the power conduits have been severed in the crash… Many of them run through the outer bulkheads, ya see?"

Douglas frowned with concern. "Have you managed to look out of the window?"

Burton shook his head. "It seems that all passages and rooms anywhere near the outer hull have been destroyed – or perhaps…"

"Yes?"

Burton looked uncomfortable. Again, he kept his voice low. "It's like the outside of the ship and Pod have been *squashed*. At least elements of the lighting circuit seem to be working – maybe a little hit and miss, but it's something."

"Aye, Ah suppose it is. You think we lost our course through the wormhole?"

"I'm not sure, James. We may be exactly where we wanted to be. It could be as simple as this end of the wormhole tunnel materialised inside a hill. Until we dig our way out of here, we just won't know for sure."

"OK, Sam. We need more information. Can you spare a couple of your guys to try and get the main hangar doors open, please?"

"We should be able to at least open the inner hatch for you. After that—"

"After that, Ah need you to check in with Dr Flannigan. You may feel fine, but if you've a concussion or internal bleeding…? We cannae afford to lose you, Sam. Set your men to the main hatch and check yourself in, please. If you are OK, Dave'll have you back in the fight straight away, yes?"

Burton looked around helplessly, considering all the work demanding his attention.

Douglas caught it. "It'll wait, Sam. Please."

The main hangar doors opened a few minutes later, revealing the vehicular airlock – or what *used* to be. Built twenty-five metres in length, Douglas barely took four strides before his way was blocked by soil, stones and rubble. Mixed in with the debris were the unmistakable structures of manufactured objects and twisted hull plating.

"What do you make of it?"

Douglas turned in surprise to see Major White standing just behind him to his right. Noting the sling, he asked, "How's the shoulder?"

White offered one of his lopsided grins. "It'll do." Checking they were alone, he stepped close. "I'm more worried about suffocating at the moment, Captain."

Douglas turned back to the landslide blocking their way out. "Aye, that occurred to me, too. Ah think we'd better get someone on a digger, as soon as we can break our personnel out of embarkation."

Concern crossed White's face.

"Dinnae worry, Ford. We've been in touch with Dewi Jones. They made it, just a few minor injuries from a rough ride."

White sighed with relief. "Do we have a head count?"

"There are still parts of the ship yet to make contact. Ah'm quietly hopeful, though. The people who designed this bird thought long and hard about passenger safety. Indeed, one of the limiting factors we had to address, with regards to getting most of our number into embarkation, was keeping the passengers well away from the window seats on this trip. It meant that some of Meritus' people had to make do with less well-equipped quarters, but with hindsight, Ah think Sam Burton's decision was inspired, don't you?

"Jonesy has reported that keeping most of the passengers as far inboard as possible has definitely saved lives. When the dust settles, Ah think Sam deserves some kind of commendation for that."

White looked impressed. "He foresaw this?"

"He's a clever man," Douglas acknowledged, simply.

"So what do *you* make of all this, James?"

Douglas turned back to the rubble. "It seems our choices are: we're either well off the map, because of the missiles that exploded on our hull as we entered the wormhole, or, we're home and have materialised underground."

"That's what I thought," admitted White. "The problem I'm having, is believing we're *when* we wanted to be."

"For crying out loud, dinnae try and comfort the auld man, will ye?"

White smiled. "Don't tell me you hadn't already arrived there, James. If the other side of that pile of earth is AD2112, then why can't we hear movement? There's nowhere on Earth, in our own time, where a catastrophe of this magnitude could have gone unnoticed. If we were home, there'd be an army of diggers out there by now, surely? Not to mention the *actual* army with air support. I just can't imagine *that* much presence being this subtle, can you?"

Douglas sighed heavily. "You think we've missed our stop, is that it?"

White shrugged. "If the Pod's totalled, I think we need to dig. Quickly."

Perhaps this won't be so difficult after all, thought Coleman. Her team had made fast work of setting up a perimeter around the lands planted with the *New World*'s crop. With guards and vehicles stationed around the fields, backed up by an outer circle of trips and anti-personnel mines, she felt they were set for anything.

Six of the mines had already gone off and been replaced, the curious unfortunates providing fresh meat for her troops. After that, the animals seemed to have got the message.

At least, she hoped so. Some of the crocodiles, or whatever the hell they were, in the lake, terrified her. At least they had not seen any further signs of the Sigilmassasaurus that killed three of her men and mutilated Captain Nassaki – so things were looking up. Perhaps all the explosions and roaring, of impossibly powerful rocket engines, had persuaded the beast to find happier hunting grounds – she certainly hoped for that too.

"Sarge?"

Coleman turned. "What is it?"

"We've found something you should see."

Following the soldier and his partner, she was led east along the beach, back towards the *New World*'s cave. They approached a largish copse on their right, which turned out to be their destination.

"Look, Sarge."

Coleman followed the man's gaze and saw a pile of stacked brush and cuttings from the bushes around. They carefully moved the foliage aside – mindful of snakes and other little surprises – to reveal a heavy steel door in what was clearly a bunker of some description.

"Looks like Captain Douglas' people have left us a little gift." An unnatural shape in the undergrowth drew Coleman's eye. "What's that?"

One of the men grabbed at something resembling a metal handle with a plastic grip. He pulled. After a second, more determined tug, it came free, bringing bits of underbrush with it.

It was unmistakably a flattened wheelbarrow.

Surprise showed on Coleman's face. "I'm guessing the bunker was the farmers' 'run-to hideout'. Looking at the condition of this barrow, I'd say they were chased in here by something big, wouldn't you, fellas?"

The steel door was immensely strong but unlocked. Heaving it open, the soldiers switched on barrel-mounted flashlights atop their rifles before stepping into the darkness.

Grey walls of new concrete lit up brightly in the flashing torchlight. The floor and ceiling were also of concrete. It felt like a military bunker, but for the lack of firing slots or gun emplacements. They also carried a creepy feeling of being inside a large sarcophagus.

Their boots rang on the floor as they searched for anything useful that may have been left behind.

About eight metres wide and at least the same in length, the room could provide protection for a significant number. As Coleman approached the rear wall, she snorted gently.

About a metre and a half up from the floor, a rough cartoon of a bald man stared back at her, his rather large nose hanging over a hastily delineated wall.

Underneath it, the concrete bore the slogan 'LOOK AFTER MY TOMATOES, YOU…' scrawled in rough capital letters. She was not quite sure what the last word read; the writer's pen had obviously given up at that point. However, she *could* make out that it began with a 'B' and was probably not complimentary.

"We'll make our camp in here," she said. "I'll send the APC to the other end of the crop enclosure – that'll give us a secure foxhole at either end. I'm not comfortable using our attack ship as a hide. If we're followed into it, one of the animals might take a run at the ship itself. Some of the creatures here are *huge*."

"Yes, Sarge."

"I wouldn't fancy explaining that to the new boss," she added, and with that, an idea struck. "Get some people over here and tell them to bring tree felling equipment."

"Hey, Jonesy!" called Sergeant Jackson, ruffling the Welshman's hair affectionately. "Glad to see you in one piece, lad."

Jones' face was not designed for smiling, but he did his best. "Alright or wha'? It was touch and go for a minute there, boy. Can we get around the ship now?"

The Sarge shook his head. "Not fully. Captain Douglas ordered us to cut a pathway to embarkation because we need diggers."

Jones made a show of taking in the soil slippage, all over the carpet at each end of large room. "I thought we might! Have you heard from everyone else?"

"Not everyone. We still haven't been able to contact the *New World*. Our analogue comms won't penetrate the hull effectively, it seems. Either that, or…"

Jones' face darkened. "You think they might be…? I mean, if we hit something, the bridge crew would be the first to feel it."

When he ran out of words, The Sarge decided that action was what they needed. "Let's go and break in, then. The construction and mining people can get back to the hangar now. The front of the Pod seems more damaged, so why don't we head back ourselves and take a couple of engineers with a cutting rig? See if we can board her through the rear connecting hatch, eh?"

"OK, the bridge is a write-off, isn't it, Sandy?" asked Baines. "So the way I see it, we need to set up operations in engineering."

"Engineering's not in great shape either, Captain," admitted Hiro, his chief engineer's pride wounded.

Baines smiled sadly, placing a friendly hand on his arm. "Nowhere is, Hiro. Somehow, we need to get comms fully working again, and any sensing equipment we can fix.

"In the unlikely event that we *haven't* ended up exactly where we wanted to be – in the middle of a convenient acreage of ag land, somewhere in twenty-second century northern Britain – we might just need to know what's going on around us."

"You don't think we're home, do you – any of you?" asked Georgio. Before the question even left his lips, his colour drained. "Oh, my God."

Concerned, Baines stepped towards the young engineer. "What is it, Georgie? *Georgie?*"

Baccini seemed to have completely shut down.

Baines shook him gently. "Georgio, what is it?"

He looked at her as if surprised she was still there. "My brother…"

Now Baines was concerned. She spoke softly, "Georgie, Mario died, remember? We didn't leave him behind, he—"

"No!" he answered forcefully. "He was still with us. Hiro, tell her!"

When Baines looked to Hiro for clarification, the chief put his head in his hands. Eventually, he said, "Georgio believes – thanks to Beck Mawar – that Mario somehow survived the passing of his physical body and has continued to help us along."

Baines' expression softened. "If you believe that, Georgie, well then, what's changed, huh? He'll still be with you, right?"

"I don't know. I need to speak with Beck, right away!"

"We'd all like to tie up with the people down on the Pod, Georgie. I'd like to get Sarah and Satnam down to Doc Flannigan, for starters.

I've put them in my quarters, but they took the crash hard. It's really shaken them."

She would have said more, but a repetitive banging echoed down the corridor, cutting her off. After a short pause, the corridor forward from engineering rang further, with the fierce, reverberating clangs of metallic hammer blows. They all covered their ears.

Baines ran down the corridor towards the commotion. As she skidded to a halt in front of the hatch that joined the ship with the Pod, the corridor ahead was filled with smoke and the burnt metal smell of fabrication. She began to cough.

Singh arrived immediately behind her, asking out, "Who's there?"

"Evening, squire!" The Sarge called enthusiastically through the fumes and haze. Stepping through a still-glowing hole in the hatch, he continued, "Sorry it took us so long. We had to cut through two layers here, and who knows how many before that, because many of the doors wouldn't even take a charge. Is everyone alright?"

Baines beamed. "We're getting better!"

Chapter 3 | Reunion

The ten-ton excavator worked hard within the confines of the vehicular airlock. Spatial restrictions forced the driver to constantly clean behind his machine and he soon ran out of room.

"OK, Red," Bluey shouted to his brother. "I'll get the bucket swapped for a spreader on one of the thirty-tonners."

Within a few minutes, the larger excavator was reaching into the airlock to clear a pathway behind Red's machine, loading the spoil into one of the Pod's eight-wheeled tipping trucks.

White watched with Douglas, as the first load was taken away and dumped at the other end of the hangar. "You know what I'm thinkin', right?"

Douglas nodded uncomfortably. "You're thinking, are we going to get to daylight before we've completely filled the Pod with thousands of tons of rubble?"

"Well, let's see, shall we?" White feigned a thoughtful expression. "If we're, say, half a mile underground and we need a tunnel about five metres wide and high – to get the machines through – that would equate to roughly… hmm, multiply that by five... carry the six… yes, that's almost exactly a *buttload* of rubble!"

Douglas chuckled. "We may only be a few feet in, let's stay positive."

"Oh, I am. I can't *wait* to see what's out there, Captain. I mean after spending a few months in Cretaceous world, this should be a piece of cake, right?"

Douglas looked at the vast excavation taking place before them. "Maybe you have a point. Perhaps we should think a little smaller, eh? More ventilation shaft, rather than—"

"Underpass?" supplied White, helpfully. "I mean, it *might* be quite safe out there."

Douglas placed a hand to his brow, covering his eyes and eventually pinching the bridge of his nose. "Oh, no' again."

Heinrich Schultz activated the homing beacon as a last resort, after waiting as long as possible for... what *had* he been hoping for? Inspiration?

There really was no way to dress his situation up. He had survived. That was it. His resources were dwindling fast. Despite his success in linking his escape pod's computer with the satellite net, he had only a partial picture of events out in the world. Douglas' ship had been somehow hidden from his spying eyes. However, he had found the recording of an explosion to his north-west. This feed showed parts of the *New World*'s giant bulk under attack – at least, that was how it appeared from the little information at his disposal. Had his granddaughter attacked Douglas' camp, then? Had she *taken* it?

As Franke's was the last capital ship of his *Dawn Fleet* still flying, maybe her officers had simply decided to leave Heidi on that island in order to make a play for themselves? There had been no communications chatter across the net, so it remained a possibility. Indeed, perhaps what the recording showed was not an attack at all, but some kind of accident? What if the *Heydrich*'s crew had simply thrown in their lot with Douglas, as that traitor Meritus had – *curse him!*

He needed information. He needed facts. He needed *help*. The very thought disgusted him, but it was a truth, nevertheless, and not knowing who was actually running the show made his situation even more perilous than it already was.

If his granddaughter had taken charge, would she even come for him? Would he want her to? He knew how cruel she could be; had encouraged, even incited such behaviour, instilling her with malice.

He remembered those games. Such a beautiful child – his creature in all things. Unfortunately, she was out now, and off the leash.

He despised cowardice. It was everywhere within his organisation. His people would quake when he so much as entered a room. However, thoughts of Heidi coming for *him*, for the first time provided just a glimmer of understanding into their condition.

He relaxed, very deliberately. Languidly, he raised his last glass of fifty-year-old malt. "Well, I shall just have to cross that bridge at the time. Now, a toast, I think."

He looked around for inspiration; the sun was setting over the river delta before him. The colours were 'art apart' from any of man's paltry imitations.

He smiled, one man alone. "Ah, yes. To *me*."

"*TIM!*" bellowed the four running teens, overwhelming their hapless victim before he could brace himself.

Almost smothered, Tim tried to answer them all at once but quickly ran out of breath. "*Whoa!* You're choking me," he laughed, trying to shake hands and exchange hugs all at once.

"I knew you'd make it!" shouted Henry, thumping him on the shoulder.

"Didn't doubt it for a second, mate," Woodsey added his sentiments.

"Oh, *Tim*," cried Rose, through joyful tears as she grabbed him around the neck.

"If I'd known I was going to receive a hero's welcome, I wouldn't have minded it all so much," he replied, grinning. Finally, his eye alighted on Clarrie.

She was holding back, he could tell, though her eyes welled with unshed tears.

With a few coughs and half-hearted excuses, Henry and Rose dragged Woodsey away to leave them alone.

"Timmy," Clarrie spoke his name tremulously.

He opened his arms and she moved into his embrace, gently.

"Not knocking me over with the others?" asked Tim, surprised.

She looked up, locking gazes with him. "I've been so worried about you. It's driven me half crazy, but I spoke with Rose yesterday – or whenever that was," she added with a wry smile.

"A hundred million years ago, hopefully, yes," he chuckled. "Spoke to her about what?"

Looking a little pensive, she explained, "Rose told me you've been through hell. That you couldn't even be yourself over there, or that *witch* would have killed you."

Tim's eyes were haunted as he looked away, but Clarrie pressed on.

"She said that you might come back changed and advised me to give you some space. Space to rediscover who you *truly* are."

He had spent some time wondering how he would feel when he saw Clarrie again. He was afraid that, after his ordeal, and with the damage his soul had taken in Heidi's camp, she might seem *young* to him now – too young, perhaps. He had been wrong.

Holding Clarrie at arms' length, he studied her. "You and Rose are very wise. I reckon you'll be leading these people one day. As for Henry and Woodsey… well, perhaps their futures lie more in digging and blowing stuff up!"

He laughed softly and she smiled up at him, causing her tears to fall.

"You're right, I do need a little space to find my feet, but don't think I've changed my mind about you, Clarrie. Thank you for understanding. You're the best."

He pulled her close and held her tightly.

Her reply was muffled by his chest. "You do what you gotta do. I can wait. I'm only fifteen, I've all the time in the world, right?"

She smiled up at him again, making Tim close his eyes with mild annoyance. "I missed your birthday, didn't I? Sorry, sweetheart. How was it?"

She wiped her eyes with feigned annoyance. "It was hell, you dummy! You better do better for Christmas!"

He laughed again. "Well, that's still months away. I'll make a note in my diary – something along the lines of 'don't get kidnapped over this period'. What if I put a line through the whole week, how's that?"

"Actually, for all we know, it might be Christmas tomorrow. We don't know what the date is outside."

Tim's eyebrows rose, impressed. "You're right, I hadn't considered that."

Her smile faded. "Have you seen your mom?"

"Not yet. The doctor wants to check her over thoroughly after the crash – before she's allowed visitors. He promised to tell her I'm safe though, so that's something. I can't wait to see her."

"Well, if you want me to come with you, or go see her alone, that's your call. Just let me know what you need."

He looked intently into her eyes, not merely with feeling, but with new respect. "Look, thanks, Clarrie."

"For what?"

"For not putting pressure on me. It might take a little while before I really feel myself again."

She linked her arm through his. "Let's find the others, then. That'll help you to remember. That and Woodsey's terrible jokes, of course!"

They set off together, at a leisurely pace, looking for trouble.

"You wished to see us, ma'am?"

Heidi sat motionless behind her smart captain's desk, staring dispassionately at the academics. It was obvious that the balding, middle-aged man standing before her had the habit of wringing his hands, but was desperately trying not to do so – there was something disturbingly familiar about this meeting for him.

The woman, younger and clearly of sterner material, returned her gaze dispassionately.

Heidi was irritated by the fear in the man's demeanour. She let him sweat a moment longer before answering, "Naturally, Doctor. That is why you are here. I have a task for you."

"Yes, ma'am," he replied, experimenting briefly with tucking his hands into the pockets of his lab coat but no, out they came again, to wring.

Heidi scrutinised him once more, a mercurial light in her eyes. Had she the choice, she would probably have replaced him, but there *was* no choice. She had only the people who came with the Dawn Fleet, those of them who still lived. Hopefully, he would pull himself together once the project began – he had gotten this far after all.

The woman spoke for the first time, interrupting her musings. A flash of annoyance crossed Heidi's face, but the woman continued undeterred. "What do you require of us, Doctor?"

Heidi glared at her for a moment. Still, the woman held her gaze. Eventually she nodded slowly. "Very well, Doctors. I have called you here to discuss a way to save our mission. As you worked with *mein Großvater*, as the principal designers of our wormhole technology, I can think of no one better."

A small slice of carrot, clumsily given, but Heidi was still feeling her way around the whole leadership versus tyranny conundrum.

It seemed to work on the bald man, at least. He visibly relaxed. She would have to see what she could do about that.

"What I am about to propose may be even more difficult, and the price of failure, very high."

That seemed to do the trick; he began wringing again. Perhaps she would find sport in this new game of politics she was exploring?

"You were given a place on this mission, a chance to become members of our new society, because of your scientific achievement. This is good, because I require your brilliance now."

Again, the woman remained impassive, suitably immune to flattery. Eventually, she spoke, "We have seen precious little of our 'promised land' so far, Doctor. Nevertheless, what is your plan?"

Heidi approved. This one had steel.

"I understand that our control mechanism is damaged, rather than the wormhole drive itself – correct?"

"Yes, ma'am," the man replied.

The woman merely nodded.

Heidi continued. "So in theory, we could open a wormhole but would have no way of controlling where it took us – yes?"

Again, the scientists agreed with her appraisal.

"I also understand that we do not have the manufacturing capability to construct a new control mechanism. So, I have been thinking, how else could we find our pathway through time and space?"

"You're suggesting some form of probe," the female scientist surmised. "Like a grapnel, fired at our destination attached to a metaphorical rope."

Heidi gave her a nod of respect. "Very good, Doctor. Obviously, I realise the reality will be rather more complicated than your metaphor suggests. Therefore, I have—"

"But, ma'am," the man interrupted her. "We don't have the equipment to construct a vehicle to send through a wormhole. It would effectively mean building a mini spaceship-cum-time-machine. We just don't—"

Heidi held up her hand and the man fell silent immediately. She eyed him coolly, disgusted by his timidity. "I am not suggesting any kind of ship or vehicle to traverse space and time. I'm suggesting something tiny. Perhaps *atomic* would be a better word? Something capable of taking the long way round, as it were."

The woman gave Heidi a sideways look, clearly piqued. "Please, Doctor, go on."

Heidi managed a wintry smile. "Very well, Doctors. I happen to have a direct link from this time to the Old Academy in Munich. This is naturally a very complex assignment already – unfortunately, it will be made even more so because of the necessity to hit our target within a relatively narrow date range."

The scientists exchanged a glance. The man gulped.

Heidi smiled. Good, now she had their attention. "We must arrive there no later than AD1943 if we are to allow ourselves a safety window."

"A safety w-window?" the man stuttered incredulously.

"Assuming you wish to avoid dying in an Allied bombing raid, yes, Doctor. Our target is a collection of fossils, 'stored recklessly and with stupid Nazi arrogance' according to my dear, and recently estranged, cousin.

"All that matters to us, is that those items will be stored just a few blocks away from Munich's Nazi Headquarters in 1943. Irritatingly, the Allies were turning the war against our courageous forebears by then and the museum will be destroyed by bombing during the night of the 24th and 25th of April, 1944. Should we arrive too early, our overtures of advancement may, just possibly, fall foul of the very arrogance referred to by my cousin. However, as the tides of fortune were reversing by that point, it should provide an ideal time to submit our offer, and for it to be taken seriously."

"Taken *seriously?*" The man could not hide his disbelief.

"Indeed, Doctor," Heidi replied smoothly. "Something I suggest you begin to do with immediate effect. While outside on the plateau, I noticed an unused grave pit. If you are of no use to me here, I might just use you to fill it in."

He gulped again.

The woman took a step forward, shunting her superior out of the way. "Tell me, Dr Schultz, what sort of vessel are you suggesting we use to carry our probe through time? And what exactly do we have to offer the *Reich?*"

It roared again. The stink of rancid fish and guts almost turned Heinrich Schultz's stomach. It seemed remarkable that his barely perceptible human scent could make its way straight to the creature's nose, past the olfactive battering of its own breath.

Regardless, his hiding place had been well and truly rumbled. Forced to live on the unappetising fruits from nearby trees, the giant had clearly caught wind of him while he was out collecting them. It had followed him up from the river.

The old man had always taken care of his physical condition, but he was nearly eighty and had not eaten well for weeks. His escape pod was almost indestructible, but he was not sure he would make it back to its safety with this creature almost upon him.

The snuffling grew ever closer. He was hidden from sight, but this would not protect him for long. Hunkered down amongst the bushes, just right of the trail his crashing escape pod had smashed through the woodland some weeks ago, he worked his mind frantically. The freshly turned earth and splintered foliage led all the way to the top of the escarpment. It was at least another hundred metres to his tiny ship and in a flat-out dash, he would lose.

His prideful intelligence had always set him well aloft of the herd, but the proximity of a fully grown Spinosaurus aegyptiacus – popular namesake to the whole spinosaurid genera – caused his boundless imagination to falter.

He needed a distraction. *Don't suppose the damned thing likes fruit?* he wondered as he cast about for an idea. Ironically, that thought provided an idea that was indeed to bear fruit.

Travelling back down towards the river was ever a risk, but it was where the edible fruits grew – although Schultz considered the term 'edible' to be relative.

Having made the journey three times during the last ten days, he had known that it was only a matter of time before he ran into trouble. The river was the source of all things here, as the Nile and its delta would be a hundred million years into the future.

The rivers flooding *his* delta were neither the Nile, nor *of* the Nile, but they governed by the same rules, carved out when life first took to the land, hundreds of millions of years before the Cretaceous – water was king, it was everything.

Schultz always approached the river with care, life becoming noticeably more prolific and diverse the closer he got, and where there is plenty, there is often *size*.

Despite this, it was astounding just how close such a vast predator had managed to get to him before he even recognised its presence. The better part of twenty metres in length, its huge head was covered with the undeniable scars of experience.

A veteran hunter, no question, and me, caught with little more than an armful of barely digestible fruit in my arsenal! Damn!

His escape pod had been equipped for basic survival, and as part of its equipment stash, there was a handgun with three extra clips. The spare ammunition was stored aboard his lifeboat – and in no danger of being useful.

Damn! Damn! Damn!

Naturally, conserving supplies was paramount to a man in his predicament, and he had assumed the remaining three bullets in his pistol would be enough. After all, a loud bang, followed by the smell of smoking gun oil, would scare away any dumb animals while he collected food, surely. However, in what was almost an epiphany, he realised that on this occasion he had better be pretty darned sure before testing the theory.

Fifteen tons of killer bearing down on his position made him decidedly *unsure*. Not even close.

The bullet would be like a bee sting, pointless. The bang might be effective – or more precisely, might produce an *effect*, but at this proximity, what would that effect be? Would it frighten the dinosaur away or anger it to lash out?

Think, Heinrich, think! He chided his inability to plan or to act as his final seconds ticked away.

He reached a decision. It would be almost impossible to miss such an animal at this range, but as an expert marksman, he had other options, allowing him to choose a different tack. Throwing one of his hard-won fruits up high, he watched it sail over the giant's head. As it reached its zenith, he fired. The bang made the creature rear away from the noise as the exploding fruit showered its face with mushy, sickly sweet shrapnel.

Shaking its head, against the ringing in its ears, and the stink and flying debris confusing its other senses, it bellowed indignation. A largely aquatic animal, its nostrils were high on its head, and it snorted violently.

While his monstrous opponent bucked in agitation, Schultz was already making his way through the underbrush. Glancing behind, he saw the creature rub its head against a tree trunk, wiping ineffectually to clear its eyes and ears. Almost halfway to the lifeboat, he tucked the remaining fruit into his jacket and, closing one eye, aimed with a double-grip towards the branch immediately beside the giant head.

Bang! A flutter of small life exploded around him, flying, scrambling and chittering away angrily from his immediate vicinity. The Spinosaurus roared again in fear and surprise.

This was Schultz's chance, and he took it. A sixty-metre dash across open ground to his escape pod – and never was anything more aptly named.

Spinosaurus, head high in the foliage and temporarily confused, took its rage out on the trees, tearing every branch and twig within reach away from their trunks as it fought to clear its field of vision.

The near universal disparity between predator-prey intelligence was all on its head, but when Spinosaurus at last spotted its quarry having it away on his toes, its vicious, selfish, ruthless reptilian mind provided an answer to restore balance – the massive application of power.

ROAR! The huge carnivore lunged forward into a run. With clawed arms well above the ground and all the power driving its massive hind legs, it quickly accelerated to a speed the rapidly tiring old man simply could not match. Each of the dinosaur's strides covered several metres, closing the distance quickly.

Schultz did not need to look round, he could *hear* the thunder of pursuit. Barely breaking step, he spun briefly and fired, hitting Spinosaurus in the face. This elicited more noise, more anger, more determination and more speed from the beast.

The old man was terrified. Still ten metres from salvation – the tiny vessel that had made survival possible through frigid space, white hot re-entry, a spine-numbing crash-landing and multiple natural threats.

Now almost equidistant between lifeboat and adversary, he had half the distance to cover, but also half the speed – breathless, with legs burning, he was almost spent.

At six metres, his exhausted limbs moved ever more slowly, the power of panic waning. On and on, he forced himself to yet greater exertion, hearing the heavy breathing of Spinosaurus like a set of industrial bellows, right behind him. Every intake of breath generated the impression of suction, dragging him back towards that maw.

Four metres, and with the last of his breath, he shouted, *"Open!"* – praying the voice activated software aboard his lifeboat would recognise the word, given his condition.

In answer to the running man's prayer, the side hatch did indeed open, just as his shadow's shadow fell across him. *"Nooooo!"*

From two metres, Schultz's only chance was to dive. Flinging himself through the hatch, he spun, landing on his back to face the enemy. Enormous, *crocodilianesque* jaws snapped, jamming his boot between a pair of opposing teeth. Mandibles already tight shut, the Spinosaurus could not bring its awesome bite force to bear, but by the same token, the old man could not free himself from its grip, either.

Locked in a hate-fuelled confusion, the challengers faced off – a momentary impasse.

The giant knew instinctively that to open its jaws for another try would be to lose its prize forever.

The man knew that to close the hatch would cost him his leg, if the creature refused to let go. No 'nanny state' sensors prevented entrapment between the external doors of spacecraft. Anyone unfortunate enough to be caught in a closing hatch would be cut in half with hydraulic efficiency, to save the vessel.

The old man looked around in wild-eyed panic. If the creature tugged him back outside, it was all over. He reached up to a touch-sensitive drawer behind him. It soft-opened, and fumbling desperately through the contents, his hand closed about a spare ammunition clip. Frantic fingers grappled with the weapon and clip, trying to make them one, while his free leg shook under immense strain as it braced him in the hatchway.

Click.

Almost silently, the clip locked into the handle and he turned the gun on the set of giant grinning teeth before him. The creature had given him a good run. "Sorry old chap, I know this is a little unsporting, but there you are…"

Bang!

Schultz's ears rang. He hardly heard his own command. Fortunately, the door controls suffered no such frailty, and the hatch sealed with alacrity.

He slumped against the storage compartments built into the opposite wall, staring balefully at the broken Spinosaurus tooth on the deck. For Heinrich Schultz, it was a token of his own mortality, whereas the giant outside would simply grow another.

"Mum?" Tim barely recognised her. Ever a slight woman, she seemed to have lost several stones in weight. "*Mum?*" he tried again gently.

Patricia Norris' eyes fluttered open, just. She was almost infinitely weary, but seeing her son's face again, realising it was he who held her hand, reignited the spark of life.

"Tim," she croaked with difficulty. Even smiling taxed her, but the love in her eyes was undiminished by pain or worry.

"Our crash landing shook her up some," supplied Dr Flannigan from across the bed.

Tim smiled, his relief palpable. "Didn't do me any favours either!"

Flannigan returned his smile. "I'll give you a minute alone, but don't tire her. She still has a way to go – but you'll get there, won't you, Patricia? Back shortly." He nodded to them and left, with a lighter step than he had managed for a while.

"Tell me…"

Tim knew what she was asking for. He also knew that almost the entirety of *that* conversation would have to wait for another day.

He squeezed her hand, attempting nonchalance. "It wasn't so bad, Mum. I was well looked after. I believe Captain Douglas already told you, that they just wanted me to teach them about the Cretaceous, really. I can tell you the details when you're stronger. The main thing is, I'm fine, Mum. Honest."

"If anything… happened to you…"

He leaned in closer, keeping her hand. "Hey, look at me, I'm fine."

"Your face… bruised…"

"It's been a bit of a rough ride for everyone, Mum. But I'm not seriously hurt, just a few bumps."

She was growing weaker again, but she tried to squeeze his hand and bring it to her cheek. He went with the movement, assisting her.

Holding his hand to her mouth she kissed it gently and fell back into sleep's embrace.

Tim sat perfectly still for the next ten minutes, until Flannigan returned.

"How are we doin—" he began.

Tim raised the index finger of his free hand to his lips, signifying that his mother slept.

Flannigan nodded and checked the pulse at her left wrist. "She's fine," he whispered. "She perked up just before our jump, when I told her you were coming back to see her. The crash has set her back a little."

Seeing concern cross the young man's face, he added, "She'll be fine, son. She's through the woods now. It'll be slow, but now you're back… Hell, give it a week and we'll have to shackle her to the bed!"

Tim gently replaced Patricia's hand comfortably at her side, retrieving his own. Standing, he offered it to Flannigan. "Thank you, Doctor. When I saw my—" he caught himself, glancing at his mother to check she still slept. "When I saw *Heidi* shoot her down, I…" he swallowed, unable to say more.

Flannigan took the proffered hand in his right, placing his left upon Tim's shoulder. "Hey, you did a hell of a job, kid, but it's all over now. We won."

The pile of soil, rock and detritus from the ship's hull was growing to alarming proportions within the hangar. Douglas approached Bluey, Red and the other workers while they took a sandwich break.

"Any signs of the sky yet, gentlemen?" he asked lightly. The air they had within the damaged vessel was finite – now most of the machinery was offline – but panicking the workers into taking silly risks would not help, so he affected nonchalance.

"Not yet, Captain," replied Bluey. "Red's doing a bang-up job in the tunnel, but more keeps falling down. There could be a whole mountain on top of us, we just don't know."

Douglas sensed the diggers' air of defeat. They would keep trying, but he could tell belief was leaving them. "Should we be digging a tunnel, rather than just moving earth? Ah'm sure Jim Miller and Sam Burton will have something around we can use for props and supports."

Bluey nodded. "Yeah, that's what we've just been discussing. Dr Samantha Portree's our chief engineer. She's in with the doc at the moment – oh, don't worry, she's fine, I think. The doc just wanted to check her over before putting her to work. When she comes back, we're gonna get into it. I think the first thing we should do is break out some of our surveying equipment – assuming it's not busted. If we can get an impression of the geology in front and above us, at least we won't be pokin' around completely in the dark."

"Aye, that sounds sensible," replied Douglas, turning to Bluey's brother. "Red, are you safe up there? Could it no' cave in on ye?"

The brothers looked at one another. Red shrugged. "What else is there, mate— er, Captain? Somebody's gotta do it. We've been taking it in turns."

Douglas had already witnessed the extent of the brothers' courage on numerous occasions over the last few months; he eyed them keenly and with respect. "Take as much care as you can, laddies. Home might be just through that pile of dirt. We dinnae want to lose you now."

They grinned back at him.

"That'll be something, eh, Captain?" said Bluey.

"Sure will, mate," added Red. "We're getting bladdy close to runnin' outta lager!"

Sergeant Coleman sat in the cockpit of Heidi's remaining orbital attack ship. She watched the *Heydrich* approach her position on the overhead monitor, courtesy of their satellite feed. Heaving a deep sigh, she wondered what sort of mood their illustrious leader might be in, upon her return.

Her people had spent most of yesterday cutting the foliage away from their recently discovered concrete saferoom. There was no one left that they needed to hide it from, after all. It had been hard work, splitting their efforts between stripping the woodland and protecting the crop, but finally the bunker was revealed in all its boxy, grey, style-less glory.

Setting aside the aesthetics, Douglas' builders and engineers had not messed around. The walls and roof were a metre thick of steel-reinforced concrete, and there was no reason to suppose that the floor slab was any less robust. It was an impressively strong little structure. So much so, that it had given Coleman an idea.

The people present had not the mathematics between them to test the theory, so when she landed the ship on top of the bunker, it had been with great care and more than a little trepidation. At a glance, it seemed the massively built structure *should* be up to the task, but proof was ever in the pudding. If she had destroyed their new saferoom, even worse their last fighter craft, it would probably have meant a firing squad, knowing Heidi. However, if the machine had been destroyed by a dinosaur while on the ground, with Coleman in charge, it would probably *also* have meant a firing squad. It had seemed worth the risk.

From the cockpit, atop the concrete bunker, it was a fair view across the lake. At four metres high, her new landing platform placed the ship out of reach for all but the largest animals, and she could not see why they would be interested in it, if the people were all below, or hiding elsewhere.

The large avians had all made a discreet exit when she fired up *her* bird, so she suspected they, too, would leave the craft alone.

The *Heydrich* was almost upon them. Coleman peered through the forward screen. "Any minute now, they should be… ah. There they are."

The forty-five-metre-long, matte black capital ship hove into view, crossing the jagged peaks that surrounded their lakeside world. "Peace is over," she muttered to herself.

The men, who helped Coleman rescue Heidi from her grandfather, seemed besotted with the German woman.

One of them even threw his life away in a vain attempt to stand before her, when the Sigilmassasaurus attacked them a few days previously. The way Coleman saw it, she was here because she wanted to live, not only past the apocalypse, but on a clean Earth that was not broken. She had saved Heidi merely because her grandfather was far worse.

She sighed again. "Everyone has to pick a side. I suppose I'd better get ready for the reunion."

Heaving herself from the pilot's seat, she walked through to the small craft's rear compartment. Checking her weapon, she opened the side hatch. Careful to close it behind her, to prevent any small lodgers from setting up home, she took the makeshift wooden ladder her men had knocked together yesterday. Once down, it was just a few metres to the beach where she began her walk towards the *Heydrich*. The vessel had already begun her landing cycle.

Coleman covered her ears, squinting against the sand blown in her direction.

The ship set down, and silence returned to soothe their ringed, mountainous enclosure. As Coleman neared, the starboard landing ramp lowered to meet her.

Heidi strode from the ship to return Coleman's salute. Could she perceive a subtle difference in Heidi's manner? What was it… positivity?

She knew that a Schultz in a good mood could be more dangerous than a Schultz in a bad one – bad being their baseline.

"Successful trip, ma'am?"

"Indeed, Coleson."

"Cole*man*, ma'am."

"Quite. Well, everything seems in order here. What is that I spy over there?"

Coleman explained what they had found.

"A good idea to keep the fighter safely off the ground. Well done, Cole*man*. You have done well here." She smiled. It was terrifying.

"Erm…" Before Coleman could struggle further with a more coherent reply, Heidi cut across her.

"We can use your new bunker to protect the more delicate items. I expect you to build a guarded compound to house the rest. Now you have more space, I will leave you a larger contingent this time."

"You're leaving again, ma'am?"

"Indeed."

"For Patagonia?"

"Indeed. There is much still to retrieve from the *Last Word* and *Newfoundland*. Even the *Eisernes Kreuz* may yet yield a little more. Oh, by the way, Coleman, I have a little surprise for you."

Heidi took out her comm. "Bring the truck out."

After a few moments, one of the *New World*'s personnel carriers descended the ramp.

Heidi smiled again at Coleman's surprise. "I secreted the vehicle away in the forest near the *Last Word* plateau. In case of emergencies. It's electric, as you can tell. I've had a second powerpack placed in the back, so you should get two good charges out of the vehicle. It is efficient, and we will have returned well before it needs recharging. An impressive vehicle. That is why I decided to keep it. There is also another tracked personnel carrier to be retrieved from Patagonia. We had reached our weight capacity, so it is locked-down on the plateau."

Coleman was astounded – not by the receipt of two extra vehicles, that was merely good fortune – she had simply never known Heidi this *chatty* before. She had certainly never witnessed her bothering to explain things to a subordinate. It was *weird*.

"Oh, I almost forgot to tell you," she added, brightly. "I have a way home. Or perhaps, a way to a new home, we shall see. Of course, we will find and crush the traitors aboard the *New World* first, especially my cousin. He must pay."

Coleman relaxed a little. *Ah, finally, the Heidi we know and loathe.*

The rumbling shook the deck. Fortunately, Red had had the sense to bring the ten-ton digger back to the mouth of the hangar doors before taking a break. Even so, the avalanche of soil, stone and other debris filled the excavated airlock completely, eradicating their hard work and burying the front of the machine right up to its windscreen. The actor and the front half of its tracks had completely disappeared.

The snacking workforce jumped to their feet and ran away from the hangar doors as soon as the deck plates began to shake, shouting for everyone near to do likewise.

After the falling earth came a cloud of brown-black dust, billowing into the hangar. With it came a peaty smell along with the stench of damp and decay as soil, buried for centuries, greeted the air.

The landslide gradually abated, allowing the crews to move back in, albeit gingerly.

Red climbed up onto the buried excavator's cab roof. "Oh, bladdy hell!"

"Is it totalled?" called Bluey from below.

"No... well, I dunno. The cab's been filled with soil and God knows what else."

"Did it put the screen through?"

"No, I opened the front screen after I backed her away from the dig face. It was getting as hot as hell in there, mate!"

Bluey grimaced at the further bad news. "I suppose it's the ground source heat. Dunno how far down we are."

Red peered down, over the rim of the cab's roof. "Not only that, bro, but have you noticed the air's getting a little more lived-in down here, already?"

Bluey nodded. He had noticed. "So, have you got any good news from up there in the crow's nest?"

Red turned away, grim-faced and then spun back almost immediately, bearing a largish clump of earth and a look of dumb disbelief. "Look at this! Here – catch!"

He dropped the tuft to his brother, who had not been ready for it, and so jumped out of the way. "You stupid baggar!"

"*Look* at it!" snapped Red, pointing down from the cab.

Still grumbling, Bluey bent to inspect it. After a brief study, he instantly straightened, staring back up at his brother with a grin that burst across his face like a size eight zipper on a twenty-two.

"*Grass!*" they shouted in unison. Also in perfect tandem, they turned and shouted across the hangar, "*Captain Douglas!*"

Baines left Hiro, Georgio and Singh trying to breathe life back into as many of the *New World*'s systems as they could. She promised Georgio faithfully that she would ask Beck Mawar to find him as soon as it was safe to do so.

Leaving with Jones and The Sarge, she set about rescuing as many of Meritus' people as possible from their mostly powerless apartments.

They soon came across Meritus himself, who thanked them profusely for helping his people, most of whom seemed largely unharmed, thankfully.

As more teams were freed to help the rescue operation, Captain Baines, Captain Meritus, Sergeant Jackson and Corporal Jones made their way down to the main Pod hangar.

What they saw when they got there took them by surprise.

Baines made a beeline for Douglas. "Have we had a cave-in?"

"Jill, Tobias, Dewi," replied Douglas, greeting them all in turn with warm handshakes and backslaps. "You got to them then, Sarge? Ah cannae tell ye how relieved Ah am to see you're all OK. No, this mound is not from a cave-in, we brought all this soil in here on purpose."

Baines looked slightly bewildered. "Are we building inside-out-world? What's happening?"

Douglas chuckled happily. It proved infectious. None of them had had very much to chuckle happily about for a while, so they were eager for more.

"We've just suffered a bit of a landslip," Douglas elucidated.

Baines stopped laughing. "OK, James. So what we're doing here is not joy, not even mirth, it's just hysterical laughter, *right?*"

Douglas laughed all the more, a deep belly laugh that seemed to reinvigorate him. "No, we've been bringing the soil in as we dug our way out of here. Dr Portree was about to use some clever scanning gear, in the hope of finding out how far down we are, when, to use your words, we had a bit of a cave-in."

Baines frowned. "I'm still not seeing the silver lining, James."

He chuckled mischievously. "That's because ye've no' looked closely! On top of that great big pile of rubbish that landed on us, was something more beautiful than Ah've words to describe."

"*Try,*" stated Baines, unmoved.

Of course, this set him off giggling again. Jones leaned in close to The Sarge. "Do you think he's had a knock on the head, boy?"

"Ah heard that," said Douglas, still grinning. "Come with me, all of you."

They followed him, crossing to the half-buried digger blocking the hatch out of the main hangar. He bent to pick up a clump of peaty soil. "Now, will ye look at that!" he declared as if pulling a prize-winning pie from the oven.

Baines wrinkled her nose at the smelly object. "Dirt and grass?" she queried. After a few beats, her expression changed. "*Grass!* Everyone, it's grass!"

"And?" asked Meritus, completely at sea.

Baines knelt to examine the grass more closely. She seemed to have tuned out, running her fingers through it, as if through the fur of a beloved pet.

Douglas explained, "If we have grass, Tobias, we must be near the top, or the side, at least. More than that, there was *no* grass in the Mid-Cretaceous – at least not that we saw. Don't you see? We're back! And just the other side of that mountain of *crap* blocking the door, hopefully, will be the human race!"

Meritus grinned at last. "Home?"

"It's where we were aiming for, was it no'?" Douglas beamed. "But we won't know exactly until we bust our way out of here. Nevertheless, this is a *good* sign! Ah've a feeling the party we had upon arriving safely in the Cretaceous will pale into insignificance compared with our reunion with the human race!"

"Are we about to start digging again, sir?" asked The Sarge, completely outside the spreading merriment.

"Any minute now, Sarge!"

"Then I'd better get these men armed, sir."

Chapter 4 | Horrors, Cope

Electric vehicles and plant were commonplace long before Douglas was born, yet there was still something frightening about such immensely powerful machines moving such heavy loads, with hardly a sound.

He watched Bluey, Red and the others handle their plant with the dexterity of dancers, swaying with the symphony of progress. Construction always begins with destruction, but this time their goal was not to shape the space around them but to join it.

Time and place awaited them, but would it be *their* time and place? Douglas folded his arms as he stood and watched. The Sarge was right to be wary. The cleverness and superhuman efforts of his engineering staff had brought them this far. Whatever happened next, that was tribute and testimony enough to their extraordinary tenacity, sagacity and capacity in the face of terrible danger. Yet it was no guarantee that they were on the money.

He shifted his weight nervously. In reality, there could be almost anything waiting outside.

A couple of Patricia Norris' botanists were examining the grasses and other plant residue, drawn in with the peat slide. The crash had put their laboratory out of commission for a while, so examination could only be made with the naked eye and basic comm-camera zooms. Their report, such as it was, was inconclusive.

This was no great surprise, but going with the assumption that they were still in the vicinity of Britain, they believed the material to be post ice age – and by that, they meant the last ice age as far as modern man was concerned.

So, somewhere within approximately ten thousand years of our own time, then. He blew out his cheeks, both frustrated and disturbed by his musings. *That's still a hell of a lot of leeway for things to go very, very wrong for us. Will this nightmare never end?*

"We may have it right, you know."

Baines broke into his thoughts. He had not even heard her approach and smiled ruefully. "How do ye always know what Ah'm thinking?"

She gave him a secret smile, which also passed him by.

"Aye. To tell you the truth, Jill, Ah'm more nervous about this than Ah was when we landed in the Cretaceous. At least we knew where we were!"

Baines nodded but had nothing to add.

"Ah just wish we could get everything working before we open the doors, ye know?"

"It's a worry," agreed Baines. "If we chanced that though, we might run out of air before we get everything back, and then not have time to dig our way out. We even stripped the life-support from the plant and vehicles to save weight, remember?"

"Aye, choose any *one* from this 'crappy list' as usual! Ah really hope this is it, Jill. Ah just want to get these people home. Ah know our world's not perfect—"

"It's dying," she interjected.

Douglas sighed. "Ah know. But we had hope."

"You mean Mars? James, we both know that Mars was too little, too late. Perhaps our race would have continued in some miserable way, but almost everyone else would be dead within a century."

He turned to face her. "You're really cheering the auld man up, here!"

Smiling, she linked her arm through his. "I'm sorry, James. What I'm trying to say is, if this is it, this is our life, then perhaps that should be enough? We have good people here and, despite the broken ship, we still have resources. I'm sure our ingenious engineers will have the power back on soon. So maybe we should stop running?"

"Oh, aye, running…" he muttered.

"James?"

"We've done plenty of that! Now Ah'm wondering what kind of disaster, stroke monster-related-madness, lies just the other side of that pile of dirt!"

"There's just no talking with you at the moment, is there?" She laughed lightly, giving his arm a squeeze. "Let's just see, huh?"

Baines' affection elicited a reluctant smile from Douglas, but his concern remained.

A horn blast from the larger of the two working diggers made them start.

Bluey grinned. "Sorry, Captains."

"You don't look sorry!" Baines called back merrily.

Bluey's grin widened. "We need you up at the entrance. We're about to break through."

"On our way. Thank you," replied Douglas.

Red took point duty in the second ten-tonner – once their first had been towed away for cleaning and repair – with The Sarge's armed response team either side and to the rear of him.

The side hatch of the machine remained open, to aid communication between the driver and the people around him. "You blokes ready?"

The Sarge looked up to give an economical nod before returning his gaze immediately forward.

Red took a deep breath, reached for the twin joysticks and lifted the machine's actor. A minor landslide poured around the bucket as it rose, and beyond it was bright, clean starlight.

Red could not remove the rubble with the soldiers all around him, so he shouted for everyone to stand clear as he pushed both drive levers forward, using the backfill blade to shove through like a bulldozer.

The might of the ten-ton excavator relentlessly pushed soil and stone out of the way, eventually rocking to a halt outside.

The air was biting fresh, but there was also something else: smoke.

Red raised the arm of the machine, moving the bucket aside for a better view. Beyond the reach of his working lights, the beautiful vista of rolling hills was well-lit by the eerie starlight, but also by a full moon.

"This doesn't smell like home, mate," he called to The Sarge.

That was when the firing began. A loud *tang* ricocheted off the digger's cab, causing Red to duck down low behind the controls. "It's the bladdy frying pan again, Sarge!"

Out of nowhere, they were everywhere. A hundred horsemen at least, most bearing fiery torches and lances, three or four metres in length. They were clearly armed with other weaponry too. It was difficult to make out details in the low light, but the short, steel-tipped bolt that thudded into the spoil, right by The Sarge's head, left him in no doubt that they had them.

His men returned fire instinctively, with a mixture of stunning and traditional weaponry.

"Fire into the air! Fire into the air!" The Sarge bellowed. "Don't kill any of them!"

Douglas, armed only with a stun pistol, made his way alongside the digger. "Red, get out of there, you're their main target. You're a sitting duck, man!"

He made to help the man down, but Red pulled away.

"Hang on a minute!" The Australian doused the diggers headlamps, muttering something about them being a 'bladdy bullseye'.

He leapt down and Douglas packed him off behind the machine. Keeping low, he moved forward. "Jill, stay with Red."

Outside was a chaos of horse and man. Shouting and shooting was all around him. His people were now firing into the air, but he could see they had already brought one of the riders down.

After the initial volley, the pistol cracks stopped. Their attackers no longer seemed to be firing. Instead, they charged, retreated and charged again, but when blue stun bolts flashed out, causing their ponies to stumble, followed by the crackle of automatic weapons fire which filled the valley, their attack faltered.

Shaggy, powerful little ponies wheeled, as men shouted insults, "Be gone! Devils!"

One voice rang clear above all others, "MAXWELL! MAXWELL! TO MEEEE!"

A few of the animals had been rendered unconscious. Although desperate not to leave them, the dismounted men were left with no choice but to grab the manes of passing ponies and run alongside. Using the power of the horses to increase the length of their strides, they made their escape.

In a moment, it was all over.

Five ponies remained on the hillside along with the man they had also brought down.

"He's alive, sir," The Sarge called.

Douglas turned to Baines. "Jill, get Natalie Pearson up here to check on the horses. Ah'll also need Beckett."

"I'm on it, Captain," she replied, pulling her comm from a pocket.

"And Jill, before he starts, tell Beckett Ah'm no' in the mood!"

Douglas carried a tray of hot drinks for the men on guard. The morning light made it immediately apparent just how much earth had slipped down into the gulley created by their machines.

As he reached the mouth of the cutting, the quality of light took his breath away. Very clearly autumnal, the landscape was clean and pure. Frost clung to the western slopes of valleys, crags and dells, where the sun was yet to chase it away.

Douglas felt like he was on top of the world. The view just kept on going – hill after valley after hill. He wordlessly passed a steaming mug to The Sarge, handing the tray to another man for distribution.

"Thank you, sir. Been a damned cold one."

Douglas felt a lump in his throat. "Ah think Ah'm home, Sarge."

"Sir?"

Douglas shook his head slightly, as if to clear his thoughts. "Something about these hills. I feel…"

Seeing that Douglas had no more to offer, The Sarge began, "Lieutenant Singh came up here last night, sir. He's a clever cookie, that one. He was taking scans of the night sky – you remember how clear it was – trying to get a fix, so he could work out when and where we are."

"Did he come back to ye?"

Jackson nodded. "Yes, sir. He thinks it's roughly halfway through the last millennium, but he wanted to crunch the numbers some more before committing."

"Fair enough, Ah suppose. However, after seeing those horsemen last night, Ah could have told ye that!"

The Sarge chuckled. "Yes, sir. Reckon we'd have all been in the ballpark. Is there any news about the man we shot?"

"Aye. And it's good news, as it happens. The round sliced him across the shoulder. Flannigan said it was a fairly simple operation to fix him up. Apparently, the real battle was trying to get him clean enough to begin!"

"Bit ripe, was he?" The Sarge asked, good-naturedly.

"Aye, he was a wee bit rum, to say the least. Beckett's interviewing him at the moment. Ah can only imagine how that's going!"

The Sarge chuckled again. "My favourite archaeologist! Still, if ever there was a time for the historian to shine…" He took a long pull of his coffee and sighed. "Have you ever seen a view like that, Captain?"

"Not really, everything was spoiled by the time Ah lived here, if indeed that *was* here. The Cretaceous was stunningly beautiful in parts, but Ah have to say, standing here, among the hills, Ah've never seen anything bonnier."

The Sarge raised his cup. "To home."

"Aye," agreed Douglas. "Home."

The clay mugs clicked together. "Have you seen this, sir?"

"What's that, Sarge?"

"Down the slope to the left – unless my eyes deceive me, that looks very much like heather!"

Douglas beamed.

Heidi sat at the desk within the captain's quarters, commandeered as her own.

"You wished to see me, ma'am?"

"Ah, Coleman. Very good. I have a mission for you."

Coleman stood to attention. "Of course, ma'am."

Heidi stood too, rounding her desk to stand before the sergeant. "Before I give you details, I wish you to answer something for me."

"If I can, ma'am."

"I am sure of it. Tell me, Coleman, if you are a pilot, why are you not an officer – flight officer, at least?"

Coleman blinked, tensing, never knowing what to expect from Heidi Schultz. It seemed the woman had surprised her again. "My flying credentials are all civilian, ma'am."

"Yes, I am aware, but you could have easily used them for rapid advancement. Why didn't you?"

"I didn't see the need, Doctor." Her answer was circumspect, and from her expression, it seemed Heidi knew it, too.

"Come, Coleman. Ally, isn't it? Let us not be coy. What is the real reason you did not wish for early advancement?"

Coleman swallowed awkwardly. "I… I merely wanted a position on the Dawn Fleet, ma'am. It seemed our world was ending and your… er… your *family* seemed to offer an alternative."

Heidi viewed her sidelong. "And exactly how did you become involved with, as you say, *my* family?"

Coleman gave a half smile. "You know how it is, ma'am. You get hooked up with the wrong guy and fall in with…"

Heidi arched an eyebrow. *"Criminals?"*

The feeling of being hunted must have shown on Coleman's face, causing Heidi to laugh one of her tinkling, almost girlish little laughs. She leaned back on her desk, at her ease. "Do not worry, Coleman. You are not on trial here."

Coleman raised an eyebrow and Heidi laughed again. Clapping her hands together she said, "No. Really. Allow me to tell you why I think you wished to avoid promotion."

"As you wish, Doctor."

"I think you forwent a commission to avoid spending more time with people who make you feel… how *do* we make you feel, Coleman? Shall we go with *uncomfortable?"*

She certainly was now, but stoked her sergeant's 'blank eyes front' look for all it was worth.

"And, of course," Heidi continued, "if you're not an officer, you don't have to make any of the really big decisions, the really *nasty* decisions, do you?"

Coleman swallowed again, but said nothing.

"I think that *you* think that you are a *good* person, don't you, Coleman?"

She had no idea how the hell to answer that one, so she opted for the truth. "I hope so, Doctor."

Heidi nodded, satisfied. "Is that why you saved me from *mein Großvater?*"

Again, Coleman had no idea how to answer that for the best, the truth on this occasion being rather stickier to explain. *I'd better make sure I know where she's going with this before I answer. I doubt being honest will win me any prizes.*

Heidi continued, "Or was it because, after *mein Großvater* arrived here, I was simply the lesser of two evils?"

Damn! Where is she getting this intel?

"Don't worry, Coleman. I'm not psychic—"

You could have fooled me!

"I have spent some time examining the files of all the people aboard this vessel. Our old ways seem to have left us with a few problems, so I am looking for people I can trust. What we have to do now will be very difficult. It will test every one of us to the limit, and I do mean every one of us – even the lost."

Coleman studied the German woman before her. *Why is she being so frank? Or is this just another set of lies, or another trap? But why? Oh, what the hell, I may as well ask!* "What do you mean, Doctor?"

Heidi smiled. It was the kind of indulgent smile one gave to a dog, while it tilted its head this way and that, trying to work out what was being said.

Any minute now the stuck-up little bitch will try and pat me on the head!

"I will tell you soon enough, Sergeant. But now, I need to brief you on your mission – it has two parts.

"Firstly, you will take some basic supplies, and one of our medics, and you will find the escape pod that crash-landed in Egypt. Its beacon is still switched on, so this should present little difficulty.

"While you are there, you will carry out the second part of your mission, which is to fly a search pattern over northern Egypt – I will provide you with the co-ordinates. I wish you to spot and plot as many of *these* that you can find within the limits of your fuel."

She waved a hand over her desktop, causing a monitor to glow to life. Touching the panel, it rose at an angle, facing them. On the screen was a picture of a dinosaur. It bore a certain resemblance to the Sigilmassasaurus, which had killed some of their number during the debacle with the *New World*, but the tiny silhouette of a man, standing alongside, made it clear that it was much larger.

Heidi could tell that Coleman was intrigued. "I suggest you cover some territory *before* you collect our survivor, however. He may not be good company."

"*He?* Ma'am?"

"I think we both know who it was that survived, don't we? You leave in the morning. Good night, Coleman."

Douglas lovingly gave his meeting room table a final wipe down with a cloth. The meeting room itself, just off the *New World*'s bridge, had been all but destroyed, the outer bulkhead crushed. The table and some of the chairs had proved salvageable, but that was all.

He sighed. "If we ever do get back, NASA will have ma head for this."

Availing himself of one of several conference rooms within the Pod, he called a staff meeting to brief everyone about their situation. The main speakers would be Lieutenant Sandip Singh and the historian, Thomas Beckett. He sighed again. "This should be entertaining."

"You know that talking to yourself isn't good, right?" said Baines.

"Where did you come from?" he asked in surprise. "Have you suddenly become really sneaky or am Ah going deaf?"

Baines laughed. "You're lucky I'm here at all. I couldn't find the place!"

"Oh. Ah wondered why Ah was the only one here. Ah was beginning to think Ah'd forgotten ma deodorant!"

"It's not quite that serious, James. However, you did choose to meet in room '4i' – what's the betting everyone else went to forty-one?"

"Oh."

Baines laughed again.

"That's right, laugh it up! Ah used to have a highly competent first officer who *knew* things like that. *She* used to stop me making a fool of myself."

"What's wrong with Commander Gleeson?"

Douglas looked at her askance. "An exemplary choice for a battlefield promotion, Jill – no question – and if Ah wanted *this* meeting room destroyed too, he would have been ma first choice!"

"Bet you regret promoting me now, huh?" Her eyes twinkled with amusement.

"Things were different then."

"Oh?"

"Aye. Ah thought Ah was going to die, *and* Ah still had a ship that needed running!"

A shadow fell across Baines' *bonhomie*. "I'm really sorry about this, James."

He brightened immediately. "Sorry enough to go and find my missing staff?"

"I'll get right on it."

He called her back. "Jill, you know this wasnae your fault, don't ye? Ye got us out of there under a missile attack. There were no other options, and most importantly, you saved everyone's lives. Ah cannae thank ye enough for that.

"We may have a few interesting days ahead, but at least we no longer have to worry about the Schultzes. Heidi looked as though she was about to get eaten by that monster before we left, and as for the old man, well, we know he's gone, don't we?"

"So, *Enkelin*, you came." Heinrich Schultz watched the icon of a ship approach on his display. Tapping into the satellite net, he tracked it down, to pull up a visual – one of his small attack ships. "Or have you come to kill me, quietly, and away from the eyes of my people? It's what *I* would do.

"Well, there's nothing for it but to wait and see. I tire of this awful fruit, anyway."

He sat back, falling into deep thought. It soon became apparent that the combat ship was no longer heading straight for him. He checked the distress beacon was still active. It was.

"*Now* what are you up to, *Enkelin?*" He toyed with the idea of opening a comm channel, but resisted, deciding to wait and see what the incoming vessel did next.

It seemed to be flying in what was surely a search pattern. This perplexed him. He knew for a fact that there were no other survivors from the *Sabre* – *he* had barely made it out.

He also knew the ship could see him, unless *its* scanning equipment was damaged. Perhaps they knew someone was out here somewhere but were unable to pinpoint his position?

Their search pattern seemed to take them hundreds of miles away and they were clearly in no hurry to close on him.

From his view screen, he could see the Spinosaurus that almost killed him; still hanging around a few days later, it kept returning to his position. He had expected it to retreat back to the river, its primary feeding ground, by now, and perhaps it would have, had it not made another kill.

Last evening, a large pterosaur had landed not far from his escape pod. The creature was clearly wounded from some sort of altercation, perhaps with its own kind, he could not tell. The Spinosaurus did not care.

Consequently, it looked like he was going to be stuck with the wretched creature for a few days.

Schultz looked dispassionately at the disgusting fruit he was forced to live on. There was not much of it left. Fetching more would be impossible, while the predator was showing this much interest in him – a predator with a grudge, it seemed.

"I suppose my luck is simply 'out to lunch' just now – wish I could say the same for the rest of me."

"Right, we're all here at last," Douglas greeted his senior staff. "Sorry about the mix-up with the rooms, there. Firstly, Ah'm going to ask Lieutenant Singh to provide us with a quick update, based on his calculations from the constellations." He smiled, pleased with his little rhyme. "It seems we made it most of the way home, people. The good news is, there are no more dinosaurs and no more Schultzes, either to ruin our days or haunt our nights. Outside, are people – real people! Sandy, please…"

Douglas sat, allowing Singh to take the floor at the end of the table.

"Thank you, Captain. I'll keep this brief. We've arrived in the Tudor period."

After an extended pause, Baines spoke out, "That was pretty brief. Is there any more?"

"We're somewhere in the North East of England, or possibly just into South East Scotland. It's AD1558, October 31st. Um... I think it's a Thursday."

"Sunday," corrected Thomas Beckett.

"No. Thursday," Singh insisted.

"Well at least it's no' a Tuesday this time," interrupted Douglas wryly.

"Indeed, Captain," agreed Beckett. "It's a *Sunday*."

"Why do we always land on a Sunday?" asked Douglas, not really expecting an answer. "No matter what day it happened to be the day before."

"I can help you there, Captain," replied Singh, brightly. "It's a Thursday!"

Beckett stood and approached the head of the table to stand next to his antagonist. "I'm sorry, but it really is a Sunday, I'm afraid. Regardless of my learned colleague's very impressive and *almost* accurate calculations and suppositions. You see, I've spoken to the man we brought down, in the confrontation last night. He seems quite cognizant – if naturally rather scared – but I see no reason to assume that he doesn't know what day of the week it is."

"Perhaps, but he is wrong, too," Singh insisted again.

Beckett sighed. "I'm sure I'll regret this, but why *is* that, Lieutenant?"

"Why is he wrong? Because it's a Thursday. Sunday won't happen for another three days. Of course, there is also the *other* matter."

"Other matter?"

"Yes." Singh leaned closer to Beckett, confidentially. "When the medical team showed our guest running hot water, he screamed the ward down, attributing it to the devil's work. Perhaps not conclusive, but surely this casts some doubt as to his state of mind."

Beckett rubbed his eyes. "I'm developing a headache. Look, and pay heed to this, please. Do not judge the people and events of this time by what we, laughingly, call the enlightenment of the twenty-first and twenty-second centuries.

"We don't have the luxury of sitting in our faculty armchairs, pretending the past was 'all lovely'. Basing opinions on *our* standards can work neither philosophically nor spiritually – nor intellectually, given that. What it *could* easily do, is get you killed!

"We tend to think of post-Nazi Europe as a relatively peaceful continent, and thank the Lord for that, but here... here and now is *very* different. Just about everyone is at war with someone in some way.

"Now, please remember what I've said. It really could save your life when we begin to integrate with the people outside. However, we've side-tracked a little.

"With regards to the day, what I *meant* was, our *guest*, as Mr Singh describes him, knows it's Sunday, because we captured him on Saturday night, you see – bit of an unassailable point... *some* might say."

Singh wore a secretive, knowing smile. "I'm afraid you are labouring under a misconception, Mr Beckett."

"Oh, do tell."

"You, and your new friend down in the med centre, are still working on the *Julian* Calendar. As we all know, the *Gregorian* Calendar is much more accurate."

"I think the learned lieutenant might be overcomplicating things perhaps?"

"No, it's quite simple. 1558's not a leap year or anything."

Beckett pinched the bridge of his nose as he fought to stay calm. "OK. Fair enough, but the not inconsequential hole in your argument, Mr Singh, is that the Gregorian Calendar will not be invented, let alone implemented, for another twenty-four years – almost to the day, as it happens!

"So there seems little benefit to insisting it's a Thursday, when the entire world out there believes it's Sunday. Wouldn't you agree?"

"Of course," replied Singh.

"Then why argue?" asked Beckett through gritted teeth.

"As a historian, you can take a stab at it and be happy to be in the ballpark. However, as a *scientist*, I was asked to work out an exact date. But of course, it makes more sense to sync with the rest of the world."

Beckett looked pained. "Thank you."

"Even though they're all wrong."

The historian placed a comradely hand on Singh's shoulder. "I'm so *very* grateful to my colleague for establishing that. Now, who would like to know what's actually going on out there?"

Spinosaurus clearly thought about making a fight of it, unwilling to give up its quarry, but in the end the noise was just too great and it fled for the comfort of the river.

Schultz stayed inside his pod while the ship hovered overhead. Once the area seemed clear of wildlife, the pilot, whoever they were, began their descent.

The craft landed with a slight bump. The old man eyed it cautiously, wondering who would get out. With a sigh, he said, "Very well. Time to see what we shall see…"

He opened the escape pod's hatch and stepped out himself. Ten metres away, a side hatch also opened in the other vessel, revealing two people – a tall man, carrying a medical pack, and a woman carrying an assault rifle. Both wore black military fatigues.

They approached cautiously and he strode to meet them halfway. They stopped and saluted.

He returned their salute with a wintry smile. "And you are?"

"Sergeant Ally Coleman, sir. This is Doctor—"

"*Why* are you here?" he cut her off.

Coleman blinked. "To rescue you, sir. To take you back to the *Heydrich*."

"Why now?"

"Sir?"

"My distress beacon has been running for days. What kept you? And what have you been doing, flying all over North Africa? You clearly knew how to find me."

His gaze seared like an arc welder. *Wow! I can feel the danger rolling off this guy,* thought Coleman.

"Perhaps, sir, the doctor can check you over and—"

"I'm fine!"

"My orders are to take you back, sir. Perhaps Dr Schultz will, erm… explain things better. Would you like something to eat, sir?"

He viewed her coolly, his stare hypnotic and utterly penetrative. It felt like falling under an evil spell, until a roar from lower down the slope unsettled them, scattering the effect.

"I suggest we continue our little chat aboard your ship, Sergeant Coleman." Schultz turned to his lifeboat and called, "Close and lock." The tiny vessel complied.

"Well?" asked Schultz, impatiently. "I would very much like to be airborne before the biggest carnivorous dinosaur I have ever seen makes its way back… ah, here it is."

"*Run!*" shouted Coleman.

"Next year, the Scottish Reformation will begin in earnest," said Beckett.

"So, what are you saying? Good for *them?*" asked Commander Gleeson.

"Not exactly. More like, bad for us. Scotland may well be about to gain its future identity as a largely Protestant nation. It may even be about to begin a dalliance with more democratic ways of thinking, even welfare and education for the poor – these were all Calvinist priorities, whatever else he was remembered for – but by our modern standards, the next hundred years are going to be hell on toast!"

"Thomas is right," agreed Baines. "Remember me saying that Tudor England's 'one place I'm glad I'll never see', James? Who could have ever guessed that glib statement might turn prophetic? Even worse than that, we've appeared in the one place in the sixteenth century I'd like to be even *less* – the border between England and Scotland."

"OK. What should we do?" asked Satnam Patel delicately, still drawn and bruised from his crash injuries.

Baines and Beckett looked at one another before answering. As one, they said, "*Arm ourselves!*"

"Is it that dangerous here?" asked Mother Sarah, also looking a little fragile and beaten, after their shocking reintroduction to the world of man.

"This contested border is one of the most dangerous places on the planet right now," Baines answered, seriously. "Added to all of the striving between England and Scotland, not to mention the religious changes, we're also in Reiver country."

"I thought Reiver was a dog?" asked Gleeson. "How do you know all this stuff, anyway?"

"When I was at uni in London, I minored in Reformation and Counterreformation Europe."

Her answer surprised the Australian, although his qualifications within the law left him little room to talk. "I'd hate to tell you what I got up to, outside my main curricular activities," he muttered.

"Were the English and the Scots still goin' at it then – or now, should I say?" asked Sarah. "I thought they'd unified about that ti— *this* time?"

"Not yet," supplied Beckett. "Not for another four and a half decades, give or take. Captain Baines is quite right. You'll have heard of the Battle of Flodden?"

He received a few nods, whereas he himself was shaking his head. "Talk about bad feeling. There will probably be people out there who still remember – may even be old enough to have been in it! And lucky us – it's just down the road from here!"

He sighed, clearly extremely concerned about what they had stumbled into. "During 1558 England is pretty much, full out, at war with Scotland – or vice versa, take your pick. There've been talks of peace and even a few agreements, but all of it coming to very little. There's just so much animosity here, and it goes back centuries!

"Also adding to Scotland's woes at the moment, they're under the regency of Mary of Guise, mother to Mary Queen of Scots. Without being too judgemental, her regency began fairly well, even bringing some measure of stability to the region. However, by this date she's become far less tolerant in religion and spends most of her energy on feathering the English throne for her daughter's nest – at least that's the dream – whilst effectively trying to annex Scotland to France.

"French herself, and while her daughter is married to the French Dauphin, she can call on military aid against any potential invasion from Spain. There are a few thousand French soldiers to the north of here already. It's funny how many times through history we see a 'helping ally' turn into an 'occupying force'.

"Although, the Spanish Empire has its own worries at the moment, what with constant problems from the Turks and a major Protestant uprising in the Netherlands.

"France, for her part, is embroiled in the worst civil fighting prior to the Napoleonic era.

"As Captain Baines also correctly pointed out, possibly even worse than all that – from our own selfish perspective, as they're right outside our door – this is indeed Reiver country.

"The Reivers lived by their own set of rules, their loyalties to their families, or clans – not to kings or queens, or countries for that matter. To offer an example, part of the western border became known as the Debatable Lands. So lawless were they, that neither country even knew who owned them!

"Most of the Reiver clans bore family names, some of them famous. The young lad we have below is a *Maxwell* – Billy Maxwell."

"Surely, with our technology and knowledge we can deal with a few roughneck families," suggested Major White. "Even if they are a little wild."

Beckett, still standing at the head of the table, leaned forward, spreading his hands as he looked White in the eye. "Maybe I misled you, Major. When I said families, perhaps I gave the impression of a set of unruly brothers? But the truth is, some of these families, like the Armstrongs for example, could put two or three thousand men in the saddle – and that's just one family!

"These people are survivors, and often they survive by stealing whatever they need from their neighbours across the border. The fluid politics and allegiances in this place and time will make your head spin! And they didn't just raid each other's cattle either."

"What do you mean?" asked Patel.

"That raid, who came upon us last night, may well have been sent to collect people, too."

"Slaves?" asked Mother Sarah.

Beckett nodded. "Please put from your mind any romantic notions about Walter Scott type heroes. They *had* heroes, of course – strife always brings the courageous to the fore – but these are bad times. We *must* not underestimate the danger we're in here. Let me put it another way, not for no reason did the Reivers give us the word 'bereaved'. You really would not want to be taken captive, believe me."

"So what do you suggest, Mr Beckett, aside from going about armed?" asked Douglas, reasonably. "If we're stuck here, we'll be found. We'll have no choice but to interact sooner or later."

Beckett looked genuinely afraid. "Then make it later, Captain. I can only tell you what I know from books, mostly written many years after all eyewitnesses to these times were long in their graves. We need to find out as much as we can before we interfere."

"You think we might interfere?" asked Douglas.

"Huh! Heaven forfend," Beckett muttered, darkly. "Anyway, for starters, it would be quite useful to know which side of the rather vague border we're actually on. Your Hawick accent, Captain, might get you invited in for ale at one hamlet, only to be gut-stabbed at the next. We must be careful. As Captain Baines mentioned, there is also the matter of religion.

"If any of you are thinking that religion doesn't really matter that much to you, then I tell you squarely, it does now!

"Again, this is essential information before any of us step outside. Mary Tudor is on the throne of England. You may know her by the more colourful moniker 'Bloody Mary' – and we're not talking about one of Commander Gleeson's old flames, I can tell you!"

Gleeson grinned. "Steady on, sport, she wasn't that bad."

Beckett gave a fleeting smile, but continued seriously. "We've landed at a time of extremely aggressive Catholicism – on both sides of the border.

"Now, to provide a little context. The reformation may have been essentially religious, but that is a massive oversimplification. Religion may not matter to many of us, but to these people it was everything and impacted on every element of their lives.

"Had Queen Elizabeth I taken the easy route and maintained the old religion, it might arguably have brought stability of a sort, perhaps even allowed further small steps towards early industrialism. However, she didn't. Forgetting for a moment Henry VIII's meandering Catholicism without the inconvenient Pope, the core of the Protestant belief is actually more about everyone – high and low – being educated to read the word of God for themselves, without the intercession or, as some saw it, *interference* of the priest. I mean no offence, Mother Sarah, just trying to provide a basis for the Tudor mindset."

Sarah smiled. "None taken – please continue, Mr Beckett."

"Well, with everyone – at least in theory – able to read and form their own opinions, you begin to see the birth of what we would call the modern world. All of our freedoms of thought and expression, no matter how sincere or how stupid, began here. And it was a most bloody and brutal beginning, I can tell you."

"But if England and Scotland are both Catholic, maybe I could reach out—"

"Don't get your hopes up, Mother Sarah," Beckett cut her off gently. "I'm trying to think of a modern comparison here, to explain the state-sanctioned religious violence of the sixteenth and seventeenth centuries.

"Let me see... Ah, yes, imagine a society in which brutal torture and killing often provide public spectacle and the focal attraction for a family day out. Now, in this time, imagine two rival crowds of football fans. Further envision them all armed to the teeth and *then* the police *instruct* them to kill one another – does that help?"

"Don't sugar-coat it for me," replied Sarah, glumly.

Beckett shrugged. "I make no apology. You all need to understand where and when we are. As I said, it could save your lives. Anyhow, assuming we do have the correct date, Mary will be dead in a little over a fortnight and the whole gameboard will be reset yet again – good times!"

A silence fell over the group as each retreated into their own thoughts.

Eventually Douglas spoke. "Mr Beckett, is there anything you can tell us about how we should greet or speak with these people – when we inevitably do come into contact with them?"

Beckett sat and crossed his arms with a sigh as he took a moment to think. "I'm no linguist, but during the sixteenth century there were some fundamental changes in the English language. Historically, this is a minefield of scattered facts and opinions, but the most basic thing I can suggest we look out for is based around, of all things, the word 'you'."

"You what?" asked Gleeson.

"No," replied Beckett. "More, 'you one' or 'you two'. And don't even get me going on you too!

"Look, at its most basic, the words 'thy', 'thine' and 'thou' in this time are being replaced more and more by the word 'you' – both for singular and plural second-person pronouns. As we also use the word 'you' in all instances, this shouldn't get us into trouble per se. However, it may be worth noting how others may use the words to address *us*."

Douglas frowned. "How so?"

"This might be difficult to wrap your head around, Captain, but I'll do my best. 'You' is beginning to take over as the polite or more respectful form of 'thou'. Again, this is a really complex area. It cannot be summed up with a simple rule, and I'm no expert. All I can say is, if a stranger, or comparative stranger, addresses you as 'thou' rather than 'you' – despite the perception handed down to us from continued 'thys' and 'thous' throughout literature – they may actually see you as socially inferior or perhaps even derisible.

"I know it's not much to arm you with, Captain, but it's something to watch out for and may at least help you guess how you're being perceived. Of course, on the other hand, 'thees' continued to be used more commonly in the north of England, particularly Yorkshire – not too far south of us, as it happens. So in summary..." Beckett shrugged, holding his hands palm up.

Now Douglas folded his arms and sat back.

"Captain?"

"Forgive me, Mr Beckett. Ah understand your difficulty, Ah was just hoping for more."

"Sorry, Captain. A potted history is all we have, I'm afraid. What I *can* say is, in a society where *thouing*[1] someone could instigate violence, we should watch our Ps and Qs!"

"Don't you mean Ps and yous?" muttered Gleeson.

---

[1] Despite the earlier and continual biblical use of thou and thine, they came to denote, amongst other things, social station, familiarity or even contempt during the sixteenth century. At best they may have been seen as rustic. Later, in 1660, George Fox wrote that Quakers, who persisted in using 'thou', were "often beaten and abused, and sometimes in danger of our lives, for using those words to some proud men, who would say, 'What! You ill-bred clown, do you Thou me?'"

Chapter 5 | Hunter Hunted

1st October AD1558

A young woman sat alone on a wooden bench under a great oak. The parkland around her was riotous with autumnal colour. Always a place of peace, but variously, of only superficial safety for her. She closed her eyes and breathed deeply, praying for an end to the nightmare.

The rumble of hooves startled her, ending her reverie. She stood as four horsemen approached. Fear clutched at her heart, as it had so many times during her short life. Just twenty-five years, and so many of them spent in such danger and such fear.

As the men drew nearer, she recognised their leader and the grip on her heart relaxed a little, but not entirely. She knew that in these perilous times, men often made shift for themselves, setting conscience aside if they wished to live.

"Sir Nicholas," she greeted, stepping away from the tree.

The man slowed his horse before jumping down to kneel at her feet. "Lady," he replied. Standing almost immediately, her visitor explained that she must pack lightly and prepare to leave at once.

30th October AD1558

"I see her… but who is she?"

"My Lord?" asked the captain of the castle guard, nervously.

"Silence!" snapped Sir William de Soulis[2], Lord of Liddesdale. The soldier fell still immediately. He knew better than to question his master, especially while in the throes of one of his trances.

"But what is this… *Strangers?* And forsooth, none stranger. Who is this that guides me? Speak thy name, spirit. Mütze… Rotmütze… *Redcap?*" After several minutes of murmuring and twitching, Sir William seemed to return from the other world.

He smiled, wickedly. His was a terrifying visage, showing weirdly pronounced canines. "We may have failed to take the crown o' Scotland, but by happy chance there is a still greater prize ripe for the taking here.

"Captain, muster up thy men. Leave only a small garrison tae protect the castle. We have much ground tae cover and all must be in place by nightfall on the thirty-first of October – the eve of the morrow!"

Heidi stared silently at her grandfather, locked in his cell. No matter how secure he seemed, she knew better.

"Well, *Enkelin?* It would appear that I am your prisoner. Did you wish to ask me anything or are we simply to glare at one another through the bars?"

"You're here because I have decided to give you another chance—"

"I am *here* because you failed to have me murdered!" The intensity of his stare seared her. "It was a very clever move, setting that fanatic free to come with us, making it look like it was *he* who turned the tables in *our* favour. Neither Franke nor I even suspected, until he began to talk, in private audience. As you well know, little takes me by surprise, and so I salute you."

She expected him to be furious, at the very least, sour, but to her complete surprise, he treated her to one of his rare nods of respect.

---

[2] The sketchy evidence regarding the De Soulis family seems to sit, at least partially, where history meets legend. However, depraved cruelty, treason and black magic are all recorded. More in 'author's notes' at the end of this book.

"You have grown, *Enkelin*. You are no longer merely the weapon into which I shaped you."

"*Großvater*, I—"

He held up his hand to silence her. Despite their relationship of prisoner and jailer, she acquiesced instantly.

"Now you have arrived at this stage, are you ready – nay, *willing* – to begin the next phase of your training?"

Remembering well the sting of being turned out, no longer required, Heidi viewed him coldly. "Explain."

The old man smiled with something approaching genuine humour, as he answered, "You are still smarting about the boy, *Enkelin*. I understand. However, that too, was all part of your development."

"Setting us against one another," she stated. It was not a question.

"To a degree, yes. Neither you, nor he, would be of any use to me if you're weak. Also, let us not forget that you'd failed in your mission – more importantly, you had failed *me*, when you lost the *Last Word* and let Douglas' rabble run rings around you. Punishment was required."

"Punishment?"

"Indeed, *Enkelin*. I gave strict orders for you to be treated by our medical staff for your gunshot wound, and then incarcerated, until you understood the full measure of my disappointment. Knowing me as you do, do you consider this a particularly harsh penalty?"

She stared balefully at him, but refused to answer.

"Who else would have lived after such a debacle?"

Still she gave no answer.

His gaze softened slightly. "However, what happened next impressed me. Your people seemed terrified of you – this is right and proper, of course – so it came as quite a surprise when loyal followers rescued you from my *care*.

"Furthermore, your attack on my transport was quite ruthless. I hoped, of course, but not until that moment did I *believe* you might be capable of completing our mission."

"And my cousin? Did you foresee his treachery, too?"

Heinrich chuckled softly. "There was nothing to foresee. Neither was there treachery – not in the strictest sense."

Heidi's brows shot up in disbelief.

"You don't agree?" he asked, testing her, taunting her. "You see, the boy was *never* on our side. I wanted to see what he was made of, and,

I have to say, that despite the pitiful upbringing he suffered, he has intelligence, resourcefulness and genuine courage. He *could* be a Schultz."

"What do you mean *could* be?" She stared, runaway wheels of machination juddering hard as the straight tracks before it seemed to vanish. With no obvious way forward, she could only reverse. Was this his plan all along? Was this his message to her? When she found her voice, disbelief added each word, one at a time, to the word behind it, like trucks coupled to her train of thought. "Was all this just some elaborate scheme to see how I would *react?*"

"Let me ask you a question, *Enkelin.* Would you be more or *less* likely to waste time and resources chasing him down, at the expense of our mission if, a, he was your cousin, or b, he was just some orphan, a nobody, with a usefully appropriate background – dragged into play as part of my overall plan for you? How do you answer?"

Heidi took a step back, involuntarily. Until her cousin came along, she had never known doubt. Now he was gone, she could barely begin to describe the damage his 'overtures of family' had done to her confidence, her surety. Tim's talk, his memories of love and friendship, had been *levelled* at her, more specifically, at her own past – levelled like a Lewis gun. It may have fallen silent with his leaving, but the inclination to keep her head down remained.

In a flash of anger, she pulled her pistol from its holster, taking a step closer to the cell. "You will tell me the truth, *Großvater.* Is he family?"

Heinrich sat back in his seat, and crossing his legs comfortably, began to laugh.

31st October AD1558

A young woman rode hard, ruddy cheeked and laughing. Twenty horsemen pursued, all spurring their mounts raucously, rapt in the thrill of the chase.

The lead rider drew level with her, also laughing as they came upon a road. Reining in, they breathed heavily.

"My lady, if you will not spare the horses, at least take pity on an old man heading into his forty-second winter! We still have ten miles to travel ere we reach the safety of Sir Ralph's castle."

Her laughter subsided. "And you have a promise to fulfil, my dear Sir Nicholas."

He sobered quickly, but nodded assent. Shouting for his men to rest and water the horses, he bade his charge follow a little way, down to a small brook. It was a beautiful place, but his reasons were entirely practical. "We may speak here, my lady. The babbling waters will mask our words."

He sniffed the air. "After another year of drought and the tempest that struck Nottinghamshire, we are indeed fortunate with our weather of late. These roads will soon become impassable. We should not have tarried so, at York and Durham, Lady."

"Chide me not, sir!" she replied, mercurially. "Cuthbert Tunstall may be of the old religion, but he is a kind man. As we walk abroad within his bishopric, we would do well to sue for his protection."

"Truly? Or didst you simply discover us to our enemies?"

Giving the man a sideways scrutiny, she spoke carefully, "I have placed myself entirely in your care, Sir Nicholas. On the friendship of our youth, I have trusted you and let you steal me away to the northernmost edge of the world. You promised to tell me *all* as we drew near our destination – I call for an explanation now, sir. Tell me."

Sir Nicholas was clearly uncomfortable, but nodded agreement. "Orders came from His Grace of Canterbury for your removal from Hatfield. Her Majesty was heard say that the further away you are, the better she doth feel. At least, 'twas the excuse spun by the queen's advisers."

The young woman's face coloured in anger. "One can always rely on Reggie to worsen matters!"

Sir Nicholas snorted, "Indeed, Lady. Although there may be some small consolation. Before I left London, the archbishop had taken to his bed – talk did abound of the influenza…"

"Be it a sin to hope, that whatever his sickness may be, 'tis nothing minor?" She was less than half joking.

He smiled wryly. "In your circumstance, Lady, I would say that 'twould not. The task of taking you north was to fall to one of his creatures, but I requested the mission for myself. In sooth, I was granted an audience with Her Majesty."

Clearly surprised, she asked, "Then indeed, sir, you have greater powers of persuasion than I!"

He shrugged. "Well, on this occasion the persuasion worked. I convinced Her Majesty that should anything befall you, while under the 'protection' of Archbishop Reginald Pole's men, then she might be implicated.

"Court gossip cares little for truth, in any case, but as her husband's final word was to treat well with you, before he left for Spain... Well, she saw the point and instructed me to remove you north."

"To the most perilous corner of her nation..."

"Indeed. Forsooth, I am sorry, Lady, but there is worse to come, and you must know it. You are to lodge with Sir Ralph Grey. I believe Sir Ralph an honourable man, always loyal to the crown – whoever wears it – as was his father before him. He will obey his orders, but will also be mindful of your importance. No, I do not think I leave you in direct peril. Not whilst you reside within his household. Her Majesty is not likely to decree publicly your execution.

"However, as you have so wisely stated, there can be no more dangerous place in the realm than this."

She took a deep breath, standing straight-backed. "Do you imply that *anything* may befall me?"

He nodded. "I believe 'twould have done so already, had I not stolen you away several days earlier than ordered."

"Perhaps tarrying at York and Durham hath confused our pursuit?" she interrupted.

He gave her a sour look. "Hmm. Forsooth, I hoped to wrongfoot our pursuit – for they follow us, doubt it not. I *had* hoped to get you safely within Sir Ralph's walls before they caught us, but as things stand, we are still on the road, and so are they..."

As Sir Nicholas tailed off, the young woman stared unseeing into the truculent waters, bubbling down three stone steps in the stream bed. "So, Mary has made up her mind at last. I ever expected it."

"Take heart, my lady."

She rounded on him. "How am I to take heart, sir? I may not have sentence of death proclaimed openly for all men to see, but plainly a price lies 'pon my head! One that will descend on me soonest. And all the way up here, blame will *never* alight on the guilty, will it?"

Sir Nicholas knelt once more, his eyes looking up earnestly into hers. "I say again, take heart, Lady. The queen is sick, very sick."

"Like to die?"

He stood. To answer truthfully would be treason, so he simply restated, "Keep your faith, Lady."

"Doctors," Heidi greeted the white coats once more.

"Ma'am."

"I would hear of your progress. Please, take a seat."

The balding man blanched, swallowing nervously. "Thank you, ma'am. We have investigated the viability of your proposal and... erm, well, we believe it will be... um."

"Spit it out, Doctor!" Heidi ordered impatiently.

"It's dangerous," the female lab coat supplied.

Heidi leaned forward across the table. "Do you think I called you here for a risk assessment?"

The woman met her gaze. "No," she admitted, directly. "We believe what you have requested of us may be possible, by utilising uranium-235. To begin with, that is the only fissile isotope that exists in nature as a primordial nuclide."

Not wishing to be overshadowed, the bald man found his voice, and a little smarm. "However, strontium-90 is better for permeating bone tissue, but has a half-life of less than thirty years. In layman's terms, ma'am, they're both radioactive. Furthermore, we can—"

Heidi interrupted him, "Be careful how far you dumb your explanation down, Doctor. I am *armed*."

He gulped, clearing his throat uncomfortably. "Of course, Doctor. I only meant that *most* radioactive elements have half-lives that measure in years, thousands of years at best."

"And refresh my memory, what is the half-life for 235U, again?"

"Erm, a little over seven hundred million years, ma'am."

Heidi smiled appreciatively. "This is good. So you are suggesting we use strontium-90 as a carrier for the uranium-235? Thus making sure we acquire maximum penetration into bone tissue? This is most ingenious, Doctors.

"Very well. How will you extract the quantities of material required?"

The female scientist took up the baton once more, "Fortunately for us, Doctor, uranium-235 exists in nature – it predates even the formation of the Earth, in fact. As you will no doubt be aware, it makes up about 0.72 percent of natural uranium. That's the good news."

Heidi's brief *bonhomie* faltered. "And the bad?"

"Collecting enough to do anything useful might take a while. We need to build some method of extraction to begin with. Uranium is not common in our solar system now, but within the rocks of our planet its consistency is about two to four parts per million. We find it in sea water too, again in tiny amounts, so you see the problem."

Heidi soured a little further. "Do you have any better news?"

"At least we have it," she answered prosaically. "It's believed to have formed in supernovae, about six and a half billion years ago – two billion years even before the formation of the Earth. Its slow radioactive decay provides the main source of heat within our planet, assisting with convection, continental drift, et cetera."

"Yes, *yes*, this is all very interesting," snapped Heidi, "but can you collect enough for our purposes and will it work as a carrier for our probe?"

The scientists glanced uncomfortably at one another.

Heidi pushed them, "*Well?*"

"Yes."

"No."

Heidi sat back, irritated. "Which is it, Doctors?"

"Yes," the woman stressed, with a little more conviction.

Heidi looked at the balding man to see if he would dare gainsay her position.

He loosened his already untidy tie, eventually murmuring, "We would need to find rocks rich in uranium first, otherwise…"

"*Where?*" asked Heidi, leaning forward once more.

"In our own time," he continued, "there are six main countries that produce the bulk of the world's supply. I know you have a distinct interest in Egypt, Dr Schultz, and as it happens, one of those countries is Niger. Not exactly next door, I know, but within a thousand miles is probably our best shot. Erm, assuming your attentions are still on North Africa?" He was clearly hoping she might have changed her mind.

She stared at him, ignoring the question. "Difficult then, but not impossible. Do you have anything else to add?"

"Yes, ma'am," he continued, hopefully. "Strontium-90 is formed inside nuclear reactors. Now, I don't advise fiddling about with our own reactor, but perhaps the *Last Word...*?"

Heidi sat pensive for a few moments. "The reactor aboard the *Last Word* is a valuable asset, too. Would it be possible to strip what you need from the ruin of the *Eisernes Kreuz?* Her core will be beyond use."

The scientists shared another glance. "It's worth exploring, ma'am," the woman answered. "As long as the source is not contaminated."

"Very well. Assuming we can produce our probe, introducing it to the fossil record will be my job – a purely military consideration. What I wish to know from you now is, how will we track it? And by that, I mean within time *and* space."

The man glanced at his colleague before answering, "We have a partial plan for that, ma'am, but it will require you to take a trip to the moon."

The surprise registered clearly on Heidi's face. "Explain?"

"What the bladdy 'ell's goin' on over there?" Gleeson stared out from the hilltop, down over the rolling lowlands to the east. Douglas had tasked him with riding a wide circuit of their crash site, to get the lie of the land and see how close they were to any trouble – and talking of trouble, they seemed to have found some.

"Hey, Jonesy, O'Brien, have a butcher's down there." He passed Jones his heavy binoculars.

O'Brien drew a pocket-set of her own, stating, "Looks like a bunch o' folks running for their lives from a bunch of other folks, to me, Commander."

"They're a good couple of miles away, sir," added Jones. "Not to mention, there's loads of 'em, isn'it, and on horseback, too. We're only six – what can *we* do?"

"Jonesy, *Jonesy*," replied Gleeson, disappointedly. "We scare the baggers half to death, o' course!"

O'Brien winced. "Is this gonna be like that time you ordered us to ride into that herd, no, that *stampede* of dinosaurs at the river crossing, sir?"

Gleeson grinned. "Nah! This'll be way better than that!" After retrieving the glasses to pack them away carefully, he grabbed a fistful of throttle and shouted, "CHARGE!"

While Heidi's science staff worked on methods of extracting uranium and strontium, she flew the *Heydrich* back to Patagonia.

This time she landed beside the hulk of the USS *Newfoundland*. Having brought their orbital attack craft on this trip, she sent her pet scientists off with a pilot and four-man security detail to the *Eisernes Kreuz* to hunt for spent reactor rods.

She lowered the boarding ramp and headed across the open ground between the two ships with a large, heavily armed contingent, surrounding a group of engineers.

Arriving under the *Newfoundland*, they used manpower and pure grunt to shift the previously ruined elevator car out of the way.

Using rope ascending grips, an advance team climbed up into the ship to rig a basic cradle lift where the elevator once rode, powered by an electric winch. When complete, people and equipment began moving inside.

Her engineers quickly spread out all over the *Newfoundland*, each with an armed bodyguard. The small hatch into the ship had been open for well over a month now; it was anyone's guess what manner of flying or climbing creatures may have taken up residence.

At times like these, Heidi harboured a guilty secret wish for her very own 'Chief Nassaki'. His brother had regained consciousness and seemed likely to live – this was good – but she knew, he was not the engineer Hiro was.

She stood on the ancient ship's bridge musing. *What a strange life this leviathan has led. Newer than the* New World*, yet much older, after decades buried under a Cretaceous forest.* This gave way to pondering the strangeness of her own life…

The sound of booted feet striding onto the bridge broke into her thoughts, making her turn. "Well?"

The engineer saluted. "The *New World* crew stripped one of her four lifting thrusters entirely, Doctor. As well as—"

"Will she take off?" Heidi interrupted.

"Maybe, ma'am."

She stepped closer to the man, making him straighten, eyes front. "I suggest you and your team go and find me a '*yes*, ma'am' and quickly."

He swallowed. "Yes, ma'am. We'll get right on it."

"I will await your report on the *Heydrich*. Be sure to impress on your engineers, that they should not become overexcited and wander off alone. There was a small infestation of pterosaurs aboard the *New World*." A wicked smile tugged at the corner of her mouth as she recalled her handiwork; a useful distraction helping to cover her escape. "Very nasty indeed, I have been led to understand. Be warned. Very well, you may go."

He visibly relaxed. "Yes, ma'am."

Heidi took one last look around the bridge. Taking in the aged, decrepit state of the consoles, her smile returned. *I must go and inform Lieutenant Devon that his new command awaits him!*

"He shouldn't be allowed out on his own!" cried O'Brien as they followed Commander Gleeson downhill in high-speed pursuit.

Dropping into a hidden hollow, the bikers came upon a grazing herd of wild deer. It was hard to say which group was more surprised – some of the deer were quite large. The animals scattered, immediately panicked. Splitting into two groups, they flocked around the rim of the hollow, only to re-join in front of the racing humans. Within moments *everyone* was heading down the slope for all they were worth.

Gleeson's team followed them, slowing to avoid injury to the beasts or themselves.

"You're right, Commander," O'Brien shouted. "This is absolutely nothing like the last time at all!"

"Why didn't Hiro give these things a hooter?" he retorted. "*Come on*, ya docile baggers! Get outta the bladdy way!"

Presently, the terrain levelled, translating gradually to woodland. They closed on the treeline fast – fortunately, the deer knew a game trail or two.

"Déjà vu, Corp – let's go! *Woohoo!*"

O'Brien shook her head despairingly. Her commanding officer's proclivity for charging into danger could be all at once exhilarating, exasperating, even estimable; it could also be downright damned-well dangerous. Checking the others were close enough to see their point of entry, she followed Gleeson into the woods.

Although Hiro's electric dirt bikes were much faster than any Cervidae out in the open, once within the restrictive forest, the riders were forced to slow significantly. The deer, on the other hand, were hardly slowed at all. A relative parity prevailed, syncing chased and chaser.

Jumping roots and ducking under low boughs, Gleeson whooped with delight as his team struggled to keep up, and then they were out – the treeline suddenly behind them.

An undulating plain lay ahead and within it sat something the soldiers from the *New World* had not seen in what seemed like a very long time – a man-made road built by someone other than themselves.

By 22nd century standards, perhaps 'road' was stretching the definition. It was a cart track. Regardless, it was a thoroughfare created by human beings, and that made it glorious to the futuristic prehistoric bikers – although upon reaching it, they quickly realised that the ruts actually made it safer to travel on the grass to its sides.

Gleeson pulled up, allowing their terrified ungulate guides to outdistance them, at last. The forest continued about half a mile to the west. To the north, the road led up and over a low rise.

"What do you reckon?" he asked, as his team drew up behind him, Jones and O'Brien to either side.

Jones nodded, smiling. "I reckon it's a road, boy!"

Gleeson cracked a grin, despite himself. "I mean which way? We got a little turned around in the woods, but I'd guess north. What do *you* say, Jen?"

O'Brien shrugged. "We could split up, search north *and* south? It's not like we have to hide our radio chatter, is it?"

Gleeson mulled. "I like your thinking, but it's too dangerous."

O'Brien's look of 'This? From *you?*' was completely missed by the Australian. He continued, "We're goin' after forty or fifty horsemen, already in the middle of their own little war. Who knows what we're riding into?"

"We could just keep our noses out, isn'it," stated Jones, as an afterthought adding, "sir."

"Yeah, I hear ya," admitted Gleeson. "But Douglas wanted us to get an idea of what we've stumbled into – as well as a good look around. Can't see how we can do that without talking to a few locals. Who knows, maybe we can even make a new friend or two. What do ya say? I mean, if we go in with that attitude, right, surely things couldn't go too badly for us, could they?"

This time he *did* notice O'Brien's look.

Heidi winched herself down. Leaving the cradle assemblage at the top, she took the simpler 'one-man' loop system, to save power; a foot through the loop, she hung onto the rope, lowering herself slowly.

The remote control for the pulley was clipped to the rope at roughly eye height, for her at least, relative to the foot loop.

Despite the sedate nature of her descent, her height above ground, measured in millimetres, fell rapidly. She watched the numbers scroll downwards while exiting the lift shaft into open air. The bottom of the shaft, built into the Rescue Pod, was about seven metres above ground. Lost in thought, watching the tiny display on the controller, she was surprised to feel her foot nudged from behind by something.

Her boot was still at least five metres above the ground. Turning, very cautiously on her rope, she found the reason standing directly below.

Gazing up at her, reaching upwards, was a dinosaur. Heidi tensed instinctively, causing the rope to sway, and her boot to bump again off an enormous nose.

The huge head also swayed, in sync, following her movement. From her eyrie, suspended in mid-air, Heidi could see all the way down the creature's spine to its tail – a tail that swished from side to side, providing a counterpoint to the movement of its head.

She felt like a ball of string, offered as a cat's plaything, but the scale was *oh* so much worse.

Frozen in place, she dared not even breathe. *If I take a shot with my nine-millimetre, it will kill me before it even feels the pinprick!*

Meanwhile, the dinosaur simply watched, clearly mesmerised by this bizarrely dangled morsel. The creature was very obviously one of the large predacious types, she did not need her cousin here to work that out. It had a wicked looking scar down the side of its snout, all the way from the bridge of the nose, crossing the maxilla, to link with an associated scar on the lower jaw.

As she swung, her boot bumped gently against its nose again, this time eliciting a soft snort.

Any second now! she thought, expecting the worst.

The jaws parted slightly, emitting a low growl followed by a whine, and Heidi realised that the giant was genuinely confused, or perhaps fascinated? Her weird position would be just part of the puzzle; she had taken a shower on the flight over, too. Captain Franke had the most appalling taste in shower gel, but right at this moment, her freakish 22nd century perfume was all that stood between Heidi and slow suffocation, whilst dissolving in stomach acid. The dinosaur was so vast, she was under no illusion that it would need to chew.

It was not one of the Mapusaurus family, she recognised them, nor was it a Giganotosaurus. Definitely not one of those horrible spinosaurids that kept attacking her people at the river crossing, either. If she was correct, that left only one suspect – Tyrannotitan. Her mental meander gave little satisfaction and made even *less* difference. She was dead.

"Doctor? Are you alright?" A voice came from above.

Tyrannotitan looked up still further and *roared* at the man, inconveniently out of reach. Heidi was of the same mind. "You idiot!" she screamed, wishing *he* was within reach instead of her. She kicked off the snout, while the beast was momentarily distracted, and began to swing. It was all she could do. As she swung, she shouted, "Keep calling! Make a noise! Bang something! *Anything!*" She played out the rope into wider arcs, ever further from the creature.

Recovering quickly from its surprise, Tyrannotitan refocused on her.

"Make some noise, you fool!" she screamed.

The man in the hatch above began to shout and bang the butt of his rifle against the metal wall of the lift shaft.

The jaws opened once more to catch the prize, but her colleague's distraction granted Heidi one last swing.

This is it! she screamed within her own mind, and at the maximum extent of her arc, she played out *all* of the rope. As her angular momentum slowed, she began to fall, not a dead fall, due to her lateral movement, but it was still a long drop. Bracing, all the while trying not to tense, she prepared to roll for her life.

The ground rose impertinently to greet her, and as she struck, all the wind was driven from her chest. She rolled for several metres, each spin revealing the dinosaur as it reached and roared towards the snack, tucked safely and infuriatingly out of its reach within the hole in the sky.

"Shoot it, you moron!" Heidi bawled hoarsely.

Tyrannotitan's gaze locked immediately with hers. "Oh, *no*," she murmured.

The man up in the ship did indeed begin firing, but with little effect. He had not the angle from the lift shaft, and Matilda was already on the move.

"So what? Flip a coin?" asked O'Brien.

Gleeson stared at her in surprise. "Have you ever *seen* one? Outside a museum, I mean."

She shrugged. "I just thought that's what you were meant to say in these situations."

The commander chuckled, but then grimaced with indecision. Help came from the crack of a pistol shot. "Huh, north it is then. Let's go!"

From that point they lost no time, riding as fast as was possible. Already five minutes had elapsed since they spotted the people in danger.

Once over the brow of the rise, the landscape opened into a wide, lowland valley. The road wended across it, following a natural ridge. About half a mile ahead, the treeline from the west encroached on the road once more, and this was where they caught sight of their quarry.

A quick glimpse through his field glasses told Gleeson all he needed to know. Those people were indeed in trouble; some of them were already down.

"Let's go, folks," he called with an arm-over gesture.

The road was not direct, but the ground to each side looked as though it became waterlogged at times. Gleeson thought it best to stick with the road. If they got themselves bogged down, theirs might be the worst cavalry rescue in history.

They managed to get within a hundred metres before anyone noticed them. Now for their next problem: who was who?

The skirmish seemed to revolve around a girl. Her long, fiery red hair shone in the autumnal sun; if she had been wearing any form of headdress, she had clearly lost it. Ten of her retainers were dismounted and grouped around her horse on foot. Whether this was by design or misfortune, Gleeson could not tell for sure, although several horses wandered aimlessly at the periphery of the engagement.

The dismounted men defended their charge with cutting swords[3] and a few rapiers. One man, wearing what to their modern eyes appeared to be even fancier dress than the others, shouted orders, while enemy horsemen closed the circle about them.

That was when someone cried a warning that a new party was incoming. This short reprieve gave Gleeson some idea as to how the parties were divided. It seemed the redhead had four men of horse and ten of foot remaining. There were at least a dozen bodies on the ground, unmoving, but as the two sides briefly parted, it was clear that her men were outnumbered.

One way or another, the arrival of Gleeson's team had thrown a spanner in the works for someone; neither group yet knew who they were or what to expect. Although it was obvious from their 22nd century fatigues that they must be foreign devils.

Gleeson pulled up within ten metres of the group. The fight was clearly on hold now, as everyone turned to stare warily at the newcomers.

The Australian kicked the side stand down on his bike and stepped off, standing in front of his people. Raising a hand, and focusing on the man wearing what he believed to be the richest attire, he greeted, "Hey, Nigel, how's it going?"

---

3   A term describing slashing rather than stabbing weapons.

Heidi ran like hell, all dignity thrown to the wind. Moving east, directly in front of the *Newfoundland*, she headed for the treeline – her only chance.

The dinosaur wasted no time in following her, the gunfire erupting behind only driving it onwards in the direction Heidi had chosen.

This really is not my day. Stop firing, Dummkopf! She could not afford the breath to shout it out loud. Already, the heavy *thump, thump, thump* of massive feet was gaining on her. Head down, she sprinted with every ounce of vitality she had, to gain tree cover.

A few metres from her goal, she almost faltered. The trees were… *moving?*

Diving to the side, she barely avoided the footfall of a vast front leg. Rolling over, she looked up, under the chin of a head surely ten times her own meagre height above the ground.

Tyrannotitan stopped in its tracks, too, roaring what suddenly seemed pygmy defiance, as the giant sauropod smashed its way through what remained of the trees between it and the beach. A deep bass rumble reverberated across the lake and was answered from further around the shore to the north. Perhaps sidetracked by a particularly good lunch, this creature had become separated from its herd.

Tyrannotitan bobbed its head and swished its tail. Heidi could see its cold, reptilian calculation as it worked out the odds. It was a ridiculous exercise; the sauropod was a mature adult in its prime and far too big, too strong and too dangerous to be tackled alone. However, survival instinct and killing instinct shared the same neural pathways within the hunter's mind. *Heidi's* survival instinct told her that her future depended almost entirely upon whatever this giant of giants did next.

She recognised it as some form of sauropod dinosaur – its massive neck and long tail left no doubt about that – and probably a member of the titanosaur family common in this part of the world. From its high-reaching, giraffe-esque posture, her study of Tim's notes led her to guess it was a Patagotitan.

She could see the cradle descending from the Rescue Pod, filled with armed men. Reaching for her radio, she opened a channel. Speaking quietly, she said, "Stay where you are. Make sure you remain well out of the dinosaur's reach. Do not fire unless it looks like it's going to get me. Acknowledge with three clicks – do not speak to me!"

She was gratified to receive her three clicks, as the cradle rocked to a halt about seven metres above the ground. Two riflemen lay flattened on the platform, aiming towards her, but no one fired.

Good, good, she thought, catching her breath. *OK, it's all up to you now, big girl, or boy, whatever you are.*

The immense sauropod stamped a couple of times. Alone, it was clearly distressed by the predatory presence growling and swishing its tail angrily before it, but seemed otherwise at a loss as to what to do next. Heidi suspected – with benefit of Tim's teaching – that this creature's vast size had insulated it from fear for so long that, confronted, its meagre intellect simply drew a blank. Eventually, it turned right, leaving the trees battered in its wake, before faltering again.

Tyrannotitan stood easily six metres tall as it leaned back slightly to look up, its tail curled barely a metre from the ground for balance. This movement placed its head more than ten metres *below* that of Patagotitan. The sauropod's huge neck was longer and heavier than the entire body of the carnivore, yet the uncertainty of isolation held it in place, the stench of the flesh-eater as disturbing sensually as it was instinctually.

Upwind, Heidi gagged.

Further trumpeting calls from around the lake encouraged the sauropod to turn north once more. It rose onto its hind legs and called. The bass at such proximity almost stunned the woman crouched below. She covered her ears, but the non-directional frequencies seemed to penetrate her very skull.

Tyrannotitan gave another disputatious *roar*, adding ear-shredding midrange to the commotion.

Slowly, Patagotitan's giant forelegs came back to earth with a thud that almost cost the slight young woman her footing. The disturbance, not to mention natural fear for her life, made it difficult to focus.

Decision made, Patagotitan seemed to forget the predator. Her unwitting protector had failed to notice Heidi at all, and now cleared the trees to plod heavily, one foot at a time, across the sandy, pebbly beach. They were heading around the reassuring bulk of the *Heydrich*'s stern.

Despite the relative slowness of the sauropod's movements, its stride was so long that Heidi had to trot to keep up. Hiding behind one of the four enormous legs, each measuring more than a metre in diameter, she moved with her 'cover' as if behind monolithic columns.

The carnivore stalked alongside easily, worrying at the much larger animal's flanks, and was not so easily fooled. If anything, Tyrannotitan became more excited and engaged in their little game.

Damn that shower gel! Heidi raged in silence while the hunter moved gracefully, bobbing to keep a constant eye on its bite-sized prey. With a sudden growl of excitement, it stepped in close, lunging for her.

Heidi screamed, in spite of herself, as she ran around the back of a leg.

Failing to reach her, the predator took a frustrated snap at the limb, leaving a wicked gash in the sauropod's flesh. A couple of seconds later, a bellow of pain and indignation came from high above, causing Heidi to dive once again for her life. The enormous creature moved its hind legs around to the left, with surprising speed, as it brought its tail to bear in a defensive swipe at the stalker.

Tyrannotitan, known by some as Matilda, was more than thirty years old and still in perfect health – which meant that, by any standards, she was *good*. Living alone for many years, she was mistress of this lake and environs, and no stranger to the *superfauna* that came to drink here. Expecting the manoeuvre, from the moment her teeth sank into the giant's flesh, she was already at a safe distance.

Once again, with an air of confused forgetfulness, Patagotitan straightened up and continued its lumbering stroll.

Tyrannotitan swallowed the lump of flesh it had stolen, without ever breaking eye contact with Heidi.

They were rounding the *Heydrich*'s stern now. She did not want to risk damage to the ship with such huge animals so close, but she was seriously in danger of losing a battle of wits with a dinosaur – and that would never do.

She continued her game of cat and mouse – or more accurately, cat and much larger cat – until they cleared the rear of the ship. Turning the volume down low, she opened a channel. *"Heydrich?"*

"This is Heydrich, *Dr Schultz. How may we help you?"* answered an infuriatingly calm voice.

"Get me Lieutenant Devon!"

Just a few seconds delay and the lieutenant's voice spoke, *"Go ahead, ma'am."*

"Devon, I am in trouble and need a distraction. Fire up the *Heydrich*'s aft, starboard landing thruster on a low-power burn. I only need a constant and very loud noise. Do not fire any ordnance. I need control."

"*At once, ma'am.*"

Within seconds, Devon was as good as his word and a single rocket motor burned to life underneath the *Heydrich*. Beside still waters, the sudden explosion of fuel was *loud*.

Both dinosaurs bellowed in distress at the shocking, alien sound, their ears built for a much quieter age. Patagotitan increased its rate of movement, making for the safety of its herd, whereas Tyrannotitan spun in a circle, unsure which way to run, its mighty tail flicking out angrily. Heidi had little choice but to follow her plodding protector, though it headed still further from the *Heydrich*.

The raw and ragged rip of rocket noise riled the giant sauropod, even more than the predation of one of nature's largest killers. The animal literally peed itself – and as it turned out, it was a boy.

"*Sweet Jesus!*" screamed Heidi, diving to escape the stinking column of brine. Fighter's reactions may have saved her from the stream, but the hose she could never unsee[4].

Almost forgetting the other peril, she watched shell-shocked as the tyrant ran back the way they came, eventually disappearing into the treeline.

Heidi stepped well clear of her giant saviour's legs, breathing deeply, hands on her knees. Unfortunately, an all-encompassing stench, like overboiled sprouts mixed with ammonia, mugged her nostrils, making her gag once more. Giving up on stealing a few seconds respite, she jogged back to her ship.

Once safely on the boarding ramp, she commed Devon to switch off the rocket engine.

Turning one last time before entering the ship, she visually tracked the most terrifying few hundred metres of her life, now fully restored to peace – the only sounds, those of breeze through trees and the gentle lapping of lake water on sand and pebbles.

---

[4] In reality, it seems most likely that dinosaurs – male and female – had a single opening, or cloaca. This has been found among the fossilised remains of a Psittacosaurus. Birds and reptiles also have this type of 'dual-use' organ for sex and excretion. However, until this is proven across all species, may it provide amusement as we ponder just what chases the wicked and murderous Heidi Schultz through her dreams.

Heidi blew out her cheeks. Never given to metaphor, she nevertheless seemed to have survived her very own 'Clash of the Titans'. Shaking her head, she disappeared inside.

Chapter 6 | Stressful Move

Beck Mawar, spiritualist medium and erstwhile 'paid-seat' passenger to Mars, strolled into the Mud Hole in a heightened state. "Thank you for seeing me. I know Georgie's been asking for me, but what I have to say involves more than just Mario."

The Pod's bar and restaurant had been much quieter in recent times. Indeed, it was almost deserted now, but for Crewman Georgio Baccini, Mother Sarah Fellows, Captain Jill Baines and Beck herself.

"Please tell me he came with us, Beck," asked Georgio, anxiously. "Please tell me we didn't leave him back in that place!"

Beck breathed deeply, centring herself. "Of all the people we've lost, my connection to Mario is strongest." She closed her eyes. "They're all staying back at the moment, but I can feel them… just."

"And Mario?" prompted Georgio.

"Yes, he's not with us right now, but he is *here*."

Georgio gave a huge sigh and visibly relaxed.

Beck continued, "As you know, Captain, Sarah, it was I who advised that Del Bond be reinterviewed. The information came not from me, but from Mario. Before you sit back and start crossing your arms, hear me out.

"He also told me other things, things he made me swear not to reveal to Georgio until we were away from that place. I don't know if we're secure here, but we're certainly safe from the Schultzes now, *right?*

"Georgie, I know you and Mario were both friends with Lieutenant Audrey Jansen – *Newfoundland*'s pilot and one of the fossilised bodies we recovered back in the Cretaceous. She was also Del Bond's niece. I suspect the Captain and Sarah may already know this. I'm not sure, did you know that his name was also Jansen – his real name, that is?"

Poker faced, they neither confirmed nor denied this.

Undeterred, Beck continued, "Anyhow, regarding Mario, apparently Audrey Jansen met with him before we left Canaveral. She warned him that a terrorist group had designs on the *New World*, but her source was a group no one was taking seriously. In fairness, they had no hard proof, either. As NASA are often under pressure from government, and the media, they sometimes choose to listen only to what they want to hear – previous disasters have borne this out. That aside, because she knew the two of you personally, she felt it best to pass the information along – for what it was worth.

"Georgie, the reason your brother was killed by the explosion was because he went to make sure no one was tampering with the drive, while the wormhole formed. That's why he was there, instead of at his usual jump station. He didn't tell you because he knew it was dangerous. We can only assume that whatever the bomber *actually* did, was done beforehand. As Lieutenant Lloyd confessed to that crime, I guess you already have those pieces of the puzzle, Captain?"

Baines remained impassive. "Go on."

"The reason Mario made me swear not to tell Georgio, was because he feared his brother might do something rash. Perhaps blow Bond's cover or go after Schultz? I'm sorry, Georgie, but it was for your own and everyone's sake that Mario kept this from you. But he wanted you to know the full truth now." She smiled, as if remembering. "He actually said, 'Tell that *idiota* not to do anything stupid. I'll see him again, but not yet!' He was adamant, Georgie."

The young Italian smiled as a tear ran down his cheek, hanging at his chin. "Tough words, but he'll be missing me like crazy, really. He was always hopeless without me."

Baines smiled too, taking Georgio's hand and giving it a squeeze. "OK, Beck. You said this was about more than just Mario, so what else do you have to tell us?"

"You're very busy, of course, Captain," replied Beck. "I'll be as brief as I can. The reason I requested this meeting was to inform you that we have another problem."

"Is this following on from the 'problems' you were having in the Pod med-centre?" asked Baines.

Beck nodded. "Dr Flannigan told you about that? Of course he did. Yes, this is related. I have been under a constant personal attack since before Captain Baines' assault on the *Last Word*."

Mother Sarah leaned forward with concern. "Attack from *whom*, dear?"

"I don't have a name. I only know that he was a Nazi soldier who didn't pass all the way. Not a helpful spirit, like Mario, who hangs around to look after his brother, until the day they join again. This creature is something else entirely."

"You told me something of this before," said Baines.

"Do you still wear the stone of protection I gave you, Captain?"

Baines dug into her tunic and produced a carved stone on a leather string. She gave an apologetic shrug. "It clearly meant a lot to you at the time, so I figured, what the hell. Besides, I've survived some pretty crazy events since, so maybe it had some juice in it after all."

Beck smiled. "Thank you, Captain. Please keep it with you at all times. You see, you're the one I fear for the most."

"I'm not sure I follow you?" asked Sarah, perplexed.

Beck gave Baines a look of apology before she spoke again. "Captain Baines saved us in some way, before we attacked the enemy. I don't have the details, but I sensed there was a real danger and the only way to prevent something coming for us was to take a life."

"I'm real sorry, Captain. I know this is painful for you, but this fact is important to what I'm about to tell you. The man who lost his life—"

Georgio's sense of propriety forced him to interrupt, "Erm, should I know any of this?"

"It's OK, Georgie," Baines replied sadly. "You remember when we launched our satellite to find the location of the *Last Word?* Well, the Nazis found it, in orbit, and tried to take it on board one of their small drop-boats. If we'd allowed them to possess that asset they might have broken into our systems, they could've…"

Baines faltered, so Mother Sarah reached across the table to take the younger woman's hand and continued the story, "The Captain had no choice but to activate the satellite's self-destruct. Unfortunately, it claimed at least one life when it blew. Although I didn't understand at first, Jill was right – it had to be done."

"Do you think there may have been others aboard?" Baines asked, wretchedly.

"It's possible," replied Sarah, "but nowhere near as many as there were down here, on the *New World*. You had no choice. If they had stolen that satellite, your mission to take that monstrous battleship from them wouldn't have stood a chance.

"Now, Beck, you were saying about the man who lost his life…?"

"OK, so like I said, he didn't pass over well. He became something dark. Now, this was a problem back in dinosaur world, but that was nothing compared with the problem we face now."

Sarah frowned. "What do you mean?"

"I mean that these things, these entities, feed off of human emotions and fears. Basically, when there were only like, what, a couple o' hundred of us? He could be controlled, but now…

"Outside our walls are many millions of souls all around the world, all acting like a giant dynamo, forever cycling. OK, so I'm no expert on these times, but I'm betting they're pretty dark, with a lot of superstition and fear, all adding to the *real* bad stuff going on all around us, yeah?"

Sarah and Baines exchanged a look, but no one spoke.

"I am Sir Nicholas Throckmorton. Who are *you*, sir?" the nobleman demanded imperiously from astride his fine black stallion.

The other group, who Gleeson believed to be the aggressors, circled slowly, also awaiting his answer.

"Commander Gleeson, at your service," replied the Australian, confidently. "You look like you're in a spot of bother, mate?"

Sir Nicholas frowned, not entirely sure he understood the other's meaning. "Do you seek to aid me or thwart me, sir?"

The second party to the skirmish – probably some flavour of mercenaries, Gleeson surmised – eyed one another shiftily. He watched at least two of them begin the lengthy process of reloading their wheel lock pistols. Both were bloody; he could only surmise their wielders used them for bludgeoning, after discharge[5].

"I'd really rather you didn't do that, mate," Gleeson spoke to one of them, keeping his tone light.

Neither man stopped what he was doing.

"Oh, bagger!" Pulling the Heath-Rifleson from around his shoulders, he dialled the power down and fired.

One of the men fell from his horse; the other worked even more frantically to load his dagg. "Mate, do yourself a favour and stop! Oh, for cryin' out loud, are you baggers *deaf?*" He fired again, dropping the other man. "Look, I'll make this really easy for you bladdy drongos. Stop whatever you're doing or I'm gonna shoot ya!"

"Devils! Black devils from the pit!" shouted one of the men, soon joined by others.

Corporal Jones did not like where this was heading and stepped up to support his officer. "Calm down, lads," he called, waving his arms. "There's no need for name-calling, isn'it."

The horses, in both camps, whirled and stamped, sensing fear in their riders.

"It's the bloody Welsh!" another man shouted.

This was apparently worse than the appearance of devils, because they immediately circled and, bringing their steeds under control, spurred towards Gleeson's team with the clear intention of riding them down.

"Fire into the air," shouted Gleeson.

Corporal Jones carried an assault rifle. Setting it to rapid-fire, he let off a couple of dozen rounds over their heads, and all hell broke loose.

A coffee-laden biscuit sagged as Mother Sarah paused halfway to her mouth. Eventually it broke off altogether, falling back into her cup with a *splosh*. "You wanna run that by me again?"

"An exorcism," repeated Beck.

---

[5] Often known as the 'dagg', a heavy, single shot, early pistol – once fired, it was often used as a club, so longwinded was the reloading process.

"Shall I break out the Inquisition while I'm at it?" snapped Sarah, incredulous.

"Obviously, I don't want you to do anything like that, Sarah," replied Beck, reasonably. "All I'm saying is, this is not our time and perhaps we should consider... well, you know?"

Sarah's eyebrows shot up. "Are you tellin' me to 'get with the programme', is that it? When in Rome?"

"I'm saying that there's a battle coming. Whether you believe it or not won't change the fact, only our chances of surviving it."

Sarah blinked. "You do know that, despite taking vows, I spent most of the last twenty years – before all this madness – as an administrator?"

Beck leaned forward, smiling kindly. "Did you see Thomas Beckett's rockery and tomato plants before we left Crater Lake?"

"I did," replied Sarah noncommittally, *really* not sure where this was going.

"He didn't even know which end of a shovel went in the ground a couple of months ago, and yet..."

"Er, this is a little different!"

"Of course it is. *You* will have at least studied *some* of what you need to know to do this, in seminary, right?"

Sarah kneaded her eyes tiredly. "Beck, you're a lovely girl, but—"

"I'm crazy?"

"I didn't say that—"

"You didn't need to."

"Look, what do you want from me?" asked the priest, exasperated. "I'm not even sure I believe in—"

"Ah! And there's the problem," stated Beck, sitting back, satisfied to have the point made for her. "Are you really gonna make me preach to a priest about belief and..."

Sarah gave her a sharp look. "*And* what?"

Beck looked at each of them in turn. "The existence of... look, the closest word we have is 'demon', OK?"

Georgio's eyes widened in alarm. "Is Mario trapped with that thing?"

"Not exactly. But your brother and the others are affected by it. If it weren't for them, I don't think I'd have made it that last time in the infirmary. The psychic blast nearly killed me. They gave everything to save my life."

"Beck," Baines cut into the conversation. "You talk about battles and dark forces – you make it sound like we're under siege, here."

"That's as good a description as any, Captain. The trouble is, this thing has just been given a practically unlimited power source. And the people in this world are likely to be way more easily influenced and affected than we are. Their very lives *revolve* around superstition!"

Baines held up a placating hand. "OK. I hear what you're saying, I just don't know how we can believe any of this. I don't mean any offence by that, I know *you* believe it, and I respect that, but how can *we?*"

"I don't know," Beck admitted, frankly. "All I'm sure of is this – if I can't make you believe now, by the time you do, it will be too late."

"Come back! Damnable cowards! Come *back!*" Sir Nicholas bellowed for his men to return to his side, but they ran like hares, in all directions from the machine gun fire. Fortunately, the group of paid assassins did likewise, leaving him alone with his charge.

Frantically, and with the light of panic in his eyes, he grabbed the reins of the young woman's horse. "Lady, with me!" he said and spurred away north.

"Oh, *don't go*, mate," Gleeson called after him.

"Well, isn't this just great!" said O'Brien, picking up a stone and throwing it away angrily. "So what now, Commander?"

"We should get after 'em. They obviously need our help, whether they know it or not."

"Better get a wriggle on then, boy," offered Jones. "Captain said he wanted us back before dark. Didn't want any weird lights spotted in the hills, he said."

"Alright," agreed Gleeson. "Mount up. Last one dead's a rotten egg, and all that."

They continued north along the road, quickly catching up with their quarry's weary, terrified mounts.

Gleeson pulled alongside. Sir Nicholas let go of the woman's reins to secure his own. He drew his rapier and brought it down in a deadly flash towards the commander's head.

Swerving away, and almost unseated by the rough ground to the side of the road, Gleeson cried out, "Bladdy 'ell, mate! There was no need for that! We did just save your lives back there, or didn't you notice?"

"Stop! Stop!" The young woman reined in her panting and well-lathered horse.

"*No,* Lady!" Sir Nicholas cried in alarm.

"We cannot outrun these devilish machines they ride, Nick, and 'twould be folly to try. We will only succeed in killing our horses, or ourselves – *halt!*"

The man returned to her side loyally, sword still drawn, though he was clearly afraid – whether for himself or for his charge was hard to discern.

Gleeson stopped his bike in the road before them, once more kicking down the side stand to step off. He raised his hands. "Look, mate. Two arms, two legs. Not devils – we haven't got a single tail between us! Just men, like you."

"*Ahem,*" O'Brien noted, grouchily.

The redhead on the horse turned to her, treating the female corporal to a wry smile. She spoke softly, "Dost thou lead these men?"

"Oi!" called Gleeson, outraged.

She turned her perfect grey gelding back to face him with exquisite control. "This realm is *led* by a woman, boy!"

"*Boy?*" mouthed Gleeson, for once unable to find his voice. His men sniggered, hiding their faces – his *woman,* merely sniggered.

"And one day soon, it may be led by another!" the redhead called out passionately.

"Lady," hissed Sir Nicholas. "Such talk is *treason.*"

"Ha!" she replied, walking her horse around to get a view of them all. "You girl! What is thy name?"

Now it was O'Brien's turn to bridle.

Gleeson folded his arms, grinning.

"Well, girl?"

"My name is *Corporal* Jennifer O'Brien."

The mounted woman frowned. "Jennifer… a quaint name. Thy speech is most unusual, whence come thou?"

O'Brien looked left and right to her comrades. "Erm… USA?"

"Yewessay?"

"America."

"Ah. I was told the native population dressed outlandishly, but not that they bore wheels."

Almost a hundred million years earlier

"We've installed the salvaged Last Word *thruster into the* Newfoundland, *ma'am,"* reported one of Heidi's senior technicians via a ship-to-ship comm signal.

"Very good," Heidi acknowledged. "Any problems?"

"Apart from the fact that it didn't fit? Yes, ma'am. It's also nowhere near powerful enough. The Newfoundland *is many times the size of the* Last Word, *as you know, but fortunately, the Rescue Pods are only a fraction of the weight of* Factory Pod 4."

"Will it be enough to get her off the ground?"

"All things being equal… no idea, ma'am. You see, the other problem we have is that one of our other thrusters has already been jerry-rigged to get the ship even this far – from wherever she's been for the last who-knows-how-long. It's a miracle she flew at all. Looks like half the fuel system to one of the burners is stolen from an escape pod, if you'll believe it! They multiplied it up, like a manifold, ma'am. Crazy!

"We're upgrading the supply – again with robbed parts from the Last Word, *ma'am. She's almost ready, but whether she'll lift…?"*

"Very well. Inform me the moment you are ready to attempt a take-off – *Heydrich* out."

Heidi turned to the *Heydrich*'s temporary captain. "Lieutenant Devon, this is perhaps a good time to join your new ship."

"Yes, ma'am," he replied unenthusiastically. "Thank you for your confidence."

She quirked a smile. "We need that Pod, Devon. Our lives at – what is it that everyone is now calling the place, Crater Lake Farm? –

will be untenable without it. The *Heydrich*, I need in Egypt. Your flight must succeed."

He straightened and saluted. "I understand, Doctor. I'll grab a few things and go now."

Heidi watched him leave, wondering whether he was up to the task. She could not risk herself, and Nassaki was still in the infirmary. There was really no choice.

"Hey *Red*, how about telling us who *you* are!" Gleeson demanded.

Sir Nicholas drew a sharp intake of breath at the Australian's impertinence.

The woman merely gave a snort of amusement. "Thou may call me 'My Lady'."

The Australian frowned in puzzlement. "*Your* Lady?"

"*My* Lady."

"That's what I said, *Your* Lady."

Her amused expression turned to annoyance. "No. I am *your* Lady – so thou shalt call me *My* Lady! Fathom this, simpleton!"

"Alright, alright, Your Lady."

"MY LADY!"

"Bladdy 'ell! It would be a lot easier if you just told me your name, lady!"

"Insolent cur!" bellowed Sir Nicholas.

"Don't you bladdy start, Nigel."

"Nicholas! *Sir* Nicholas to you—"

"Enough!" shouted the red-headed woman. "Bess! Thou mayest call me *Bess* – flap-ear'd knave!"

Gleeson smiled broadly. "See? That wasn't so hard now, was it? OK, Bess, and er, Nick, was it?"

"Sir!" Sir Nicholas retorted.

"S'OK, mate. Commander will do."

"*Thou* wilt call *me* 'sir', ye baseborn rogue!"

"Alright, skip."

"SIR!"

"No worries, mate. Where were you guys heading, before those other baggers jumped you, anyway?"

Sir Nicholas and Bess exchanged a look of bewilderment.

"Where...were...*you*...going?" he tried again, speaking slowly and, to his mind, helpfully.

Bess began to answer, "We—"

"Have a care, Lady," interrupted Sir Nicholas.

"If these people wished us ill, forsooth, we would own it by now," she retorted.

"Yeah, Nick. Take a bladdy onion and cry later, will ya? Go on, Bess, please continue."

Bess frowned in puzzlement, shook her head and continued, "We travel to the castle of Sir Ralph Grey."

"Is it far?" asked Gleeson.

"A league or so nor'east," replied Sir Nicholas.

"We could escort you there, or at least until you're within a safe distance," Gleeson offered reasonably. "We probably should stay away from the castle itself."

"Art thou outlaws?" asked Bess.

"Not exactly, it's just that the Captain wants us back before nightfall."

"Thou hast a ship?"

Gleeson scratched the stubble on his cheek. "Er, yeah… kinda."

"Speak plainly, man!" snapped Bess, irritably.

"Yes, we have a ship!"

She exchanged a look with Sir Nicholas before continuing, "Where art thou moored?"

"Yeah, about that. It's complicated, lady."

"Complicated?" repeated Sir Nicholas.

"You see those hills over in the west there? It's kind of *inside* one of those."

Sir Nicholas leaned back in the saddle. "Mock me not, sir!"

"Nah, like I said it's just a bit—"

"Complicated?" the nobleman finished for him, raising an eyebrow.

"Would you take us back to your ship?" asked Bess.

"*Lady!*" Sir Nicholas was suddenly horrified.

She returned his gaze levelly. "Should we place all faith in Sir Ralph Grey – a man I have ne'er met, nor have real cause to trust? We know well that his was not the hand that cast poor Jane to the wolves, yet small love do I bear the name of Grey.

"Or perhaps I am to conceal myself here? Until the winter snows take me, or the long reach of His Grace, the Archbishop of Canterbury, grasps to close about my throat. These people may offer a third way, sir."

"But, Lady. We know not these men."

"Again, with the men!" O'Brien grumbled.

Bess studied Gleeson's team, treating each to a bold, disconcerting stare. Slowly, she shook her head. "Look at them, Sir Nicholas. These poor souls are more lost than I. Perhaps 'tis fate that drew them to our aid, at this hour, and in this lonely place."

...The *New Worlders* stared at her. For that moment, it felt as though she were the axis about which the whole world revolved. Even the machinery of the universe seemed to realign. An inflation of breath expanding space–time to its limits, only to deflate with a sigh, reality recompacted – remade almost, but not quite, the same. Something so intrinsic that it could neither be seen, felt, nor even measured, had been *adjusted*...

Gleeson felt like he had just changed channel, then clicked back, but back too far. Jumping over his original choice, he suddenly found himself watching a channel he never knew existed, and it was a revelation.

"Commander," said O'Brien. "Can I have a word?"

They huddled.

"Did you feel that?" asked Gleeson, slightly dazed.

"Feel what?"

"Like everything was just taken apart and put back together again..."

"*Sir?*"

"Never mind. What did you want to say?"

"Commander, I'm concerned about the timeline. Who knows what we've done here today, already? Maybe she was *meant* to die?"

Gleeson took a long look at the young woman, perched side-saddle on her glimmering grey palfrey. He shook his head, almost dumbly. "I don't know, there's something about her... I just can't imagine a timeline when she was meant to die."

O'Brien's brows rose in surprise. "Are you *smitten*, Commander?"

"Nah, it's not like that. Are you kidding? She stinks like a yak. No, there's just an aura – I mean, other than the smell."

As if to reinforce his words, Bess' horse turned to, and the westering sun haloed the young, red-haired woman in pure gold.

O'Brien shrugged. "OK, that's a *look*, I'll grant you that, but what are we getting involved with here?"

"I dunno, Corp, but after everything I've seen over the last three months, I'm willing to go on a little faith and see where it leads."

Dr Natalie Pearson's animal enclosure now housed Mayor, the small hypsilophodontid dinosaur rescued by Captain Douglas; the pack of mammalian Cronopio that Henry Burnstein had insisted on 'saving' from their own environment[6]; and now she had a new charge in her care – a stout, shaggy-haired, barrel-chested fell pony.

During the altercation, the pony had taken a number of stun bolts. Consequently, he remained groggy long after the others had already regained their feet. Natalie had requested he be carried inside, rather than leave him prey to wolves. Doubtless, the other ponies had found their way home by now.

She had no idea what the chestnut brown's name might be, so she called him Barney. It was time for mucking out and Woodsey had promised his services. Along with the doubtful assistance of Reiver, she also had a third helper, an extremely nervous-looking young borderer named Billy Maxwell.

"I suppose you'll know a lot more about tending to these ponies than I do, Billy." Natalie smiled encouragingly.

When he did not answer, she tried again. "I notice they're unshod – I suppose you rarely ride across hard surfaces up here, eh?"

He sniffed her, which was disconcerting to say the least.

"*Billy?*"

"Are ye a witch?" he asked, seriously.

---

[6]   They had already been rehomed once, as Hank Burnstein Snr completely lost his shorts when Henry tried to 'introduce' them into the Burnstein apartments.

Trying not to bridle at the insinuation, she replied as calmly as she could, "Whyever do you ask that?"

"Yer wearing breeches."

"Do witches usually wear trousers?"

"I dinnae ken, I dinnae wish tae meet one!"

Natalie raised an eyebrow, mildly annoyed. "Well, you still *haven't* met one – just so you know! Now, are you going to help me muck out the animals or not?"

He did not answer, but when she turned towards their enclosure, he followed. The main hangar was a chaos of diggers and lorries, moving the collapsed earth back outside.

Douglas had decided to use it to build a plateau in front of their new front door, so that they could deploy vehicles and – despite hoping it would not be necessary – maintain a clear field of fire.

The first time Billy stepped outside Flannigan's infirmary, the mere sight of such giant yellow machines made him scream. He actually swooned. Natalie marvelled at the obvious toughness and hardiness of these people, yet in other ways, ways that she would take for granted, they were so fragile.

She smiled at him once more. "I have a few animals under my care now, Billy. Come, I'll introduce you. This is Mayor—"

"Aaaargh!" the boy screamed. "*Dragon!* The serpent!" He fell on his backside as he scrambled to leave the converted steel container.

Natalie reached out, attempting to calm him. "It's OK, Billy, it's just Mayor. He won't hurt you. Look, he's friendly."

Billy turned his terrified eyes on her. "You consort with demons – monsters from the pit!"

"No. Mayor is just an animal, like Barney over there."

"Barney? One o' our Galloways is yer *familiar!* No wonder Ah'm trapped in this hell!"

"Now just you hang on a minute!" retorted Natalie, crossly. "We're inside a ship, just a ship, nothing to do with magic or devils, OK? These are just animals – Barney is one of yours, as a matter of fact. Surely you can tell?"

"Barnabas, the devil's hobbler!"

"Look, will you just calm—" Natalie stopped and stared. "Back up a second. You're saying his name *is* Barnabas?"

He nodded, struggling against her grip on his collar.

"OK, that's weird, I'll grant you. But he's just a pony. He was stunned in the fight and left behind. I had him brought inside, so that he'd be safe, is all."

"What's *oh-kay?*"

"It means it's *all* right – all is well." She relaxed her grip. "Will you help me groom him? He doesn't look like he's ever been brushed."

Billy looked at her askance. "Galloways dinnae need tae be brushed. Ye'll offend the lad."

"OK, now that's something else I've learned," replied Natalie, once again in friendly tones.

Reiver had taken himself for a sniff. Barrelling back into the container, he skidded to a halt in front of the borderer and curled his lip, the beginnings of a growl in his chest.

"Wheesht, away with ye!" said Billy, brushing past him to approach Barnabas the pony.

Reiver sat, confused, looking to his mistress for instruction. Natalie merely stroked his head, so he relaxed, yawning voluminously.

"Hey, Natalie! Still need a hand?" asked Woodsey, strolling into the container, confidently late. He nodded to Billy, "How's it going, dude?"

Billy nodded nervously.

"You're just in time to muck out," replied Natalie, brightly.

Woodsey's enthusiasm wilted. "Oh, great."

Natalie grinned. "Thought you'd arrived just in time for feeding, did you?"

"Well, I kinda hoped, you know? So who's our new friend?" Woodsey held out his hand to the stranger.

Billy stared at it critically, sniffing again. "Have ye ne'er worked, lad? Ye smell like a bawbee[7] whore."

Woodsey's jaw dropped as Natalie exploded into raucous laughter[8].

---

[7] Bawbee was the Scottish word for a debased copper coin worth sixpence. It was introduced by James V in 1538 and roughly equal at the time to an English half-penny, or ha'penny. The low price stated would probably have wounded Woodsey's pride more than the insult itself, had he understood it.

[8] Having already being accused of being a witch, it would have been unsafe to cackle at this point.

"This feel like a trap to you, Corp?" asked Gleeson.

"You mean the way we have torch-bearing riders to the left and right of us, but the middle way is suspiciously clear?" replied O'Brien.

"Yeah, that'd be the one."

Sir Nicholas reined in his mount to their side. "I, too, believe this to be a trap, Commander."

Gleeson was both pleased and surprised to be addressed with courtesy by the nobleman for the first time. *Maybe I should throw him a bone,* he thought. "So, what do you think, Sir Nick? This is your world, after all."

Sir Nicholas viewed him strangely, eventually shaking it off as just another 'oddity' of these foreigners. "I can see no way out but *through* the trap."

Gleeson grinned. "I like your thinking, mate. Listen up, people! We're gonna have to charge straight down the middle—"

"That'll make a change," muttered O'Brien.

"What?"

"Nothing, sir. You were saying?"

"Right. Like I said, we're gonna have to go for it – straight down the middle, if we're to get back to the *New World*. Remember our orders – fire over their heads, try not to hit anybody."

"Sir Nick, how much life is left in the dobbins?"

When he did not answer at once, Bess cut in, explaining, "'Tis a new Scotch term for horse, I believe. In answer to your question, I think they will not gallop more than a mile."

Sir Nicholas viewed Gleeson with sudden suspicion. "Scotch?"

"That's kind, but never when I'm on duty, mate." He looked up at them both. "If your horse starts to pack in, shout out. One of us will have to take you pillion for the last bit of the journey. That *means* you'll have to sit behind one of us, got that? Right, let's go!"

In the privacy of his own mind, he added, *Bagger strange lights – Douglas is gonna have a cow when we drag these two back with us!*

Daylight was dropping quickly now, the sun already hiding halfway below the hills in the distance. It was rough going and the horses were already spent.

The torch-bearing riders came on regardless, but they too seemed to be sparing their mounts. Gleeson knew, from Beckett's talk, that some of the border raids covered so many miles in a night as to become the stuff of legend. If the newcomers were also weary, he dared hope that they might just have a chance.

At that moment, the surprise they had all been waiting for surprised them anyway.

A couple of dozen men stood up from the heather, blocking their path, waving swords, axes and long spears. Down a little way to the left, Gleeson could now see where their horses were tethered behind a rocky outcrop, and with them – at a safe distance from any impending violence – was a huge man wrapped within a black cape, a silver clasp at the throat. He was far larger than anyone else they had yet encountered, possibly even as great in stature as Corporal Jones.

Something about him gave Gleeson the urge to take a pot-shot at the man, but firing a rifle from the saddle of a homemade, electric dirt bike over rough terrain was impractical to the point of suicidal. They would have to push through or make a stand.

As the commander ran limited options through his mind, another was taken from him. Bess' horse reared when the men nearest her jumped to their feet, roaring a battle cry. She was thrown hard from the dubious security of her side-saddle.

The distinctly feminine scream caused Sir Nicholas to turn recklessly, desperate to go back for her, but the tight manoeuvre caused his mount to stumble in the heather and throw him too.

"Take the woman yet alive!" bellowed the black-clad man. "Should any man inflict a harm upon her, I shall *flay* his *entire* family!"

Corporal Jones stopped his bike and fired several rapid bursts into the air, shocking and backing off the men nearest him. He reached down for Sir Nicholas. "Get on!"

"I cannot leave her!"

"You heard the man! They want her alive! That means there'll be another chance, isn'it! Get on now, or you *will* die, and there'll be no saving her then, boy!"

Nicholas grabbed the giant Welshman's hand, allowing himself to be pulled onto the saddle behind. Jones stood, surrendering the seat. "Hold on to me," he called as the bike shot forward.

A few pistol shots cracked in their wake, but they seemed hopelessly inaccurate. A bolt from a latch[9] caught between the spokes of O'Brien's rear wheel, bending a few and causing her to skid, but the powerful electric motor snapped it and, skipping over a few heartbeats, she resumed her flight.

"Pray God, forgive me," cried Sir Nicholas as they scrambled for their lives.

---

[9] A small crossbow, mostly used in preference to the longbow by the Scots.

Chapter 7 | The Dog of War

"Open a channel to the *Heydrich*," ordered Lieutenant Devon.

"Aye, aye, Captain."

He smiled inwardly, enjoying the naval tradition that granted the title of Captain to a ship's commander, regardless of rank – although the vessel herself left a lot to be desired.

The USS *Newfoundland* was huge, 550 metres in length, sharing the same body plan as the *New World*. An extremely impressive ship by any standards, ordinarily, but time and injury had left her in poor shape.

The comms officer nodded to signify he had his connection.

"Dr Schultz, this is *Newfoundland*."

"*Go ahead,* Newfoundland."

"Doctor, we are go for launch. Suggest the *Heydrich* takes to the air and creates some space between us." He hardly needed to add, 'in case we explode and leave a hole in the ground the size of Washington State.'

"*Acknowledged,* Newfoundland." Devon nodded; typical Schultz, curt and to the point, but then she surprised him with the supplementary, "*Good luck, Captain Devon.*"

"Yes, ma'am," he replied, hoping the surprise in his voice did not carry through the comm.

The *Heydrich* launched in a cloud of dust and rocket smoke, the noise of her engines shaking the ground and carrying for miles. After a few hundred metres of vertical climb, she turned to starboard and headed north, eventually stopping to hover about two kilometres away.

Devon steadied himself. "Right. Our turn. Begin the ignition sequence."

The *Newfoundland*'s remaining intact engines, positioned vertically opposite, fired almost immediately. Devon was impressed and could not hide it – she was a very old and undermaintained ship, after all. The third engine, jerry-rigged by Douglas and Hetfield, coughed to life sporadically but eventually fired too, adding to the noise.

"Now for *our* handiwork," said Devon. "Fire engine four."

A huge bang rocked the ship as fuel, an excess of fuel, exploded in a manner too far outside of their control for her new captain's liking.

"It's just a start-up flash, sir," called one of his engineers. "She'll burn."

Devon gave him a look carrying some misgiving, but the rocket did indeed fire, eventually gaining a measure of equilibrium – and with it, they began to lift.

A cry of celebration tore from the crew.

"Quiet!" roared Devon. "This isn't an office party, *damnit!* Helm, is she stable?"

"Sluggish, but answering, sir."

"Fire the main engines." This was it. The phrase 'go big or go home' crossed Devon's mind, but of course, going big in this situation was likely to mean a fireball several miles in diameter, leaving precious little to return to sender.

He said a quick prayer – he had no idea who to – but apparently whoever it was had their ears on, because three of the main engines fired. The upper engine of the quad-diamond sputtered and flamed but would not stay lit.

His pilot turned to face the captain's seat. "Sir, engine four is sporadic and unpredictable."

"Will she fly on three?"

"I think it will certainly be safer to try, Captain."

"Very good, shut it down and move us out – course north-north-east."

"Incoming!" someone shouted, but before Major White could react, Corporal Jones had already zipped past him, down into the Pod, an outlandishly dressed passenger on pillion.

"Jones?" he shouted after him, but was quickly forced to press himself against the dirt wall as several other bikers shot past. They were most decidedly *not* sparing their horses.

Turning around, he was forced to jump out of the way yet a third time as Gleeson skidded to a halt, narrowly missing him.

"What the hell?" White called out in alarm, holding his damaged left arm protectively within its sling. He peered in the low light. "Gleeson?"

"Yeah, it's me, mate. We need to talk. But before we do, turn out the guard. They're right on our asses!"

"STAND TO!" bellowed White, not waiting for further explanation. Using his good arm, he pulled out a comm to call up reinforcements, before returning his attention to Gleeson. "Been making a few friends, huh?"

Before the Australian could answer, the partially complete plateau, constructed during the day from spoil removed from the hangar, was suddenly alive with shouts and calls blended with the whinnying of horses.

They came at speed, mounted on the rugged little ponies clearly favoured in this region, and charged towards the duty guard.

"Fire over their heads!" shouted White. "Don't hit them unless a life depends on it!"

White did not want to kill any of the people from this time, but neither did he wish to hamstring his people completely, preventing them from defending their own. He was only willing to go *so* far for the grandfather paradox.

His people dutifully fired into the air, and at the ground around the horses. This did lessen the ardour of the initial attack, but it was soon replaced by further disruption.

Firstly, the roar of a massive diesel engine echoed along the gulley excavated out from the ship. The armoured personnel carrier seemed almost to leap from the mouth of the cutting. The boxy, black monstrosity spun around on the new plateau, throwing clumps of loose earth all over the place, provoking screams from men and horses alike. When the fifty-calibre machine guns opened up into the starry blue sky, panic ballooned into anarchy.

Spinning around on terrified ponies, the attacking force began noticing the *other* burning torches in the distance.

White noticed them too. From his viewpoint, looking out from the mouth of their cutting, a ridge led away north-west, to his right. Along it came a stream of flickering lights, seemingly without end.

Along with the machine gun fire, this proved the final straw for the horsemen. With rallying calls they wheeled their ponies around and rode them hard, down into the valley. Dousing their lights, one at a time, they vanished into the deepening shadows.

White stepped out onto the plateau. "Get the other armoured vehicles out here and set up a blockade! I want everybody behind cover and with clear fields of fire. Remember folks, we can't free up any air support yet, so it's eyes and ears only."

At least a thousand strong, the approaching group hugely outnumbered the previous band; this was an army.

"If we have to fall back, do it by sections, or use the APCs if necessary. The armed APC will back down and bring the rear, but let's not let it get that far, people. For all we know, they might get ideas about bringing up a cannon to work on what's left of our hangar doors! So, dig in and stay sharp! Whatever happens, do *not* fire first – we may yet be able to talk our way out of this."

"Oh, no," Gleeson spoke quietly, focusing on the last of the fleeing horsemen.

"What?" asked White.

"Did you notice a young woman with them?"

"Can't say that I did, but I was a little busy."

Gleeson nodded without taking his eyes from the valley below. "What about a massive dude with a black cape, a silver brooch and pointed teeth?"

White stared at him. "*Come on!* I've been told it's Halloween, but this is no time for games."

"Straight up, mate. This is what passes for real life these days."

"OK, Commander, what haven't you told me yet?"

"We came upon a skirmish. Another set of mongrels, out to kill a young girl was what it looked like. This is a really unfriendly place we've dropped into, mate.

"Obviously, we didn't know what was happening, but it's a hard thing to stand by and not act, you know? So we gave pursuit and intervened.

"That bloke Jonesy just took down into the ship, is some cove named Sir Nicholas Throckmorton. He's a bit of a stiff, but he seems genuine. His loyalty to the girl certainly was.

"When we came over the hills, we were trapped between two columns of riders. That was when yet another bunch jumped us. The girl and Nick lost their horses – those thieving dags have probably taken them. Jonesy grabbed Nick, but we couldn't get to the girl. I didn't see her here, so chances *are* Black Cloak has already whisked her away."

"Or she's been killed," suggested White. "Like you say, these folks seem none too friendly."

Gleeson shook his head. "No. Black Cloak made a big, blood-curdling speech about what he'd do to any man who laid hand to her. I reckon the Sheila's safe for now, but I don't know for how long. I feel responsible for her."

White's expression darkened. He knew how it felt to lose someone in his care; whose actual fault it was never came into it. He patted Gleeson on a meaty shoulder. "Maybe this Sir Nicholas can provide a lead. That guy you identified – Dracula? He sounds like the kinda dude with a reputation, know what I mean?"

"Yeah, well, we'd better deal with this latest army first. I suppose it would be too much to hope that they're simply on their way somewhere, and nothing to do with us. This will be the third group to just *happen by*, since we crashed here – this place is like Melbourne city centre on a Friday night, mate! If we're stuck here, I might open a Walkabout Bar!"

White stared at the approaching horsemen with trepidation. It was almost dark now and when he turned back to Gleeson, his face was a mask of concern. "Third time lucky?"

Heidi watched the *Newfoundland* lift off, slowly turning to a northerly heading. She permitted herself a nod of grim satisfaction, and ordered her pilot to follow at a safe distance. The day was clear, and even at ten kilometres, the vast bulk of the ancient ship could easily be seen with the naked eye.

Assuming we all arrive back at Crater Lake, this should be phase one accomplished. Her thoughts now turned to phase two – production of the isotopes.

Rising from the captain's seat, she left orders to be called immediately should there be any change in the *Newfoundland*'s status.

The ship's corridors were busy these days, filled with extra crew members and survivors from the other Dawn Fleet vessels. The vastness of the *Newfoundland* and its Rescue Pod would help balance that.

Once landed, in what would one day be Britain, she would probably never fly again, but that did not matter. She still had a vital role to play in their survival.

Lost in thought, Heidi had walked all the way through the ship to her destination, almost without realising it.

Standing square shouldered, with arms crossed, she glowered. "*Großvater*. You will now tell me what I wish to know."

Heinrich Schultz gave her one of his cool smiles. "And what would that be, *Enkelin?*"

"Is the Norris boy my cousin?" Heidi was furious with herself for not running a DNA test on the boy. It had simply not occurred to her that the whole story might be a fiction created to suit her grandfather's ends.

Judging by Heinrich's expression, he understood this well – and was enjoying it.

"You never answered *my* question, *Enkelin*. If it turns out he is not, will you still pursue him, at what I am sure will be great cost?"

"You are correct, *Großvater*. I did not. This is because *you* are here to answer *my* questions."

His stare penetrated her, as it always did. He did not answer for at least a minute as he calculated and plotted his next move. Eventually, he answered simply, "No. He is not."

Heidi's gaze was hooded with loathing. She had expected this. "Thank you."

The old man's poker face twitched, just a millimetre. "Perhaps there are other things you wish to learn?"

"No," she replied, flippantly. Treating him to a knowing smile, she left. His expression would have been unreadable to anyone else, but she knew him as well as any creature alive knew him, which was by no means completely. However, it was just enough to see that she left him perturbed.

He is *my cousin, then. I thought it was so. Fifteen-all, Großvater, and the ball is back in my court, I believe.*

Dr Natalie Pearson used a multiplex utility knife to cut the ties she had used to bushel Cretaceous ferns. These were the mainstay of Mayor's diet and she had stockpiled a reasonable supply. Nevertheless, finding a suitable local replacement would soon be paramount.

Mayor seemed unsettled. Perhaps it was not surprising, after all he had been through with the crash, but he also seemed very wary of Barnabas the pony.

Natalie found this strange. Although they were wildly different physically, they lived similar lives and fulfilled similar natural niches – pre-domestication.

She would have expected there to be far more hostility between Mayor and the Cronopios. They were also mammalian, but more significantly, were carnivorous. However, behaving like individuals from the same place who were simply unacquainted, they left one another alone – neither a threat to the other.

The Cronopios seemed to have accepted Reiver into their pack, quite quickly, and with minimal fuss. He was far bigger in stature, and obviously they scented that he was also a carnivore, but their wariness soon eased as they sensed his playful nature. This genuinely surprised Natalie. Wild carnivores very rarely develop interspecies relationships. Perhaps their shared affiliation, or connection, with humanity provided a bridge? It was worthy of study.

Reiver, for his part, was so used to Natalie being involved with all kinds of creatures that he mostly took it in his stride; he barely registered the pony.

It was a very weird dynamic they had going here.

Bending to offer Mayor a fistful of ferns, she pondered the complexities of their interactions, her knife left open on top of the feed storage container.

So lost in thought was she, that the sudden blade at her throat caught her completely off guard, causing her to cry out. A second hand clapped to her mouth, stifling the call instantly.

Woodsey looked up from across the container, where he fed some dried meat to the nine rescued Cronopios. "Hey!" he called out, startled to see Billy Maxwell with a penknife to Natalie's jugular.

"Wheesht! Or Ah'll cut the witch's throat!"

"Steady on, mate. No one here wants to harm you."

Reiver instantly abandoned the meaty treats to run to his mistress' aid. He skidded on the metal floor and began jumping and barking menacingly.

Billy's left shoulder had been nicked by a bullet upon his arrival, and his arm lacked its usual strength. However, he slipped a practised hand down over Natalie's chin to grasp her around the throat, thrusting the knife out in front to defend himself. As Reiver jumped, he slashed, catching the dog's front leg.

Fortunately, the knife was not particularly sharp, and his thick fur further reduced the effectiveness of Billy's strike. Even so, he squealed as the blade bit into his skin.

Limping now, he barked not only with anger but with pain. Regardless, injury dulled his purpose not a jot, nor did it curtail his doggy valour. He continued to bark and threaten, looking for another opening to dive straight in. Whatever the cost, all that mattered was the defence of *she* who was his entire world. Mayor too began honking, jumping and flicking his tail skittishly, as the pony stamped and whinnied.

Barely able to draw breath, Natalie managed, "Billy, what are you doing?"

"Ah'm leaving and ye'll be ma key to tha' giant steel portcullis out there." His eye left the collie for an instant, but with superior reflexes now on full attack, a split second was all it took. Reiver pounced once more. The time for warnings had passed, and his teeth sank deep into the young man's arm for effect. As they found bone, it was Billy's turn to scream – needless to say, he dropped the knife instantly.

Barnabas had also clearly had enough and bolted for the exit. The heavy, steel container doors were only slightly ajar, but this provided no barrier at all to the charging pony. He burst through and Mayor bolted after him, quickly catching up with the panicked hobbler.

Once out in the main hangar, giant alien machines moved around while men shouted orders. It was a terrifying environment for a horse, but doubly so for a small herbivorous dinosaur. Scenting the fresh air from outside, they both sprinted for the doors, barrelling men and women out of their way as they fled.

Within moments they were up through the cutting and out onto the new plateau, forcing Major White, once again, into the wall.

"What the bladdy hell was all that about!" Gleeson shouted, angrily. He could not afford further distractions now; the thousand horsemen were within a few hundred metres of their position.

Bess could barely breathe. Tied at the wrists and ankles, she was slung unceremoniously across the shoulders of a giant black stallion. Bouncing across the darkened landscape, even her bruises seemed to have bruises. It was agony, but physical discomfort was the least of her concerns, for she fancied that she could put a name to her captor – Sir William de Soulis.

She had listened hard, every time anyone spoke. His men called him Sir William and there surely could not be two such men in the borders – or indeed, anywhere. A black-clad giant with pointed teeth...? Yes, she had heard all about this tyrant.

Although afraid, Bess was determined not to give in to that fear. Sir Nicholas had escaped, after all.

Their journey north had afforded Nick every opportunity, should he have meant her harm. He had proved himself to be loyal, courteous and gallant at every turn. She had watched as the newcomers' giant Welshman snatched him to safety. That was the last she saw of her little party after being thrown by her mount.

She knew not who Sir Nicholas' rescuers were, but there was something about them. Just what, she had no idea, but she felt that they would not abandon her, either. Sir Nicholas certainly never would. So there was hope.

They must have been travelling for close to three hours now. If she was correct, and this was indeed De Soulis, they would have to make camp for the night. Hermitage Castle was still far from here.

She would not necessarily have known that, were it not for the infamy of its owner.

Bess had taken hospitality with the eighty-four-year-old Prince-Bishop of Durham on her ride north, Cuthbert Tunstall. Although of the old religion, she had found him a kind man, and taken advantage of his offer to avail herself of his rare and extremely valuable maps of the North.

Bess was not a woman to fly blind into the unknown if she could avoid it, and by her reckoning, she guessed they still had more than forty miles to travel west. If she could only create an opportunity to escape into the night.

Despite riding to war, De Soulis had clearly planned an ambush. His men therefore travelled light and brought no dogs with them. In that lay her last hope.

Hunting dogs would have been on her in a heartbeat, but men...? Perhaps she could outwit men, given half a chance. If she could only vanish into the darkness...

Her thoughts tailed off as De Soulis reined in their mount and did indeed order his men to make camp.

This was her chance. Once within the walls of Hermitage Castle, she would be lost forever. Few left the embrace of those cold walls alive, it seemed. Her captor's reputation was terrible.

Taken by surprise, she found herself snatched from the horse and flung to the grass by a vile, rat-faced man, who stank of sour ale and urine.

"We'll find ye a nice bed for the night, lass," he cackled. His lecherous grin forced Bess to shrink away.

Creature that he was, Bess was glad De Soulis was there. He was, for now, her only protection. *So this is the end dear Mary hoped for me, is it?* The thought made her so furious, she failed to even notice the damp, freezing ground, upon which she had been so casually cast down.

"Just what's been going on here?" Douglas shouted, angrily. "And who is this?"

Corporal Jones saluted before answering, "Captain, this is Sir Nicholas Throppington—"

"Throckmorton, knave!"

"Throckleting, Throt—Thropple... This is Sir Nicholas, Captain, isn't it. We rescued him and a young lady named Bess from... er, well, I suppose you could call them *robbers?*"

"I would call them mercenaries – murderers for hire," supplied Sir Nicholas.

Douglas looked back to Jones. "So where's the girl?"

"Taken by another bunch of..." he looked to Sir Nicholas for confirmation, "mercenaries?"

"Robbers!" snapped Sir Nicholas. He focused on Douglas. "Thou speak'st with the tongue of the Scotch, sir, and thou hast clear affiliation with the Welsh. Am I in the hands of England's enemies?"

Douglas and Jones glanced at one another. The moment dragged...

Eventually, Douglas cleared his throat and shrugged mildly. "That usually depends on who's left in the tournament and how much beer we've all had."

"What?"

"Relax, ye're among friends here. Now who's this lassie you've lost?"

With that, Sir Nicholas looked shifty but remained silent.

"Look, Sir Nicho—"

His comm binged, cutting him off. Reaching into a pocket, he answered, "Douglas."

Sir Nicholas' eyes widened in horror. "Witchcraft!"

Jones attempted to calm the man, while Flannigan's disembodied Brooklyn accent explained why the young borderer was back in his infirmary – this time with a particularly nasty dog bite – along with Natalie Pearson, who had a minor cut to her throat from a knife attack.

"What!" roared Douglas.

"*Afraid so, James. I'm having a little trouble giving her stitches because she keeps fighting me, so she can go and stitch a cut to Reiver's leg.*"

Douglas could hear scuffling and squabbling from the tiny comm speaker.

"*Let me go...*"

"*Look, honey, I know you've more blood to lose than he does, but...*"

"No, you can stitch me later! Let... me... go!"

Another scuffle.

"Nurse! Assistance here... Sorry, Captain. I'm back with you now. I had a dog once, I understand her priorities, but I wondered if you might have a word...?"

"Ah'm a little tied up with our other guest at the moment, Doctor. Do you have the Maxwell laddie secured?"

"Yeah, the kid's landed himself at the top of Corporal Thomas' list. He'll be giving us no more trouble this day."

Douglas nodded with satisfaction. "Good. Ah'll get along to ye as soon as Ah can, Davy, but at the moment Ah've just been told about a missing person, and Ah have to urgently view our defences – apparently we've an army just outside, about to move against us now!"

"Really?"

"Aye."

"Well, it never rains, does it, James, because I've just been informed that the dinosaur's escaped, too."

"WHAAAT!"

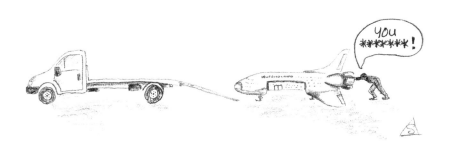

Chapter 8 | Reasons and Reason

Captain Aito Nassaki awoke. The pain from his hand seemed intense. *Seemed* intense; it was no longer there. He had been warned about this kind of 'phantom' pain, often associated with amputees. In a way the pain was helpful. It distracted him from the nausea.

Ever since he first awakened from the general anaesthetic after surgery a few days ago, he had suffered with bouts of sickness.

Today, he felt a little stronger, the dizziness a little more under control. He considered rising from his sickbed to take his first steps since a large, carnivorous dinosaur had flung him against a cave wall.

The loss of his hand had sent him into severe and immediate shock, rendering him unconscious before he even struck the rock face. This 'limp' state had probably prevented far worse injury from the collision and consequent fall.

Despite this, his body behaved more like a rigid frame than a multi-jointed machine, shocking him with pain from bits seldom noticed before.

Observing his struggle, a nurse rushed to his side with the practised aplomb of a wine waiter spotting a glass in the air. A second nurse appeared out of nowhere bearing crutches.

"Why don't my legs work?" Aito asked, hoarsely.

"They do work, Captain," replied one of his helpers. "Apparently, after being thrown against the cave wall, you fell about five or six metres to the sand. Also, you haven't moved a muscle in days. It's not surprising you're a little stiff. You were lucky, sir."

"Lucky I landed on sand?"

"Just lucky all round, sir," supplied the second nurse. "Here, let me help you with these crutches."

"What about my hand?"

His helpers glanced meaningfully at one another. "Lost, sir," replied the first.

"The dinosaur ate it... erm, apparently, sir," supplied the second, awkwardly.

Aito sighed, looking at his bandaged stump. "Right. So what am supposed to do with that second crutch then, nurse?"

She looked embarrassed. "I'm sorry, Captain. Maybe we could find a way to—"

Aito cut her off. "Never mind. I'll manage with just the one, thank you."

"I'll help you on your left side, sir," added the first nurse. "Come, let's take a walk to the observation lounge. We're flying over the Atlantic. It's a beautiful view." She smiled. "And you're alive to see it."

Aito sighed again. "Lucky me."

The first horsemen fanned out around the plateau on another crisp night in the Scottish Borders. Torches burned steadily in the still air, sending smoke curling upwards into the darkness.

A richly dressed man stepped his mount forward, two attendants closely at his flanks.

"Show yerselves!" he commanded. "Be ye devils?"

Douglas eyed White questioningly.

White shrugged.

Douglas sighed. "Take charge here, Major." He nodded for Sergeant Jackson and Commander Gleeson to follow and stepped out from behind their hastily thrown together barricade.

The Sarge was armed with a Heath-Rifleson while Gleeson carried an assault rifle, borrowed from Captain Meritus' cache.

Douglas signified his peaceful intentions by holstering his stun pistol as he approached the mounted men. The *New Worlders* fanned out before their counterparts.

"Ye dinnae look like devils," stated the apparent leader of the army ranged before them.

"Will ye no' step down here?" Douglas snapped, tetchily. "Ye'll give me a bad neck!"

The horseman stiffened slightly and then relaxed, the briefest flutter of amusement crossing his face. "So, ye're a Scottish devil, eh?"

"Douglas," stated the captain in answer. "And you are?"

The man swung quickly and expertly from his saddle, handing the reins to one of his men. He strode to face Douglas. "A Douglas, eh? Ah'm Maxwell and Ah believe ye're holding one of ma men. Is he hostage?"

"That depends."

"On...?"

"Why you, and your army here, are at my door," declared Douglas.

"Ah'm here because ye're holding ma man."

Douglas glanced theatrically around Maxwell. "Ye seem to have many more."

Maxwell let go a bark of laughter. "Aye, Ah do at that."

"So the man that we hold is important to you." Douglas' reply was confident, offering nothing.

Maxwell gave him a calculating look. "The lad is to sell then?"

"Perhaps."

A flash of impatience crossed Maxwell's face. "Damn it, be done with yer blathering and speak yer price, man!"

Douglas was unperturbed. "This is a large force to reclaim just one man, Maxwell. A young one at that. Your son, is he?"

Maxwell bridled slightly. "Perceptive, Douglas, but he's no' ma son, he's ma—"

"Nephew?"

Maxwell's expression soured further. "Hmmm."

Douglas craned slightly, clearly visible in the bright moonlight. "Sorry, Ah didnae catch that?"

"Aye!" snapped Maxwell. "Noo, speak yer price, man!"

Douglas stroked his chin thoughtfully. "We need information and we need friends, if we're to stay here." He offered his hand. "What do ye say, Maxwell?"

Bess worked her wrists, biting back the urge to cry out as tendons and skin burned with the effort.

That filthy rogue knows his knots, it seems! she fumed silently.

While she wriggled and squirmed against her bonds, her kidnappers, six of them including De Soulis himself, worked on building a large fire at the centre of their camp. De Soulis sat on a wooden box, closed with a large iron hasp and lock, staring at the stars. He was unmoving, as if in a trance state.

Bess felt her hands slip. Her struggling had caused them to sweat a little, lubricating her efforts and allowing some movement. If she could just pass her thumb...

"Let's just check those ropes, lass," said a hated voice from behind her.

Bess undid her work and slipped her hand back into its original position, just as the ruffian forcefully flipped her onto her stomach to inspect his knot.

He grunted, seemingly satisfied, and left her face down on the freezing earth. She turned back onto her side, aiming a silent curse at the scoundrel's back as he walked away. Working her wrists again, one hand slipped through to halfway along the thumb.

Almost there, she thought with desperate hope.

A respectable pyre grew while she struggled. Far bigger than any campfire would normally warrant.

What do these curs intend? Am I to burn?

De Soulis gave nothing away. His only movements were to glance occasionally towards the growing stack of timber.

One of his men drew some dry kindling from a pouch and knelt to pack it into the base of the fire. Taking one of a pair of dags from his belt, he used its flintlock action to create a spark. Bending still closer, he blew on the gently smouldering material, causing it to fully ignite. He fed those first tongues with yet more dry kindling, producing yellow flames that soon began to lick the timbers above. Larger timbers hissed and popped as the sudden heat flash-dried them. Within minutes the blaze took hold, blanketing their campsite with an eerily drifting layer of smoke and steam.

Bess closed her eyes tight against the brightness of the fire to retain her night vision, but hearing movement, she opened one of them, just slightly, studying De Soulis through her lashes.

He stepped to the fire and pulled some manner of substance from a pouch at his belt. As he threw it into the flames, coloured sparks flew into the air with a fizz.

Closing her eyes once more, Bess knew this was her last chance. With the men blinded by the fire, she would have several seconds advantage on them. Her hands slipped free suddenly, allowing her to work frantically at the ropes binding her ankles. Still clumsy, from cold and the tightness of her bindings, she knew that any second now her movements would be noticed.

De Soulis began an incantation. Distracted, his men shrank away fearfully as Bess fought with her final knot.

His words gained in pitch and volume, becoming frenetic. Some of the words were in Latin, Bess recognised those, while others were of no language she had ever heard before. Almost by way of a finale, he suddenly broke into English, "Robin Rotmütze, Robin Redcap, I now have thy name and summon thee! I *command* thee – appear!"

A vast *whoomph* of flame and smoke exploded from the fire, sending sparks flying several metres from the main conflagration, and De Soulis' men diving for cover.

The final knot gave and Bess lay still, panting for breath. Counting to five silently, her mind screamed, *I must escape now or ne'er shall!* She jumped to her feet and ran into the darkness, not daring to look back.

"Tea or coffee, dear?" asked Mary Hutchins, the *New World*'s janitor and cook. "I expect you'll be a tea man, being British and all?"

Sir Nicholas stared back in bafflement.

"Sorry, dear. Is it my accent?"

"Forgive me my impertinence, madam. I am an *Englishman* – and know not this 'teeorcafey' of which thou spake. Be that a beverage from the new colonies?"

Unsure how to respond, Mary decided to stand on good, solid American hospitality, and offer something else. "Erm... sparkling water maybe?"

Sir Nicholas sat back. "Water is for the horses, madam!"

"Try this, Sir Nicholas. We call it 'tea'," Beckett interjected, stifling a chuckle. "Sorry, Mary. Hundred years too soon."

For Mary, the penny suddenly dropped. "Oh, I'm sorry, Sir Nicholas. Can I offer you a cookie to make up for it?"

This was too much, and Beckett burst out laughing.

The ship's cook placed a cup and saucer before the English nobleman and poured for him the closest approximation NASA had provided to tea. "Milk, Sir Nicholas?"

After a sharp intake of breath, he countered with, "Milk? Milk is for babes, madam. Would you have me disgorge?"

"Oh dear, I'm not doing too well at table service today, am I? I'm sorry, honey."

"I need neither honey, milk, nor teecafay, madam. I thank thee kindly!"

"Please forgive us," tried Mother Sarah, kindly, patting Sir Nicholas on the hand. "We're a little confused by your way of talkin', too. I'm sure we'll grow used to one another."

"Indeed, Sir Nicholas," added Patel, with a disarming smile.

The effect on Sir Nicholas was anything but. "The heathen Moor speaketh our tongue!"

Patel stiffened and Sarah placed a gently restraining hand on his arm. "Whoa there, big fella. Let's make a few allowances for more than five centuries of adjustment, huh?"

Patel relaxed and smiled once more. "You are wise as ever, Sarah. Mr Beckett, perhaps we should hand over to you for these talks?"

"Very well, I'll do my best," agreed the historian. He spoke slowly and as clearly as possible, "Sir Nicholas, you told us about the kidnapping of your ward. I'm sure that we will help you if we can, but could you tell us who she is?"

Sir Nicholas frowned, concentrating with all his might as he followed the stranger's words. Eventually, he admitted, "Forgive me, but I may not speak her name, sir."

"She is a person of some importance, then?"

"'Tis truth, the lady is of the highest."

Beckett tried a different tack. "Commander Gleeson mentioned that she gave her name as 'Bess'? In order to help us understand the situation, can you at least tell me where it was you were travelling – before the attack, I mean?"

"I have orders to deliver my lady safely into the protection of Sir Ralph Grey, at Chillingham Castle."

Beckett leaned forward. "Orders from whom?"

"From Her Royal Majesty, Queen Mary herself."

Beckett caught his breath. He stared, wide-eyed. "And this 'Bess', she is naturally someone of note to the queen, also?"

Sir Nicholas nodded cautiously.

"Oh, my God." Beckett buried his face in his hands.

"What is it, Thomas?" asked Mother Sarah.

Looking out from between his fingers, Beckett pierced Sir Nicholas with a searching stare. "Are you telling me we've lost the Princess Elizabeth?"

Patel spilt his coffee. "*Princess* Elizabeth," he managed. "As in—"

"As in the future Elizabeth I, yes. As in, the Elizabeth who should be at Hatfield House, down in Hertfordshire. Waiting for a message to arrive in a couple of weeks, proclaiming her Queen. A message carried by Sir Nic—" he froze. "Sir Nicholas?"

"What ails you, man?"

"Are you Sir Nicholas Throckmorton?"

"Indeed, sir."

"Oh, my God."

"What is it, Thomas? Thomas? *Mr Beckett?*" Sarah scolded.

"Something bad," muttered Patel. "Just how bad, I think we may be about to find out. Everything is unravelling. All of our history."

The conversation going on all around him set Sir Nicholas completely at sea. "I pray you, tell me what is it you all seem to know without words?"

"Yeah, *telleth* me as well, will ya?" added Sarah, perplexed.

Beckett pulled himself together, briefly. "I believe that one of the most influential monarchs in European history has just been captured by a lunatic Satanist, infamous for acts of torture and butchery, and taken away into the wilderness and beyond, just as she was about to *become* one of the most influential monarchs in European history – that's all!"

Sir Nicholas' brow creased in confusion. "Elizabeth the *first*...?"

99.2 million years ago, Britain was a chain of tropical islands; a lagoonal landscape of wide deltas, crisscrossed with many rivers. It was a time where large-scale chalk deposition began, due in part to rising sea levels.

Aito Nassaki relaxed in a comfortable chair, staring out from the *Heydrich*'s observation lounge, his crutch leaning against the arm. He had never visited Britain, but he suspected it did not look like this. Following the white beaches north over a coast kissed by the bright turquoise Atlantic, he began to dwell upon his whole reason for being there. The very idea of turning away from such a view displeased him, yet they would soon be over their destination, and he was still too fragile to be shaken about by a rough landing.

The *Heydrich* had slowed already; he had just minutes before a nurse came to secure him.

This world is more beautiful than I imagined. What right do we have to ruin it the way that we did, or perhaps more accurately, will? I have to stop it.

I wish you could see, Hiro. Working against the system, for the common man, and smashing the corporations that have ruined our world seemed like the right thing to do, but it's not enough. Not nearly enough.

The irony that Heinrich Schultz would not have given him the opportunity to join their mission, were it not for Aito's connections within the corporate world, did not occur to him.

Indeed, the more we improve conditions for the masses, the more successful and destructive we become. No. I need to stop that from ever happening. This is what our planet was meant to look like, what she was meant to be *– a living, breathing organism, a single unit of life with fifteen octillion cells to her body.*

Everything we make blocks those cells from working together. We're a toxin that has almost killed her. If we succeed, a light could go out of the universe that might never be relit!

I miss you, brother, but that is better than watching you die. When we all return to cosmic dust, I hope we will be together—

"Captain? Are you OK, sir?" asked a professionally calm voice.

Aito looked around sharply to find his chaperone, waiting to take him back to the medical bay. "I'm a little better, nurse, thank you."

"Sorry for startling you, sir. You looked a little lost just now."

"Yes, but now I'm found. Thank you."

"Information and friends?" Maxwell repeated. "That would depend upon yer terms, sir."

Douglas nodded. "Indeed, but first, let me make some introductions. This is Commander Gleeson, and this fine fellow is Sergeant Jackson. Ah'm Captain James Douglas, at your service, sir."

"James, eh? A king's name. David Maxwell, o' the Kelso Maxwells." Maxwell grinned, suddenly. "Shall we no' get down tae business, Captain? What d'ye wish tae ken, in trade for ma nephew's safe return? Ah assume he *is* safe?"

"He is safe, sir. You've my word on that. The first thing Ah'd like to know, is that you'll take your army from here in peace, when we're done."

Maxwell gave the three men an appraising look. "Before making any promises, Ah would need tae ken *why* yer here, Captain."

"That's fair," agreed Douglas. "But the truth is, we're here by accident."

"Accident, say ye? Would that explain why this bonnie wee mountain is twice as high as 'twas a few days ago, Jamie?"

Douglas glanced at the hillside behind them. Turning back to Maxwell, he said, "If that's the case then, aye, that would be a fair assessment. Twice the size, eh?"

Maxwell smiled wryly. "Ah've no' measured it, but aye. 'Tis grown. This drovers' path is well ken tae us, Captain—"

"A reiver trail?" Douglas regretted his interjection immediately as Maxwell visibly stiffened. "Sorry, we're no' here to judge your people, sir. Please continue."

"Hmm... Well, imagine our surprise when we came this way a couple o' nights ago, only tae find the top o' the hill was suddenly only part way up – and ma men, all sent a-runnin' for their homes in a black fear!"

Douglas winced. "After being confronted by one of our bright yellow digging machines. Yes, Ah can see how that may have been disconcerting."

"Oh, aye, 'twas all that! We thought this must surely be an open gateway tae hell itself! 'Twas why Ah returned with a full retinue."

"Understandable," Douglas admitted. "We're sorry to have surprised your people the way we did. Please believe me when Ah tell you that we had no idea where we were. We were as surprised as you."

Maxwell scrutinised Douglas and his men. Stepping closer, he reached forward to feel the material of Douglas' flak jacket. Looking around him, he stared at the rifles of the men behind. "Those are yer weapons, gentlemen?"

"Yes, sir," replied The Sarge.

"May Ah?"

"No, sir!"

Maxwell smiled again. "Is that one o' the ones that make light, as if from the very air? Or one o' the ones that make bangs tae deafen the dead, Sergeant?"

The Sarge looked to Douglas for guidance.

Douglas merely shrugged.

The Sarge hesitated. "This is... one of the ones that make light, sir."

"So, 'tis a weapon o' fear, Sergeant Jackson?"

"Not exactly, sir. It uses an electrical charge to incapacitate, or if dialled up sufficiently, to kill, sir."

Douglas coughed. "Perhaps we could save further detail for another time."

Maxwell returned to face Douglas. "Ye say ye didnae ken where ye were, Captain. Is that true, or did ye truly mean, *when* ye were?"

Douglas blinked in surprise. "Sir?"

Maxwell eyed him shrewdly. "Och, 'tis as plain as the nose on yer face, man. Ah'm no' a fool. Yer rifles are far ahead o' our flintlocks. If we're tae be friends, Captain, please tell me where ye came from, and why."

"Where?"

"Oh, aye. Ah'm guessing ye werenae inside our hill all this time, eh?"

Douglas thought for a moment. "Where exactly *are* we?"

"In the Borders. The Cheviot Hills. This is Old Cheviot himself. Although, Ah'd nae be surprised if locals started a-callin' him 'Great Cheviot' after this. He must be head and shoulders o'er his breethers noo. So, that's where ye are, noo where did ye come fram?"

Douglas pulled at his ear, unsure how to answer for the best.

"Dinnae fash, man – Ah can take it!"

Douglas looked to his men for support. "A couple of days ago, we were... erm, it's a wee bit complicated."

A couple of days ago, Bess had been safely installed in the guest quarters of the Bishop of Durham's palace. A consequence of the time spent poring over maps and family trees, within his extensive library, was that she now knew for a fact she was running in the wrong direction.

Shouts came from behind, but as yet, no sounds of pursuit. She dared hope that whatever De Soulis had conjured was keeping them all busy. She further hoped that whatever it was would not come after her.

The five men at arms scattered away from their fire and its emanation. De Soulis stood, arms outstretched, a wide grin splitting his face. "Welcome, my servant!"

Rotmütze felt a sudden power surge such as he had never known or believed possible. The energy of raw belief from an entire world flowed through him; millions of souls, all living in fear of the dark. His laughter boomed across the campsite. "*Master*," he allowed, eyes twinkling with secrets and mischief.

"Bring me the girl!" De Soulis snapped at his guards, who cowered at the periphery of the firelight. The rat-faced man suddenly found his senses, calling out, "She's gone!"

"Find her! Now!" bellowed De Soulis. Turning back to the fire, he continued in a calmer voice, "Show me where she hides, Rotmütze, I command thee—" His words turned to a strangulated cry of pain and alarm as he fell to his knees. "What *is* this?"

Robin Rotmütze stepped easily from the flames, untouched by their heat. "I have something else to show you first, De Soulis."

De Soulis screamed as a demon of monstrous proportions bore down on him, its vicious maw full of teeth the size of daggers, its burning eyes crested by livid red, horned brows. The 'Earth Lizard' towered over the petrified nobleman, frozen in place on frigid grasses that transformed at once into large-leafed ferns and cycads before his very eyes. The air itself warmed to a cloying humidity, as low-lying mist began to shroud the world around him. Terror tore from the man's lungs again, and in answer, the majestic Mapusaurus roseae leaned in to strike, jaws wide, roaring its fury across time and space.

Balled up on the ground, De Soulis cried like a baby as he braced for the end. When it failed to arrive, he risked a look upwards. Slowly lowering his cloak from his face, he could see only bright starlight, twinkling through the smoke of his campfire. The creature was gone.

Several hundred metres away and climbing breathlessly, Bess could hear the sounds of a bad situation in her wake. She kept running, not daring to stop or look round. If she could just reach the top of one of the hills, and with this Halloween full moon, she just might be able to find a ridgeway leading back towards people who, perhaps, would be able to protect her.

In a place that would, in the far-flung future, become the borderlands between England and Scotland, the USS *Newfoundland* came in to hover over the shore of a lake. Another explosion sounded through the ship as the landing thrusters were lit.

"Report!" demanded Devon, hiding the panic he felt.

"The thruster we installed from the *Last Word* has a fuel leak, Captain," his pilot supplied. "It's firing, but sporadically. The explosions are due to fuel build-up and ignition, sir."

"Will it get us down?"

The pilot turned. "Only one way to find out, sir."

Devon nodded. "Do it."

Tasking the veteran ship's four rickety thrusters to maximum, the pilot began his landing cycle. The vastness of the *Newfoundland* caused her to straddle the beach out into the water, her rockets beating Crater Lake's surface to a turbulent mist.

Where land and water met, the air swirled with sand and steam as flames superheated everything below them. Silicates fused together in an instant pressure cooker as the behemoth drew closer to the ground. The roar of the ship's engines cleared the area of wildlife as fast as they could run, swim or fly.

Newfoundland listed suddenly as the fuel system, hastily rigged by Douglas and Hetfield, burst a valve and lost power. The extra strain on the remaining three caused the *Last Word*'s jerry-rigged motor to struggle and splutter. Five metres from the ground, the 550-metre-long marvel of NASA engineering barely remained airborne. Her two original thrusters were ancient, and completely over-taxed. The heat generated by their fight with gravity turned the beach to glass beneath them.

When the *Newfoundland* left Patagonia, her crew had struggled to get one of the landing stanchions to retract – now it refused to extend.

"Captain, we still can't get more than three of the landing struts down!" the pilot shouted across the bridge, above the roar of rocket noise.

"How long can we hold this position?" asked Devon.

"Really not long, sir."

"Keep her steady, Lieutenant. Comms, get some engineers to meet me outside stanchion 2's access hatch – on the double!"

"Yes, sir!"

Devon ran flat-out through his ship. He had been captain for no more than a few hours and was determined not to lose his first official command. They were so close to the ground that, although crash-landing would be rough, he was not unduly concerned for the survival of his crew. His concerns were about a hundred thousand tons hitting the ground, hard. The Rescue Pod was much less massive than the Pod carried by the *New World*, but even at just five metres per second, per second, she might break her back, utterly destroying the old girl as a working vehicle. He did not want to lose her.

He arrived on station to find a small team of engineers already poking around inside various access panels. "Report," he ordered, breathlessly.

"Sir, the hydraulics seem to check out. We think it's a bad connection somewhere within the electrics."

"Can you isolate the problem?"

"I think so, sir," a second engineer called, his voice muffled as he reached through a hatch into the bulkhead. "The problem is with the landing gear bay doors. If the bay won't open, all power is cut automatically to the strut, to prevent it from pushing out and buckling or destroying the surrounding fuselage."

"Can you reactivate the bay door?" asked Devon.

"Not within the time we have, sir."

"Why did no-one work on this during our flight over here?" Devon demanded, angrily.

"It was deemed less of a risk to land, carefully, without the strut, than to have part of the fuselage deformed or jettisoned over the Atlantic, sir."

Devon cursed. "So how can we save her?"

"Really, sir, it would be best if we simply override the hydraulic cut-outs and force it down. Any damage to the fuselage or landing gear would be far less than the ship would suffer from a crash. Even from such low altitude, Captain. Her mass is so great that—"

"OK, do it!" snapped Devon, cutting him off. "Do it now!"

The man's head disappeared back inside the access chamber. There was a *pop* of electrical sparks and an "Ouch!" followed by the hiss of a hugely powerful hydraulic system. The boom and rumble of buckling metal plates preceded a *bang*, and with that the man extricated himself from the bulkhead, blowing on his fingers.

"It's done, sir. Not sure how much damage we've caused, but it's the lesser of two evils."

Devon patted him on the back. "Well done. You'll need to get that burn treated, but for now, everyone, hang on.

"Bridge, this is the captain. We're ready. Set her down as gently as you can."

Newfoundland's landing thrusters had spiked almost fifty percent above their acceptable running temperatures and were beginning to burn out. Following the captain's order, the pilot reduced power to his remaining engines very, very gradually. From outside the vessel, she appeared to wobble at first, before beginning her final descent, painfully slowly. Less than a metre from the ground, one of the engines peaked to critical and shut down. The whole vessel dropped on that corner. Fortunately, Devon's team had managed to lower the landing strut and its hydraulics soaked up most of the punitive force directed against it, until the other three could take up he strain.

It was hardly Heathrow, but the USS *Newfoundland* had finally made landfall in Britain. Furthermore, she was still largely in one piece.

The *Heydrich*'s landing, a kilometre away, was altogether less dramatic, but equally noisy. Heidi's crew made well sure the *Newfoundland* was not about to explode before coming too close, but once both ships were down, her ground crew resurfaced from their hiding places.

Heidi marched down the boarding ramp to be greeted by Sergeant Coleman, as was becoming usual.

"I see you were successful, Dr Schultz."

"So it seems. I intend to turn the *Newfoundland* into our permanent base here. A permanent 'settlement', if you will, to defend our crops. Our engineers have brought a hold full of cabling and wire stripped from the *Last Word* and *Eisernes Kreuz*. My intention is to build an electrified perimeter – quite lethal. Any animals stupid enough to touch it will provide us with dinner!

"I also intend to make you commander of this base, Coleman. Do you accept?"

The sergeant's eyes widened in surprise. "Yes, ma'am. I, er... thank you."

"Good. You can begin by organising our new perimeter, incorporating the *Newfoundland*, naturally."

"Of course, Doctor. Are you to set off again?"

"Yes. As soon as possible. I have people going through the logs you brought back from North Africa. You did well to spot so many Spinosaurus aegyptiacus, but they may still wish to confer with you at some point.

"It may take some considerable time to catch up with Douglas' rabble, so I want our 'Crater Lake' settlement to be a going concern within three days, Commander. Carry on."

Five teenagers sat gloomily in what remained of the Mud Hole.

Gloomiest of them all, Tim hung his head. "I can't believe you lost him."

"Oh, come on, fair go, mate. That bloke held a knife to Natalie's throat. I couldn't have calmed the animals down with tranquilisers!"

Rose held up a placating hand. "Don't worry, Woodsey, Tim's not blaming you. He's just upset because Mayor ran away. I do hope the pony's all right too," she added thoughtfully.

Woodsey looked both truculent and upset when he answered, "I'm more worried about Reiver."

"Why did you let him go for a man armed with a knife?" snapped Tim.

"Steady on, mate. Natalie's his family, I couldn't have stopped him if I'd tried—"

"But you didn't try!" Tim cut him off.

Woodsey closed his mouth, stood and walked out, wiping his eyes.

"That was bang out of order, dude," said Henry.

Rose placed a hand on his arm to quiet him. "Tim's been through a lot. Go after Woodsey, he looks like he needs a friend."

"Sure." Henry pushed back his seat and left too.

"What is it, Tim?" asked Rose.

Clarrie was yet to speak; she simply held Tim's hand.

"I just can't believe he's gone. He won't survive out there, in the winter, and as for Reiver—"

"That really wasn't Woodsey's fault, Tim. Natalie's life was in danger. He was focused on trying to talk that lunatic down."

"He should have done *something!*"

Rose stiffened, but then let her annoyance go with a sigh. "Tim, what's really wrong?"

"I just want to be alone."

Rose reached across to take his other hand. "Well, when you do need to talk, I'm here. OK?"

He nodded but said nothing.

After Rose left them, Clarrie finally spoke, "Are you worried about your mom, Timmy?"

He sighed deeply. "A bit, but she's much stronger today. Dr Flannigan thinks she'll make a full recovery."

"I'm so glad for you. We've all been real worried about her." She lapsed into silence once more, allowing him to speak, or not, as he pleased.

"It's just..." he began.

"Take as long as you need." Clarrie laid her head on his shoulder. "I'm not going anywhere, not unless you want me to."

"It's just that I feel like I'm losing everything. I still can't take Mum home, not that we have a home. Now I've lost my last dinosaur, too. I'm really worried about him. I hope Reiver is OK. He's my friend."

"Do you miss the dinosaurs?"

"Yes, bitterly. I know everyone else will think I'm insane, but that place – in fact, that time, before I was kidnapped – was about the happiest of my life, since Dad died." He sniffed and wiped at his eyes.

When there seemed no more, Clarrie replied, "I understand. And you're not crazy. Those were the happiest days of my life so far, too. I got to make some real friends for the first time. And I met you, Timmy."

He glanced at her, finding tears welling in her eyes. "Do you mean that?" he asked.

She nodded vigorously.

He looked away from her, staring into space. "Don't you wish we could go back? I know it's dangerous there, and this probably goes against all reason, but..."

"Yes, I do. I also wish we could go back because..."

Tim gave her a searching look as she faltered. "Because?"

It was Clarrie's turn to look away. "Because I think a part of you was left behind there, Timmy. Will you be able to find it again here?"

Tim looked uncertain. "What do you think I've lost?"

"I don't know, but I think it has something to do with what happened when that mad woman kidnapped you. What did she do to you, Timmy? What did she tell you?"

Tim swallowed. "She told me about my past, my family."

"Patricia and Ted Norris? What about them?"

"No. My *biological* family. My real parents, who died in what I believed was a random terrorist bombing."

Clarrie frowned. "Believed?"

"Yeah. It was murder. They were murdered."

Clarrie breathed in sharply, squeezing his arm tighter. "Tell me."

"They were killed, assassinated at Schultz's order. The old man, that is, not Heidi."

"Oh, my God, Timmy. I'm so sorry. But why did they kill them – how did they even know them?"

He took a deep breath, organising his thoughts. "Apparently, they were Schultzes, too."

Clarrie stiffened, wide-eyed. Tim studied her, allowing her some time to process.

Eventually, she managed, "Are you saying that you...?"

He nodded slowly. "I was born Timothy Schultz – apparently."

Her eyes widened still further. "*No!*" she breathed.

"Do you hate me now?" he asked, voice quavering with emotion. "Do you think I'm a monster too?"

She was already shaking her head. "Of course not. This doesn't change who you are. Doesn't change anything. I mean, what's in a name?"

"What's in a name?" he asked in disbelief. "I'm the grandson of one of the worst men of the twenty-second century. He's a mass murderer, a vile creature – my grandad!"

He pulled his hand away from her and bowed his head, sobbing as he slid between heartbreak and rage. Clarrie placed her arms lovingly around him, holding him tight.

"It's OK, Timmy. You can let it out. You shouldn't have carried this around alone. We're your friends and we love you."

Tim's reply was muffled through his hands. "How can you? *His* blood is in my veins. Who knows what I'm capable of?"

"Are you sure?"

"*What?*"

"Seriously, are you sure?" she asked again. "Those people *lie*, Timmy."

He wiped his eyes, swallowing deeply. "I did think that might be a possibility, but..."

"But what? You're afraid to check? In case it's proved, and you no longer have doubt to lean on?"

He nodded silently.

"Who else knows about this?"

"Captain Douglas and a few of the most senior people, I think. Why?"

"Well, for two reasons. Firstly, Captain Douglas thinks the world of you. That's gotta count for somethin'. Secondly, with all this craziness and crashing, and who knows what's happenin' outside now, they've been too busy to check on this."

"Probably. What's your point?"

"Don't you see? Captain Douglas obviously doesn't care whether it's true or not. He trusts you, cares for you, for the man you are – this just isn't a priority for him. Furthermore, there's the possibility that this is all just a bunch o' garbage cooked up by the bad guys to mess with your head!"

"But why would the old man have wanted me to take Heidi's place, Clarrie? He wanted a male heir – me – by his side!"

"Wow, really? He offered you all that power and you didn't take it?" She looked thoughtful for a moment. "And all those beautiful blonde women...?"

Neither of them spoke for a while, until Tim felt her eyes boring through him. "What?"

"You didn't take him up on any of his... offers, did you?"

"No!"

"OK, OK, I'm sorry. It's just that I can't believe many men would hand back the keys to the entire world, and... other stuff, too."

"Well, I didn't want anything to do with it, OK? But I had to pretend. Heidi made me teach her people about the Cretaceous. To survive, I had to *be* one of them. I even got her to accept me, under the pretence of siding with her. I'm a collaborator!"

"Nonsense!"

"How do you know?"

"If Captain Douglas thought you'd betrayed us, you wouldn't be here. And I will never believe you're one of them – I don't care what your name is! Come on, let's go."

"Go where?"

"To see Doc Flannigan. He'll have access to Heidi's records with a DNA sample on NASA's database. We need to put an end to all this guessing, once and for all."

"But what about my mother?"

Clarrie stood, pulling him to his feet. "Patricia? What about her?"

"How will she possibly be able to deal with this?"

"It may be all lies. But even if it's not, she will still love you, just like I do. You were a baby when the Norrises took you in. You grew up as a Norris and you *are* a Norris, Timmy. Now, come on!"

Bess scrambled through a patch of gorse, crying out as it caught her dress and tore mercilessly at the skin beneath. Heart hammering, she fought her way up the steep incline on hands and knees, all dignity forgotten in her desperation to escape.

After a hard climb, she crested the hill to stand upon a ridge. Bent double, panting, her shadow was cast into sharp lines by the full moon. This would be a perilous path in the dark, certainly, but on this night, the brightness might prove equally deadly. She straightened, to look around. No sign of pursuit yet, but she would stand out atop this ridgeway, under such a Hunter's Moon.

Should I run or hide? she wondered. If she hid, De Soulis' men would swarm these hills looking for her. No. She must use the moonlight to make her escape.

I pray the hunter's light will favour the hunted, this night. We must surely have ridden for three hours. Hence, I could happen upon the help I need in another six – if I keep moving. I am young, I am strong, and I am the daughter of the great Henry. I shall make it so. Right, east then!

Gritting her teeth with determination, and to stop them from chattering, she put her back to the pursuit and cried out in sudden alarm.

A man blocked her path. Arms folded, he was clad in black, also wearing a mocking expression. Conflicting emotions whirled within Bess. The shock of finding herself in company warred with the reassuring recognition of the fatigues in which he was dressed. Hesitantly, she asked, "Are you with the new people?"

"The new people?" he repeated, as if chewing the idea over. He smiled. "Yes, I suppose you could say I came with them. So, you have met some of the *New World*'s crew, Princess?"

A deep cold, which had nothing to do with the frigid air, struck Bess to the heart. "My name is Bess, sir. Just plain Bess."

"Oh, I think we can forgo modesty here, girl. You are, after all, the future Queen of England, Elizabeth Tudor."

"Future queen? *Really*, sir..."

The man smiled again, but it was as though human features slid over something altogether inhuman beneath. Again, she shuddered.

"Indeed," he answered. "Despite many trials, you are destined to bring a golden age to this land. More than that, you're to play a most instrumental role in ushering the beginnings of enlightenment to this part of the world. At least, what will one day be as close as mankind ever gets to such a state. Your tolerance towards religious practice – by the standards of your day – and your interference, encouraging people to read from that *book* in the hope of understanding its ramblings for themselves, will be acknowledged as the beginnings of free thought for the common man." He chuckled nastily, "And one day, even for the common woman! There will be others, of course, but you are important."

"If by 'that book' you meant the Bible, sir, then this d-does not sound s-so ill," Bess stammered through cold and her growing fear of this man, whom she was no longer sure *was* a man.

"For you and your kind, perhaps," he replied sourly. "Speaking for myself, I think things are absolutely perfect just the way they are. All this fear and superstition is raw, naked power for a being who knows how to direct it."

"You did not come upon me here to help." It was a statement; Bess already sensed the answer.

His smile hitched up a little higher, a little too high for a human face, in fact. There was also clearly some form of dementia present in his gaze. She was afraid, but her blood froze with the final realisation that he cast no shadow.

"What art thou? A figment?" Bess asked tremulously. "Do I speak with mine own fears, alone? Or art thou a spirit come to taunt me, at the beck and call of De Soulis?"

He became more solid, seeming to grow as he spoke angrily, "I am like nothing you would ever understand, girl." He approached her, somehow without moving. His eyes, shadowed beneath heavy brows in the moonlight, became clearer.

Bess could see no humanity in them, no soul at all, like the dead eyes of a predatory fish. "What is thy purpose with me?"

Robin Redcap laughed. Bess was stricken with terror, finding herself paralysed. She had been afraid for her life many times, but this was something more. She simply could not move. His laughter was replaced by the rumble of hooves.

"I commend you, Master Redcap," De Soulis called down as he slowed, reining in his mount. He gave an abbreviated bow to the creature. To his men, he shouted, "Take her!"

Chapter 9 | Perennial

Allison Cocksedge activated the control cluster's viewscreen mounted beside the entrance hatch to her apartment. Once the engineers restored power after the crash, she had quickly found herself bundled back into her apartment and locked away again. Her door was sealed from the outside with a security code she could not break. However, something was clearly afoot. The last few times she had checked the door cam, there had been no guard.

Cocksedge sensed an opportunity; possibly the only one she would get. Picking up a few papers, she strode to the kitchen and switched her grill to maximum. The papers, she placed underneath. The smell of burning followed almost immediately, activating automatic sensors that disabled the grill and triggered fire suppression systems. Unless she missed her guess, the computer would also enact one final safety protocol, too. Returning to her front door, she heard the clear and reassuringly mechanical *clunk* of locking bars being withdrawn.

Cocksedge hit the open button and stood back as the door slid smoothly aside. Grinning triumphantly, she poked her head out into the corridor, checking both ways: deserted.

Nothing to lose, she left residential and headed towards Pod operations. Despite expectations, no security showed up to apprehend her. Indeed, there did not seem to be *anyone* around at all. Further emboldened by this good fortune, she opened the hatch to operations and strode in, preparing a yarn about needing help with a fire in her quarters, but ops, too, was completely deserted.

Finding a security terminal, she wasted no time in getting to work. Cocksedge's personal comm had been confiscated upon her initial incarceration, but joy of joys, there was a whole rack of them in ops. She palmed a couple, connecting one wirelessly with her terminal to download everything she read and more.

She needed to know what was going on. As everyone knew, the ship was buried, so anything that could draw their entire security contingent's attention must be happening outside, and it must be something big. A quick scan through the Pod's systems showed that most of the civilian population was currently confined to quarters, but there was no log explaining why.

Whatever has happened must have happened quickly, she thought. *I wonder if...?*

She searched through all the comm codes until she came to 'Captain J Douglas', reasoning that whatever was going on, he would be in the thick of it. Perhaps she could listen in?

[ACCESS DENIED]

Damn, clearly the kung fu surrounding the Captain's security was too strong. She thought for a moment, *Who else will be in the middle of whatever is happening out there? That wretched Baines woman? No. If Douglas is out there, he would leave her in charge in here. Aim lower. Hmm...*

She found 'Sergeant J Jackson'.

[ACCESS DENIED]

"Aargh!" she exclaimed in frustration, and then her eye alighted on another name: 'Commander E P Gleeson, *temporary* security access codes'.

"Worth a try."

Within moments she could hear voices from her comm's tiny speakers. *Result!* she thought, pleased with her own ingenuity.

There was a conversation happening somewhere; she could hear Douglas and another male she did not recognise. The second voice was quite difficult to understand at first, but as her ear became attuned, she realised that he too spoke with a Scottish accent. The voice seemed harsher than Douglas', the dialect more archaic.

After a few moments of eavesdropping, Cocksedge began to grasp what had happened to them. They were indeed back, but not all the way. Perhaps not ideal, but if they were once again in the world of man, with communication at least possible, that would open up all kinds of opportunities for a politician. Especially if she happened to be a *rich* politician. The Pod carried many resources of value – goods possibly even more desirable within a primitive society. She knew that these included precious metals, even diamonds, for electronic and engineering applications.

This might not be so bad after all, especially with the knowledge I possess of the future. I must download the ship's entire historic database while I plan. She began to smile as an idea formed in her mind. *Yes, that might work, but I'll need help.*

She mulled the problem over a few moments more before beginning to type frantically. Her first query retrieved details of 'Lieutenant R Weber' – still safely installed within the *New World*'s brig. Could she use him? She could not be sure, but it seemed likely that he was the agent who had contacted her regarding the stealing of Pod security codes from Hank Burnstein. She quickly scanned a report about the hostage situation that took place within the new infirmary some weeks ago; a failed attempt to break out Old Man Schultz from his confinement, apparently.

"Hmm," she considered. This choice would be vital to her survival, and Weber's almost religious following of the Schultzes would make him difficult to control, impossible to trust. Furthermore, as she read the final conclusions of his bungled jailbreak, she was forced to her own conclusion that he was perhaps not the sharpest tool in the shed, either.

Cocksedge thought furiously, and then it came to her. *I wonder if she might help...?*

The protocontinent of Africa, Gondwana, 99.2 million years ago
"So this will one day be Niger?" asked Heidi, looking out from the *Heydrich*'s observation lounge. She was again joined by the man and woman she simply thought of as 'the whitecoats'.

"Indeed, Doctor," the man replied. "Part of Niger sits on the Sahara meta-craton. That means the underlying geology here remains very stable, even as the continents 'wash' over and around it, during the constant drift over millions— *billions* of years."

Heidi nodded absently, watching the world pass beneath them at blurring speed. Eventually, she turned to face them. "Doctors, I have but one question. Where is the land?"

The whitecoats looked at one another, and then out of the observation port.

"*Well?*"

"It... erm," the man began.

"It's under the sea," confirmed the woman, tonelessly.

The balding man felt obliged to add, "This must be the Tethys Ocean—"

"I do not care what it is called!" snapped Heidi. "I thought you had rejected the idea of extracting uranium from seawater?"

"We did, ma'am," he quailed.

"We did not realise that much of Niger was under the ocean at this time, Doctor," the woman clarified.

"Imbeciles!" shouted Heidi.

The female lab coat looked her in the eye. "Did you know, Dr Schultz?"

Heidi's eyes narrowed, her mouth tightening as she spat the words, "It was not *my* plan! Careful, Doctor – no one is irreplaceable!"

"That's not true, is it?" the woman replied undaunted. "We're all irreplaceable now. So do you wish to take out your tantrum on us, or would you rather we came up with a new strategy?"

Heidi clenched her fists. "You would be wise not to push me, Doctor."

"If we use the ISL method, we could still extract uranium-235 from the coastal areas – perhaps even the shallow beds," the man interjected.

"ISL?" asked Heidi.

"Yes, ma'am," he agreed, his colour returning as a scientific problem drove his fear just a little further away. That's 'in-situ-leaching'. We inject the uranium-laden strata with a soluble chemical which separates the uranium from the surrounding rock, binding it within the solution. It's then possible to flush the uranium out."

Heidi stroked her chin thoughtfully. "Yes, I have heard of this method, but is it not unpredictable where groundwater is present?

As I understand it, any secondary current acting upon the uranium solution can dilute, even redirect the flow, spreading it everywhere, contaminating the land. As we are talking about an operation at, or even below, sea level, how would you control this?"

"Do we care about contamination?" he asked, unreasonably reasonable.

"I do not," admitted Heidi. "However, a major event could change the course of history. It seems that we now need to get back to the future to gather equipment and supplies we need to complete our mission. I also intend to catch up with our enemies and extract retribution for the trouble they have caused us."

The whitecoats looked at one another. "What about the moon?" asked the woman.

"Go on," Heidi prompted.

"We know there's a buck load of uranium-235 on the moon."

"Ah, yes," the man elaborated. "Japan's Kaguya satellite discovered it in 2009, I believe."

"Yes, *yes*," his counterpart agreed impatiently. "The important thing is, we can make as much mess as we want to up there, without affecting the natural order of things down here. It's not like it's out of our way, we'll have to go there anyway to leave our time capsule."

"Do you still believe that will work?" asked Heidi, less confident after this latest setback.

"Yes," replied the woman assertively. "Once we have our manufactured isotopes, we simply leave the capsule behind. You may *then* begin your operation, Dr Schultz – to find and shoot every Spinosaurus aegyptiacus you can in North Africa. Once you have completed your task, we simply open a wormhole, blind, and scan for traces of our isotopes."

Heidi nodded. "You explained that to me the last time we spoke. Perhaps this time you will explain the rest of your plan?"

The female lab coat raised an eyebrow. The way she remembered it, Heidi had been 'too busy' to hear about the fruits of their labours last time. "Yes, Doctor," she agreed sourly. "If you have the time?"

Heidi nodded again.

"Our scans through the open wormhole should be able to trace any isotopes that become fossilised within the rocks of the Earth. It will also keep track of our 'time capsule' on the moon.

"It is possible that more than one of the affected skeletons will become fossilised and survive in some way to be discovered in the twentieth century. However, only one of them will end up in Munich."

"Yes, but how will we be able to follow that movement? How will we even know it has occurred—"

The female scientist held up her hand to hush her. Heidi bridled, but she needed to hear this, so made an allowance. "Continue."

"*So* kind. In order to track when Ernst Stromer moves our bones from the deserts of Egypt to Germany, we need some method of triangulation. The point of leaving our isotope on the moon, is that the moon moves around the Earth. In effect, we can take two readings from the moon every rotation of the Earth – and compare them to our known co-ordinates. This will completely tie up every bit of processing power our computers can deliver, but it is possible."

"Yes, but—"

The woman held up her hand again. Heidi glowered, but stalled her interruption.

"We know the co-ordinates where the bone will be found during Stromer's AD1911-14 expeditions. Naturally, we also know where Munich will be in 1943. By triangulating with two points from space – that is from the moon, one hour apart, once a day – we can fix the time when the bones move to Europe. We already know the place."

Heidi sat back in one of the lounge's sofas. "That's clever. Indeed, so clever, that I have decided not to jettison you from a fast-moving spaceship."

The lab coats glanced at one another with concern. "Erm, thank you, Doctor," hazarded the balding man, as always, wringing his hands. "We'll, erm... we'll begin scanning the moon for uranium-235, then."

The female lab coat raised her hand to forestall him. "Not quite. There is still the *other* matter."

"Explain," Heidi commanded.

"You intend to shoot every Spinosaurus in North Africa with our radioactive isotope, yes?"

"I do."

"What about the others?"

Heidi studied her for a moment. "You are alluding to all the specimens not *currently* alive?"

"Yes, Doctor. This species may have been around for hundreds of thousands of years, perhaps longer. On average, any given species can persist two to four million years, if successful. What are the chances of Stromer finding an animal in 1911, or whenever, which conveniently lived *exactly* now?"

Heidi gave a nod of understanding and agreement. "I have considered this, and yes, it could be a problem. However, we do have 'more than one bite at the cherry', I believe that is the saying?

"Stromer's expedition discovered two other dinosaurs from roughly the same place and period. I understand they were also theropod predators that he eventually named Bahariasaurus and Carcharodontosaurus. Although the exact pedigree of Bahariasaurus remains in some doubt, all the fossils were shipped to the same museum a few years after the First World War."

"I see, Doctor. So if we fail with the Spinosaurus, we can try shooting those up?"

"Exactly. However, as they were also enormous apex predators, and having no burning desire to solve the Bahariasaurus question, I would be happy if we did not have to!

"On the other hand, if even that failed, there must be many other animals alive in this time and place that will turn up in the twentieth, twenty-first or twenty-second centuries. It might require research, but would not be impossible for us to follow them. Nevertheless," Heidi paused, a secret smile on her lips, "something tells me we will not need to."

"Doctor?" the male scientist asked.

Before answering, Heidi gave one of her tinkling, girly laughs, that usually preceded one of her shocking, grisly acts. "What are the odds against one of those giant, deadly reptiles outside our door, ending up just a couple of blocks away from Nazi headquarters, Doctors? Do you believe in fate?"

They cleared their throats awkwardly.

"Of course you don't, and quite rightly so. However, it seems to me that Douglas' rabble managed to survive again and again on little more than hope and belief, in themselves and their overwhelming 'righteousness'.

"Our mission is just and necessary. Perhaps we should put more faith in our own cause, Doctors? Now run your scans on the moon."

The white coats eyed one another with concern. Heidi merely waved them away, otherwise ignoring them as she resumed her vigil, staring out over the perfect aquamarine of the Tethys Ocean as it passed beneath the *Heydrich*.

Allison Cocksedge sat back in frustration. Most of the ship's security cameras were out of commission. On the other hand, so were most of the security doors and hatches. In theory, she could walk straight to her destination, unhindered; it would have been nice to know *what* she was walking into, though.

She drummed her fingers on the desk. Reaching a decision, she swept the stolen comms into her pocket and rose. Giving ops a last look around, she was disappointed that no one had been considerate enough to leave a weapon of some sort; not so much as a taser. Never mind. If challenged, she would just have to think on her feet. She was good at that.

Ops computers had highlighted which access corridors were passable and which were damaged or otherwise blocked. A thought struck her, and she sat once more, calling up the schematic for the entire ship and Pod.

It was fortunate that she did so. Immediately, she could see that something fundamental had changed since her incarceration. The Pod now faced the opposite direction with regards to the *New World*. This threw her, forcing a moment's reorientation. The computer had obviously adjusted portside to starboard automatically, almost certainly when the ship redocked with the Pod a couple of months ago, after Baines' attack on the *Last Word*.

The schematic showed two routes to the guest quarters that were still open to her. This was a long shot, and she was working blind, but there would be no one around to hear her message, saving any guards she hoped to deflect.

She opened a tannoy link to the corridor outside guest quarters 2, "*All security to the Pod main hangar, repeat all security to Pod main hangar. This is an emergency – no exceptions!*"

OK, that ought to do it, she thought, *if there's anyone there*.

As it happened, there had been someone there, but by the time Cocksedge arrived, a few minutes later, the lone security guard had left his post, 'as ordered'.

She peeked around the corner and smiled slyly. The corridor was empty. She had deliberately chosen the less direct route for herself, reasoning that any guards would make a beeline to their ordered destination.

And that, my friends, is the downside of military thinking – ultimately, they take their orders from people like me. In a rare moment of introspection, it occurred to her that she was *really* off the reserve now, heading further out all the time. *Needs must*, she justified. *I feel sure this world will soon be in need of a saviour – may as well be me!*

Having filched the codes for the remaining security doors from ops, she entered the code to guest quarters 2 and stood back as the doors parted. "Hello?"

The quarters were dimly lit, but Cocksedge could make out an astonishingly attractive blonde woman on the sofa, plaiting her hair.

She looked up. "Yes?"

"Erica Schmidt?"

"I am."

"I have a proposition for you."

"Perhaps we could offer you some hospitality inside, David?" asked Douglas.

Maxwell seemed unsure. "Ye already have ma nephew. 'Twould seem folly tae offer ma'self into yer hands as well."

Douglas nodded. "Fair enough. Sarge, get someone to the bring the laddie up here from the infirmary."

A shadow crossed Maxwell's face. "Has Billy been hurt?"

"He was nicked by a stray bullet on the night of your first attack. Our doctors have fixed him up – he's fine."

"Apart from the dog bite, sir," added The Sarge.

"Billy ne'er was good with animals. What happened?"

Sergeant Jackson looked to Douglas. "Go on, Sarge. You may as well tell him."

"Yes, sir. It seems the lad got scared and tried to take one of our ladies hostage. Unfortunately, he didn't factor for the lady's dog. He'll be smarting for a time, but he'll mend."

"Ah see," replied Maxwell, frostily.

"Aye," said Douglas. "But it wasnae the dog's fault. Your boy was in no danger. There was no reason to act the way he did, other than out of fear. These are strange times for us all, you'll understand, and that's why the lad wasnae punished – except by the dog. And as The Sarge says, it's a lesson, but he'll mend."

Footsteps sounded behind them, as Billy Maxwell was propelled towards the gathering by Corporal Thomas. "The prisoner as ordered, sir. I thought it best not to let him run free after the incident, Captain."

"Quite right, Corp. You can remove his binders now, though. We're placing him under the care of his uncle, Lord Maxwell of Kelso, here."

Thomas looked uneasily around the armed men, massing at the edges of their plateau, but released his charge with a simple, "Sir."

"Ye seem mostly in one piece, Billy."

"Aye, Uncle. 'Tis only a wee dog bite. Do we attack them noo?"

Maxwell gave the young man a disapproving glare. "For what reason?"

"They're devils, Uncle. Devils and witches and they consort with monsters!"

Douglas sighed. "Let's get some light on the situation – Major White! Floodlights!"

The plateau lit up like a stadium. Unsuspecting, the locals were temporarily blinded. A stir of fear passed among them as they worked at calming their skittish horses.

Douglas pointed at the young agitator. "Now let's get one thing straight, laddie. You came at us. We offered you medical care and you repaid it by attacking one of ours, who was only trying to befriend ye. So if ye've nothing helpful to say, keep yer damned teeth together!"

Maxwell placed a gentle hand on the young man's shoulders. "Go and stand back with the others, Billy." The young man obeyed, leaving Maxwell squinting into the lights as he faced Douglas. "These day lights ye have, Captain. Impressive. D'ye have other miracles tae show us?"

Douglas was not blind to the guile in the man's words, but he had little else to work with. Clearly Maxwell had evaluated Douglas and his strange party, rating them formidable. Although he did not seem overly afraid, and this was a surprise, especially as his men would have doubtless told him all sorts of tales about them.

An exceptionally clear thinker, this man, mulled Douglas. He assumed Maxwell would probably not attack, at least not yet. Like any good commander, he would learn as much as he could first, and he was clearly both concerned and fascinated by the *New World*'s many toys.

"Ye'll be curious to learn more about us?" asked Douglas, obliquely. "Will ye no' come with me, into ma ship? Bring your two retainers here, if ye wish. We mean ye no harm."

It was a strange thing, but after just a few minutes dialogue with this man from 'home', Douglas could hear his own accent thickening up.

"And ye'll let me back out, any time Ah wish it?" asked Maxwell.

"You've ma word," replied Douglas, offering his hand. "Ye've an army at your back. What's there to fear?"

Maxwell glanced meaningfully at the weapons borne by Douglas' men. "Ah'll say again – Ah'm no' a fool, Captain. Ah can see the strength of yer war gear."

Douglas' expression softened. "Then will ye take ma hand in trust and friendship? My God, man. Ah was born just down the road from your house!"

Maxwell snorted and then began to laugh, causing the tension around the plateau to ease, at least for a little while. "So were most o' the men who want me dead, Captain!"

Douglas led Maxwell to the seats and coffee table arranged outside the infirmary. These were the only comforts on offer in the main hangar, and he had no intention of showing any more of the ship to this man until he knew a good deal more about him.

Watch the timeline, Douglas, he berated himself. *Be careful what you say and watch the damned timeline!*

The view of the main hangar with its myriad vehicles and equipment alone was enough to awe their visitor speechless. "Incredible," he murmured at last.

Douglas seated himself comfortably, but before the thought even crossed his mind, Mary Hutchins appeared, slicker than any butler, to offer their guest refreshment. Not wishing to cause another faux pas, she simply set a cup before the stranger and poured some tea as Captain Baines joined the little group.

"Ah, Jill, let me introduce you. This is David Maxwell, Lord of Kelso. David, this is Captain Jill Baines."

Maxwell looked more astonished by the idea of a female captain than he was by the thirty-ton excavator, parked near their seats. "*Captain.*" His greeting was more than half a question, but he rose slightly, respectfully taking Baines' hand as she sat.

"It's a pleasure to meet you, sir."

Her semi-American accent confounded him still further. He winked to Douglas, "Yer woman's no' a local lass then, Jamie?"

Baines laughed, both at the audacity of their guest and the embarrassment it seemed to elicit in Douglas, who felt the need to explain the situation. "We're both serving officers..."

Maxwell grinned. "So there's no' anything untoward between ye two then, eh, Jamie?" He offered his teacup in salute. "Ha ha, God forbid! Ah'll raise a dram tae that!"

Baines laughed again. "I do believe you're blushing, James." She leaned forward and clinked her cup with Maxwell's.

"Perhaps Ah should just leave you to continue the negotiations," Douglas muttered sourly.

Maxwell continued to chuckle while quaffing his drink. As the tea went down, his smirk was replaced with a look of amazement. "What's this? Another miracle?"

"It's called tea," supplied Baines. "Get used to it! Top-up?"

"Aye!"

Mary poured a second cup with unmistakable relief. This second introduction to her wares had gone much more smoothly than the last – and Sir Nicholas an Englishman, too!

Baines sobered slightly. "There may be a way we can help each other, sir. Not long after we arrived here, some of our people met up with a man escorting a young woman to Chillingham Castle."

Maxwell soured slightly. "Ah ken Sir Ralph Grey. What of it?"

"Well, sir, they never got there. They were ambushed by bandits, or that's how it appeared to our people. The woman was captured and taken."

"And Ah suppose yer asking for ma help in getting her back, eh?"

"Perhaps. Some guidance, certainly. Her bodyguard is here with us, but he's from the south and unfamiliar with this land and its people."

Maxwell leaned forward menacingly. "When ye say 'southern' are ye really saying 'English'?"

"Of course—"

"Ah cannae help ye," he interrupted her.

"You say that now, sir, but there's a bigger picture you need to see before you decide."

He looked mystified. "Ye want tae sell me a painting? Ah've a grand hoose full o' tha damned things, and ma wife keeps buying more!"

Baines chuckled. "No, sir. I'm sorry. What I mean is there is more to this situation that you know." She turned to Douglas. "I think it might be best if we interrupted the meeting with Sir Nicholas and got Thomas Beckett down here."

"Aye, Beckett should be able to stop us tripping over our own feet perhaps," Douglas remarked with chagrin.

Baines nodded, opening a comm channel.

Maxwell stiffened, eyes wide in alarm when the tiny box answered her back. "Speaking in tongues...?" he asked nervously. Voices from the air was one miracle too many, it seemed.

Baines waved a hand. "No, that was just Mother Sarah. Sorry, sir. I didn't mean to surprise you."

"Mother Sarah? Ye have nuns aboard this vessel o' yers?"

Baines' eyes narrowed in thought while she considered the safest way to answer. She knew from her studies as a young woman, just how dangerous any kind of religious affiliation could be in this time and place. "We have no nuns, that's just what we call her."

He looked suddenly distrustful.

"Do you follow the reformist faith, sir?" she asked, carefully.

Maxwell still appeared unsure. "What's that tae ye?"

Sensing the sudden tension, Douglas spoke to diffuse it, "Dinnae worry, David. No one here will judge you, whatever faith ye follow."

"And what faith *dae* ye practise aboard yer ship, James?" he asked directly.

"Oh, we've all sorts, here. You've nothing to fear on that account."

Still unsure, Maxwell attempted to clarify, "Yer sayin' ye have both faiths here, in harmony and tolerating each other."

"No. Ah'm saying we have *many* faiths here," Douglas stated. "We've a man on his way down who'll be able to explain things a little more in context, perhaps."

"This Thomas à Becket? Have ye mastered death and time itself, too?"

A shadow of confusion momentarily crossed Douglas' face. "Not *that* Thomas Beckett, sir. Another one. As for mastering time, not exactly, but we've certainly seen more than our share of it."

Maxwell looked at him askance. "Is that a riddle, sir?"

"Not exactly, but Ah'm sure we'll be able to explain more over time – no pun intended."

Now Maxwell looked confused.

"Perhaps we should wait for Mr Beckett to explain," Baines concluded quietly.

Schmidt lay on her sofa with the languid air of a classical goddess. Cocksedge's innate jealousy found an extra gear, choking her on fumes while common sense struggled to catch up.

"My dear," she began through a brittle smile. "How would you like to get out of here?"

Cocksedge explained their situation as best she could, from the little she had gleaned from Douglas' eavesdropped conversation, and the stolen security files.

Schmidt listened in silence, unmoving. Indeed, she seemed economical in all her movements, exhibiting the catlike grace of either a dancer or a fighter. Cocksedge put her money on the latter, or possibly both.

"Very well. I understand. What do you want from me, Mrs Cocksedge?"

"That's Ms!" Cocksedge snapped automatically. Quickly painting an unctuous smile onto her face, she added, "But please, you must call me Allison, dear."

Schmidt neither moved nor replied; she merely stared.

Eventually, Cocksedge cracked. "The people aboard this ship will never trust us, but two women such as we, could do well in this world."

"You want my help to escape?"

"In a way, but I thought we might take a little something for our trouble, first. It has to be tonight, though." She smiled again. "Apparently, it's Halloween. That said, it would seem remiss of us to leave without a little 'trick or treat', wouldn't you say, Miss Schmidt?"

The astonishingly beautiful young woman, Heinrich Schultz's personal aide, continued to stare. The moments dragged. Eventually, she answered, "Call me Erika. Now, tell me your plan, Allison."

Ally Coleman walked alone alongside Crater Lake, high up the beach, where gritty sands touched the green line of cultivation. She breathed deeply, taking in a wonderful view of mountains across the water.

Apparently, deeming Coleman trustworthy – as much as a Schultz ever trusted anyone – had been more important to Heidi than protocol. Consequently, Coleman had risen from lowly sergeant straight to commander, and was now charged with running their home base. More importantly, she was charged with the defence of their food supply; the steadily maturing crop she ambled past on her right.

Being honest, this was not how she had imagined her future. Having never sought such a thing, her meteoric rise from enlisted soldier to the exultant rank of commander was never considered, but it did not matter. She was here now. Although, with both feet firmly on the ground, and swanky titles set aside, it occurred to her that she was really just the manager of a farm.

Once again, being true to herself, this suited Coleman well enough. Upon joining the Schultz campaign – firstly having had little choice and, secondly, with expectations of nothing very much – she had hoped to survive the end of the human world, that was all. However, she began to realise that, with Heidi and her grandfather thousands of miles away for the foreseeable future, she was happy.

Feeling the reassuring weight of an assault rifle strapped across her shoulders – she might be an officer now, but old habits die hard – she stopped by a huge cycad to admire an intricate spider's web, stretching from leaf to leaf. It swayed slightly, a gentle breeze catching the morning dew that weighted the silken strands with silver.

Mesmerised by its complex beauty, a question crossed her mind. It was an old question, but as no expert, she could not help wondering, *How do such small, fragile creatures endure for hundreds of millions of years, while some of the most robust animals this world has ever seen fail to do so?*

She could not see the spider, but knew it was there – rather like her mistress, Heidi Schultz.

Coleman sighed. She was falling in love with this place. If only her people were alone here, what lives they could make for themselves. She knew many had had a belly-full of all the destruction and strife – all the waste. Douglas and Baines had proved surprisingly adept at preventing the Schultzes from ever bringing their vastly superior forces to bear. Then, of course, there had been the internal problems. The old man obviously saw himself as the next *Führer*. Well, plenty of his own side tried to kill the last one. It seemed nothing could stop history repeating itself, even when you took it out of sequence.

She shook her head sadly. Perhaps their own future would be brighter.

Despite the largely derelict condition of the *Newfoundland*, her powerful reactor had clearly been looked after and was in a surprisingly good state of repair; capable of providing as much power as they needed, for many lifetimes.

Yes, she could see a future for them here, were it not for the spider at the other end of their web. Regardless of the many switchbacks and dead ends thrown in their path to confuse them, they were here. Was that not the whole point? *This* world was not ending, and it could support a small community of humans practically forever. Why should they get dragged into this ridiculous grudge-match Heidi seemed so set upon?

Coleman knew she had some good people under her care. They tended to be the less militant types, or scientists, with skillsets more suited to biology and farming than killing. Heidi had taken what she considered to be 'the cream' with her. There were, of course, still a few she would have to watch out for – the Schultz camp was liberally salted with fanatics to their Nazi ideals, after all.

Even if that were not the case, any kind of stand against their masters would be logistically impossible and almost certainly suicidal. However, she felt the people here deserved a chance to continue this pastoral existence into which their fate had, despite all the odds, delivered them. If *she* was falling for this place, she could only assume many of her people were, too.

They had a job before them, and she would see it done, but a determination settled in her chest, an intention to hold on to this gift they had been granted.

She turned away from the web, and its connotations, to take in the *Newfoundland* at the lake shore. So alien, and yet so perfect.

"I'm not leaving here," she muttered. The words surprised her, yet somehow, she felt them to be true. "This place will one day become Great Britain – perhaps we could leave a message for the future...?" She would think on that.

It was a beautiful, early summer's morning; a day made for dreams, but Coleman forced her thoughts back to the job in hand, for today, they hoped to lower the Rescue Pod to the ground. Once down, it would form the final link in their new perimeter fence. It would also prove essential to everyday life.

Access via winches and pulleys had proved time consuming and difficult. Especially when a quick getaway was required. There were still many dangerous animals in the vicinity, easily capable of becoming man-eaters – and some of them could fly.

Mothballed among the various clutter within the Rescue Pod's hangar, Coleman's people had found much of use, including a mini digger within Captain Bessel's mission equipment stash. There were also inflatable boats, but whether they would be trustworthy after so many years was hard to say.

However, after a service and a recharge, they found the digger still worked, setting it to level the beach beneath the Pod. The machine was undersized for the task, so the operation had proven to be one of several days' work and many breakdowns. Despite this, and with only sand to shift around, a team of drivers and mechanics had eventually managed to create a flat plateau in readiness for the Rescue Pod.

Things seemed to be going well.

Coleman checked the skies to find them completely clear. No clouds, no monsters, just a few entirely respectably sized birds. She lowered her gaze to the lake's gently lapping waters, barely disturbed by a mild breeze; a liquid blue looking-glass surface, rippled only by the occasional leap of a fish for a fly.

Peace...

She pulled her rifle from around her shoulders in a smooth, practised motion, holding it in a ready position – but why? Tiny hairs prickling on the back of her neck, she looked all the way around her position, checking land, sky and water: nothing.

Confused, she pondered, *What's wrong with me?* Slowly, it dawned on her. She, *they*, had lived on their nerves for so long, that there was but one reaction left to reach for. Good news or bad – brace yourself – that was it. They were programmed by their pain.

Deep breaths.

She willed herself to relax. *I need to stop expecting the worst, but what if lowering my guard gets me killed?* Coleman was no philosopher, and so had no answer to that.

"I need to retrain my nerves," she spoke to herself aloud. "We've lived through a nightmare, some might say of our own making, but vigilance doesn't have to mean pessimism – that way mental illness lies. I must allow myself to experience happiness when and where I can find it. Our world may have changed forever, maybe not, but there's still so much wonder and goodness surrounding me that I can be a part of."

Realising that she might appear slightly batty, should a perimeter patrol come across her speaking to herself, she internalised, *Bad things come and go, but life goes on. I'm so blessed to be here at this time, with this view, and how do I relate to it? By worrying about monsters that at the moment aren't here, and Heidi Schultz – which pretty much amounts to the same thing! Take stock, woman, this is the first day of the rest of your life!*

A comm bing startled her. "Coleman."

"Commander, we're ready to lower the Pod. Do you wish us to proceed, or wait for your return, ma'am?"

Mulling over the man's request, she felt momentarily split between the beams. Her sense of duty prompted her return to *Newfoundland*'s bridge – now their centre of operations – and yet, this short-lived physical and psychological enjoyment of her surroundings argued otherwise. Perhaps she should hang on to it a while longer...?

Reaching a decision, the base's 'new boss' smiled. "I'll monitor the descent from here. You may begin – Coleman out."

"We must take this route, Erika," stated Cocksedge, checking the map on her comm screen. "It may be tight in places, but apparently it is passable. Everyone else will be keeping to the main thoroughfares, and while most of the internal sensors are down, we should be able to travel unnoticed."

Schmidt craned to look at the tiny monitor in Cocksedge's hand. "Very well, Allison. Shall we?"

The two women made their way down through the ship. With only one operational access point remaining between the *New World* and the Pod, this was also the point of greatest danger for them. They approached cautiously, Schmidt in the lead, braced for a possible confrontation. However, the hatch through to the Pod was also unguarded.

Either it was their lucky night or whatever was going on outside was big indeed.

"Before we cross into the Pod, can you show me our preferred route?" asked Erika.

Cocksedge called up Pod schematics from her downloaded database. "We can follow the portside access corridor for about a hundred and fifty metres. After that, it appears to have been crushed. However, there is a cut-through into residential deck five."

"But the civilians—"

Cocksedge spoke over Schmidt's interruption, "*Are all* ordered to remain in their quarters. Let's hope they do as they're told."

Schmidt gave her a sideways glance, speaking volumes about how much stock she placed in people 'doing as they're told', even when their own safety depended upon it.

Cocksedge shrugged. "We need to do this if we're to make a clean start – what choice to do we have?"

Schmidt sighed but nodded reluctantly, and they began their journey through the empty, often darkened corridors of *Life Pod 4*. In places there was clear evidence of what could only be crush damage.

"We really did materialise inside a mountain," Cocksedge whispered in awe. "I can't believe we survived it."

"It seems these people build well," Schmidt admitted, grudgingly.

They groped their way along. In some places they had only the light from Cocksedge's comm to guide them. Within minutes, the corridor before them closed to a crawlspace. The women looked at one another with equal misgiving. "How are you with confined spaces?" asked Schmidt.

Cocksedge looked uncertain. "Not great. You?"

Schmidt shrugged. "I am willing to proceed. How far is it to our junction?"

Cocksedge checked the schematic once more. "Less than ten metres, but I can't tell if it's blocked ahead."

"I will go first," Schmidt assured the older woman. "Give me your comm, I will need the torch."

"Oh, here." Cocksedge reached into a pocket. "I have another."

"Excellent. Wait here. I will call you when I'm through. Either that or I will shuffle back if our way is blocked."

Cocksedge looked uncertainly back along the darkened and damaged corridor. She swallowed.

"Allison?"

"Of course, here you are. I'm not great in the dark, either. Sorry."

"Courage. I will call soon."

With that, Schmidt scrambled into the narrow tunnel, all that remained of a corridor where four men could once have walked abreast.

"Ah, Thomas. Thank you for coming," Baines greeted the historian, offering him a seat around the table. "This is Lord Maxwell of Kelso. Lord Maxwell, this is Thomas Beckett, our historian."

Maxwell accepted Beckett's hand cautiously, but did not rise. "Do historians a'ways conduct yer people's business, Captain?"

"Not ordinarily," replied Baines. "But recently, we've had to draw on the knowledge of people with, shall we say, a superior understanding of our past."

Maxwell gave her an appraising look. "Yer telling me yer from the future, is that it?"

Baines gave her most disarming smile. "You're a clever man, sir." She looked to Douglas, who nodded agreement. "It seems you've worked out our problem. You are correct, we're not from your time."

Maxwell sat back, eyes widening not with surprise, but with shock. "Ah was right?"

Baines nodded.

"Dinnae be afraid, David," offered Douglas. "We're here by accident, but we mean your people no harm."

"What year is it, where ye call home?"

"*Captains*," warned Beckett.

"Ah think it may be too late to U-turn, Thomas," admitted Douglas, sadly.

"Might I have a word?" asked Beckett.

"Of course. Would you excuse us for just a moment, David?" Douglas apologised. "Mary, perhaps ye could offer Lord Maxwell, and his boys here, a wee snack?"

Beckett and the two captains huddled a little way off. "This is dangerous," he began without preamble.

"What isn't?" retorted Baines.

"I don't think you fully realise what we may be starting here, Captain Baines. You've studied these times – what was it you told us, you've a minor in Reformation and Counter Reformation Europe? You must have an understanding of the, shall we call it, 'Tudor mindset'? If these people find out about our technology, it'll start a war. Anyone taking control of our knowledge and our weapons, even just a few of them, could take over the world! We *must* be cautious."

Douglas nodded soberly. "Agreed, Mr Beckett, but we'll also need friends and allies if we're going to be stuck here – and the *New World* will never fly again, that Ah can promise ye.

"Furthermore, we seem to have lost a young lady to some bandits up on the moors. A local lassie Commander Gleeson rescued from another set of bandits over the way – friendly times these!"

Beckett bowed his head into his hands. "Thomas?" Baines prompted. "What is it?"

Beckett looked up wretchedly. "That 'lassie', as the captain calls her, is none other than Elizabeth I – or at least she will be in about two and a half weeks' time. If she lives through this current madness. And if she doesn't, then may God help us."

Douglas' eyes widened at Beckett's revelation. Eventually, he asked, "What do you mean by that?"

"Simply that we're outside our timeline, Captain. And if she dies, we will be *so* far off the map!"

Douglas pinched the bridge of his nose and closed his eyes against the world. "Why is it never good news?"

"Good news, Natalie! He's gonna be just fine." Dr Flannigan smiled as he approached the young zoologist across the ward. "Sorry it took a little while to get back to ya. As you can see, we've put the infirmary on high alert, in accordance with Captain Douglas' orders."

Dr Natalie Pearson positively flopped with relief, not realising just how taut she had been. Intellectually, she knew the injury was minor – but this was her dog! "Thank you, Dr Flannigan—"

"Call me Dave. We've worked together long enough now, surely?"

"Thank you, Dave. How many stitches, and are they neat? Did you make them yourself? Will they dissolve?"

Flannigan held up his hands, laughing. "Take it easy, he's fine. Yes, I stitched him personally – I dared not do otherwise. And it's just the ten. They'll dissolve once they've done their job. Don't worry!" He grinned broadly. "I've picked up a thing or two with the needle over the years."

Natalie smiled, slightly abashed. "Sorry, Dave."

"I understand. He's a tough little guy, though – didn't even whimper – but I gave him a local anaesthetic anyhow. He'll be groggy for about thirty minutes, as you'd expect. You may want to have a little chat with Jim Miller, later. I'm sure he could spare a little polymer to make Reiver a cone of shame – to stop him nibbling and licking, 'til the wound's knitted. He was takin' a nap when I left him. You wanna look in on him?"

"Please."

Flannigan led Natalie into one of the small theatres, hastily built for surgical procedures. Reiver lay on the table, his tongue lolling, a bald patch on his right forelimb revealing stitches.

"Hello, baby," she cooed.

Reiver, as always, woke up tail-first. The process began with a couple of wags, followed by the fluttering of lashes as his eyes widened. His head lifted to allow a vast yawn, all culminating with his gorgeous border collie smile.

Natalie had tears in her eyes, her voice thick with emotion. "Thank you for saving me from that crazy man, boy. I don't know what I would have done if..."

"Hey, he's all *fine*," soothed Flannigan, giving her shoulder a friendly squeeze. "He'll be none the worse for his little adventure."

Natalie turned to him. "But what about Mayor? I'm sure the pony will be OK, this is his home, but poor Mayor won't know how to survive in these lands."

A glint came to Flannigan's eye. "James has his hands full with those armed men outside at the moment, but I don't think there's a chance in hell that he'll abandon Mayor, do you?"

She smiled again, a tear escaping. "The captain *is* very fond of him."

"He saved James' life – he'll never forget that."

Natalie looked over his shoulder. "I think someone's trying to get your attention."

Flannigan turned. "Excuse me."

Leaving Natalie and Reiver, content in one another's company, he approached a very agitated looking Tim Norris, standing with Miss Clarissa Burnstein, who also appeared concerned. "Hey, Tim, Miss Burnstein. You here to see your mom? You know, you kids shouldn't really be here, right?"

"I'd like to see her, Doctor, but there's something else I need to ask you about first. Please?"

"It couldn't wait," interjected Clarrie, seriously.

"Sure. Come into my office and we can speak privately."

The teenagers followed Flannigan. He closed the door behind them and beckoned them to take a seat. "Now, what's this about?" he asked kindly, although he already had a suspicion forming in his mind.

"It's a little embarrassing," began Tim.

Flannigan's lip twitched as he tried not to smirk. "Don't worry, son. Whatever you say in here will remain private. No one else has to know, not even your ma."

"Thank you, Doctor. Yes, I would appreciate it if you didn't tell her. At least not before I can bring the subject up... I mean, when she's well enough to take it."

Flannigan's eyes twinkled. "I'm sure she'll be able to handle it, Tim. Now, what is it?"

Tim looked down at his hands. "Like I said, it's a bit embarrass—"

"Oh, for goodness sakes," snapped Clarrie. "Shall *I* ask him?"

Flannigan chuckled. "Don't worry, Tim. You won't be the first young couple I've advised about—"

"*No!*" Tim cried out. "It's nothing to do with *that!*"

Flannigan sat back in surprise. "It's nothing to be ashamed of, we all... well, you know."

"Doctor, *please,*" Tim interrupted him again, his face forgoing tomato red and shooting straight for beetroot. "I'm talking about my... my *heritage.*"

Flannigan's jaw dropped with the penny. "Oh, *that.*"

Clarrie was grinning. "But while we're here, perhaps we could kill two birds with one stone?"

Tim was aghast, scandalised. "*Clarrie!*"

Flannigan threw his head back, letting go a bark of laughter. "Perhaps first things first. OK, Tim. I kinda expected you to ask, sooner or later. Very few people know about your alleged relationship to the Schultz family, and in truth, we've been so busy, the question got back-burnered. But I guess now's as good a time as any. Give me a minute."

He waved a hand over his glass-topped desk, causing a monitor to rise from its surface while a keyboard glowed to life. Flannigan typed several queries while activating secondary applications via the touchscreen itself.

After a few minutes he sat back, stroking his chin thoughtfully. "Hmm," he said at last. "It seems that someone's been to work on Heidi's files."

"Doctor?" asked Tim.

"There's an outside chance we've lost files to crash damage, but yours were easy enough to access. Let me try something."

More typing...

"Yeah, it seems more than coincidence that we have every DNA profile I request, crew *and* passengers, all *except* Heidi's. She must have screwed up the files before she left."

"But why would she do that?" asked Clarrie, perplexed.

"So that we can't prove anything either way," answered Tim in dead tones. He became suddenly angry. "Textbook Schultz! Lies and misdirection with the occasional nugget of truth thrown in to blow your mind! *Damn them!*"

"So what can we do?" asked Clarrie, looping her arm through his, supportively.

"We might try her quarters," suggested Flannigan. "It's been billeted out to a small group of Meritus' people, so I don't hold out too much hope, but there might still be something."

Tim placed an elbow on Flannigan's desk, cradling his head in his hand. "I need to know if it's true," he muttered wretchedly. Looking up, he faced the doctor once more. "I must know who I am, before I broach this with Mum."

Flannigan nodded. "I understand, son. We'll get to the bottom of this somehow. Trust me. We'll begin with a forensic search of her quarters, as soon as the situation outside has passed, OK?"

"Yes, sir," Tim agreed sullenly. "I think I'd like to see my mum now, please."

The army doctor reached across his desk to pat the young man's shoulder. "Sure. Follow me."

"The way's clear. You can come through now, Allison."

Cocksedge, standing alone in the darkness, jumped. The weird acoustics made Schmidt's voice sound eerie, like it was coming from behind her. She did not need telling twice, and scrambled quickly into the dark tunnel.

Claustrophobia, nyctophobia and paranoia all gnawed at her as she caught her clothing on a jagged stone, or was it a piece of the hull? She could not tell. Panic bloomed, threatening to consume her, when a light shone down into her crawlspace.

"Quickly. Just another few metres," Schmidt offered, encouragingly.

Cocksedge tried to take a deep breath in the confined space, closing her eyes. *No one's after you*, she assured herself. *They don't even know we're out. Come on, nearly there.* "I'm coming," she answered, her voice wavering.

All at once, the scramble way opened out into a full-height corridor and intersection. Schmidt helped Cocksedge to her feet. Their way forward was indeed blocked, but the corridor leading right was still open and fully accessible – and joy of joys, from about ten metres in, it was lit, too.

"Now we will see if people are indeed obeying the order to remain in their quarters," Schmidt commented darkly. She set a fast pace, with Cocksedge almost skipping to keep up. "I studied the schematic while waiting – we turn left in about fifty metres to take the 'spineway' up the centre of the Pod. After another thirty metres we take a second left and head back towards the portside. There we will find a set of elevators."

"Elevators?" asked Cocksedge with alarm. "But surely, there's no power to them?"

"Actually, some of them appear to be active according to the information you downloaded. If we cannot find a working lift, we will have to climb down. Either way, we need to get to the ground floor if we are to break into the factory spaces."

"Do you know how far down that is?"

Schmidt gave her a cool look. "As a matter of fact, I do. Come."

They reached the spineway, Schmidt checking carefully around the corner before they fully revealed themselves. "All clear."

"This is the main thoroughfare through the residential area," whispered Cocksedge.

"Indeed. We must hurry." Without waiting, Schmidt set off at a jog. Cocksedge sighed and ran after her once more.

They reached the next intersection without incident. Taking a left, they made all haste toward the portside elevator terminal. Almost home, a door slid open to one of the apartments lining the left-hand side of the corridor.

A man appeared. Distracted by a conversation over his shoulder, he failed to notice the women. "I'm not staying in here – being ordered to my room, like some damned kid! Who the hell do they think they ar—" Then he saw them. "What the... hey, I thought we were all meant to be confined to our— *You!*" bellowed Hank Burnstein Snr, recognising Cocksedge at last. "What the hell—"

The words quite literally stuck in his throat as Schmidt chopped, knifehand, into his Adam's apple. Burnstein went down, choking.

"Hank?" A woman's voice called from inside the apartment, with just a hint of concern. Within moments, Mrs Burnstein was at her husband's side, trying to lift him back to a sitting position. "Hank!" she cried desperately. Only then did she notice Cocksedge. "Allison? What's happening? What's wrong with my husband?"

"That crazy bitch!" Burnstein managed to wheeze past his damaged throat.

"I'm sorry, Chelsea," replied Cocksedge. "I wish you hadn't seen this – I really do."

Schmidt darted forward, striking Hank a hammer blow to his temple. Burnstein was a big man, but he went down like an eight-ball.

"*Hank!*" screamed Chelsea.

"Shut her up!" demanded Schmidt as she dragged Burnstein from the threshold, back inside his quarters.

Cocksedge acted, grabbing her former friend around the neck with the crook of her right arm, while slapping her left hand around the prone woman's mouth. She dragged her to the sofa and threw her down.

Schmidt closed the apartment's door before they attracted any more attention.

"Allison, what are you doing?" demanded Chelsea, not quite believing this latest turn of events.

Cocksedge ignored her. "They have two teenaged children," she told Schmidt.

Schmidt leaned menacingly over Mrs Burnstein. "Where are they?"

"My daughter's with her friends and my son's with his girlfriend. Why do you want to know? Allison, what's happening?"

"Nothing for you to worry about, dear," replied Cocksedge. "We'll soon be out of your hair, but we'll need you to keep still and quiet for a while, I'm afraid."

"What have you done to my husband?"

Schmidt took his pulse. "He lives. Assuming you wish this trend to continue, you will shut up and remain where you are. Allison, go into one of the bedrooms and start tearing some sheets into strips. We'll tie them up."

"What? No!" Chelsea Burnstein's protestations were cut short, as Schmidt's fist lashed out in a roundhouse punch to lay her out cold across the sofa.

"Finally, some peace! Get the sheets. I'll keep an eye on these two, in case they awaken. *Go!*"

The Burnsteins were quickly trussed up and gagged, allowing their attackers to proceed to the next stage of their mission.

The heavy winches groaned disturbingly as the Rescue Pod lowered towards the beach. Hardly surprising after several decades buried beneath woodland, Coleman surmised. However, the descent continued smoothly enough until three loud, metallic booms rang across the lake.

The Pod tipped as one corner halted its travel.

Coleman dug in her pocket frantically, locating her comm. "All stop! All stop!"

Her people aboard the *Newfoundland* must have discovered the problem and acted at the exact same instant. The arrested descent left the Pod swaying, massive cables creaking.

"What happened?"

"*Not sure yet, Commander. I've got engineers checking, but it looks like one of the four winders gave out.*"

Coleman closed the connection before swearing roundly. Her diatribe was not even halfway finished when another boom sounded, followed by the screech of metal on metal. A loud creaking followed. The Rescue Pod juddered, its high corner dropping a few metres. No sooner had it levelled out than a *crack*, like a vast electrical explosion, wracked the silence. Immediately, the same corner began to tip, downwards this time as its cables snapped, making the entire mechanism scream in protest.

Coleman reopened the channel, "Resume! Resume! Continue lowering the Pod – quickly as you like!"

Once again, the people on the bridge seemed to be ahead of her, and the remaining winches began delivering slack. The sounds of mechanical torture made Coleman wince, even from fifty metres away. "Heidi is going to kill me!"

Another boom, the loudest yet, and the Pod dropped, lowest corner first, onto the sand. The reverberation through the ground caused

Coleman to stagger. Even from a distance, she could see crumple damage where it struck.

"Yep, I'm dead."

That was when the remaining winches decided to let go.

The boom, as the rest of the Pod hit terra firma, rolled across the land like an earthquake, instantly creating a dust cloud that billowed towards Coleman faster than a raptor could run. With nowhere to hide, she had no choice but to cover as best she could. Having tied her jacket around her waist earlier, as the morning air warmed, she now tore it from her midriff, and covering her head, hit the ground, just a moment before the sandstorm buried her.

The sudden grit-blast made her arms feel like they had been through a cheese grater, but the main force passed by quickly, leaving her buried alive. The effect was strangely allegorical for how she felt in her heart.

Coughing, she shook sand from her limbs and body, unsteadily regaining her feet. Pulling up her tunic to cover her mouth and nose, she waited for the dust to settle. It would take a while. She could make out the vast bulk of the ship through the cloud, of course, but no details as yet. Her bare arms were red raw, covered in sand and grit. Gingerly, she wiped her eyes, briefly considering a quick dip in the lake, but then regained her senses. "I think I'm in enough trouble as it is, without being crocodiled!" The words made her cough hoarsely.

After a few moments searching, she found her rifle and comm. Blowing the dust from them as best she could, she noticed several missed calls. Opening a channel to the *Newfoundland*, she asked, "What happened?"

"*Oh, thank God!*" came an immediate response. "*We thought we'd lost you, Commander! Were you well clear?*"

After another wracking cough she managed, "Not exactly. What happened to the Pod and what shape is it in?"

"*We've despatched teams to ascertain damage, ma'am. As to what happened – catastrophic failure of the winch system would seem to fit the bill, but we'll have more detail soon. Do you require assistance, ma'am?*"

Coleman dropped heavily onto the sand, her buttocks complaining. A deep sigh made her cough some more.

"*Do you require assistance, ma'am?*" he asked again, more insistent this time.

Coleman picked up a stone and cast it towards the lake despondently. "Oh, probably... Why not?"

Chapter 10 | All Hallows' Heist

"This one has power," Schmidt announced with satisfaction.

"Maybe, but should we trust it?" asked Cocksedge. "The ship's been crushed and contorted into who knows what shape."

Schmidt raised an eyebrow. "There are *many* decks..."

Cocksedge sighed. "Call it."

Within moments, the lift car shuddered to a stop at their deck, the doors sliding apart. The right-hand door failed to open fully. Juddering to an eventual stop, it made an electrical whirring sound before finally cutting out altogether.

The women looked at one another. Cocksedge rolled her eyes. "Great. Come on."

Once inside the car, Schmidt said, "Ground." Nothing happened. Remembering the ship was built by NASA, she tried, "First."

Nothing.

Cocksedge reached for the control panel and pressed '1'. The damaged door juddered again but failed to close. Fortunately, the inner set, that were part of the car itself, closed correctly.

They felt the split-second weightlessness of lift travel, before gravity synced them once more with the movements of the car. Within seconds, the doors opened again, to reveal a space that was considerably more utilitarian than the carpeted lift terminal, now several decks above.

Cautiously, they stepped out. Looking right, towards the aft of the ship, they could see the huge vehicular hatch that led into the Pod's main hangar. Its giant steel doors were still firmly closed, completing the structural rigidity of the bulkhead, in line with standard NASA landing procedure. The manufacturing bay seemed deserted.

Cocksedge smiled nervously. "So far, so good."

"Yes, so what," Schmidt intoned lifelessly. "If we are to carry out your plan, we still have to find what we need, retrace our steps back to my quarters, cut through the hull and dig our way up to the surface."

Cocksedge bridled slightly. If politicians *had* sensibilities, then the directness of Schultz's aide – if that was all she was – went very much against them. "In that case, what are we waiting for?"

Setting off towards the bow of the ship, they soon arrived at 'Manufacturing Stores'. The control panel for the connecting hatch was dead. Cocksedge cursed, beating her fist on the door. "Now wha—"

Her question was interrupted by a *clank* as Schmidt noisily applied a large crowbar, magically acquired from somewhere, to the crack between the doors. "Get another bar," she ordered through gritted teeth.

Together, they managed to pry the doors apart and step through. Manufacturing Stores turned out to be a large warehouse filled with racks. Wandering among the aisles, this area was clearly an engineer's toyshop.

"There are some very valuable and useful items in here," Schmidt noted with approval.

"Never mind all that – we want the precious metals and diamonds if we can find them."

Schmidt gave her a cool, disapproving look. "The diamonds will only be suitable for industrial use."

"Fine, well perhaps it's gold that's a girl's best friend, after all? Come on. Whatever's keeping them all busy won't last forever."

They split up; there was much to search through, and Schmidt's pockets bulged with many useful items by the time they met up again.

"I've found the precious metals," said Cocksedge, "but I need a container."

"Here." Schmidt pointed towards a stack of flight cases. "We can empty a couple of these."

"What's in them?"

"Who cares?"

"Right."

Helping themselves to as much as they could reasonably carry, they loaded three kilograms of gold dust, along with several ingots of silver and even a little platinum into two cases.

Locking the containers, Schmidt said, "We're going to need survival gear."

Cocksedge shook her head. "We can't get to the military stores from here. We'd have to go out into the main hangar and head for security."

"I thought you had already *been* to security, when you stole all that downloaded information?" asked Schmidt, again, directly.

Cocksedge chewed, a sourness creeping across her face. Her answer was typically brittle, "I did not *steal* anything. As a Member of Parliament, I have every right to the information I *procured!*"

A raised eyebrow fleetingly interrupted the perfect symmetry of Schmidt's face. "Is that so? Well, regardless, we will not survive out there as we are. It is winter, you say?"

Cocksedge nodded. "Or very nearly so."

"Indeed. Then perhaps we shall have to be bold."

"Erika? Whatever do you mean? Have we not been bold enough already?" Cocksedge's expression was both pleading and appalled as she spiralled ever further out of her comfort zone.

The younger woman extended a hand, gracefully. "Show me the schematics again."

Cocksedge handed over the comm.

Schmidt studied the Pod's factory floor layout, at last commenting, "It is as I expected."

"What is?"

"The things we require to survive, in the short term at least, may be found through there." She pointed towards the large vehicular hatch leading to the main hangar.

Cocksedge paled. "You can't be serious! It's little short of a miracle we encountered no one in *here*. It will be a hive of activity through there. Have you forgotten that Douglas is trying to talk down an entire army outside?"

"Exactly. A hive of activity, as you say. So who would notice two more bodies going about their business?"

Schmidt's 'matter of fact' reply annoyed Cocksedge, stretching her anxiety until it twanged. "Two escaped prisoners, you mean!"

The young woman smiled back coldly, causing a shiver to run down the politician's spine. "Heinrich Schultz had a saying, Allison – people see what they expect to see, more often than not. The reverse must surely also be true, yes?"

"What do you mean?"

"If they think we are locked up, half a ship away, they will not believe we could possibly be in their main hangar, relieving them of their goods. We will be seen, of course, but suggestion will serve us like a cloak of invisibility."

Cocksedge could not have mustered a more horrified stare if the metaphorical chocolate biscuit, dressing the saucer of her ministerial teacup, were suddenly substituted for something emphatically *not* made of chocolate. "No, Erika, they will *serve* us with a hefty prison sentence!"

"You surprise me, Allison. I thought you would be used to the cloak and dagger approach – you *are* a politician."

"Let's just say that I'm familiar with chocolate..." Cocksedge trailed off as Schmidt frowned in confusion. "I mean metaphor – I'm familiar with *metaphor*. There's no double-meaning in what you're suggesting! We're going to be caught – or shot!"

Schmidt tapped a few commands into the comm, speaking without looking up, "Did you think we would be able to carry out this plan of yours without risk?" She turned the screen towards her partner in crime. "You see? This is a camera feed from the hangar – the only one I could get to work, in fact. Everyone is quite busy, as you surmised.

"The majority of traffic is focused around the hangar doors – this is perhaps no surprise. There is also a gathering outside what is labelled on here as the 'Infirmary'. You have an infirmary in the main hangar?"

"We, *they*, were forced to adapt, when your Captain Meritus and his people joined the ship."

"I see," replied Schmidt, coldly. "Accepting that, and with an army outside, everyone should be well away from where we need to go. Look."

Schmidt pointed out the security department, where they would be able to procure equipment.

"Yes, yes, I know where security is, thank you," Cocksedge acknowledged, crossly. "I still don't believe we'll get away with what you're suggesting."

"Allison, do you really believe missions like this are anything new to me? I was Heinrich's personal assistant. I can assure you that my skills were required to go well beyond a hundred words a minute and a short skirt!"

Cocksedge eyed the obscenely beautiful woman acidly. "But naturally, you excelled in those skills too?"

The briefest of smiles. "Of course. Our main problem, however, will be in making a fast getaway."

"You're thinking about some kind of vehicle?" asked Cocksedge.

Schmidt nodded, studying the tiny screen in her hand. She directed the camera to sweep the bay, from its position above the hatch through to manufacturing. "Unless I am mistaken, that appears to be Captains Douglas and Baines – over by the infirmary. The talks must have moved inside. At least they're both in one place – good to know."

Cocksedge craned to see. "Maybe, but look, all the vehicles are blocked in by the construction plant near the main doors. We won't be able to get anything out quickly, if at all. I'm pretty sure that if we move one of those lorries someone will notice!"

Her accomplice was forced to concur. "If we could just get our hands on a pair of motorcycles."

Cocksedge gaped.

Schmidt looked up sharply. "*What?*"

Douglas, Baines and Beckett sat with David Maxwell, Lord of Kelso, each waiting for one of the others to break the silence.

"Is naebaddy going ta tell me about Captain Baines' 'big picture', then?" asked Maxwell, grinning at their obvious awkwardness.

Baines chewed her lip. "Hmm, about that. We're going to have to put our cards on the table here and trust you—"

"*Captain,*" warned Beckett.

"No, Thomas, there's simply too much at stake. If the girl dies..."

"Who is she?" asked Maxwell, leaning forward with interest.

Baines looked right to Douglas, who shrugged, and left to Beckett, who buried his head in his hands.

"She's the future Queen of England," she admitted.

The bombshell seemed to render Maxwell as speechless as Douglas and Beckett for a moment. Eventually, he managed, "Are ye talking about Mary's wee sister, Elizabeth?"

Baines nodded. "Half-sister."

"A fair prize and nae mistake," continued the borderer in wonderment, and mostly to himself as his mind raced through possibilities.

Beckett almost squawked, "*Captain!* Now look what you've done. If she's captured by the Scots, it will change everything!"

"No!" Baines brought her fist down on the table. "Enough! This isn't about some petty border struggle or even about messing around with the succession – this is about the whole future of Scotland, as well as England."

"And if this man controls that succession, what then?" Beckett retorted angrily.

"He won't!" Baines admonished. "And I'll tell you why, tell you both why – although you'd have the answer already, Thomas, if you'd just take the time to stop and think clearly for a minute!"

Maxwell sat back, surprise on his face. "She's a wee firebrand, this one, eh, Douglas?"

"Ye've nae idea."

Baines straightened in her seat. "If you don't mind, gentlemen. What I'm saying is Elizabeth is vital to the stability of these isles. She will not only help soothe the terrible fracture caused by the break from Rome, but she'll also – very soon, as it happens – save Scotland from French occupation. If she lives. The Scottish reformation you hope for will be set back severely if she dies. There's even a possibility it won't happen at all."

"How d'ye ken that?" asked Maxwell.

"Because for us, sir, this has already happened. If Elizabeth isn't crowned, she won't be able to send an army and a fleet to Scotland's aid. And without your reformation, freedom of thought, not to mention help and education for the poor and sick, will be lost for years, decades, centuries! Who knows?"

"Whoa, now! Hang on, lass. This young queen is ganna send an English army and a fleet tae Scotland, and Ah'm supposed tae believe that's a good thing?"

Baines nodded sombrely. "We've seen it, David. If we're to save her and put her back where she should be, we'll have to trust you. And if you want your reformation, and a better future for your people, you'll need to trust us. The division between the two nations from Edward I's reign was a long time ago. Change is upon you."

"So yer reformers, then?"

"No," explained Baines. "This might be hard for you to accept, but religion is just the springboard for the reformation."

His look of confusion forced her to reiterate, "I'm sorry, I mean it's the starting point for reformation. People will be taught and encouraged to read the Bible. Taught to read! Encouraged to form their own opinions from what they learn! And that's just the beginning. Religious division may never completely heal, there may always be differences of opinion between the nations, but the reformation – for better or worse – will usher in the beginning of a new world. A world of freedom of thought and expression, of travel and discovery beyond your imagination – it all starts here."

"Yer saying this wee English lass will bring reformation tae Scotland? 'Tis already here!"

Baines was shaking her head. "No. That's not what I'm saying. The reformation in Scotland is a uniquely Scottish thing. All religion aside, it opens the door to education for the masses, welfare for the poor and the sick – you've no idea how advanced that is for this time. Your people have much to be proud of. All I'm saying is, Mary of Guise will attempt to make Scotland subsidiary to France – and solidly Catholic once more. Some may even welcome that, but I'm fairly sure her agenda is not yours, Lord Maxwell.

"Look, gentlemen, I'm not trying to tell you who's right or wrong, here. I'm just saying that we need to put things back on track, the way they were meant to happen, otherwise..."

"Otherwise?" asked Douglas.

"Who knows?" Baines shrugged, returning her attention to Maxwell. "Mary of Guise may have been fairly tolerant so far, but she'll get worse – believe me. I can't tell you how much of the future can be assigned to the actions of any single individual. Until now, we've only had one version of history to learn from. All I can say with certainty is, whichever way you look at it, Elizabeth is important."

"An English army. In *Scotland?*" repeated Maxwell.

"Well, it willnae be the first time, will it?" Douglas commented, drily.

Baines' answer was impassioned, "No, no, *no!* You're focusing on the wrong thing. In a couple of years, believe me, you will welcome her help! And furthermore, it will lead to a Scotsman on the thrones of both England *and* Scotland – the same Scotsman!"

That got his attention.

"Captain, really!" protested Beckett.

"Thomas," she rounded on him, "it may have escaped your notice, but something has really screwed up here, and dollars to doughnuts it's to do with our arrival! What do you suggest? We just hide in our mountain and let it all go to hell out there? We need these people to trust us, but how can they if we don't trust *them?*"

Another silence.

"And what's in this for ma people?" asked Maxwell. "Ye need food tae help ye through the winter, Ah hear, and help finding the lass – what do we get?"

"We can help you with education, advancements in medicine and crop yield—"

"Weapons?" he interrupted.

Douglas and Beckett straightened in alarm.

"Not exactly," Baines answered obliquely. "But that's not to say that you won't benefit from them."

Maxwell looked at her sidelong. "Explain."

"Retrieving the Princess Elizabeth should leave no doubt in people's minds that they would do well not to upset us – or our *friends...*"

He nodded slowly, considering. "Can ye prove any o' this? Ye'll understand if Ah ask for a wee bit more than yer word."

"We can," stated Baines.

"Oh, *God*," muttered Beckett.

Schmidt took Cocksedge by the shoulders, locking gazes to add weight to her encouragement, "Nonchalance. It's all about nonchalance."

Cocksedge was already breathing heavily as they stood next to the pedestrian hatch to the main hangar. "But they'll see us."

"Of course, that's the point. If we look like we're trying *not* to be seen, they'll have us. Trust me. I've done this many times. I was a thief before Heinrich found me."

"He picks the nicest people."

Schmidt gave a brief laugh. "I was the *best* thief. He picks *only* the best. And by the way, a thief is what you are now – if you were not before."

Cocksedge frowned, not for the first time having reservations about this young woman. Her only surety was that life in such company would never be dull, her concerns over longevity shone through far too brightly to allow it.

"Are you ready, Allison?"

She nodded nervously.

"Good. Relax. And remember, *nonchalance*. We are merely about our business, yes?"

Schmidt turned away to activate the hatch. It slid open noisily, but the hangar was indeed busy, and no one seemed to notice. It closed behind them as they strode purposefully away, heading starboard towards the entrance to Pod security.

Cocksedge was almost hypnotised by the liquidity of the young woman's movements, while she herself followed nervously, concentrating on every step to avoid tripping over her own feet. *Damn her!*

She promised herself that whatever happened, she would not look round. Unfortunately, her curiosity, if nothing else, was worthy of the catlike grace of her partner, and she glanced over her right shoulder anyway. Between various large vehicles, she occasionally glimpsed Douglas, Baines and the historian, Beckett. The final member of their little quartet took her breath away; a man dressed in all the finery of 16th century Britain. Not a picture, nor an actor – an actual nobleman from history. It was unbelievable. It was also distracting, and she tripped, sprawling across the hangar floor.

A man appeared from behind one of the lorries, wiping his hands on an oily rag.

Rumbled, Cocksedge cried out, "Oh, *sh*—"

"Should have been looking where you were going, madam," he said lightly, misinterpreting her distress as the result of her fall.

"Ms!" she corrected, mechanically.

He offered a semi-clean hand to help her up.

Cocksedge glanced at her companion. In the merest instant, the supple poise of a dancer morphed almost imperceptibly into the tautness of a warrior.

For her part, Cocksedge took the man's hand with a thank you, but failed to recognise him. It occurred to her that he must be one of Meritus' people. Immediately on the heels of that thought, came a more worrying question. *I wonder if he will—*

"Don't I recognise you, miss?" the man greeted Schmidt.

Oh, crap!

By contrast, Schmidt was completely unfazed. The smile that lit her face in answer to his question, was that of an angel. It damned near took Cocksedge's breath away – it certainly worked on the young man, who hit the deck before his own smile even had chance to relax from his now unconscious face.

Schmidt took a hasty look around them, all business. "Quick! We must carry him with us!"

Cocksedge had barely recovered from the shock of the attack when the force of Schmidt's words hit. "Are you kidding?" she hissed. "What did you hit him for? He was smiling at you."

"He recognised me!" Schmidt hissed back. "Or soon would have. Come *on!* There may be others."

Also taking a quick look around them, Cocksedge grabbed the man's other arm and pulled. They were almost at the hatch through to security, when she spotted the very things they had been looking for. She caught Schmidt's eye and nodded towards half a dozen of Hiro's homemade, mud-spattered dirt bikes.

Schmidt acknowledged with a smile, hitting the opening button for the hatch. "Take him through."

"On my own?"

"It's a smooth floor, just drag him!"

Cocksedge was very close to freaking out. "Where are *you* going?" she whispered harshly.

Schmidt had already left, heading for the bikes.

The erstwhile politician-turned-commando shook her head in exasperation as she struggled the man across the threshold and into the corridor. *I should have stayed in my quarters! I had books and music, and even hot chocolate! Damn!*

Douglas looked round after a noise from behind them. Craning to see past one of the large vehicles, he shrugged and settled back into his seat.

"Yes, we have proof," Baines stated confidently. "So, will you help us?"

"Ah'll *see* yer proof first, Captain Baines. Besides, we dinnae ken where the lass is. D'ye even ken who has her?"

"Yes, we do."

"Well?"

"Apparently, his name is Sir William de Soulis."

"Oh, *God*," repeated Beckett, placing his head once more in his hands.

Maxwell's eyes widened in disbelief.

"You've heard of him," Baines prompted, hopefully. "Can you help us find him?"

"Oh, aye. Ah've heard *that* name. He's a depraved, twisted creature – a devil worshipper! Ye dinnae ask much, d'ye, lass!"

Baines frowned. After a moment's consideration, she waved a hand around the giant excavators, lorries and spacecraft docked in the hangar. "Look around you, sir. If we're stuck here, it must be obvious to you that we'll make the very best allies you could possibly hope for. We're asking for your help to find a young lady who's been kidnapped. She's alone and will be terrified. Will you help us or not?"

"I am not afraid of thee, vile creature!" Bess bellowed like a sergeant at arms. "Release me this instant!"

De Soulis smiled wryly. He had never met the Great Henry, though all who had, said he was a giant, and terrifying. If he had doubts about the pedigree of this slip of a girl, they were certainly laid to rest in the face of her mercurial Tudor temper.

"This instant, damn thee! Open thy deaf ears!"

Robin Redcap rumbled a deep belly laugh.

"Ye'll fetch a fine price, wench," said De Soulis, joining in with the laughter.

"Idiot!" snapped Bess. "My sister sent me hither, she hath no *cause* to pay ransom. Thine efforts shall not bear fruit, sir!"

De Soulis stepped closer to the bound woman, strapped to a dismounted door for convenience.

His men had commandeered a remote farmhouse, forcing the tenant and his family out into a barn while helping themselves to their host's pottage.

When he spoke, his voice was low and dangerous, "That rotten auld bitch will soon be in Hell, girl. But imagine what the English state will pay for *ye*, when she's gone."

"No," said Redcap with finality.

De Soulis looked around in surprise. "But the wealth o'—"

"I said, no. And you will obey me."

De Soulis' knees seemed to buckle, and he went down as if pressed by an unseen hand. "Then why do we need her?" he asked through gritted teeth.

The pressure released and with a gasp, he fell onto his hands, breathing deeply.

"You will find out all you can from her, then she is to be destroyed."

Despite his pain and discomfort, De Soulis' eyes widened in surprise, but he looked up to find only empty space where Redcap had stood just a second ago.

"Thou art a fool, De Soulis," Bess hissed angrily. "Dabbling with powers beyond thy control. Now, look what thou hast set free in thine arrogance!"

"His power will wane with the light o' dawn, and the passing of All Hallows' Eve."

Bess smiled cruelly. "So *thee* say'st. Either way, I think thou hast a long night ahead."

"This is going to be a very long night!" Cocksedge grunted, straining as she dropped the pannier onto a purpose-made frame over her bike's rear wheel. "I don't even know how to ride one of these things."

Schmidt twisted the right-hand grip on her own bike. "I have never seen these before, but it seems they share some standard features. This is the throttle – as it would be on a motorbike. The brakes are the levers on the handlebars, as with a bicycle. I assume this button is for... yes, the headlamp. That's pretty much it. Nice and simple. You've ridden a bicycle before...?"

Cocksedge looked at the contraption with misgiving. "Not for a long time. Bicycles were banned from central London a decade ago, due to the astonishing number of accidents and infractions of the law. Obviously, as a politician, I had to be *seen* obeying the law – especially when so many of my colleagues were caught on camera, flouting it."

Schmidt chuckled. "And now here you are, stealing a bike to use as a getaway vehicle after a gold heist. Is it not refreshing to step out into the light, Allison?"

Cocksedge smiled. A career liar, she had to admit, it was. "Shall we?"

Schmidt nodded. "This switch disengages the motor, transforming it back into a standard bicycle."

"We're to *pedal* our way out of here?"

"No, we're to push. As soon as we are near the main hangar, engage the motor, mount and hang on! Electric motors often deliver surprising torque and acceleration. Are you ready?"

Dressed in a stolen flak jacket and boots, Cocksedge nodded. The situation outside had stripped the security department of all weapons – at least she had been unable to find any – but fortunately, the necessities for living rough were still in abundance. The women split the gold between them, in case one or the other were taken down.

"This is going to be a wild ride," said Schmidt, grinning wolfishly.

They stopped at the hatch connecting with the main hangar, giving their equipment one last check over before their flight to freedom.

"What if the man you knocked out wakes up?" asked Cocksedge.

"No one will hear him—"

Schmidt's answer was cut short as the hatch before them slid open, revealing another man, also dressed as a mechanic.

"Francis? Hey, Frank! Oh, sorry ladies, I didn't realise there was anybody... Hey, what's going on here?"

"You're just in time," Schmidt answered smoothly. Standing her bike against the wall, she invited the man into the corridor. "You see this sprocket?"

Thud.

"Are you planning on knocking the entire *New World* staff unconscious?" asked Cocksedge.

"Only the stupid ones, and I can tell you, there is more sport in shooting ducks!"

"Hey, what's going on here?"

Another pair of mechanics arrived, perhaps to check on their colleagues.

Schmidt stepped forward, out into the massive hangar to give herself room. "Do you gentlemen all have the same script?"

"*Huh?*"

She attacked, quick as sight, collecting them both with a single spinning-hook-kick.

"What now?" asked Cocksedge, panic-stricken.

Schmidt shook her roughly. "*Ride!*"

They mounted their bikes, speeding down the clear run, alongside the hangar wall. In seconds they reached the hatch leading back into the manufacturing bay, and this turned out to be all the time they had.

Shouting struck up from behind them. Schmidt's kick had been ferocious, but at least one of the mechanics seemed to have recovered and was calling out.

Soon, the men and women in front of them also woke to a situation in the making.

Seated across the hangar, Douglas held up his hands to halt conversation. "What *now?*" he asked in annoyance. He raked his gaze along the opposite wall, and then he had them. Two people, moving quickly between the parked vehicles, on heavily laden bikes. "No you don't." Jumping to his feet, he bellowed, "*Stop them!*"

The hangar service and maintenance team closed in to surround the riders. They seemed to have them, when the foremost popped a wheelie and rode straight at the three mechanics blocking her way. One man dove to his right. A second was slower and caught a wheel in the face. The third, a woman in mechanics coveralls, tried to grab the rider from the opposite side, but received a kick to the crotch for her trouble and doubled up. As an experienced martial artist, Schmidt was only too aware that this trick worked on women, too.

Cocksedge slipstreamed through the confrontation, following Schmidt's violent bow wave. The remaining three service engineers threw themselves out of the way. Douglas drew his stun pistol. He did not know the identities of the runaways, but it hardly mattered – they had to be stopped.

He fired and missed, the stun bolt slipping neatly between the two bikes. For his second shot, he held the weapon in a double grip, leading the target.

One of the service engineers saw a last chance; regaining his mojo, he leapt for the second biker. His dive coincided with Douglas' shot, blocking it. Worse, the man crumpled in mid-air from the bolt and fell to the floor like a sack of spuds.

"*Balls!*" shouted Douglas in frustration. He turned immediately. "Jill, get Ford on the line, tell him to stop them!"

Baines obeyed immediately, but the riders were already at the mouth of the gorge created by their diggers.

Major White took out his comm in surprise. "Jill? Is that you?"

"*Ford, you have incoming. Secure the—*"

"Watch out!" shouted The Sarge, diving to grab the major.

For the nth time, Major White found himself flung against the mud walls of the man-made cutting, cursing roundly.

Although several soldiers turned at the commotion, the riders were already slithering out of the muddy opening and onto the plateau.

"Keep going!" screamed Schmidt.

Cocksedge had neither the breath, nor the concentration to offer a response. It was taking all she had just to hang on. Her bike skidded and slalomed between the remaining men as she flatlined it in pursuit of her insane companion.

"STOP THEM!" roared The Sarge, loud enough to unsettle many of the men and their mounts around the plateau's edge.

"Oh, my *Go-o-o-o-d!*" screamed Cocksedge, shuddering to a forced slow by the rough surface. Reaching the edge, both riders dodged between the ponies suddenly rearing and bucking in their path. "*Aaaargh!*" Cocksedge screamed again.

Schmidt flattened over her handlebars, darting below a pair of thrashing hooves. Cocksedge was not so fortunate. She was forced to veer left, but her front wheel lost traction on the icy mud.

Several things happened at once, all within a split second. Schmidt vanished. There was no time to qualify this event, let alone ponder it, she was simply gone. The rearing pony landed, catching Cocksedge's back wheel on the way down. The nudge flicked the bike upright, although this was of little help. Her wheels were no longer sliding, nor had they found traction; they were flying.

The very last words spoken by Allison Cocksedge MP, upon her disappearance from the USS *New World*, were recorded on Halloween, 31st October AD1558, and they numbered just three – although technically a panicked repetition of the same word over and over, they were as heartfelt and succinct as they were timeless, despite having but four letters between them.

Chapter 11 | One Small Step Before Man

Hiro Nassaki lay on his bunk. Bone-weariness would normally have taken him instantly to sleep, but not this night.

Now well into the small hours, it had been one hell of a day. Working alongside Georgio Baccini and Sam Burton's people, they had focused most of their efforts on restoring power to the Pod. Hiro believed that most of the *New World* herself would remain in a state of ruin, little more than a spare parts cache, going forward. He felt great sadness about that. They would keep some of the living quarters, such space was at a premium, but it would be a waste of resources to repair a ship that could never fly again.

A tear escaped down his cheek and he wiped it gently. The only positive to come out of losing his beloved ship was that it allowed him to push back the grief he felt over losing his beloved brother – for a second time.

He reached out, could almost feel Aito's face. *Why?* he thought miserably.

Aito Nassaki lay on his bunk, staring unseeing at the ceiling. His small quarters aboard the *Heydrich* were assigned after the accident, when Heidi had taken his captain's quarters for herself, but he hardly cared about that.

Had he made a mistake? He could have stayed aboard the *New World*, perhaps as a prisoner, but his brother would have lobbied tirelessly to change that state – he knew he would.

His brother... and how he had hurt him. His mind drowned in the guilt his actions manufactured. Hiro probably thought him dead, again, after that dinosaur had bitten off his hand and thrown him against the rock face. Sigilmassasaurus; apparently that was the thing's name. He hardly cared about that either.

He reached out, could almost feel his brother's tear-stained cheek in his hand.

"I'm sorry, Hiro. Truly, I am. I used to believe in making life easier and better for all, but the easier existence becomes for humans, the more we destroy the world around us. The planet has recovered so many times from so many trials and mass extinctions – I used to believe it would survive us, but now I'm not so sure."

Aito spoke aloud, and it almost felt as though Hiro was with him, disapproving as always.

"Now I'm not sure *any* life will survive *us*, and I may be the only man alive with both will and opportunity to change that. I have a job to do. I have to save the world – not mankind. I hope you'll forgive me. I'm sorry, brother. I love you."

Aito closed his eyes, replaying his last full conversation with Hiro, from a prison cell aboard the *New World*. Had there been someone listening? Had he said too much? He could not afford his position to be compromised. He would need the resources of this ship. He would also need to know he could keep them, and that would require some proof against any duplicitous action levelled against his control.

All at once, he reached a decision and sat up, spinning his legs around to dangle from the bunk. It was time to act.

The old man acknowledged the salute with a nod. The sergeant about-faced and strode away smartly. Heinrich Schultz watched him go, deep in thought. *Such intricate webs we weave. Having arrived in a world with no people, who would have thought it would be so difficult to stop them from killing one another...?*

Benedictus Jansen waited for the command to release the massive rock from its sling. He sat in the co-pilot's seat next to Heidi Schultz, who had the controls of their small but lethal attack ship.

Strapped into one of the 'occasional' seats behind them, the balding scientist in his white lab coat perspired. He scrutinised the readouts scrolling across one of the screens set into the tiny bridge's side wall.

"Two minutes," he said.

"Are you sure about this, One?" asked Heidi.

"I, erm... yes, quite sure, ma'am. Er, ma'am?"

"Yes?"

"Why have you begun calling me 'One'?"

"I think of you as 'lab coat one', and your counterpart, the woman with the attitude, as 'lab coat two'."

"You never learned our names?" he asked peevishly.

Heidi's response was matter of fact, "No. I had a dalliance with 'A' and 'B' for a while, but eventually settled on 'One' and 'Two'."

"I see... er, thank you, ma'am."

"Time?" demanded Jansen.

"Sixty seconds," One supplied.

Surrounded by a bright starscape, they flew towards an object still only visible on their monitors. 2,997,684 kilometres away from Earth's moon, they headed out rimwards, away from the sun. The object they sought was a comet. Currently, it followed a trajectory that would pass by the Earth and moon several hundred thousand kilometres out. The vastness of space made this a near miss – Heidi's plans made it perfect.

She brought the little ship about in an arc, to cross the comet's path, using angular momentum to augment their rock's velocity in a slingshot action. If their mathematics were correct, it would be travelling at 50,000 kilometres per hour when it impacted the comet.

Under constant acceleration from the vast gravity of the sun, the comet approached from the opposite direction at roughly 80,000 kilometres per hour. When they met, the anticipated explosion would be impressive. Powerful enough, in fact, to alter the comet's trajectory and set it on a collision course for the moon.

One began a countdown. No sooner had he said 'mark', than Jansen released the hitch underneath the ship, freeing their payload. Untethered, the doomed rock began one final journey through space.

Heidi powered away from the comet's path as Jansen increased the rear-view camera magnification to maximum, making sure the feed was recorded.

"Now we wait," Heidi commented drily.

"Not for long," he replied.

They headed back towards Earth and her only natural satellite, but despite the exquisite spectacle of the dual spheres, their attentions fixed on the rear-view monitor.

Even at full magnification, the rock they launched was no longer visible against the brightness of the comet's reflected light. However, when they struck one another, the *effects* of that rock were most evident.

They squinted, despite the automatic dampening filters. The collision, and size of the subsequent explosion, awed them.

Heidi gave a nod of satisfaction. "I'm bringing us around. Record *everything!* Now, how are we? Did it work?"

The scientist behind Heidi typed frantically, calling up the results of their experiment.

"Did it *work?*" she asked again, impatiently.

Trying to read and speak at the same time, the whitecoat stammered, "It – it's changed trajectory— hang on..."

Currently with nothing to do, Heidi unlocked her pilot's seat and spun it round to further intimidate him. "One, I'm waiting."

Jansen, now Heidi's new bodyguard it seemed, turned in his seat too. "It would be very unfortunate if you bungled the calculations, Doctor," he added menacingly.

"Not helping," spat One, indignantly. After a run through several more screens, he sat back, taking a deep breath. "I believe we're on course."

"Excellent." Heidi also sat back, steepling her fingers in a mannerism unpleasantly reminiscent of her grandfather.

"Oh dear."

"What is it, One?"

"The *Heydrich* has only just begun to lift. They should be long gone by now, several minutes ago, at least."

"What?" Heidi's usual anger was tempered with anxiety.

"Something must have delayed them." The middle-aged man looked up from his monitors to see all eyes upon him. "It's not my fault! How could I slow the comet down to give us another chance to hit our mark? This was a one-shot deal – you knew that, ma'am!"

Heidi growled. "Where is the *Heydrich* now?" she demanded of Jansen.

He shook his head. "Still in the pull of the moon's gravity."

"How long do they have?" Jansen snapped at the scientist, in turn.

He swallowed hard. "The comet is passing us... one, two, three, *now*. That means they have roughly seventy-five seconds."

Cretaceous Gondwana – T-minus five days
The *Heydrich* eventually put down east of a vast inlet from the Tethys Ocean. East of where they *had* expected to find Niger. Discovering that it was under the sea in this time had been an unpleasant surprise, especially for the scientists who suggested travelling there.

After running from Heidi's stateroom, before the bullets began to fly, they met with their subordinates to find an urgent solution.

Despite their recent bad luck, one idea led to another, allowing serendipity to smile on them at last. However, their new plan had a problem, and that problem was the moon. It was *damned* cold there. Their idea of in-situ-leaching uranium from the rocks, depended on the higher temperatures required to allow a liquid chemical to pervade the rock and collect the uranium. Their solution was at once complex and astonishingly blunt.

The balding, middle-aged scientist burst into Heidi's quarters. "We have an answer, ma'am," he said by way of explanation, greeting and apology.

"Really."

His enthusiasm was slightly derailed by her flat, caustic response, but he persevered. "Yes, ma'am. We believe we have a way of heating the lunar surface at our mining site. We can then sift the uranium direct from the steam cloud. Much easier! You see, we used our satellite net, pointing some of the units out into space—"

"And you found something?" Heidi cut him off, with just the glimmer of interest.

"Indeed, ma'am. There's all manner of debris spinning around out there, mostly left over from when the solar system formed. We found a near-Earth-object that may just fit the bill!"

He beamed...

Heidi had never visited the moon. It was a strange thing, a trip so easily undertaken by a wealthy 22nd century citizen as to be hardly worth the bother. Although Captain Jill Baines was on record as the first lunar birth – or 'loony' as they were known colloquially – there were already people born on the moon, in their own time, who had never even been anywhere else; it was just 'old hat'.

However, it occurred to Heidi that, should she set foot on the moon *now*, she would be the very first human being ever to do so. This seemed suddenly worthwhile. In fact, should their mission to mine uranium from the moon fail, however unlikely, it might almost be worth leaving a capsule for NASA. Perhaps containing a short note. Maybe something along the lines of 'Sorry Neil'.

A smile twisted her lip as she lowered her helmet's sun visor. "Depressurise the airlock."

The atmosphere began to evacuate immediately, buffeting the space-suited moonwalkers, and within moments they were in vacuum.

Heidi gestured for Jansen to open the hatch. The vibration through their boots demonstrated the mechanism's engagement, but otherwise the doors parted in absolute silence.

Jansen was about to step outside when Heidi reached out to roughly shove him behind her. They could not see one another's faces behind the sun visors, but she knew he would be staring at her; looking for some clue as to what he had done wrong.

By way of explanation, she said, "This time, I think we will go with 'one small step for woman', yes?"

Without waiting for his response, she leapt out onto the lunar surface. The transition from Earth standard gravity aboard ship, to approximately one-sixth of that gravity on the moon, was an almost osmotic experience. As Heidi passed through the invisible barrier, her stomach lurched. A feeling further exacerbated by her complete failure to land on target, approximately one metre from the ship. She kept on going, eventually setting boots on the ground several metres out.

A cloud of moon dust puffed up from the loose surface where her feet dug in, floating eerily in the low gravity.

Despite herself, Heidi giggled like a schoolgirl. After a moment's elation she realised that Jansen was saying something. "What was that?" she asked.

"One small step for *a* woman," he corrected her truculently.

"What is this?"

"Neil Armstrong swore that he said, 'one small step for *a* man', not the more commonly quoted 'one small step *for* man'. Although the transmission never unequivocally proved that, there was a tiny electronic sound detected that would have been too quick for the human ear to discern. It's possible he actually..."

Heidi's silence began to deafen Jansen, stifling his explanation. Eventually, she said, "Neil *who?*"

"Right, of course, Doctor. Sorry if I spoiled your moment."

"Well, you may as well step out yourself now!" she spat, irritably.

Jansen stepped out of the *Heydrich*'s pedestrian airlock, located near the bottom of the ship. With her hydraulic landing stanchions only minimally extended, the drop was little more than a metre. He stepped out, gracefully alighting on one foot to continue at surprising speed, his steps like the last strides of a long jumper before take-off. Despite the low gravity, his gait obviously came naturally.

Once more, the sun visor hid Heidi's annoyance. "You have been to the moon before?"

"Of course, Doctor. Haven't you?"

"This is the area the whitecoats suggest is richest in uranium," she changed the subject.

Jansen kicked a boot into the ground, sending moondust billowing away. Like disturbed sand on the ocean bed, it seemed to hang suspended, before eventually coming to rest. "Doesn't look like much. Why are we out here?"

That question threw her for a moment. "Haven't you ever just wanted to be the first to do something? Especially when that something is extraordinary?"

"No, and *certainly* no. The first people to do things, especially extraordinary things, tend to be the ones who get killed. I've become good at surviving, Doctor."

"So it didn't bother you that I pulled you back, to take the first step myself?"

"Not at all. If you had sunk below the sand or been fried by a solar flare, I would have been quite comfortable where I was."

Heidi's answer was equally prosaic, "Perhaps I should have chosen someone else to share this moment with!"

The Moon – T-minus three days
Heidi looked doubtful. "And you expect this to work?"

The female lab coat stepped forward. "No one has ever tried this before. On the face of it, it's a crazy notion, but why not?

"We were able to manufacture ammonium carbonate from carbon dioxide and aqueous ammonia, and sulphuric acid from the oxidation of iron sulphide, before we left Earth. We'll utilise both systems in case one performs better than the other. The drums are being emptied across the area of the expected crater. We will reuse them to store the water created by the impact – which we hope will also contain our chemical treatment, diluted by meltwater from the comet impact. With any luck, our solution will be laced with uranium.

"The steam will condense and freeze very quickly. So when the time comes, we should act with alacrity – but water or ice, it ought to be possible to extract what we need from the blast site."

Heidi ran a long blonde plait through her fingers as she absorbed the woman's explanation. "And from there we simply return to North Africa and open the lids, evaporating off the water?"

"Leaving us with the uranium. Yes, Doctor. This is an incredibly violent and wasteful process, but it will be quick – if dirty. The strontium-90, we managed to extract from the ruined core of the *Eisernes Kreuz*, as you know."

Heidi nodded thoughtfully. "How long will it take to create our marker isotope, so that we may begin the second phase of our operation?"

"A few days, ma'am," the male lab coat answered.

Heidi treated each of them to a brief penetrating stare. "This is a most audacious plan. I only hope that I am able to compliment you... upon its successful delivery."

"Erm, yes, ma'am," he answered hesitantly. "About the execution – I think I will need to fly in the attack ship with you, just in case any last-minute calculations are required."

Heidi rose from behind her desk, smiling coldly. "I could not agree more. I would hate to have to go looking for you, should this not work. And if your execution fails, I promise you, your second execution will not. Thank you, Doctors. I am impressed – for now. You may go."

An hour after the final meeting with her scientists, Heidi busied herself overseeing the loading of their orbital attack ship. The journey planned was long for a short-range craft, about six million kilometres, but the operation on the moon was still underway, so the *Heydrich* had to remain where she was.

It would take them a little over five days to reach their target, launch their projectile, and return. By the time of that return, the mission clear-up teams should already have completed the post-impact operation.

Jansen and the male scientist appeared at the doorway to the hangar, bearing duffle bags.

"I see you are packed, gentlemen. Good. We leave within the hour."

Heidi seemed distracted, but as good as her word, she launched soon after, circling to find their quarry – which perhaps ironically was a giant rock.

After meeting with her scientists, she had visited her grandfather to scatter seeds of reconciliation, suspecting his help would be invaluable where they hoped to journey next. Their conversation had set her nerves on edge. Her concentration suffered still further as a white sleeve, revealing the white cuff with brown check of a maths teacher, landed suddenly across her shoulder – hairy hand all pointing and cheap deodorant. "That one."

Wrinkling her nose, she batted the arm aside. "Thank you! I see it."

As they neared their designated ballistic, Heidi noted its impressive size. "What is the mass of that stone, Doctor?" she asked.

"About forty tons, ma'am. It's rich in iron ore, which can only help to create more sulphuric acid on impact – waste not, want not."

"Indeed. How do you suggest we lift it?"

Immune to sarcasm, the man answered precisely and truthfully. "We moonwalk, wrap our sling around it, and take off again."

Heidi turned in her seat. "Does the rock have to be that big to create the effect we need?"

"Yes, ma'am."

"And did you trouble yourself with the specifications of this vessel, before you put all this into motion?"

He gulped, knowing he was in trouble but unsure why.

In the spirit of helpful cooperation, Heidi continued, "For your information, the maximum payload of this vessel is *ten* tons."

His expression cleared and he visibly relaxed. "On *Earth*, ma'am. We're at one-sixth gravity, remember?"

Heidi blinked. "Of course."

The men looked at one another, their surprise evident. "And once we break the gravitational hold of the moon, it will be virtually weightless—"

"Do not speak to me as if I were a fool!"

Whitecoat gulped again.

"Are you feeling well, Doctor? Enough to fly, I mean?" asked Jansen. It was unclear whether his concern was for her, for their mission or for himself – in the hands of an unfit pilot.

Dr Heidi Schultz straightened, eyeing them coolly. The conversation with her grandfather had shaken her more than she realised, it seemed. "Get suited up, I want that sling in place directly. We still have two and a half days' flight ahead of us, just to reach our target. Now, move!"

The Moon – T-minus thirty-seven minutes

Lieutenant Devon sat in the command chair on the bridge of the *Heydrich*. Out of the corner of his eye, he noticed members of his bridge crew snapping to attention. He turned. "Captain on the bridge," he barked, standing himself.

Aito Nassaki nodded to his officers as he approached the captain's chair, the empty left sleeve of his jacket swinging free while his injured arm remained in a sling. "At ease everyone, I only came for a look around and to get some exercise. Please, Lieutenant, retake your seat. I've spent too much time on my backside lately."

"Sir."

Aito stood alongside his command chair. "The ship seems in good order, Mr Devon. Now, what's the situation?"

"Yes, Captain. However, we seem to have a complication. The spreader teams returned aboard thirty minutes ago, ready for our launch. But one of them is missing, sir."

Aito showed surprise. "Missing? Where in the wor— *moon* could they have got to?"

Devon could only shrug. "The missing man is not showing up on our scanners, nor is he answering our hails – he's just *gone*."

Aito frowned. "I understand that I'm a little behind events, Lieutenant, so please correct me if I'm wrong, but won't this location resemble molten lava in a pressure cooker about half an hour from now?"

"In about thirty-six minutes, sir, yes."

Aito stroked his smooth cheek distractedly; it had taken him longer than expected to wet shave with one hand, something else he could no longer take for granted. "We're no strangers to sabotage on this mission," he began at last. "If that's what's happening, what could this guy be up to out there? Ideas? Anyone?"

The bridge crew looked from one to another for inspiration. The officer manning the sensors turned back to her console and began to reconfigure their scans.

"What have you, Lieutenant?" asked Devon.

"Sir, moon rock is rich in metals, including aluminium, iron, magnesium and titanium. If the missing man has taken a fall, our scans may be blocked by the surrounding rocks."

"And who *is* our missing man?" asked Aito.

"Sergeant Denholm Haig, sir," supplied Devon. "Lieutenant, can we adjust our scans to compensate?"

"Trying, sir, but the metal content in the rock reflects any signals directed at it. I've tried infra-red, but our EVA suits are so efficient that we probably won't spot any heat loss, either."

"I suppose his suit's homing beacon has been deactivated?" asked Aito.

"It seems so, sir."

Aito straightened; his next order would probably make him unpopular. "Very well, then we must assume that whatever Sergeant Haig's purposes are, he does not wish to be found. Our first duty is to our mission and the ship – it's all we have. We should leave the moon immediat—"

He was interrupted by a call from sensors. "I've found him, sir!"

Devon left the command seat to approach. "Good work, Lieutenant! Where is he?"

She opened a camera feed of the moon's surface, where the ammonium carbonate and sulphuric acid spreading had taken place.

"What am I looking for?" asked Devon.

"Our suits contain a very specific aluminium alloy, sir. I attuned our scanners to search for that, ignoring the elements found in the igneous rock, and I found this."

The camera feed zoomed, pixelated, cleared and zoomed again, as the optics worked with digital sampling to bring the object into view from several hundred metres away. It was a boot.

"Man down!" called Devon. "Get a team suited for EVA on the double!"

Aito, still standing by the command chair, shook his head. "We don't have time for this, Mr Devon. We have our orders and must leave on schedule."

"But we can save him, sir," said the Lieutenant at the scanning controls, spinning her seat to face him.

The whole bridge crew stared at their captain. Aito looked around uncomfortably. "Very well, but be quick. We must leave!" He turned and left the bridge.

"Ben, contact the *Heydrich*. Priority one!" barked Heidi.

Benedictus Jansen opened a channel.

"Dr Schultz, this is acting Captain Devon. We have a situation here, ma'am."

"You have sixty seconds to live! Get my ship out of there!"

"We know, ma'am. Everything is at maximum, but even on the moon this is a heavy ship—"

"Never mind that! What the hell are you still doing there? You were ordered to leave an hour ago!"

"There's a bit of a story attached, ma'am, but if we don't concentrate you won't get to hear it!"

"Very well, Schultz out." She turned to the scientist behind her seat. "One, can they ascend in time?"

Already doubtful, his confinement and proximity to a known psychopath made him doubly so. He cleared his throat nervously. "I give them, maybe, fifty-fifty?"

Heidi bristled. The men edged away.

The *Heydrich* rose slowly, her vast weight countered by many hundreds of tons of thrust from her rocket engines.

"Helm?" Devon called out across the bridge.

"We're lifting, but not fast enough, sir." He turned to his superior in fear. "Sir?"

Devon thought for a second. "Time to impact?"

"Fifteen seconds, sir!" came the frantic response from sensors.

Aito Nassaki had left the bridge, taking himself back to sickbay. Devon was once again captain of the *Heydrich*. There was no help, it was all on him. Reaching a decision, he barked, "Helm, cut power to the aft section thrusters by half."

A look of terror crossed the helmsman's face. "*Sir?*"

"DO IT!"

The pilot spun back to his controls. "Aft thrusters at fifty percent, sir."

The *Heydrich* immediately began to rise at the nose. Out of the front viewports, Devon watched steep-sided lunar cliffs sink below his false horizon. "Fire main engines! Push them all the way, past their stops! Go, go, *go!*"

The sudden acceleration outstripped the inertial dampeners' ability to compensate, and several Gs pressed the entire crew into their seats as the *Heydrich* leapt forward. She passed close enough to the ancient, jagged peaks of a vast impact crater for her rockets to send a plume of lunar aggregate flying into space.

They were barely past the rim, when blinding white light fully encompassed them, just ahead of a shock wave that flung the *Heydrich* out into space. The crater rim deflected much of the blast force upwards and over, but her stern lifted nevertheless, engines fighting immense forces to prevent them from being flipped end over end.

"MAX IT!" screamed Devon.

"We're at a hundred and thirty percent, sir!" the pilot cried out above the rattle and shake of everything around them.

The blast wave was actually the product of hundreds of lesser explosions. They hit the ship's stern in violent succession from multiple vectors, causing the *Heydrich* to shake her tail like an exotic dancer, while pilot and computer struggled desperately with attitude control. The fight to keep her level and true continued for a few clenched seconds of bowel-twisting discomfort. Gradually, she began to stabilise, unpinning the crew from their seats.

"*Woo-hoo!* What a ride!" the pilot whooped in sudden elation. "Sir, we just hit seventy-eight *thousand* kilometres an hour! That's the fastest man has ever travelled, Captain!"

Several of the bridge crew were vomiting, some explosively. Devon gagged, covering his mouth. "It felt like it," was all he could manage.

A couple of days had passed since they surfed the blast wave. Devon sat alone in the observation lounge, staring out over the immense plume left by the impact. It hung in space like a vast cone, though its interior was still a maelstrom of fast-moving objects. It might take years for the moon's weak gravity to reclaim it all. However, Devon's immediate concerns were much closer to home.

When Dr Schultz returned tomorrow, they would use her small craft to harvest the uranium solution, or more probably, uranium ice. He did not doubt she would want them to begin as soon as the little ship was refuelled. He would have to explain why they cut it so close before leaving the surface, but they did find the missing man, and the damage to *Heydrich* was minor. That concerned him less than explaining about the murder.

He sighed, not for the first time regretting his decision to rescue Heidi from that island in the middle of the Atlantic.

Sergeant Haig's oxygen supply had been adulterated with arsenic. Whoever did this had access to, and extensive knowledge of, ship's systems, stores and equipment. This gave him several suspects, but as yet he could see no motive.

It seemed fair to remove Heidi from his list, as she was millions of kilometres away when the tampering was carried out. Although perhaps that was underestimating her. He knew the Schultzes wove webs of intrigue complex enough to make any normal person's head spin. The old man was locked in the *Heydrich*'s small brig, but Devon had to question the efficacy of any holding cell where its architect was concerned. The Dawn Fleet had been constructed to Heinrich Schultz's personal and very exacting specifications, after all. They had already seen him shut the vessels down remotely – what else was he capable of? Was he actually their prisoner, or were they his?

When Heidi returned, he must be seen to be taking action, but if he revealed his suspicions, how would she take it?

He placed his coffee mug on the low table before him. While considering their situation, the drink had gone cold in his hand. He sat back, taking a deep breath. *I wish Captain Nassaki would take back command.* As the thought came, it collided with a memory. *Nassaki would have left that man to be incinerated by the explosion. OK, so Haig was dead, but we didn't know that at the time. It could be argued that Nassaki's first concern was for the ship and getting it free of the impact zone. This would be difficult to argue – it would certainly be an approach endorsed by their mistress. So why am I concerned by it?*

He had checked the ship's logs to retrace Sergeant Haig's movements up to the time of his death and found that he had met with Heinrich Schultz, a few days prior to his moon walk. Although the camera feeds from inside the brig were conveniently missing, he had footage of Haig entering and leaving a few minutes later. This was an oddity. If Haig had issues, or suspicions, he should have brought them to him, as acting captain. Why go to the old man? Upon Heinrich's capture, Heidi had passed a standing directive of no communication. She obviously considered him dangerous even when locked away.

Devon's suspicions were further compounded, or confounded, by Heidi's own visit with Heinrich, shortly after Haig.

If these facts are connected, then maybe the Schultzes wanted Haig out of the way, and it'll be business as usual, when Heidi returns.

This thought seemed plausible. However, If Haig had fallen foul of the Schultzes, Heidi would have had no problem in executing the man, very publicly.

There must be something else going on here.

A number of people had been around the stored suits and oxygen tanks before Haig took his final walk. It seemed he would have to follow Sergeant Haig's movements back much further if he were to get at the truth. He knew Haig was among the men and women captured aboard the *New World* with Captain Nassaki; perhaps he would start there.

Sir William de Soulis stared balefully up at the Hunter's moon. He had no concept of deep time, but believed in the existence of the 'Old Ones'. Creatures who lived long before man. According to the Bible, man and the world were less than 6,000 years old, but he knew there were creatures older than this; creatures who still dwelt in the dark places. He had no idea where Robin Rotmütze had actually sprung from. The creature seemed greatly amused by the name Redcap, taking it to himself almost like an epiphany of sorts – like he suddenly realised who he was. He looked less than thirty years, but his knowledge and power suggested otherwise, and were clearly not of this age. He terrified De Soulis.

"You look for answers in the full moon?"

De Soulis started. Turning quickly, he stepped back. "I heard not your approach."

Redcap smiled secretly, also looking up into the heavens. "That's a mischief-moon. For more time than you can possibly imagine, its effects have been interwoven with the fate of this world. Affecting everything from the tides of the oceans to the emotional rhythms of the creatures below her. But now she has a new secret, and it will bring chaos."

De Soulis did not understand. "What d'ye seek?" he asked, nervously. "Power?"

Redcap looked at the man before him, a giant of a man, but nevertheless his expression softened as though he spoke with a child. "I *have* power. Although, I was once just a man, like you. In ways, and for reasons, you would never understand, that existence was taken from me before I had the chance to fulfil my potential."

"So ye seek revenge?"

Power radiated from Redcap, driving the impression of heat haze. "Doesn't everyone?"

Chapter 12 | Dinosaurs!

"I want to go with you!" Woodsey continued to badger Dr Natalie Pearson all through breakfast.

Strict rationing had forced Sam Burton to centralise their food stocks within the galley and set up a temporary canteen. Some favoured this move, as it brought people together after their confinement to quarters. It also created a new lease of life and purpose for the Mud Hole – the Pod's bar and restaurant, partially reopened after structural damage sustained in the crash. Woodsey had spent many happy hours here with his friends, but it held no comfort this morning and he was glad to leave, having hardly touched his breakfast.

A little surprised, Natalie helped him finish it. From what she knew of the New Zealander, this could only mean that something was seriously bothering him; an impression borne out by the way he pursued her, all the way down to the animal pens. She sighed. "I understand, Woodsey, but I don't make the rules."

"It's my fault he got away."

She stopped, favouring him with a direct look. "How d'you work that out?"

"When that crazy dude attacked you, I let Mayor run straight past me. He's used to temperatures thirty degrees warmer than we have outside. We need to find him fast."

His expression was so earnest, and Natalie suddenly realised how much this meant to him. "We shall. The captain has given permission for me to ride out with Commander Gleeson's squad to look for him."

"Really?" His tone was doubtful. "I heard they were going after that crooked Pom politician and that crazy Nazi chick."

Her response was circumspect, "Well, perhaps. But *my* agenda is to find Mayor. Surely you believe me."

"I do, I just don't think he'll be a priority for those military guys. I need to get him back, Natalie."

"Why's he so important to you?"

Woodsey looked away, guiltily. "I know how much he meant to Tim. I let him down."

"Nonsense. I know Mayor meant a lot to him, but you didn't let anyone down. You tried to intervene when a man had a knife to my throat." She reached out to grasp his arm. "I'll always remember that."

"Yeah, well it's Reiver that deserves the credit there. All I did was lose Mayor."

She studied him for a moment. "Do you know how to ride a bike?"

"Yeah, 'course."

"And what about your father? What does Tom have to say about you going out?"

"I haven't told him yet. Look, Henry went after Rose into a world full of dinosaurs with virtually no help – what are we gonna find out there?" He gestured through the walls. "A few crotchety badgers?"

"There are wolves," Natalie pointed out. "In this part of the country they still roam wild, in packs. But that's not the biggest danger."

"So what is?"

"Same as everywhere else we've ever been – people!"

She turned to leave, but he held her arm. "Look, Natalie, please. I need to do this."

She kneaded her brow thoughtfully. "Alright, I'll ask the captain, you ask your dad. We'll let them decide, yeah?"

99.2 million years earlier, a harvest was taking place on the moon – a most unusual harvest. "The first shipment of barrels is aboard, ma'am," said One, now comfortably reunited with Two.

"This is good. And the quality?" asked Heidi.

The female whitecoat nodded confidently. "Looking hopeful. We will accelerate evaporation here, to create the small amount of uranium-235 required to seed the moon."

Heidi held up an index finger as she asked, "Ah yes, about that. What sort of vessel are you suggesting we use to contain the isotope? It will have to remain intact for a *very* long time."

One and Two looked at one another.

"*Well?*"

"We have a couple of ideas in that regard," the balding man took the lead. "Firstly, a simple steel box, or plastic for that matter, might block our signal – making it hard to track the item. Therefore, we firstly suggest burrowing our package into rock, placing it in its own cave, if you will. Hopefully, this will keep the radioactive object where we place it, protecting it from things moving about outside, without completely blocking it to our scans. We suggest leaving a few of these in various locations – you know, in case the moon is impacted by another foreign object, or something."

"That seems wise," Heidi allowed. "And your second option?"

He swallowed, looking to his counterpart for support.

Two rolled her eyes and began, "Our second suggestion is that we utilise the same medium we're hoping will avail us down on the planet below."

Heidi frowned. "*Bone?*"

"Indeed."

"But that would necessitate a trip back to Earth, unless you feel like donating one of your— *Ah...* I see."

"You have an objection?" asked the female lab coat.

Heidi shrugged. "Not if it works. You will need to check that Lieutenant Devon is finished with the corpse, as a courtesy. I believe he is still trying to identify the killer."

"Yes, ma'am," Two continued unemotionally. "We plan to leave some of Sergeant Haig exposed and some in a suit. You see, the vacuum suit should allow at least partial mummification – we're unsure which will have the best chance of standing the test of time.

Once again, a small cave will be found, or created, to house the body parts. You don't approve?"

"It seems costly."

The male scientist once again took the lead, "We understand that using that poor man's remains in this way is distasteful, but his life is already lost. We thought you would appreciate the saving in fuel. I mean, from tripping back to Earth—"

"I don't care about his corpse," snapped Heidi, cutting him off. "I'm talking about sacrificing one of our EVA suits. *They* are irreplaceable."

"We believe these measures will give the best chance for success," interrupted Two, impatiently. "The choice is yours."

Not for the first time did Heidi bridle at the female scientist's tone but, for now at least, she needed her. "Very well, Doctors. Make it so."

Bess could no longer feel her hands or feet. For several hours she had travelled, hog-tied, across the shoulders of De Soulis' giant charger. Judging by what little they could see of the sun, it was afternoon when they forded the river. From the air of expectation in the men around her, she assumed they were close to home.

De Soulis' main force had caught up with them by mid-morning. From what she could gather, Sir Nicholas and the new people had eluded them somehow. They also reported being driven off by the approach of a much larger force.

She knew so little of the families and the politics in the barbarous north. While perusing Cuthbert Tunstall's library within the Prince-Bishop's palace at Durham, her attentions had focused on the very few maps of the area and the specific interests around her destination – Chillingham Castle. Now, she was far to the west of there, on the opposite side of the Cheviot Hills. Although the border had little validity, nor even meaning to the people who lived there, she was now in Scotland – a young woman alone, in the clutches of a madman, in a country of enemies.

A wave of desperation threatened, but she fought it back. She must survive – for England.

If I survive these tribulations, I shall travel to London and throw sister dearest into the Thames! Be she living still.

It was painful, but by craning her neck, she could see ahead. What she saw made her heart sink even further. The earlier sun had vanished behind heavy snow clouds, cloaking the valley in an unnatural half-light; and nestled within it, alongside the river, known as Hermitage Water, was the towering monolith of Hermitage Castle[10].

Bess shut her eyes against the vision. Once those gates closed behind her, she felt certain she would never see the world again.

The *Heydrich* lifted in a far more controlled and stately fashion than on the previous occasion, almost a week ago. Heidi sat in the captain's chair and toggled one of the ship's belly-cams to view the lunar surface as it seemed to race away from them; aggregates becoming rocks, becoming craters, becoming a pockmarked landscape, becoming a sphere.

It had taken several days to harvest the material they needed, but she had been willing to allow it; they had time. It was not like the future was going anywhere.

They left behind what her scientists dispassionately described as isotope caches; five of them. These caches were actually the dismembered remains of Sergeant Denholm Haig.

Heidi reflected on her visit to the moon; it had been interesting, but now it was time to focus on the future. A future that, weirdly, would be full of dinosaurs. She leaned forward in her seat, eyes alight with anticipation. It was time to go on safari.

Lord Maxwell's camp was breaking up as he sent most of his men home. It had been a hard, cold night, but these men were used to that. They had lit campfires and borne it without complaint. By lunchtime,

---

[10] Not for nothing would this structure one day be described by a Scottish broadcaster as 'sod off in stone'.

the landscape bore only the imprints of their presence, along with a few gnawed bones left for the wildlife to pick over.

"Ah'll remain, with ma best scouts, James," he said. "Ye'll be needing guides."

Douglas took his hand and shook it. "Thank you, David. We have maps, but it'll be useful to know whose territory we're in."

Baines joined them. "Beckett says Sir William de Soulis is the master of Hermitage Castle."

"Hermitage?" asked Douglas.

Maxwell looked surprised. "Ye know it?"

"Aye, but only as a ruin. It's just a wee ride from the A7."

Maxwell frowned. Baines grinned. Douglas apologised.

"There will be a main road... look, never mind. Ah know where it is on the map, that's what counts."

"Without GPS that won't be so easy," Baines noted. "Our maps will be, in a weird way, out of date."

"Ma men will be able to guide ye," replied Maxwell confidently. "There's no' an inch o' the Middle Marches they dinnae ken."

"The Marches was a term used to describe the border between England and Scotland, or Wales," explained Baines, for Douglas' benefit.

He smiled wryly. "Ye do know who ye're talking to? Ah was born just up the road there, remember? If there was a road."

"Sorry, Captain. I was born on the moon – all this looks alike to me!"

Maxwell's jaw dropped.

"Erm, perhaps we should stay on topic," said Douglas. "We'll need to put together an expedition to rescue the lassie Elizabeth."

"I've been thinking about that, James." Baines had the light of mischief in her eyes now. "Remember when you were held aboard the *Last Word?*"

Douglas closed his eyes and groaned. "You know Hermitage is a national monument, right? At least tell me this plan of yours willnae involve Commander Gleeson."

Baines grinned.

Gleeson and his squad followed a pair of cycle tracks. Cocksedge's leap from the plateau had impressed the Australian. Viewing her drop in the morning light, he marvelled that an inexperienced rider had even survived it, let alone made their escape in full darkness.

Five miles west of the *New World*, the tracks stopped at a broad stream, bubbling through a narrow glen. It would be a beautiful spot in summer, no doubt, but black clouds gave the place a dark, ominous feel on this day.

"No tracks the other side, Commander," stated O'Brien. "They must have dismounted and carried the bikes a while, knowing we'd come after them."

Gleeson grinned, imagining the soft British Member of Parliament, carrying a loaded bike through a freezing stream in the hills. "Bet Cocksedge is having the time of her life."

Snowflakes had blown on the wind for the last couple of miles, becoming heavier the further west they travelled. The opposite side of the stream was already beginning to white over.

Gleeson spat, disgustedly. "Devil's luck."

Woodsey left his bike on its stand to step close to him. "Commander, we spotted Mayor's tracks back the way we came, can we look for him now? Doesn't look like we can go on."

Gleeson was clearly agitated by their failure to catch the prisoners.

"Commander?" Woodsey tried again.

"I'm just wondering what kind of trouble those two could cause out here, in this time," he replied eventually.

"But we can't follow tracks buried in snow, Commander. Whatever they *may* do, Mayor will *definitely* die if we don't find him. It will be a miracle if he survived last night... Please?"

Retracing their tracks proved more treacherous than the journey out. Despite the snow, the temperature had risen slightly, turning the frigid earthen trail to mud. After several slips and falls, and many oaths, they eventually came upon some very large, very distinctive, three-toed footprints.

"Are you sure this is the critter we're after?" asked Gleeson.

Corporal Jones and Natalie Pearson looked at one another. "What else could it be?" she asked.

"Dunno, mate. Ostrich? Dodo?"

Jones laughed. "There's no ostriches in Scotland, boy."

"Well, how am I supposed to know?" Gleeson bridled. "More than ninety-five percent of all birds were bred in batteries for food, in my time."

Natalie soured. "Yes, we've still got that to look forward to, haven't we? What a mess."

"Can we just go and find the dinosaur?" asked Woodsey, tetchily. "I'm no expert, but it seems clear to me that these tracks were not left by a pony, they were *not* left by a cow, they were *not* left by a badger! What are we waiting for?"

"He's right. Come on," agreed Natalie, setting off slowly, following the tracks.

They appeared to wind aimlessly for a while, crossing and recrossing themselves. After another mile they came across other, more numerous tracks.

"Cattle," said Natalie. "It looks like Mayor was following them."

"This fella's not a carnivore, is he?" asked Gleeson, cautiously.

Natalie shook her head, no. "He's probably looking for the best places to find food. He's also used to travelling in a large group. Perhaps he's looking for the only help he understands – the herd?"

The snow continued to grow heavier as they headed north. Another mile on, they came to a rise. Behind it, in the distance, was a plume of smoke.

"Fire," said O'Brien.

"A chimney?" offered Jones.

"Looks like," agreed Gleeson. "OK. When we get to the top, dismount and stay low. We don't want to freak out the locals, especially if there's a lot of them."

They left their bikes just below the brow of the hill and approached on foot. Down on his haunches, Gleeson pulled out his field glasses. "Just one house and a couple of barns. Must be a farm."

"Dangerous place for a farmstead," Natalie mused. "Seems like everybody's at war with everybody else in this place."

"Like Caernarfon town centre on payday Friday night, isn' it," muttered Jones.

Gleeson pointed. "I can see a woman. At least, I think it's a woman." He lifted his binoculars once more. "Hmm, not bad, bit rough."

"*Commander!*" snapped Natalie.

Before she could remonstrate further, they heard screams carried on the wind. The tiny figure in the distance burst out of one of the barns like the devil himself was on her tail.

The *New Worlders* looked at one another. "I think that's our cue," said Gleeson. "Let's ride!"

Following the cattle trail at breakneck speed down into the valley, they skidded to a halt in the yard before a relatively small, but massively over-built, stone farmhouse.

They arrived, just as three men ran out of the house brandishing spears. Both groups froze.

"How's the saying go? The more things change?" grumbled Jones.

Gleeson took a step forward. "Erm... G'day there. How's it hanging?"

North Africa was much closer to the equator in the middle of the Cretaceous Period, and the summer's heat quickly evaporated the comet ice, leaving yellow-brownish uranium powder. Heidi's scientists would use this 'yellow cake' in the first stage of the process to create their uranium-235/strontium-90 compound.

"Will this radioactive isotope kill the animals?" asked Jansen, overseeing preparations of the tracked vehicle and their orbital attack craft.

Heidi watched a man load a battery of small, heat-seeking rockets – one could not be too careful – and answered distractedly, "No, it's only a marker. We need them to live out their lives naturally. For our plan to work, we must preserve the timeline."

It had made good sense to land the *Heydrich* near Heinrich Schultz's crashed escape pod. It was a valuable item and worthy of salvage. It was also very near to a river delta where their quarry was numerous.

Hunting Spinosaurus aegyptiacus had to be one of the most dangerous endeavours imaginable. Heidi smiled.

"Ma'am?"

"Ben, this will be sport!"

A week had passed since the Rescue Pod had been dropped from the *Newfoundland*'s belly. The recently minted Commander Ally Coleman had foreseen her new position ending abruptly, along with her life, when Heidi heard about their 'butter fingers' incident.

The damage to the Pod's exterior appeared severe at first glance, when she inspected it with a couple of her engineers. It would certainly never be space-worthy again. However, aside from some noticeable distortion at the corner that hit the ground first, and accepting that it did not *need* to be space-worthy again, much of the damage was actually cosmetic. The structure had retained its rigidity albeit at the expense of some of its contents.

Despite some crumpling to the lower deck, the two upper decks remained largely intact and, most importantly, habitable.

Heidi had taken her pick for the crew of the *Heydrich*; forty or so individuals Coleman had been largely glad to let go – she certainly had a 'type'. Now Coleman was responsible for the *Newfoundland*, their crops and sixty-four of their least fanatical followers – including herself within that philosophy.

The first thing she needed to do was identify any spies Heidi had left among her people. There would be some, but she would need help in weeding them out.

As she considered this, someone called out in alarm from behind her, out in the crop fields. She turned but could not see what had caused the sudden commotion. Some of the crops were already as tall as a man, and despite the slight upward slope of the fields from the lake, she had no advantage from the beach. Calling her guards to her, the four of them ran towards the sound of voices, and what was clearly the bellowing of a large animal.

The sharp crack of rifle fire compelled an extra spurt out of them. Once through the taller crops, they pulled up sharply, taken aback by the bizarre altercation less than a hundred metres ahead. Half a dozen crop tenders were beating on the sides of a large animal with shovels and rakes.

Although easily the size of a rhinoceros, it was squatter and heavily armoured. There were no horns on its face, but two rows ran all along its back and down its tail. From what little she knew, Coleman guessed it was some kind of Ankylosaur. About five or six metres in length, the animal plodded through the barrage of shovels and shouts, hardly seeming to notice.

What *she* could hardly fail to notice, was that it was *inside* their perimeter fence, and scanning left, it was easy to see why.

Following in its tracks were another eight of them, all of varying sizes and all heading for Coleman's crops. Behind them, a tenth animal lay across their electric fence, probably dead either from the current or from the automatic rifle fire. Its bulk had smashed the fence down, allowing its brethren to stroll in.

"Come on!" shouted Coleman. Approaching on the run, they saw the crop handlers' guard and suddenly understood why the gunfire had stopped so abruptly. The man's chest had been virtually flattened, almost certainly by a giant footfall, and in all likelihood, by accident.

Coleman closed her eyes against the grisly sight. She pulled out her comm. "*Newfoundland*, this is Coleman. I need a ten-man, armed detachment, a box of halothane gas grenades, some strong rope and the *New World*'s personnel carrier sent to the southeast perimeter, asap. Oh, and bring us another one, two, three... *ten* gas masks – that's one-zero."

"*Right away, ma'am.*"

The dinosaurs were happily munching on their crops, while their winded antagonists leaned on shovels to get their breath back.

Coleman shook her head. Living here was not going to be easy, but killing every living thing they came into contact with was not the answer, nor the way. The Ankylosaurs had not acted from malice. She heaved a heavy sigh; they had lost another of their people. Their only solace was in the fact that they had all seen a world where most animals were extinct; this was better. There was no such thing as perfect.

Presently the large, ten-ton four-wheel-drive lorry appeared from the trail between the crops.

"Get masked up, everyone!" bawled Coleman, every inch the sergeant once more. "Come on, move it!"

The gas grenades upset the animals, making them sneeze and shake, like wet dogs. Eventually, they began to stagger and lie down.

Coleman stepped up to one of them, opening its eyelid. The eye was rolled up into its head.

"OK, get the ropes. We should be able to drag them two at a time with the truck. I want them all outside the perimeter fence before they wake up – *move!*"

She pulled out her comm once more. "*Newfoundland*, this is Coleman again. We need a medical team – one casualty. Also, get a crew out here to fix the perimeter fence, would you?"

"*At once, Commander.*"

"Thanks – Coleman out."

The unfortunate beast, still hanging across the wire, was like a silent, disconcerting memorial from the trenches. It was certainly dead, as was the poor soul lying before it. She turned her back on the spectacle. Watching the sleeping dinosaurs being towed away was much more preferable.

Her mind returned to planning their stay here. It was a beautiful world, but it could be cruel. Nevertheless, whatever Heidi and her band of fanatics decided, she had no wish to go back with them. This was indeed better. Besides, there was always the chance that unfortunate creature might taste like chicken?

"Who are ye?" demanded the oldest of the three men, his voice deep and accentuated with rolling Scottish 'r's.

"The name's Gleeson. And you are?"

"Ah'm a Johnstone, lad, that's a' ye'll need tae ken!"

This was clearly important, but for reasons that entirely escaped the Australian. "Look, mate, we heard the Sheila screaming and thought you might need some help." He held his hands out, palms up, unthreatening.

The 'Sheila' screamed again, "Father, there's a devil in tha barn – Lucifer himself!" She crossed herself in the manner of the old religion[11].

---

[11] Reformist or papist, a thousand years of Catholicism could not so easily be shoved aside. Throughout the religious changes of the period, there was much confusion among commoners and gentry alike as to where doctrine and ritual actually lay. In extreme cases, being out of step with the latest trend could leave people with more than burning cheeks.

Gleeson turned slightly, keeping a wary eye on the spearmen before him. "Jones, take two men and see what's in there."

"Yes, sir."

The soldiers pulled stun rifles from around their shoulders and jogged toward the nearest barn.

"We'll check this out for you, sir," Gleeson calmly assured the farmer and his family. He noted that the massive walls of the house had but tiny windows, and to the upper floor only. The doorway from which the men ran was narrow, the door itself of heavy oak. What was particularly strange, to the Australian's eye, was that there seemed to be no way into the upper storey, other than via a rope ladder hanging down the outer wall – which was clearly meant to be drawn up after use. Through the ground floor doorway there was just one room, as far as he could tell. It had fetid air, stinking of animals and smoke from a single torch. As he marvelled at the heavy timbers in the ceiling, one of the younger men took a step forward, levelling his spear.

With the newcomer's numbers reduced by Jones' departure for the barn, the youth must have seen an opportunity. Gleeson snapped his own rifle from around his shoulders, also levelling it in one fluid, practised movement. "Steady there, mate. Let's not ruin what could be the start of a beautiful friendship."

"Father?" asked the young man.

The older man placed a restraining hand on the younger. "Haud yer wheesht!" he snapped harshly.

Jones and his men slowed as they neared the barn. The girl had left one of the large doors ajar and the Welshman craned to see in. The interior was very dimly lit from vents high in the timber walls and by cracks between the rough planking. It took a moment for his eyes to adjust, and then a broad grin spread across his face.

He pulled the door open further, throwing what there was of the gloomy daylight inside. The barn was large. At least twenty head of cattle made it smelly too, but nestled within a haystack at the far corner, and fast asleep, was Mayor. "Commander, we've found him!"

"Shall we go and look together?" Gleeson asked the older man. "We mean you no harm, sir."

The farmer nodded and they all approached the barn. He entered, stopping in his tracks. "Whit in tha name o' *God?*" Unconsciously, he crossed himself, too.

"Don't worry, sport, he's with us."

The man levelled his spear once more. "Devil worshippers!"

The son raised his spear to hurl it at the Australian, but Jones was ready for it and fired. His stun-bolt hit the man in the back, and he collapsed forward. It was ungallant, but he had no choice but to shoot the other young man, too. Whether he was family or a farmhand, he was about to strike. The shot felled him immediately. The older man roared in fury, raising his own spear.

Jones stepped up from behind; Johnstone was a sinewy bear of a man, but nevertheless dwarfed by the Welsh corporal, who seized his wrist and plucked the weapon from his hand.

The girl screamed again as her family fell or were seized. Natalie stepped forward. "Don't be afraid – please."

Perhaps unsurprisingly, this did little to belay their fears, so she tried a different tack. "Your brothers, or friends – whatever they are – will be fine, they're only stunned. And the animal's not a devil, he's..." She faltered, looking to Gleeson for support.

"He's a large flightless bird from the New World," he finished for her, in a flash of inspiration.

"Well *done*, Commander," murmured Natalie, fully respecting the veiled dishonesty of this blatant truth. She knelt to take the pulse of the fallen men. "You see? They're fine."

Unslinging her rucksack from around her shoulders, she pulled out her first aid kit. Placing smelling salts under their noses brought them round quickly, if indignantly.

She helped them stand and held out a hand to the girl. "I'm Natalie. What's your name?"

She looked to her father, before dropping to a curtsy. "Aila, m'lady."

Natalie raised her to her feet. "No need for that, Aila. And just Natalie will do." She turned to face the girl's menfolk. "We really don't mean you any harm, gentlemen." She pointed to the dinosaur, who was stirring awake. "We call him Mayor. He's kind of a pet."

They frowned at her, doubtless trying to work through her strange dialect and syntax.

Turning back to Aila, she said, "Come. He's waking, let's say hello."

Woodsey followed as they approached Mayor. Natalie could see that he was shivering groggily and reached into her pack to draw out two small packages. She gave one to Aila. "For you. It will keep you warm these cold nights."

The girl took the strange gift, gingerly, not knowing what to make of it.

Natalie smiled at her. Taking the second package, she broke it open for the girl to see, unfolding a tightly wrapped silver blanket.

Mayor recognised her instantly and allowed himself to be wrapped up without fuss. "You'll be OK now, Mayor. You've also given Mummy some intriguing evidence about dinosaur physiology. If you were a straightforward ectotherm, you wouldn't have survived this long, you clever boy, you. I suppose the jury is still out on ectothermic homeothermy..."

Woodsey knelt by her side. "What does that mean?"

"An ectotherm relies on ambient temperatures to control their own – what we term cold-blooded, like the reptiles from our own time. Animals that maintain a steady body temperature through their own effort, despite being cold-blooded, are called ectothermic homeotherms. If that *is* how Mayor is plumbed, it's possible he could survive a while in this climate – as long as he kept moving. Of course, it's quite possible that some dinosaurs, possibly even Mayor himself, are – *were* – simply homeothermic, like you and me."

"That's warm-blooded, right?"

"Correct. He's plenty small enough, with a large enough surface area to body mass, to shed any excess heat his body generates – again, like you and me."

Woodsey grinned. "Whatever he is, he was clever enough to hang around with these guys and get a nice warm bed of hay for the night." He opened his coat to reveal a priceless artifact – a small bushel of Mid-Cretaceous fern. Cropped just a few days and 99.2 million years ago, it was still green and vibrant with life, and with the code of life.

Natalie could almost hear every palaeobotanist and every palaeobiologist who would ever be, screaming down the ages, but said nothing, as the young man delivered it tenderly into Mayor's mouth.

He nipped at the offering with his horny beak and crunched noisily, hungrily mincing the leaves and stems to pulp with his battery of grinding teeth. Eyes wide and greedy, he craned forward for more.

"Tim's gonna be well pleased to see you again, mate," the New Zealander murmured contentedly.

One of the cows came over to investigate, nudging Woodsey with her nose. He stumbled forward, regaining his feet with the dexterity of youth. "Hello, Mrs Moo." He petted her nose gently. "Thanks for all the milk!"

Natalie felt a slight stirring. She had long held a candle for The Sarge; ten years her senior, his no-nonsense honesty was as attractive as his courage. Woodsey was ten years her junior and shared very few characteristics with The Sarge, but for an innate kindness of spirit – also well hidden – and a tendency to say whatever was in the front of his mind. She was not sure either man was appropriate for her, but there was certainly something...

Perhaps she should stick to animals; she always seemed to know what *they* were thinking. Men were said to be simple creatures, but Natalie felt sure she had missed the memo explaining the details.

The farmgirl tucked Natalie's gift into her shawl, but remained a step back, watching everything with eyes wide.

"Come, Aila." Natalie smiled again. "He's quite friendly. He's just a little cold, not being used to our Bri— our *Scottish* climate. You can stroke his head."

Tentatively, Aila reached forward, her hand gently patting his snout as she would a horse. Mayor yawned widely, making her gasp, but then she giggled, smiling broadly.

Natalie chuckled too.

The girl's father approached. His spear may have been taken away, but he was far from disarmed by the scene before him. "How did tha' *thing* get in here?"

Aila shied away, but not quickly enough and the man's backhand knocked her to the mucky barn floor. "Ye left tha damned doors open again, ye glaikit mare!"

"Really, sir!" shouted Natalie, rising to her feet.

"Dinnae tell me howfur to govern ma own, lass, or ye'll cop tha back o' ma hand, tae!"

Natalie balled her fists, about to lunge at the man when Gleeson snatched her from the air, mid-flight. "Whoa there! Remember what Beckett told us before we left. Don't interfere. Come on, it's time we got Mayor back, before dark. We'll cut the blanket into a coat and strap it to him. You brought a leash?"

Natalie glowered at the farmer but allowed Gleeson to lead her away. "It was nice to meet you, Aila," she called over her shoulder.

Gleeson's team left much more slowly than they arrived, with Jones pushing Natalie's bike along with his own, while she led Mayor back up the rise, retracing their tracks. It would be a cold trudge home, but Natalie was thrilled to have found Mayor alive.

Woodsey, unnaturally subdued throughout the day, seemed to have brightened noticeably.

O'Brien rode ahead, taking a man with her to scout their path. These were dangerous and violent lands. It was not hard to see why the farmhouse behind them was so massively built in stone[12]. The family needed its protection, from both steel and fire.

Erika Schmidt watched them disappear over the rise with a satisfied smile. "What a happy coincidence." Lowering her stolen binoculars, she handed them to Allison Cocksedge.

"What is?"

"Simply that we have spent all day trying to lose our pursuit and find a place to hold out, and now we bump into them by accident only to watch them march away, leaving behind just what we need."

"If they've looked there, they probably won't be back, either," Cocksedge agreed, her teeth chattering against the cold.

"Precisely. I see three men and a girl."

"How shall we deal with the men? We don't have any weapons, other than knives and a few tools," Cocksedge dithered.

Schmidt smiled slyly. "They're men – I won't need weapons."

---

12 Heavily built and fortified stone farmhouses in the Scottish Borders were, and still are, known as bastles – thought to be from the French 'bastille'. During the reiving days, the family would pack their animals into the ground floor and bar the door, sometimes climbing to their living quarters through a hatch in the ceiling. Many surviving structures have stone staircases on the outside, built in more recent centuries to access the upper storey. However, back in 'the good old days' upper floors were accessed by ladders, that could be pulled up frantically behind, during times of attack. There the family would huddle within their massive stone walls, praying for the Reivers to go away.

Mid-Cretaceous Egypt

"*Run!*" shouted Heidi, putting action to words as she tucked her notepad back into her breast pocket. It was doubtful the giant even felt the prick of the steel dart; more likely, it seemed that all spinosaurids were simply *born* angry.

"Run where?" Jansen panted at her side. "We won't make the ship."

Her eyes narrowed as her more powerful bodyguard sprinted away at a pace she could not match. This was categorically *not* the time to be the one bringing up the rear. She redoubled her efforts. A human scream came from behind as she outpaced her remaining guard.

When you are right, you are right! she thought, not daring to even glance over her shoulder.

The thunder of fifteen tons on the move, right at their heels, abated. Hiding in a nearby copse, they looked back to see what had happened to their companion. He was five metres above the ground, clamped in the jaws of Spinosaurus. The animal shook him violently to break his neck, but Heidi felt certain that this was unnecessary. The man had already left this life.

Spinosaurus seemed to forget the chase and turned back towards the river, bloody prize in its jaws.

Jansen watched the beast in some consternation, while Heidi appraised her bodyguard. She had picked the strongest and the best to accompany her on the ground. A natural choice, perhaps, but one that had almost got her killed. She needed people who could handle themselves, of course, but perhaps a more mixed set of abilities would increase her chances of survival. Making sure she was never at the back of the herd seemed a good place to start.

She tapped Jansen on the shoulder. "Come. We must leave. There are many Spinosaurs in this region—"

ROAR! The stink of rancid meat almost felled them, as a huge crocodilian head reached between the trees; but this was no crocodile, it was another Spinosaurus, possibly even their last quarry's mate.

Heidi and Jansen fell to their haunches, ready to spring. Time slowed. Like something from a nursery rhyme, Heidi could not help contemplating the slyness of crocodiles – where the hell had it come from?

The tree creaked and then cracked, falling towards them. They dove right and left as the trunk crashed into its neighbour. The monstrous head pushed closer, the reek of death causing Heidi to gag. Jansen scrambled to his feet, backing off into the trees, and she could hardly blame him. What could a man do against the power ranged against them?

Kicking her feet and grappling wildly with her hands, she slid away from the monster, on her back. The Spinosaurus lunged, its shoulders jamming between two trunks. A roar of frustration burst from its lungs, spraying the young woman with spittle that stank like the gutters from an abattoir.

The trees groaned as the beast forced its wrath upon them, perhaps too stupid to go around, perhaps too enraged.

Heidi stared in horror, straight down the vast maw, as death smiled back at her. There was nothing for it, she would have to disobey her own directive, but then she *was* the boss. Buried within the mind-numbing stress of being responsible for everything and everyone's actions, there had to be a few perks, after all.

She broke the rules.

Rolling over her shoulder, she came to her feet, just as the tree to the dinosaur's left gave way and the predator surged forward, roaring triumphantly. Heidi launched the grenade down its gullet a splinter of a second before launching herself behind a large tree trunk.

She did not see what happened next, but she heard it. The explosion was muffled yet still loud at such proximity, and combined with a percussive thud. The crash that followed was unmistakable; the creature was down.

Risking a glimpse from behind her cover, she saw the animal sprawled, its midriff semi-suspended by broken trees, its head not two metres from where she stood. The tongue lolled, bloody, from the side of its mouth, clearly pierced by jagged teeth when the massive skull hit the ground. The eye sockets and nostrils were pits of gore, left by shrapnel exiting the head via its weak points, on a wave of explosive force. Further shredding had taken place in the neck and throat but astonishingly, the head seemed largely intact. The inner braincase probably resembled raspberry conserve. *Not even this remarkable creature could survive that*, she mused.

Heidi felt something touch her shoulder and jumped, in a manner most unbecoming for a Nazi dictatress. Once she realised it was only Jansen, she almost buckled with relief. Leaning forward, hands on knees, she waited for the world to stop spinning.

"I thought you wanted them alive?" Jansen asked, reasonably.

She glowered at him. "Give me the rifle!"

Loading another dart, laden with their uranium-strontium cocktail, she stepped around the deceased dinosaur's head and walked eight metres to draw level with the largest of the spines along its back, which gave Spinosaurus its name. "The strontium would normally carry the uranium-235 through the blood stream and into the bones. However, without a heartbeat, we shall have to improvise."

"Improvise, ma'am?"

Heidi nodded and fired the dart into the largest of the spines. "Indeed," she answered while reloading. "We know that Ernst Stromer found some of the larger spines in the deserts of Egypt." She fired again. "I don't want to miss an opportunity, especially one as costly as this. You will inform the dead man's friends of his fate – if he had any?"

"Yes, ma'am. Would it not be easier to simply kill these animals from the air and then shoot them up, as you just did?"

"No, Ben. That could upset the whole ecology of the continent, altering the future. Unfortunately, we must carry out this task the hard way." She handed the rifle back to him, once more taking the notepad and pencil from her breast pocket. Looking both ways along the vast creature's length, she turned back to face him, demonstratively licking the pencil's tip. "One Spinosaurus," she said, marking the page with a flourish.

Jansen struggled with feelings of inadequacy as he gazed upon the beautiful princess and the dragon she had slain, deliberating on which scared him the most.

Captain Aito Nassaki leaned against a bulkhead, studying the scientists as they busied themselves refitting the wormhole drive. It seemed that their illustrious leader no longer intended to take the entire ship forward in time, but to use its power to hold a much smaller wormhole open for a protracted period. He shook his head in awe and frank disbelief. She actually intended to step into a wormhole and travel, unprotected, almost a hundred million years into the future. Whatever else she was, Heidi did not want for courage.

Now it was for him to make sure he was in a position of power once she stepped through. Only then could he derail their efforts. As captain, taking command was his right. However, since their return from the moon, he had sensed a distance growing between Lieutenant Devon and himself. Did his first officer suspect his motives, or was it simpler than that? After all, Devon had run the ship during his convalescence; perhaps he was less than keen to hand power back?

Aito held rank, but the *Heydrich* was Devon's ship; most of its crew had been together since the beginning, under Captain Emilia Franke, and would likely cleave to him if push came to shove – especially with all the top brass out of the frame. Then there was the lingering unpleasantness about the murder of Sergeant Haig.

Aito sighed. He fervently believed that the boot of mankind had to be removed from the neck of the natural world. Yet he was just one man and it seemed that almost everything was against him... almost.

Sometimes it would be so easy to simply give up, but I mustn't. Wonder if I could cause an ecological disaster severe enough to change the future with this ship? Africa is the so-called 'cradle of life', after all? Or perhaps all I need to do is convince these people to just 'fade away'?

Still weak from his injuries, his musings began to overwhelm him. *Bide and wait*, he thought. *An opportunity is bound to present itself.*

The crewman passed a tray through the hatch in the bars, leaving it on the small ledge provided. Heinrich Schultz ignored the food, gazing directly at the man. "I would have something to read, fellow. I know my granddaughter has forbidden you to speak with me, so merely listen. I would have everything in the ship's library about world history from AD1918 to 1947. I assure you, my granddaughter will be glad of my 'brushing up', and I... I will be *grateful* to you."

The crewman kept his eyes lowered. He turned and left without acknowledgement.

Heinrich watched him go, a secret smile on his lips. Taking the tray, he sat at his small table and tucked in. It was rather good. He had not seen Heidi since their conversation several days ago, but his rations had certainly improved. Nor had he foreseen her plan to recapture the future, but it was brilliant, worthy of his family name. He approved. In fact, its audacity could place them in a position of control beyond anything he had originally hoped. Just one or two adjustments would be necessary, adjustments of which his dear granddaughter would certainly *not* approve.

It was time to start flexing his intellectual muscles; he had rested for long enough.

"I suggest we get reinforcements before we go back down to the river, ma'am."

Heidi could not argue with Jansen's assessment, although this time she would pick a little more carefully. She nodded. "Let's get back to the ship."

As they walked, Jansen asked a question that had been growing on his mind, "Dr Schultz, why are there so many large predators here? We've seen some huge sauropod herbivores in the distance, up on the plateau to the west, but most of the creatures here seem to be carnivorous."

"Yes, that was a riddle that plagued the palaeontologist, Ernst Stromer, for many years, according to the documentary evidence. It took a while before anyone realised that the vast Spinosaurs here were largely aquatic, bingeing on a vast array of giant fish found in the waters below us. It's easy to see why he was fooled for so long, as it is hard for us to imagine this vibrant green delta as the Egyptian desert. A hundred million years is a long time."

Jansen whistled. "You're right, Doctor, it's hard to take in. I could easily expect to find an Aztec pyramid amongst the jungle here, but Giza, never."

"We should hurry, Ben. That corpse we just made will draw all manner of creatures to feast."

"Yes, ma'am. Let's hope they don't eat the spines." Heidi was about to respond when Jansen touched her elbow. "Look, what are these other tracks?"

Giant, three-toed footprints crossed their path. Jansen was a head taller than his mistress and saw them first.

"Another Spinosaurus?" Heidi ventured, but as they drew closer it became clear these tracks belonged to something else.

"They don't show any marks of webbing between the toes, ma'am. The Spinosaurs leave tracks more like enormous waterfowl, if less splayed, perhaps. These look more like the tracks of the creatures I thought we'd left behind in South America."

Heidi smiled wryly at his description. "Enormous waterfowl?"

He grinned sheepishly. "I don't pretend to be an expert, ma'am. I know we'll be 'Donald Ducked' if whatever left these catches us, though!"

A roar in the distance quelled their humour instantly. It was just far enough away to forewarn them as to how much trouble they were in.

Heidi grabbed Jansen's arm. "I hate to repeat myself, but *run!*"

Aito made his way to the bridge, still mulling over the pros and cons of retaking command sooner, rather than later. On the one hand, if he waited, the crew would only become more used to 'Captain' Devon's command, weakening his position. However, if he waited to step in at a critical juncture, that might cement his position far more than simply demanding back the reins.

The key was the old man. If Schultz could be somehow muzzled, his way would be clear. He already had an idea in that regard, and if things played out the way he expected, the benefits to waiting might be twofold.

Stepping on to the bridge, he approached Devon, who had his back to him but turned as he drew near.

"Captain Nassaki," Devon acknowledged coolly, making no attempt to stand this time.

Aito opened his mouth to answer when the whole bridge appeared to shut down.

"What the hell?" demanded Devon.

"We've lost main power, sir," called out helm.

"This is exactly like what happened when Heinrich Schultz sent the kill code to the *Heydrich*." Aito spoke evenly, but he was genuinely surprised at how quickly the old man had made his move. "Captain Franke passed it to the fleet through the comm."

"She had no way of knowing what would happen," Devon replied, defensively. "She called the other ships to prevent the *New World* from escaping – she was following procedure."

"Indeed. She behaved exactly as the old man expected. I certainly don't remember Heidi being impressed by her actions, though. I *was* considering taking back command today, but suddenly I feel a little faint." Aito patted the temporary captain companionably on the shoulder. "Good luck, Mr Devon."

It was hardly a sprinter, but its vast stride allowed the animal to cover the ground between them at an alarming pace, nevertheless.

"Oh my God!" panted Jansen, as he ran.

"I told you not to look back!" snapped Heidi.

"That's the biggest meat-eater I've seen yet!"

"Save your breath and *run!*"

They scrambled up the side of a small bank, using its bushes and tufts of undergrowth to pull themselves while their legs pumped hard to drive them onwards. At the top, they stopped for breath. Their pursuit was close now. Unfortunately, as surely as they could see it, it could see them, thrown sharply against the skyline.

On a positive note, their vantage point also allowed them to see their ship. The small attack craft was nestled in the valley below, amongst a copse of large cycads. Heidi had flattened a space in the centre, hoping that the dense overgrowth would provide some protection from any large animals and a place to retreat to, should the need arise.

The need had arisen.

Unfortunately, although they could see their destination, the fluvial nature of their environment created rivers that came and went with the seasons. Their ship was parked on a small island surrounded by the cracked, sun-dried mud of what was, and would likely be again, a river. They stood atop another such island. Stalking around its base was a patriarch among truly giant, terrestrial killers, Carcharodontosaurus saharicus.

"Well, it seems that particular question may now be laid to rest."

Jansen could barely tear his eyes away from the huge creature less than fifteen metres below them. "Ma'am?" he asked.

"An early twenty-first century palaeontologist and biologist, named David Hone, theorised that the large theropods may have continued to grow throughout their lives. He postulated that some living examples could have achieved sizes exceeding those suggested by the limited fossil record. It seems he was right."

"Nice one, Dave!" spluttered Jansen, sourly. "Lucky us, for being at the forefront of scientific discovery!"

Heidi's lip quirked a wry smile.

"You seem to know a lot about these animals, ma'am."

"I have my cousin to thank for that, Ben. Tim was extraordinarily learned about them. He was exceptional..." She sighed, lightly. Her grandfather had vouched that there was no familial link between them; it had all been a ruse to set her on the path she now followed – making her a stronger leader.

However, she did not quite believe him. The boy was a genius, after all. He had also betrayed her, and just as she was learning to trust. Before departing for this mission, she had ordered a full search of the boy's quarters. With a little luck, there may survive some scraps of DNA, perhaps within his clothing. Heidi vowed to get to the truth of it, once and for all – if they made it back to the *Heydrich*.

"Do you think we can make it to the ship before that thing catches us?" Jansen broke into her thoughts.

Heidi considered for a moment. If they ran, she knew she would be the slower, and the most likely caught. If she sent him on alone, to see if it were indeed possible, he would probably be killed. She would sacrifice him if necessary, but that course would only leave her alone and in the same predicament. She answered slowly, "I don't believe we can."

"Don't suppose you have any more of those grenades?"

She shook her head, no.

"Ma'am, with respect, I believe you should rethink our policy of hunting the biggest carnivorous beasts ever with only a dart gun they rarely even feel."

"I do not want my people going around killing the animals I need to inject," she replied harshly. "However, you may have a point."

"Perhaps we should leave a pilot with the ship, next time?" he suggested. "In case we need a quick evac?"

"If there *is* a next time. No. We cannot trust anyone with our lives in that way, Ben. My grandfather's influence is still strong and there may be other elements among the crew, too."

He gave her a sideways look. "You're talking about the murder on the moon."

Before she could answer, a roar of frustration burst from the dinosaur's throat, scattering their thoughts.

"Perhaps we should focus on one problem at a time," Heidi brought them back.

"Oh, I don't really think that's possible," replied Jansen distractedly.

Heidi turned to see what had snagged his attention. She sighed, deeply this time. "Oh, no."

Mid-Cretaceous Britain

"We've cleaned the tanks thoroughly and given the pumps a full service, Commander. As soon as we've laid the pipe, we'll be able to draw water direct from the lake and filter it, in-house, as it were."

"Excellent, Crewman," replied Coleman. "Progress at last."

After the incident with the Ankylosaurs smashing their way into their crop fields, and the death of one of the guards, morale had suffered. One of her science staff had theorised that the animals penetrated the circle of mountains surrounding Crater Lake by following the riverbed, largely dried up now summer was fully upon them. The creatures may have been unintentionally destructive, but seemed otherwise peaceful and very dull-witted. However, Coleman could not help wondering what else might follow the herbivores' tracks. Would this happen often? Would it be a yearly event? They had much to learn about their environment.

Her thoughts were interrupted by a comm call. "Coleman."

"*Commander, Lieutenant McBride. I've recalled the field workers, ma'am. My apologies, but it was an emergency.*"

"That's OK, McBride. Go with your judgement. What's happened?"

"Difficult to describe, ma'am. Have you ever heard of an ancient movie called 'The Birds'? I think you need to see this, Commander."

Coleman stepped out of the Rescue Pod's pedestrian hatch into the waiting personnel carrier, stolen from the *New World*. "We'll need its protection, ma'am," said one of her sergeants, giving her a hand up.

"What are we looking for, Sarge?"

"You'll see soon enough, ma'am." They walked from the rear hatch through to the vehicle's cab. The sergeant took the wheel and drove them away from the Pod between fields of tall crops. After a few hundred metres, they reached the crossroads at the centre of their operation. He executed a three-point turn, allowing Coleman to look back at the *Newfoundland*.

"Oh, *my...*" she murmured.

"I believe they're called Ornithocheirus, Commander." He shrugged, admitting, "At least, that's what I was told."

Reaching along the entire spine of the vast ship, like a row of crows, perched more than a hundred giant pterosaurs. Absolutely motionless, some were as large as giraffes, and *all* stared down huge, wicked-looking beaks, heron-like, right back at them.

"You know what, Sarge?"

"Ma'am?"

"I don't think I'll sleep tonight."

Mid-Cretaceous Egypt

"Ah, Captain Nassaki! How *are* you now?" Heinrich Schultz greeted, warmly. "Did you hear about our recent murder? On the moon, no less. How remarkable."

Aito returned his smile in the gloom of emergency lighting, while studying the old man intently. "I'm mending, sir, thank you. Unfortunately, I know very little about the situation on the moon."

Heinrich smiled blandly.

"But do I take it this is your handiwork?" Aito gestured generally at the darkness around them.

"Modesty forbids me, Captain."

Aito snorted gently. "I see you have your tablet, sir?"

Heinrich turned, noting the device on his small table as if seeing it for the first time. "Oh, that. Just a little light reading."

"Indeed, sir. So where does this leave us?"

"I assume, Captain, that as you are here, my granddaughter is off hunting dinosaurs – yes?"

"I believe so, sir."

"I would be very grateful if you would recall her, please."

Aito pretended to consider the request. "And what should we tell her?"

Heinrich noticed the 'we'. "Not too keen on facing my granddaughter's wrath alone, eh?"

"Let's just say that doing so is not usually conducive to a long career, sir."

Heinrich chuckled lightly. "Tell her it's about my suite, here." He looked about the stark, gunmetal walls, taking in the spartan furniture and the seatless loo. "I wish to discuss an upgrade."

Circumnavigating their small island, the huge Carcharodontosaurus now stood directly between Heidi, Jansen, and their ship. The creature had no idea that it stood sentinel, dead-middle of their escape vector; it was simply circling them, looking for an advantage. Far too massive to scale the steeply riven sides of the outcrop, carved by yearly floodwaters, it did not need to, for its tiny prey were about to be flushed out.

From the south they came, on the run, and they moved quickly.

Jansen turned to Heidi with a 'this is it' finality to his gaze. "What are they?"

"Not sure, but let us not panic." She searched her memory of Tim's notes for the area. "The tiny vestigial forelimbs suggest an abelisaurid, I believe. My cousin would know, but I think maybe... *Rugops?*"

"With them to the south and that monster cutting us off from the ship, north, perhaps it's time to panic *now?*"

Heidi shook her head. "I think it's worse than that, Ben."

The Rugops approached in a pack of eight. At little more than a twentieth of the Carcharodontosaur's mass, these smaller theropod dinosaurs were still as tall as a man at the hip, and maybe five metres or so in length.

"They're meant to be scavengers," Heidi continued her commentary as if in a dream, "but that won't stop them attacking anything that appears weak."

A flash of memory struck her – an altercation in the main hangar of the *New World*, where she accused Douglas of being weak, came home to roost.

"Like us, you mean?" Jansen filled in the subtext. "So why do you think things are worse than being surrounded by these, these *gorgons?*"

"Because they are small enough to... ah." There was no need for her to continue. The scavengers had their scent, there could be no doubt, as they began to climb towards them.

Jansen nodded. "You were right, ma'am. *This* is the time for panic."

A relative of South America's Ekrixinatosaurus, their forelimbs were also virtually useless, but their strongly muscled hind legs powered and clawed their way up the embankment. Animals without use of their 'arms' grew naturally adept and dexterous with their mouths. Theirs was a strange gait of bite, scramble, bite. The watching humans were almost transfixed as the pack grabbed tree limbs and heavy underbrush with their mouths. Once anchored, they caught up with their hind legs to leap forward again – every spring bringing them closer to the tasty morsels up on the ridge.

They must have been waiting for the Carcharodontosaurus to go away, thought Heidi, mesmerised. "They've been stalking us. Only the stench of the larger animals kept them at bay, until now," she spoke her thoughts aloud.

"*What?*" snapped Jansen, the edge of terror in his voice. They were close now; no matter how awkward their perambulation, they would soon be on them.

Heidi grabbed his arm. "Be ready! We have but one chance, and even that is—"

"Please – no need to finish that thought. What do we do?"

"When they reach the top, we throw ourselves down the other side as quickly as possible, using the brush to slow our descent. Once at the bottom, run towards the large dinosaur."

He looked at her as though his long-held suspicions about her sanity had finally come to a middle. "Run *at* it?"

"Sort of."

"*Sort of?*"

"You break left and I will break right," Heidi explained. "Timing will be everything."

"That's it? That's your plan? A fifty-fifty deal?"

"Not if we're lucky. If we're lucky, those stupid reptiles will follow us down and run into the waiting *teeth* of that monster!"

"Oh, my God." Jansen put a hand to his brow, feeling his chest tighten with fear.

"Be ready!" she hissed. "One, two, three, *GO!*"

Heidi threw him down the bank and gambolled after. Behind them, the snarling, grunting, expectant Rugops roared in fury to find their quarry gone, and after such labour. Three of them crashed down the slope straight after the fleeing humans, smashing their way through the foliage in a frenzied attempt to catch them before they reached the bottom.

Heidi and Jansen arrived first, barely. Not stopping to check behind, they set off on their agreed tangents, right under the gaze of the Carcharodontosaurus. The giant stamped massive, clawed feet and swished its tail, bobbing its head in excitement. It had the aura of a spectator at a big game, beside itself with anticipation.

The three Rugops tumbled out of the greenery onto the parched riverbed and rolled to their feet, shaking dust from themselves. So lost were they in the hunt, in the moment, that they set off immediately after the man and woman. Two followed Heidi. The wiliest of the three set off after Jansen, and hopefully, a meal-for-one. One at a time, they realised their peril and faltered.

The rest of their pack, behind in the ascent, reached the crest of the embankment to find everyone gone. Instinctually, they stole the moment and gathered their senses to re-evaluate. A pack of eight Rugops was no small danger for a lone Carcharodontosaurus, even one so huge, but that was by no means a guarantee. Even a win was no good to you if you were dead, and the five, leering from atop their ridge, calculated the probabilities with intuitive cunning – and decided to leave it.

This effectively hung their more impatient packmates out to dry, a fact they had now fully awakened to.

The three smaller predators, already split into two, circled cautiously. They followed in the tracks of the escaping humans, but their attentions were all on the titan in their midst.

Carcharodontosaurus lunged and snapped for Jansen as he ran past. He dove and rolled to leap back to his feet, not bothering to look behind. Lowering his head, he ran. The giant dinosaur took a step to follow him, but its immense weight had broken through the crust of dried mud to the soft bed beneath and its feet moved clumsily, encased in muck. It roared in fury as the titbit had it away on his toes.

Jansen's Rugops also saw an opportunity and sprinted after the man directly, so directly, that it passed under the head of the Carcharodontosaurus. The vast skull dropped like a wrecking ball – if wrecking balls gaped mouths full of daggers. The hapless Rugops was not quick enough, and the jaws closed around its spine, crushing ribs and puncturing lungs. It screamed once, but after being lifted bodily from the ground and shaken, it fell silent immediately.

The Carcharodontosaurus was clearly enjoying its afternoon's entertainment now – soon to be followed by a feast. In high spirits, it spun clockwise through 180 degrees and flung the 750-kilogram corpse at the other pair of Rugops.

The giant's spinning tail narrowly missed Heidi, whose small size and agility allowed her to duck underneath while it tripped her pursuit. The first Rugops landed on its chin, breaking its comparatively weak jaw. The flying body smashed into the second, knocking it to the ground, winded.

Roaring in triumph, the huge predator stepped heavily towards the stricken animals, massive clods of mud flying from its taloned claws. It walked as though its feet were too big for it, but any humour was lost on Heidi and Jansen, who ran, too terrified for their lives to look round. However, when the first foot came down on the winded animal's chest, smashing bones and organs almost flat, the surviving animal cried in terror. It scrambled with its hindlegs, churning up muck as it tried to regain its feet.

The Carcharodontosaur's other foot landed between the two prone animals and it simply leaned forward to snap at the pathetically mewing Rugops, almost severing the head from the body.

Carcharodontosaurus raised its head, bloody maw dripping nameless fluids to drench the parched earth. Jaws parted in victory, its roar made Heidi and Jansen cover their ears.

The watchers from the ridge looked on stoically, before turning away to descend the opposite embankment.

Heidi was already on the island where their ship was parked. She called out for the hatch to open and threw herself inside. Jansen, his the less direct route, landed beside her an instant later.

"Close!" he shouted at the door.

They sat side by side on the deck for a moment, chests heaving. Regaining her breath, Heidi began to laugh – they had survived.

Jansen vomited.

"You can clean that up!" she snapped, unhelpfully clipping him around the ear.

"You look exhausted, *Enkelin*," Heinrich welcomed her, smoothly. "I thought you would have come to me sooner."

"*Großvater*," she greeted warily. "How do you know how long I have been back? Main power is still down."

He smiled unconvincingly. "Is it?"

"I had Tim Norris' quarters and belongings searched, *Großvater*."

"Oh? How did that work out for you?"

Heidi grated her teeth against his *bonhomie*. "There was a little DNA found in his clothes. You told me he was not my cousin, your grandson."

"And...?"

"The results were apparently conclusive. Although we are obviously the same species, there is no familial link between us."

Heinrich's smile broadened. "Excellent, *Enkelin*. So now perhaps we can continue with the job in hand. I have decided to accept your kind offer of reconciliation, but with just a couple of small addenda – I hardly like to call them amendments."

"Such as?"

"Such as, I want the best quarters aboard this ship. The second is so obvious, I hardly like to even mention it, really."

Heidi glowered. "Go on."

The old man relaxed into his solitary seat, crossing his legs comfortably. "I will be in charge from now on, until, well... one of us is dead, I suppose."

AD1558 Scottish Borders

"Welcome back, Commander," Douglas greeted Gleeson's team cheerfully. He reached down to stroke Mayor's muzzle. "Hello, boy. Ah see you were at least partially successful?"

Gleeson nodded. He looked exhausted; his whole party did.

"You look all-in, Commander. Why don't you get cleaned up and take some rest? We can debrief then."

Gleeson nodded again. "Thanks, Captain, but food first. I could eat the backside out of a dead rhino!"

Tim Norris stepped into Dr Flannigan's office with the weight of the world on his shoulders. Flannigan looked up from his desk and greeted the young man warmly, offering a seat. "Your mother is doing very well, Tim. She'll be out of here in a day or two – as long as she promises to take it easy!" He smiled disarmingly.

"That's great news, Doctor, thank you."

Flannigan could see that the news had been well received, yet Tim remained taut with anxiety.

And well he should, he thought sadly, but did not let it show on his face. "You'll also be wanting to know about the 'other matter', huh?"

Tim nodded stiffly.

"We searched Heidi's quarters. Now, you must bear in mind that they had already been cleaned and six other people are sharing them at the moment, yeah?"

"I understand, Doctor. Was there any sign of her?"

Flannigan's jaw muscles bunched. "We found something, but this is not conclusive, OK? We found one long blonde hair."

"And the people sharing the quarters at the moment are...?" Tim led.

"Of darker colouration or short haired," Flannigan admitted.

"So there's a good chance it belonged to Heidi." Tim's was a statement rather than a question.

"It's possible, but as she scrubbed her DNA from our files, we can't be sure."

"I understand, Doctor. What did your tests reveal? Is she my cousin? Am I a Schultz?"

Flannigan chewed his lip. Bad news was part of a doctor's life – the worst part. "I cannot prove that definitively. However, the hair that we found contained DNA which shares a close link with your own."

"A familial link?" Tim had to be sure.

"Yes, son. I'm sorry."

Tim left Flannigan's office and dragged his feet across the ward in a dream. Opening the hatch, he stepped out into the Pod's main hangar and walked, he did not know where.

Halfway across the hangar, he heard a shout. "Hey, Tim! Look who I found!"

Turning slowly, still in a daze, Tim saw Woodsey bearing down on him, and with him on a leash of all things, was Mayor.

Tim buckled to his knees and threw his arms around the bewildered animal's neck. Mayor looked to Woodsey for guidance, almost dog-like, but for once Woodsey had no words.

Eventually, Tim got back to his feet and grabbed Woodsey in a bear hug. "Thank you," he said, tears running down his cheeks as he sobbed soulfully.

"Hey, steady on, mate," replied Woodsey, hopelessly patting his friend's back.

Chapter 13 | Turkeys and Christmas

Another time...
Family is my enemy,
An enemy within me,
Who am I?
Whoever those who need me need me to be,
One at a time,
My soul draws debts like carcass to crows,
My past is lost, today is for sorrows,
So who am I?
A man from the past who hopes for tomorrow.
Sleep now...

...excerpt from the private diary of Tim Norris.

"We can track them now, Dr Schultz," said the white coat designated 'Two'. "Your teams have done a remarkable job. In just two weeks they, and yourself, have tagged more than a hundred and fifty Spinosaurs."

Heidi acknowledged the woman's praise coolly. "And what does your data tell us?"

"That you have introduced the isotope into two-thirds of the local population – when I say local, I mean over the northern continental deltas, an area of nearly half a million square miles."

Heidi raised an eyebrow in surprise. "So few? Over such a vast area?"

"Yes, Doctor. There are many other predators here competing with our quarry. And of course, the Spinosaurs keep mainly to the rivers, not venturing far on land. Despite their size, when out of water, it appears they're outcompeted by some of the other large carnivores, better suited to terrestrial living.

"Within their main environment, they're also in direct competition with the many species of crocodile indigenous to this region. Some of them are huge, too. The ecosystem can only support so many large predators. Were it not for the apparent abundance of giant fish, there would be fewer still."

"Interesting," Heidi replied slowly, absorbing the information. "And what have you learned about the habits and movements of individual animals?"

"Well... the Spinosaurs don't seem to travel far – at least they haven't during the short window of our study. It seems the constant flow of the river provides for all their needs, bringing everything to *them*. Despite an innate ability to scrounge – as with any carnivore – they otherwise seem rather specialist in their hunting practices, following the shoals within their local river systems. They leave the rivers now and then, to sun themselves or when an easy picking offers itself along the banks, but otherwise prefer the water."

Heidi frowned, recalling how many times she had almost become just such an 'easy picking'. "Very well. As my teams' efforts approach saturation, there exists the obvious risk of pursuing the same animal twice – and when I say risk, I do not choose my words lightly! I need you to create an application for our comms that can track the isotope. We have lost four people during the hunt already – it would be unfortunate to lose more merely to cover old ground."

Cut from the same cloth, Two displayed no emotion towards Heidi's blasé attitude regarding the loss of her men. "Of course, Doctor. We have already begun programming a search algorithm for installation on our orbital attack vessel's sensors. The computer will flag, but otherwise ignore, animals with the isotope. However, it will use its whole suite of sensors to locate *new* animals. The infrared scan should also prove useful to locate any submerged specimens."

Heidi nodded sagely. "Yes, these creatures can be sly, cunning even. How long will all this take?"

"Forty-eight hours, Doctor."

"Very well. Don't let me keep you."

As the female scientist left, Lieutenant Devon held the door as it began to close. "May I speak with you, ma'am?"

Heidi invited her temporary captain to enter. "Devon. Is this about Captain Nassaki taking back his command tomorrow?"

"Yes and no, ma'am. He was about to take command yesterday – that was before *dein Großvater* shut down our power core—"

"And he suddenly remembered he was too ill to take command after all? Especially as I was due back any time?"

Devon squirmed a little. "Perhaps, ma'am."

"How *flexible* that man can be when his own survival is at stake."

"Yes, ma'am."

"Still, you seem to have lived through the incident, Devon. Indeed, I have found you..." she paused, leaving him hanging a moment, "competent, over the last few weeks."

The military way does not require 'thank yous', however, his surprise was evident as he answered with a simple, "Yes, ma'am."

"Was there anything else you wished to tell me about Captain Nassaki?" She leaned forward on her desk, staring intently at the young man before her as she fished.

"Yes, ma'am. It has to do with the murder of Sergeant Haig."

"Go on."

"I've traced the movements of everyone who came into contact with Haig's equipment. Unfortunately, none of them have an obvious motive for killing him. So I went back further. Haig was captured with Captain Nassaki aboard the *New World*, and I wonder if he knew or heard something he shouldn't."

"You believe Nassaki is intriguing against us?"

"I was hoping you could tell me that, ma'am."

Heidi sat up straight, a smile twisting her lip. "A bold question, Devon. Why do you suspect I have the answer?"

"Because Nassaki spoke with the Old— *dein Großvater* right before you did, ma'am. The video footage was missing for both conversations, of course, but I know they took place."

"And you think I should tell you what passed between us?" she asked, the twinkle of amusement still present in her eyes.

"If Captain Nassaki is a threat to this ship, then yes, ma'am."

She gave him a calculating stare. "Captain Nassaki reported an overheard conversation between his brother, Hiro, and Sergeant Haig aboard the *New World*. He suspected Haig of planning to use this ship to create a major ecological disaster that, while not endangering all life on this planet, would certainly present it with a new set of challenges. Challenges that could ultimately lead to a different future."

"So Nassaki murdered Haig on your orders, ma'am?"

She sat back again, relaxing. "I honestly don't know. Perhaps *mein Großvater* has the answer, but I doubt he will share. You still suspect Nassaki?"

"Yes, ma'am. His record for joining dangerous and subversive political groups speaks for itself. Maybe it was Haig who 'overheard' the conversation?"

Heidi sat in thought for a moment. "I will endorse Captain Nassaki's reinstatement to duty later today. However, I am not deaf to your suspicions. I need *mein Großvater's* knowledge on the journey I am soon to take, so I hereby give you secret orders. Listen carefully."

Tim woke refreshed. The brutal truth may not have set him free, but neither was its weight paralysing him any more. He understood that what he was, did not change the man he had to be. He would stand, so that others might stand behind him. He was Tim Norris – he hoped his friends would feel the same way.

Since the army at their door had dispersed, people had resumed their freedoms about the Pod, structural damage notwithstanding. To that end, Tim made his way to the Mud Hole and to an arranged meeting with the others.

He stepped through the doors feeling no small trepidation. The Schultzes, his kin, had effectively upended all their lives and put everyone in mortal danger. This was going to be a load, and he really did not know how his friends would take it.

Clarrie had organised things, explaining that he had an announcement to make. They were clearly intrigued. Despite being early, Tim was the last to arrive.

"Hello, everyone," he began, taking a seat next to Clarrie.

"Hey, Tim," greeted Henry.

Rose smiled.

Clarrie squeezed his hand.

Woodsey grunted. By the look of him, the others must have got him out of bed.

They all had steaming mugs of coffee before them. Tim turned to order a drink just as one arrived for him.

"Didn't think I'd forgotten you, did you?" asked Clarrie.

Tim smiled, taking a sip of extremely hot cat-pee-tea. He grimaced. "Now we're back in England, I wonder if we could—"

"Too early," Woodsey cut him off. "Won't be a decent brew here for another hundred years. I checked."

Tim sighed. "Oh. It's just that this stuff is like the tea they serve in those expensive coffee boutiques – not fit to paint a fence with."

"What's wrong with the coffee, dude?" asked Henry.

"It tastes like dirt!"

Rose laughed. "Come on, Tim. Never mind the beverages, what did you want to tell us? Is it about your time as a prisoner – among the *enemy?*"

Tim took another slug of his tea, held his nose, and swallowed; he needed the caffeine. "Sort of," he wheezed. "There's something I have to tell you. I'd rather this stayed between us. I've no idea how everyone else will react, but I need you to know."

He lapsed into silence once more.

Rose leaned across their usual table, a happy survivor of the crash, and took his hand. "It's OK, Tim, you can tell us..."

Baines frowned. "*You?*"

Lord Maxwell chuckled. "Dinnae worry yesel', Captain. My nephew Billy, here, kens those lands as well as any man."

"We herd tha Johnstone's cattle through there – every noo and then," the young man elucidated.

Baines' frown deepened. "When you say 'herd', I assume you mean steal?"

Billy Maxwell grinned. "We take back what's ours."

She looked to his uncle. "Does anyone actually milk or eat these cows? Or do you all just move them around?"

Maxwell laughed. "At least 'tis only beasts, lass. Ah dinnae allow the taking o' people any more."

"You mean slaves?"

"Aye. Ye could call them that."

"Well, at least that's something."

"Aye. They're more trouble than they're worth."

"Hmm." Baines' distaste showed in her face, but Maxwell's smile deepened, his eyes twinkling secretively.

"Ye dinnae approve of our ways, Captain."

"It's not for me to approve or disapprove," Baines sniffed, superciliously. "All that matters is that your boy can lead us there without attracting too much attention."

Billy bristled at the word 'boy', but his uncle stayed him with a hand on the shoulder. "We're ready to leave, Captain."

Baines nodded, gesturing for the two men to follow her out of the Pod and up to an armoured personnel carrier waiting on the plateau. Overnight snow had softened the landscape. She squinted while her eyes adjusted to the rolling sea of white.

Captain Douglas stood next to the vehicle, chatting with Captain Tobias Meritus, Commander Gleeson and The Sarge. Also standing with them, outlandish beside the officers and their 22nd century transport, was Sir Nicholas Throckmorton. Corporal Jennifer O'Brien and Private Adam Prentice loaded supplies through the vehicle's rear hatch from the large spreading bucket of one of the diggers. Bluey jumped down from the cab to help them, while their superiors stood around talking in the interests of maintaining the stereotype.

Douglas turned to greet them. "Jill, David, Billy, good morning. As a paid-up member of Historic Scotland, Ah was just explaining to Commander Gleeson about the importance of Hermitage Castle, about the uniqueness of its construction."

Baines smiled for the first time. "I promise we'll be careful. Might need to break the door down, though."

Douglas sighed. "Our effect on the timeline is to be – and Ah choose my words carefully – 'low impact', Jill. If Ah find a pile of rubble where our national monument used to stand, so help me, you and Gleeson will be put in charge of rebuilding from photographs!"

Her eyes lit up. "So, we'll get to decide where we put the hot tub, the en suites, things like that?"

"Hey," piped up Gleeson, "and we could reuse the dungeon for the heating and air conditioning plant, you know? Get it tanked. Or maybe turn it into a bar? And what about a pool table? 'Course the spiral stair would have to go—"

"Enough!" Douglas cut them off. "As it is will be just fine, thank you."

Still smirking, Baines held up her hands to placate him. "Don't worry, James. The natives will be no match for our men. We'll just blow the doors and rescue the princess – what could go wrong?"

"Just make sure there are no Douglases inside," Douglas pleaded, wearily.

"Why?"

"Because Ah dinnae wish to vanish from existence in the middle of ma dinner. That's why!"

"Actually, now you come to mention it, the south-west tower is... erm."

Douglas eyed her keenly. "*Jill?*"

"Oh, nothing, James." Baines replied innocently. "Don't worry, we'll..." She trailed off as she spotted Beck Mawar, running towards them.

The spiritualist medium pulled up in front of Baines, panting. "Captain, you mustn't go."

"It's OK, Beck. We'll all be back tomorrow. How did you know we were leaving?"

"Mario told me."

Baines and Douglas exchanged a glance.

Beck inhaled deeply to stabilise her breathing. "He told me you're going on a rescue mission, but *you* must not go, Captain."

"Why?" Baines asked simply.

"It's too dangerous."

"Beck, thank you, really, but there's no need to worry. I'm going in a tank – what could go wrong?"

Douglas winced. "Ah wish ye'd stop saying that!"

Baines placed a comforting hand on his arm and the other on Beck's. "We have to do this. It's really important."

"I know," Beck replied immediately. "I'm just saying that *you* shouldn't go."

Baines attempted a smile, but frustration began to gnaw at her. "It'll be fine, Beck. Thank you. I'll see you tomorrow, OK?"

Beck looked to Douglas, who also seemed uncomfortable with what was happening, but it was clear that Baines would not be dissuaded. "Keep my stone with you, Jill. Please."

Baines patted her chest where the stone hung on a leather string about her neck. "I have it right here."

Gleeson called from the back of the vehicle, interrupting them, "Hey, Captain Baines. Thanks to Lord Maxwell's generosity, they're having roast beef here tonight. Meanwhile, we're on survival rations, so can we get on with it?"

"That's my call. Mind the shop, James." She took his hand in her own. "Back soon."

Douglas' eyes were full of concern. "Be careful, Jill."

She tossed a casual salute. "You know me."

Five teens sat alone in the Mud Hole, wrapped up in a deafening silence. Woodsey placed his forgotten coffee back on the table, absently. "Are you sure you're Heidi's first cousin? I mean, she's... you know," he mimed the German blonde's voluptuousness, "and you're, erm..."

Clarrie glowered at him. "Woodsey, stop digging before you fall in!"

"I'm just saying..."

"Look, the point is," Rose interrupted, "that Tim has evidence, but not conclusive proof. It might not be true at all."

"I believe it is," Tim admitted, quietly. "Heinrich is the sort of man who wants a male heir. I think he would have killed me otherwise."

"Bet that Nazi chick went crazy when he offered her place to you, eh?" asked Woodsey.

"Something like that. She started a mini civil war." Tim shook his head wryly, remembering her fury with the old man.

Woodsey held up his hand as if in class. "Question: are you gonna go psycho on us as well?"

"Don't be stupid!" snapped Rose. "Tim is our friend. We all know everything he did for us. More than that, we know Tim's mum, too. He was brought up by the Norrises – good people – there's no way he'll become like... like *them!*"

"Woodsey's right," said Tim. "I *am* of their blood – who knows what I'm capable of?"

"Rubbish!" Rose slapped her hand down on the table. "Henry, tell him!"

"Rose is right, dude. Not only were you brought up by Patricia and Ted Norris, but we also know that your real parents ran away from the Schultz regime – hated it! They wouldn't have done that unless they were different, right? So the way I see it, whether it's environmental or genetic, you got it covered!"

"That's a really good point, Tim," Clarrie added quietly. "You're a good man."

"But how do we know what was done to that good man?" Woodsey butted in. "He was in their hands a long time. Sorry, mate, but you haven't been the same since you got back, have you? I mean, what if they did something to you?"

"Woodsey!" hissed Rose.

"No. Once again, Woodsey is right," replied Tim. "Which in itself is weird. Every now and then, amongst all the blather, he occasionally spouts something perceptive – insightful even. I know my experience changed me, I'm just not sure how, yet."

"So what do you need?" asked Rose.

Tim bit his lip; he had no answer.

"He probably needs us to give him a little time to work it out for himself," said Woodsey. "Look, I don't believe he's gonna go running around setting off bombs. I just think he needs some time-out, to remember who he is." He looked at Tim directly. "What you need, mate, is some fun!"

"What sort of fun?" Tim asked, hesitantly.

Woodsey grinned.

"We have a proverb," said Lord Maxwell, darkly. "It's like turkey cocks voting for Christmas[13]."

"We have a similar saying," replied Baines. "What are you referring to?"

"Us helping the future Queen of England escape a Scottish castle, so she can send her army and navy north tae 'free' us!" The bitterness in his voice was clear.

"What is this story?" asked Sir Nicholas, instantly alarmed. He was seated opposite Lord Maxwell, although they had spoken not a word to one another.

Baines laid a hand lightly on Maxwell's arm, making him start. He was clearly not used to such familiarity. Taking in both of them, she explained, "I understand your concerns, gentlemen. But trust us, please. We believe that our coming here has changed things – don't ask me how – but we need to try and put it right. We won't let you down."

Maxwell nodded, but Baines could tell he was not fully convinced. "Getting rid o' De Soulis is no' a bad thing, anyway," he admitted grudgingly.

Baines was shaking her head. "We can't kill him. We don't know what effect that might have."

Maxwell stared at her in disbelief. "Yer going tae try *talking* tae him? And say what? Let the lass go?"

"But your weapons art most powerful," Sir Nicholas added, hotly. "And you have promised to save the princess."

"I'm sure De Soulis'll understand, if we just say please," Gleeson chipped in.

"Not helping, Commander," Baines reprimanded. "Look, De Soulis will be dealt with, but not by us."

Maxwell gave her a sideways look but let the matter drop.

"If you should choose not to help, then I must go on alone," Sir Nicholas vouched stoically.

Baines turned to look at him squarely. "We will help. I promise."

---

[13] Turkey became popular for Christmas dinner during the 16th century. It is believed that Henry VIII was the first monarch to enjoy it as such. The verb 'vote' originates from roughly the same time. How turkeys used government pencils to leave their mark is not recorded – perhaps due to problems using pencils. Once the votes were in, they tended to be plucked either way.

After more than two hours of being thrown around in the back of the tracked troop transporter, several of the passengers were a little green around the gills. O'Brien chose the best routes she could through the rough landscape, but it would be centuries before proper roads would crisscross the Cheviots. They kept to the ridges where possible, on a south-westerly bearing. A thin blanket of snow covered the tracks of man and animal alike, making it difficult to judge the terrain. Were it not for Billy Maxwell, their progress would have been slower still, or possibly halted altogether by a hidden bog or brook.

Twenty-five miles and several sick-breaks later, they trundled to a halt before a stream.

"This is tha North Tyne," stated Billy. "We're no' far from the source, so this is a good place tae cross."

"How much farther to our destination?" asked O'Brien.

"Another five miles – maybe six. Due east."

She nodded, pushing the control levers forward. The machine splashed into the stream, crunching pebbles under its tracks. Gnawing deep grooves into the opposite bank, it climbed out the other side, steam pluming from the exhaust system. Although they were leaving the Cheviot range behind, the terrain continued to follow a succession of hills and valleys. Billy guided them skilfully between the boggiest areas, despite the worsening of the weather. They were just coming up on noon, yet the sky was black with snow; the sun, nowhere to be seen.

The ridge they followed ran west-south-west. A steep-sided valley, riven with streams gouged from the hillside, made a more direct route impossible.

Gleeson leaned forward in his seat to see over the driver's shoulder. "I hope you're taking notes, Jen? Our tracks are gonna be under a foot of snow an hour or two from now."

"Don't worry, Commander. We may not have satnav, but the computer's recording our route. The APC could drive us back on its own."

"I don't like the sound of that!"

O'Brien smiled. "Relax, sir. If we have to get out to check our route, nothing's going to eat us here. It's a dinosaur-free zone!"

"What's this 'dinosaur'?" asked Billy.

"A big, ugly, angry lizard," supplied Gleeson. "Erm... that lives in the New World."

"Ye've been tae the Americas?"

"Once or twice," he replied sardonically. "Of course, I'm from Aus—"

"Somewhere else," Baines completed, cutting him off. "How close are we to the castle, Billy?"

"About another three miles. We'll cross the Liddel Watter[14] soon. We're lucky the autumn's been dry 'til noo, or we'd be away in white watter."

"There are no bridges?" asked Gleeson.

"No' many. And they'll be guarded by De Soulis' men. Ah doubt they'd carry this steel beast anyway."

"Found it," called O'Brien. "Looks a little deep here. We'll need to find a shallow crossing. Do we go upstream or down?"

Billy reached out to point south-west. "There's a shale beach nae more than a furlong downstream."

"A furlong?"

"An eighth of a mile," said Baines. "It's an old measurement, but it began to be used in conjunction with horse racing around this time."

"I'm surprised you didn't know that, Jen," quipped Gleeson.

She turned and gave a wry smile. "What can I tell ya? Where I grew up, there weren't too many kids with ponies!"

Presently, they came to an oxbow in the river, where the bed broadened to about fifteen metres. Most of it was a dry shale bank, ramped against the eastern shore.

"It looks like the river cuts deep at the other bank," O'Brien stated with concern.

"We swim our ponies through here when 'tis deep enough," said Billy. "See the track leading up the opposite bank?"

"We cut across diagonally?"

"What does that mean?"

"*Not* perpendicular," offered Gleeson, grinning.

Billy frowned. "Perpendicular? Like the designs o' Kelso Abbey?"

---

[14] Liddel *Water*. In the Scottish Borders and Northumberland, water is often pronounced as watter, or in some cases witter – depending which side of the border you straddle, or even if you happen to be in the uplands or lowlands.

"Eh?" asked the Australian, baffled and boomeranged by his own wit.

"Just cross the damned river!" Baines ordered, witheringly.

"Yes, ma'am." O'Brien engaged the drive once more and they crunched across the pebbles to the water's edge. "We have a snorkel, but if we start to float, we may be in trouble."

"Don't these crates let the water in to stop that?" asked Gleeson.

"No," Meritus spoke for the first time. "They're proof against gas attack – airtight. We're on recycled air unless someone opens a hatch."

"Good to know," muttered Gleeson. "I suppose it's for the best. That river's gonna be freezing. Think heavy thoughts, everyone!"

It was hard to discern day from night. The prison tower within Hermitage Castle was the grimmest place Bess had ever been, but her first floor apartment was not the worst of it. She had a tiny window, out of which she could see a heavy black sky. She also had access to a latrine. The poor souls in 'the hole' below her were considerably less fortunate. Not since she was forced into the Tower of London via Traitor's Gate, some four and a half years earlier, had she felt so utterly lost. At least she had the company of her servant, Kat Ashley, then. Now she was alone, in a foreign state, and locked within surroundings far less agreeable.

From her cell she could hear the cries and screams of children below. She shuddered. This monster, De Soulis, was truly without God. The guards were filthy creatures. Were she not protected by their master's orders... No, she could not bear contemplate their actions. Her imagination ran wild with the horrors of this place.

From what she could tell, the children were selected from the local populace to become part of De Soulis' twisted rituals. She heard the guards laughing about bleeding them. Also in the hole with them was a man. Bess may not have seen him, but she certainly heard his screams when guards took him from the hole and tortured him, only to throw him back again. As far as she could understand their speech, he was accused of inciting a peasants' rebellion against De Soulis. Despite her natural aristocratic aversion to such risings, in this case she did not doubt they had good reason. The prisoner was a brave man. After hours of agony, he had finally fallen silent, without giving up the names they were after.

The sergeant subsequently ordered that he be pressed, and this morning – if this was morning – Bess heard a low moaning coming from an adjacent room, where the torturers seemed to have their fun.

She shuddered again, a nervous reaction beyond her control. *Dear God, please help that poor man*, she prayed.

She knew what being pressed entailed. The man would be laid with his back upon a sharp stone. A board would be placed on his stomach and chest while the guards questioned him, all the while adding weights on top of the board. Eventually, if he refused to speak, his spine would break, but he would know so much pain before that happened.

Bess sobbed silently into her hands. *How can I ever escape this place? How can we allow such evil to exist in our land?*

The sounds of bolts being withdrawn forced Bess to her feet, backing against the far wall of her small cell.

The heavy, ironbound oak door creaked open slowly, to reveal the rat-faced man who had first bound her upon her capture. He smiled nastily. "*My lady*. My lord would speak with ye noo, *if* ye'd be so kind?" He gestured for her to leave the cell, bowing in indolent mockery of civility.

Having no choice, she straightened, attended to her hair and dress, and strode from her cell into the passage, without acknowledging her vile jailer.

Mid-Cretaceous Egypt

"We thought it would be wise for the wormhole created, to remain outside the ship," said Two, sheltered from a blazing equatorial sun by the *Heydrich*'s prow. She and Heidi stood surrounded by armed guards, all sweltering in their combat gear, as the female scientist continued, "You will be aware that the ship creates a wormhole ahead of itself, and slips into it. The wormhole would normally exist for just a few seconds, however, after many simulations, we believe that by attenuating the wormhole, we can keep it open much longer."

"How long?" asked Heidi.

"At the moment, we believe it's possible to hold it open for an hour – maybe an hour and change."

Heidi nodded. "Very well. That would give us a brief window to look around and report back. Although we will need to work on extending that time if we are successful. Begin building your stockade around this point. When we do go, and return, I would rather not step out in front of a dinosaur!"

"Yes, Doctor. I have men felling trees as we speak."

"Good. Then my teams will round up our final catch. I shall return in two days. I expect you to be ready."

Beck Mawar came upon Mother Sarah and Dr Satnam Patel in the corridor outside the Pod's main kitchens.

"Either way, we will have to wait until the spring, Sarah," said Patel, anxiously. "But I just don't see how we can last that long without help. Ironically, our crops are probably thriving back in the Cretaceous."

"I understand that, Satnam. I was thinking more about hydroponics. It was something Jill was talking about last night, and we still have vast seed stocks, don't we?"

"Yes, but look around you, Sarah. The Pod and the ship have been smashed to pieces. We're lucky even to be alive—"

"Ahem. I'm sorry to interrupt," said Beck, guiltily wondering whether anyone ever meant those words.

"What is it, Beck?" asked Sarah, looking a little harassed.

"Sorry, Satnam, but I need to speak with Sarah, urgently."

"I should get on, anyway," stated Patel. Before he left, he added, "Look, Sarah. I agree with you, it is just... well, let me have a word with Jim Miller's people – see what we can come up with. How would that be?"

Sarah smiled. "Thank you, Satnam. I know you'll come up with something."

Patel nodded to both women and strode away, clearly disgruntled.

"Short of food, are we?" asked Beck.

"Not yet, but soon. Now what did you need to see me about that was so urgent, huh?"

"Captain Baines."

"Ah."

"I know you don't believe me, Sarah, but she really is in danger."

"They're all in danger, honey. The mission to save that poor girl, well... it makes you wonder what we've all gotten ourselves into. And that William de Soulis sounds a real sweetheart!"

"He's not the problem."

"Oh, it's going to be one of *those* conversations, is it?"

"Sarah, I don't say this lightly. We brought something back with us into this world. Something evil."

"From what I've heard about this place, Beck, it'll just be a face in the crowd!"

"Please take this seriously."

"Beck, honey, I told you. I don't know *how* to perform an exorcism – and have no intention to learn. I'm not even sure I believe in such things."

Beck fell silent, suddenly thoughtful.

"What?" prompted Sarah.

"Perhaps that's the answer."

"What is?"

"Look, Sarah, there must be dozens, even hundreds, of priests in this region alone, despite the religious changes. *They* will definitely believe."

Sarah leaned back, staring at the younger woman in disbelief. "You can't be serious?"

"There must be dozens of churches around here, too. Surely we can find a priest willing to—"

"Willing to *what?* Huh?"

"I understand that the rite of exorcism requires two priests?"

Sarah held her head in her hands. "You know what? I'm worried about feeding our people right now, I just can't—"

Beck took Mother Sarah by the hands, forestalling her. "What if I could prove it to you?"

A black object, conjoining lethal lines with cutting angles, flew along the North African shoreline where it met the Tethys Ocean – the fastest body ever to move through Mid-Cretaceous skies. Unnatural and deadly, the roar left in its wake rumbled across the landscape like a skyquake, trying and failing to keep pace.

Beneath its shadow, a confluence of rivers and streams flowed endlessly, drawn ever onwards by the meagrest of slopes in the low-lying topography. The air, shredded by the ship's passing, triggered an adrenaline response in every vertebrate creature below. Huge crocodilians tossed and rolled, seeking sanctuary under the waters. Small enclaves of land divided the streams into homes for myriad birds, mammals and reptiles, all fleeing for their lives and often to their deaths, in the snap-happy confusion.

Slowing, the craft came in to hover, its pilot searching for a place to land where there was little land to be had. A sluggish river, heavy with silt en route to the sea, passed languidly underneath them. A steep-sided island stood out prominently, further upstream.

"I think we have something, Doctor."

Flying low, they followed the river, closing quickly. A preliminary circle revealed how the flow, forced around the island's sides, had cut deeply over millennia, creating a heavy stone jut at its point. The solid overhang projected out at least four or five metres, at approximately twelve metres above the water.

The rocky island sloped downwards from the jut's point, to no more than two metres above the current waterline at its trailing edge.

The little ship landed near the jut, and Heidi's small crew stepped out, blinking, into what was for them, a baking hell of humidity and flies. For Spinosaurus aegyptiacus, it was home.

"Knowing the size of our quarry, I doubt the security of this position," she noted with concern.

"It's the best perch in the area, ma'am," replied the pilot.

"Our new sensor algorithm has flagged three contacts within two hundred metres of our current location," said Jansen. "Tool up, everyone, and stay sharp."

He called Heidi aside, out of earshot of their men. "So what now? Wait here all day, 'til we spot a sail?"

She frowned for a moment, then her expression cleared, and she smiled. "Perhaps you would like to turn around, Mr Glass-is-half-empty?"

He followed her gaze, and jumped, in spite of himself. Gliding along with the current, snout under the water, was the huge, many-spined sail of a dinosaur. The only other signs above the waterline were a pair of nostrils, near the top of its head, and the occasional flick of an exceptionally long, muscular tail.

"Crap!" blurted Jansen. "Get your... fire your... *shoot it!*"

Scrabbling for his own rifle, he fumbled for a dart loaded with their unique isotope, and fed it into the breach. He dove to his belly, crawling to the rocky edge of their promontory. Sniper fashion, he took aim at the impressive sail along the creature's back and fired.

Unlike the South American Oxalaias' reds and flame-oranges, the skin stretched over Spinosaurus' sail had a greyish green base, overlaid with wicked-looking stripes picked out in reds, yellows, oranges and purples. Jansen could not see below the waterline as the river was a slow and filthy, completely opaque brown, but as far as he could tell from glimpses, the colouration continued down onto the animal's body.

Heidi drew a small pair of electronically enhanced field glasses from a pocket and saw Jansen's dart connect with the trunk of the largest spine along the beast's back.

"Got it, Doctor."

"I would hope so. It must be more than fifteen metres long."

"Yes, ma'am. You know, if we served one of those this Christmas, it would feed our entire contingent."

"With enough for sandwiches on Boxing Day," she agreed.

The giant head of the Spinosaurus broke the surface at that point, letting out a roar of pain that dissembled into a rumble of indignation.

"I believe it felt that, eventually," Heidi noted, wryly. "Or was that your belly complaining?"

Jansen shrugged. "I might be a little peckish."

"There's another one!" A shout came from the other side of their ship.

The crown of the island was no more than forty metres across, maybe twice that in length, and bore numerous rocky outcrops surrounding their landing site. Heidi and Jansen ran and scrambled towards the call. Sure enough, another large sail was cruising the river on the opposite side of their island.

A small puff of propellant gas from the rifle's muzzle was all that gave away the steel-tipped dart as it flew towards its target. "Got it!"

Heidi rolled her eyes. "How fortunate I am to be surrounded by such eagle-eyed sharpshooters. What will be your next trick-shot? A barn door?"

Her ire was cut short by a roar from the northern and lowest point of their little island. She exchanged a brief look with Jansen, and they turned slowly.

"They don't usually notice the dart," he said.

"Hmm. I suspect you caught yours in a sensitive spot. If I am not mistaken, that is the sound of many tons of bad temper and teeth, climbing onto our island."

"What are your orders, ma'am?"

"We must not let it damage the ship." She turned to include the other three personnel, two men and a woman. "Lead it. Keep away from this end of the island at all costs."

"Then what, ma'am?" asked the woman.

"Hide!"

"Our backside's floating!" called Gleeson. "We're drifting and coming about."

O'Brien called over her shoulder as she fought with the controls, "I know. The engines are in the front of these to allow greater access at the back."

"That's great information and I'm sure we're all the better for it," he retorted. "What do we do now, break out the oars?"

"Come *on!*" snarled O'Brien, unconsciously throwing her weight forward to encourage the tracks to bite on the bank. She gave it full throttle. Sacrificing torque for speed would have cost her traction on land, but as their connection with land was tenuous at best, she decided to use the steel ribbed tracks like the buckets on the wheel of a paddle steamer. Although the rear of the vehicle was drifting and slowly spinning them around, the trick worked and edged them closer to the bank. Once the tracks dug in, with the weight of the engine and armoured nose of the vehicle providing downforce, it was like laying their own road. The wheels turned within the tracks and they wound their way up the steep embankment on the other side. The APC burst over the top with such force that its nose was airborne for a second before it crashed down, rocking on its suspension. The bank was cleared of snow and turf by the violence of the manoeuvre, their tracks shovelling muck into the air and throwing it behind them, back into the river.

"Woo-hooo!" cried Gleeson. "Are we having fun yet, or what!"

"Yeah!" called O'Brien, turning briefly to give him a high-five.

Lord Maxwell and Sir Nicholas dug their fingers into the arms of their seats, staring at one another in horrified incredulity.

"Let's do it again!" shouted Billy.

"Let's not!" snapped Baines sourly. "I suggest we find another place to cross on the way back, Corporal. Now, resume our heading."

"Yes, Captain."

The next couple of miles passed without incident and presently O'Brien drew up alongside the bank of another river. "Billy? Where are we?"

"This is Hermitage Watter."

"*Hermitage* Water?" Baines checked she had heard correctly.

"Aye, we're close noo," added Maxwell.

"OK," she said, reaching a decision. "It's possible we're about to go into a combat situation, so we'll stop here for thirty minutes and take a light meal. Oh, and by the way, if you need to *go*, now's the time!"

Gleeson clapped his hands. "Right, you heard the lady, open the rear hatch and let's stretch our legs for a few. Don't suppose anyone brought a shovel?"

Thirty minutes later, Maxwell joined Baines back aboard the APC. "Are we about tae receive that wee demonstration ye promised, Captain?"

Baines shot him a questioning look.

"The demonstration o' why yer friendship is going tae be so valuable tae the Maxwells?"

Understanding crossed Baines' face. "I fear you may, David. I can't see this being easy, but I hope we can make it as bloodless as possible. Either way, I'm sure folks will get the message."

"Aye? And what message will that be?"

Baines snorted with a half-smile. "You've yet to spend much time with Commander Gleeson. Believe me, the word will soon spread that we are not to be messed with – and neither are our *friends*."

A sly smile of understanding spread across Maxwell's face as a cry came from outside.

"Everyone back aboard!" yelled The Sarge.

"Captain, a word?" asked Gleeson.

Baines stepped out of the vehicle as everyone else piled in. She waited until they were alone. "What is it, Commander?"

"You know, somebody's gonna notice we're here, sooner or later," said Gleeson, staring balefully at the deeply riven tank tracks, cutting through the snow to the muddy grass beneath.

Baines chewed her lip thoughtfully. "Hmm. Can't help that. We've done well to get this far. Maybe our luck will hold – perhaps it'll snow again."

"Yeah, I don't like it but can't think of an easier way to hide them. After you, Captain."

Leaving behind their tracks, many footprints, an accidentally-dropped biodegradable food wrapper and several patches of strangely yellowish snow, they set off once more.

"Just follow this bank o' the river. It'll take us right tae it," advised Billy. "Less than a mile, noo."

As good as his word, they soon saw the huge, blocky presence of Hermitage Castle in the distance.

It did indeed begin to snow again, ruining visibility.

"Well at least they won't see us 'til we're virtually on them," Baines remarked, heaving a sigh. "Would've been good to get a better idea of what we face though."

"What about our diesel engine?" asked Meritus. "They'll still hear us, even if they don't know what on earth we are."

"I don't know, Captain," countered O'Brien. "The wind's coming pretty fierce. I'd bet it's howling round those stone parapets now. We're driving into it, too, so the engine noise should be carried away from them – for now at least."

Gleeson sat in the front passenger seat, calling up an image from the vehicle's cameras. The blizzard distorted his view and zooming in did little to help. He switched to infrared. "Yep, I can tell you with absolute confidence that there's a giant grey block of something about half a mile in front of us."

"That's good to know," replied Baines, lightly. "Any other insights?"

"Yeah, it seems that the front door is in the shape of an arch."

"So?"

He turned to face her. "How tall are these people?"

Baines' brows beetled slightly, as she wondered what he was getting at. "Oh, yeah," her expression cleared as she answered, "Don't worry, they're not giants. No monsters in this picture, Commander, just men."

Gleeson raised an eyebrow. "I hope you're right, Captain, but in my defence, I stood next to a creature that would've had to *duck* under that arch – just a few days ago, as it happens. So forgive me for being a little edgy."

Baines chuckled. "Fair enough. Beckett showed me a picture of this place, even had a ground floor plan. Apparently, those arches aren't the doorway."

"No?"

"No. They're flying arches that carried a timber fighting platform across the narrow spaces between the towers. Apparently, the platform wrapped all the way around the top of the castle."

"Fascinating – a *fighting* platform, you say?"

"It's OK, Commander. They were a late medieval addition. I don't think they'll be there any more."

"Oh well, that's alright then. So, no timber fighting platform. Just one small question, Captain – hardly like to mention it, really."

"Go on," prompted Baines.

"As we're now," he snorted softly, "in a more 'advanced' time. What are they likely to be using instead?"

"Erm... yeah. OK. It's likely to be, erm..."

"Sorry, Captain, didn't quite catch that?" He cupped his ear sarcastically.

She sighed. "Yes, it will almost certainly be a stone battlement around the top by this time. At least that's what Beckett believed."

"No defence cuts up here then?" he asked, raising an eyebrow.

"Huh, you've seen this place," she retorted. "These people don't seem big on liberalism – at least, the living ones aren't."

He gave her a look. "Right. So, what was all that *talk* about *not* blowing this place to hell, then? Yeah, I'm pretty sure I remember a conversation along those lines with Captain Douglas, just this morning, as it happens."

Baines chewed her lip uncomfortably. "Yes, so do I."

"So," continued Gleeson, relentlessly, "we're back to asking this guy to give up the girl, then, yeah? Still, I suppose there's always plan 'B'."

"What's plan 'B'?"

"Saying please."

"OW!" shouted Tim as a snowball exploded against his chin. "What the hell was that for?"

Woodsey laughed maniacally while preparing a second missile. "I know you haven't had snow in Britain since the twenty-fifties, and there wasn't a lot of it in Cretaceous World, so I thought I'd introduce you to the noble art of snowball fighting, dude!"

"I don't like it," Tim mewed pathetically, ice dripping down his chest under his coat and shirt. "You promised me some fun— Ouch!"

"If you don't defend yourself, you're gonna have a really bad day, mate!"

"Ow! Stop it!"

Woodsey continued to laugh as he poured on the assault. "When we're done, I'll show you how to build a snowma— Aargh!"

A snowball, launched with vicious accuracy by a giggling Rose, hit Woodsey squarely between the eyes. "Yay! I love this! Come on, Henry, join in!"

Henry's face was battered from both Rose and Woodsey before he even realised what was going on. Stumbling, he fell onto his back. In strict adherence with the arts of war, his attackers used his prone position to their advantage and hammered him with snow. Clarrie rolled one to the size of a football, waiting for Henry to sit up. That was when she dropped it on his head from behind.

"Aargh!" he screamed as ice ran down the back of his neck. *"Clarrie! Right! You guys are gonna get it!"*

Tim raised a wet collar, his face screwed up in misery. Perhaps it was a little piece of Schultz that glinted in his eye, but as Woodsey turned to seek out a new victim, Tim's expression took on the squint of vengeance. Rolling a snowball, he used the heat of his hands to melt and compact it as he ran towards his friend's back. Approaching from the rear, he battered the solid ice ball off Woodsey's freezing cold thigh.

The New Zealander squealed at the sudden burning sting and instant dead leg, following it up with a squawk of indignation about underhanded tactics.

"Says you!" Tim retorted. "You attacked without warning."

"It was pre-emptive, dude – ouch!"

Rose slammed him again, enjoying her victim's inability to defend himself. "Come on, Tim," she called. "England versus New Zealand!"

As Rose and Tim ganged up on the hapless Woodsey, Henry and Clarrie struck up with "U-S-A! U-S-A!"

"Look what you've done now!" shouted Tim, laughing breathlessly as he divided his attentions with this new enemy.

"Hey! Stop picking on the little guy!" cried Woodsey as he tried to get up, slipping once more onto his backside.

Rose was laughing so hard she almost fell, too, but turning her slip into an opportunity, she scooped a doublehand of snow and forced it down the back of Woodsey's neck.

As the New Zealander screamed, Tim threw a snowball, rather ungallantly, at the back of Rose's head.

"Ow!" she bellowed, straightening her bobble hat. "You're on *my* side!"

"I know, but why wouldn't you?" Tim laughed.

"That's treachery! Treason!"

"Don't worry. It's just allegorical. We're still on the same side."

"What?"

"If we ever get back, I'm going to lobby for snowball fighting to replace politics. The results will be the same, but this is loads more fun to watch!"

"That makes no sense."

"And?" Tim did not get the chance to further elaborate, as Woodsey's reprisal from the ground hit him on the nose, filling his mouth with snow. It was hardly a white paper, but it did end all debate.

The free-for-all that followed was not pretty, but all parties seemed to thoroughly enjoy themselves, nonetheless. Right up to the point where another half a dozen freezing missiles flew into the bundle from outside.

"What's going on?" shouted Henry, on his knees and desperately trying to cover his face.

That was when the barking began. The new players were Natalie, supported by five of the six sentries guarding the plateau, and of course, Reiver.

"Stand back-to-back," Tim called out.

"Who put you in charg— *Ow!*" Woodsey's complaint was truncated by an iceball on the nose, making him rethink. "GET THEM!"

It is often said that there are few rules in love and war, but as it turned out there were none at all in a snowball fight, and the conflict soon became confused and dirty, with the inevitable drift towards girls versus boys.

Reiver, not content with an umpire's role, was the only one not struggling to keep his feet. However, he soon proved extremely adept at taking the other protagonists off theirs – especially when their missiles were launched Natalie's way.

"Aaah! That's cheating, dude! Get off me!" Woodsey shouted and squirmed as Reiver leapt, pinning him to the ground. He licked the New Zealander's face mercilessly, the cone of shame about his neck scratching the young man's freezing cheeks. "Your breath stinks, boy! Have you been licking your—" Before he could finish, his mouth was cleaned out by a snowball from Natalie.

Reiver sneezed, shaking his head to clear the slushy shrapnel. Victim down, he seized the opportunity to lunge at another man, trying to beat a hasty retreat from a combined attack by Natalie and Clarrie.

Whilst trying ineffectually to wash his face with snow, Woodsey saw the man go down. Drenched, freezing and miserable, he wondered whether he should have kept this particular pastime to himself. *Maybe I should have just gone with the snowman?*

Tim sat on the snow where he had slipped, laughing still, snowmelt from wet hair running down his face and neck to obscure his tears.

"He's sunning himself! Can you believe it?" hissed Jansen in exasperation. He slid back down behind the rocks where they were hiding. "What do we do now?"

Heidi craned around the side to take a look. Lounging comfortably in the fierce afternoon sunshine, the vast Spinosaurus yawned lazily. "Can we make our way around the edges of the island?"

"What? Past Smaug, over there? You know, I plum forgot my ring of invisibility, did you bring yours?"

Heidi frowned. "Sarcasm does not become you, Ben. Besides, he, or she, seems to be dozing now."

"After the last time we were cut off from our ship, you agreed to find a pilot we could trust. Now I suggest we use him. If he starts the engines, maybe they'll scare that thing away."

"*Maybe* – that's the problem. Our ship is still on the ground. What if the pilot startles the beast, causing it to lash out and smash it to pieces? Do you fancy our chances, trying to live on this island until we are rescued? *If* we are rescued – we cannot fully trust *mein Großvater.*"

Jansen's eyebrows rose.

"What?" Heidi demanded.

"Do you think we can trust him at all?"

"No. But we will need him where we are going – assuming we survive this. There is also the matter of the other Spinosaur in the area we have yet to collect. I want the set before we leave."

A scrambling, grunting sound made them turn. They heard earth sliding and sploshing into the river. Jansen climbed to look over the rocks once more. "Oh, no. You had to say it, didn't you?"

"What is it?"

He gave her a look of fear. "The rest of the set! I think we're going to be stuck here a while – if we're lucky..."

Chapter 14 | The Burning Times

"You wished to see me, Doctors?" asked Heinrich Schultz, comfortably ensconced in a leather armchair within the captain's quarters. After the agreement with his granddaughter, he had indeed taken over the best suite the *Heydrich* had to offer.

Heidi was less interested in material things than her grandfather. Fully engaged in her Spinosaurus safari, hers was only a small acquiescence.

The whitecoats experienced a disquieting déjà vu. The balding scientist wrung his hands.

"Yes, sir," he managed. "We're concerned about volcanoes, sir."

Heinrich frowned slightly, leaning forward to retrieve his glass from the small table at his side. "Do go on, Doctor," he prompted, taking a sip from his slightly chilled, crisp Chablis.

"We believe that the rivers here are much lower than they should be for the time of year, sir. Much lower. As if the monsoon has not arrived for perhaps two or three years."

"And why do you suspect a volcanic eruption?"

"Volcanism, particularly north of the Tethys Ocean in Laurasia, could have wide-ranging effects on this region, sir, because they tend to push the tropical rain belt further south. Over the last few millennia – from our own time, that is – reducing rains in the headwaters of the Nile have led to droughts that have been documented historically. They may well have caused civil uprisings and even ended a few wars, back in antiquity, as troops were called home to quell the unrest.

"Obviously, this isn't the Nile, but we have no reason to believe that the delta systems in this age will behave any differently than they do in our own, sir. The volcanic gases may reflect some of sun's power, but if they drive the monsoon rains further south, we may even be witnessing the beginning of a localised extinction event. These may actually be the last beasts of the kind Dr Schultz hopes to find, for the purposes of her... *experiment*, to live in these parts."

"Added to that, sir," the female lab coat took up the explanation, "we're seeing many small eruptions to the north-west of our position, via our satellite net."

"You think we may be in some danger here?" asked Schultz, sipping languidly.

The scientists looked at one another. "We're not sure, sir," answered the female. "That would depend upon the *size* of the eventual eruption and where it takes place. For example, geologists have never been able to exactly pinpoint when the Nabro caldera was formed, to the south of here – that's modern Eritrea. My point is, there are many, many active volcanoes in this period of Earth's history, and many of *those* have unknown origins. Some of them could quite conceivably have begun, well, nowish."

"However, even that is not our main fear, sir," continued the balding man, taking back the baton once more. "In the short term, we're more concerned about the path your granddaughter's planned wormhole is to take."

Heinrich's frown deepened. "I always understood that wormholes exist outside our space–time? Why would the pathway matter?"

"That's correct, sir—"

"We *think*," interrupted Two.

Heinrich raised an eyebrow.

One sighed. "We don't fully understand the physics involved, sir, no one does. But sending a wormhole through a very unstable section of the mantle, and skimming the top of the core to create a direct line from Egypt to Munich, could be..." he floundered.

"Unwise, sir," Two finished for him.

"So, are you suggesting we create our wormhole elsewhere, Doctors?"

"We think sending a wormhole through the planet could be dangerous from anywhere, sir," replied One, beginning to perspire.

"So it really doesn't matter where we begin, does it?" asked Heinrich, all reason and civility.

The female scientist known as 'Two' shook her head. "Sir, we suggest opening a wormhole, either from space, or at very least from the same geographical coordinates."

Schultz leaned forward again, with interest this time. "From Germany? So we travel through time but *not* space – is that what you're suggesting?"

"We think it would be safer, sir," they answered together.

The old man sat back, glass held delicately by its base as he swirled the liquid, breathing in the aroma. "I understand your concerns, Doctors. However, there are other considerations. If our plan doesn't work, my granddaughter intends to try for secondary targets, here in North Africa. We'll also need to resupply at our base in Britain. Our fuel reserves are finite and dwindling. And," he added tersely, "as you people failed to secure the resources of the *New World*, we have no way to easily refine more. Can you provide me with any solid evidence for your concerns?"

They looked at one another. "No, sir."

"Then you have very little time to find some, Doctors. Otherwise, we proceed as planned."

Douglas was red in the face. Perhaps it was the worry he carried for their situation, or concern about Captain Baines' mission, but the unscheduled changing of the guard – to prevent them from developing pneumonia after a snowball fight – had left him furious.

After dressing them down, he sent them to undress, and wrap up with warm towels.

As he stormed across the hangar, he heard the distinct sounds of sardonic laughter, away to his right. He stopped and turned to see Geoff Lloyd, piloting a wheelchair in charge of a sarcastic expression.

Douglas took a deep, calming breath. "Geoff. Out and about, Ah see. How are you feeling?"

Lloyd grinned. "All the better for seeing you, Captain."

Douglas' expression soured further. "Well, Ah'm glad you're on the mend." He turned to leave.

"James, wait. Please."

Douglas sighed. "What is it, Geoff?"

"I'm just wondering what I can do."

"From a wheelchair?"

It was Lloyd's turn to sigh. "Not exactly. My insides took more stitches than my fatigues – hence the chair. Flannigan is concerned I might exert myself. I see a lot of physio in my future – assuming we survive whatever it is you've gotten us into now, of course."

He smiled, but Douglas saw the cracks in his carefully crafted demeanour. When Lloyd continued, he spoke quietly, in confidence, "I meant, what can I possibly do to set things right – as much as anyone can, at least?" His eyes were imploring, searching desperately for any chance of redemption.

Douglas studied him a moment; a tragic, friendless, broken man, and despite their recent history, he felt a rush of pity.

"Ah'll never forget how you saved young Georgio from that dinosaur, Geoff."

"Neither will I."

Douglas' lip twisted into a smile. "Ah suppose not. Ah thought you'd died. Ah'm glad Ah was wrong."

"I think you're alone in that assertion, James. The people here... well, I can hardly blame them for hating my guts. This *is* all my fault, after all."

"No, Geoff. You made a bad decision, one unworthy of you, that much is true, but you were just a cog in the machine. You've also paid, very nearly with your life on several occasions. What Ah'm trying to say is redemption is always there, for those who truly wish to receive it."

Lloyd's face screwed up in disgust. "What the hell is that? Zen? I want to know what I can do, man!"

Douglas' colour, so recently subsided, rose again. "Damn it, Geoff! Why are ye always so obnoxious when people are trying tae help ye?"

Lloyd smiled wickedly. "That's better, more like my old comrade in arms. I thought I'd accidentally dialled the Samaritans for a minute there."

Douglas snorted, defusing, despite himself. "Clearly you've things to think about. If you come up with a way to contribute, Ah promise Ah'll consider it. How's that?"

"Good enough."

"Right." Douglas made to leave.

"Hey, James. Thanks."

Douglas nodded and left.

"So much for them not seeing us coming!" shouted Gleeson, as missiles rained down on them, ricocheting off their transport's armour in a barrage of bangs and pings.

"They're only crossbow bolts and a few musket balls—" Baines' explanation was forestalled by a huge, deafening *clang!*

"What the hell was *that?*" demanded Gleeson.

"Cannon!" Sir Nicholas shouted, his eyes round with trepidation.

"A glancing blow," Baines concurred.

"I thought you said the main cannon loop was on the opposite side?" retorted Gleeson.

"It was, I mean, it is— Look, what do you want from me?"

"They must have wee cannons up on the battlements," added Maxwell. "Breech-loading falconets they can shove aboot."

Baines pointed at the firing controls for the turret-mounted, fifty-calibre machine guns atop their vehicle. "Commander, take out that cannon, but don't hit anybody!"

Gleeson's disbelief was matched only by Lord Maxwell and Sir Nicholas. Speechless for once, he turned to the controls and raised the weapon while their attackers up on the battlements fought the blizzard to reload.

When the armoured personnel carrier's guns sounded, the concussion shook the passengers to their very bones. It was, however, far worse for the men loading the cannon, high above.

Doing his best to comply with what he considered ludicrous orders, Gleeson chewed away at the crenelations. Stone and hot shrapnel showered the garrison along the eastern rampart, causing them to abandon their cannon. As they ducked or otherwise saved themselves, he went for the weapon itself. The small falconet exploded into sparks and shards as iron fragments scattered across the wall walk, exacerbated by a powder primer poured by the cannoneer.

A hail of crossbow bolts and small arms fire bounced ineffectually off the personnel carrier's armour in response.

Gleeson targeted the remaining men and returned fire; once more gnawing on their stone defences, he sent them running for their lives.

Lord Maxwell watched the destruction on the vehicle's heads-up display with awe bordering on lust. "Ah think yer right, Captain Baines."

"Oh?"

"Aye. Ah think people will soon get the message!"

"Yes, well, tell your friends – and your enemies – that these are only a *small* guns!" She grinned wolfishly.

Gleeson whooped with delight as he stopped firing. "Douglas is going to have a mare! What do you want me to blow the crap out of next, Cap?"

"Actually, I thought we'd try talking at this point." Once again, Baines was answered only with looks of incredulity.

"You're gonna go out there?" asked O'Brien, at last.

"Not just yet, we have a public address system on board, don't we?"

"Erm, Captain," Meritus piped up from the rear of the vehicle. "I'm no expert on these times, but won't those people believe that the booming voice belongs to a 'giant, impregnable, unstoppable monster'?"

"Is he referring to the APC or Captain Baines' predilection to cause trouble?" muttered Gleeson.

"Heard that, Commander, thank you!"

"What I'm saying," Meritus persevered, "is that they're more likely to throw everything they've got at us or cower in terror, than come out to talk. For them, it'll be like the Devil himself is knocking on the front door."

"*Her*self..."

Baines clipped Gleeson around the ear.

"Ow!"

"Keep your eyes on those battlements, Commander. They may have more than one cannon." She turned back to Meritus. "So what do you suggest, Tobias?"

"Well, if you're serious about doing this, I think we're going to have to get out and talk to them."

"Captain," interrupted The Sarge, "if we go out there, we'll be completely vulnerable. Bows and arrows have been killing people quite handily, for thousands of years, ma'am. We should not give up our advantage."

Baines pondered. As she did so, torchlight streamed from an opening in the fortress wall. They could not see the opening, only the light thrown.

The Hermitage Castle of AD1558 was in its final stages of development, and in floorplan resembled a large 'H'. The centre of the 'H' remained largely from the first phase of the stone structure, with four towers added later, completing the shape – although preparation for the prison tower was part of the earlier design. The western towers were larger, with the south-western the largest of all – the *Douglas* tower.

O'Brien had driven in from the east. According to Beckett's plan, this meant that the towers facing them were the well tower in the south-eastern corner, to their left and, more ominously, the prison tower, in the north-east corner, to their right. Baines felt sure the prison tower would be where De Soulis held their prize.

On both the eastern and western sides of the castle, the towers were joined at high level by giant, flying arches. Baines had been correct that, although initially built to carry a timber fighting platform between the towers, they now carried stone battlements that circumnavigated the entire top level of the fortress.

The doorway throwing its light across the recess between the eastern towers was in the north wall of the south-east 'well' tower. Of more interest to Baines, however, were the shadows cast by the men stepping out of it.

"Looks like they have the same idea," said Gleeson. "We're up, Captain."

"No," Baines replied, placing a hand on his shoulder. "You stay here and keep your mitts on those firing controls."

"Good luck, Captain," he offered seriously.

"Fire!" hissed Heidi, triumphantly.

Jansen started, but instantly pulled his dart rifle to the shoulder in readiness. "Who? Where?"

"*Nein*. I mean we *need* a fire. They are only animals, after all."

"There are no trees on this island, Doctor. Firewood's going to be thin on the ground. Do you have anything combustible?"

"In the ship."

"We could get the pilot—"

"No," she cut him off. "I don't want to draw any attention that way."

"I have an idea," he tried.

"Well?"

"There are three of those monsters out there, sunbathing between us and the ship. One of them, the smallest – and I'm guessing, youngest – we're still to inject with the isotope."

"Your point?"

"If I hit it where I shot the big one, in a sensitive spot, it might upset it enough to turn on one of the others."

Heidi's lack of congratulation was deafening.

"You disagree, Doctor?"

"What if you simply struck the larger one at the point of an old injury, or an infection? You said yourself that they do not usually feel the dart."

"Right," he agreed dejectedly.

"However, your stupid idea has given me another one."

"*Another* stupid idea?"

She stared at him, coolly, despite the burning heat of the day. "Another *idea*. Talking of sensitive spots, perhaps we could use such a thing to our advantage."

"What do you suggest, ma'am?"

"Waiting for an opportunity."

Jansen's attention turned to the river sliding indolently beneath them and a vast tree trunk slipping by with the current. His eyes widened in horror as the end of the log yawned wide and became the gaping maw of the biggest crocodile he had ever seen – even here.

Heidi snapped round to see what had clearly unnerved him. "You again," she breathed.

"Are these the same damned things as the other damned things – that lived in the river, back in Patagonia?" asked Jansen.

"Similar. According to my cous— According to Tim Norris' files, those were Sarcosuchus hartti – these are Sarcosuchus *imperator*."

"Well, isn't that a fancy handle?" he replied nervously.

"Indeed – certainly paints a picture, does it not? These are bigger."

"I can see that."

The object Jansen had taken for a free-floating log was now clearly under power, and heading for the northern tip of their island.

"You've got to be joking!" Jansen burst out. "Haven't we got enough to deal with?"

Heidi was shaking her head. "I doubt he could climb up here like the Spinosaurs did. Actually, I do not believe it is us he is interested in."

"You mean...?" Jansen tailed off, gesturing towards the lounging giants behind them.

"Perhaps the youngest."

"An opportunity?" he asked.

"Chaos often provides them. As soon as everything is in motion, new avenues are created, new strategies become apparent. And speaking of such, I believe we have one now."

The opportunity she spoke of was heralded by a smell. It was the worst stench they had ever experienced. The carnivores ate a lot of fish, often rotting fish, decomposing on riverbanks beneath an equatorial sun; the processed *disjecta membra* was lively enough to have gotten up and walked, let alone swum. It almost brought Heidi and Jansen to their knees.

"*Jeez!*" he exhaled, almost losing his last meal.

Heidi pulled her shirt neck up over her nose. "Quickly, shoot the small one now."

"*Wha...?*" Jansen was squinting like his eyes were about to bleed.

"Shoot it *now!*"

He fired. "Hit it!"

"Yes, yes, of course. Reload! Reload!"

He did as ordered, choking on bile. "Now what?"

The smallest of the Spinosaurs had indeed failed to notice the prick of the dart. However, the largest of the three should only be so lucky. Heidi grabbed the rifle from the unresisting hands of her bodyguard, leaving him to turn away and vomit. Meanwhile she took aim, and as the giant dinosaur's tail rose to complete its indelicate operation, she fired.

The animal's sphincteric relaxation shot forth an unholy stream of white liquid, which could only have been something it ate. Before the creature had chance to breathe a sigh of relief and contract, Heidi's missile struck with the cruellest accuracy, not to mention intimacy, imaginable. The resulting bellow of agony and fury scattered every bird within half a mile.

Sweeping its vast tail in a deadly arc, the closest of its brethren was knocked sideways, forcing the smallest of the three from the edge of the island, where it exited with a colossal splash. As modern era crocodiles can sense the gentle lapping of a deer taking on water, Sarcosuchus imperator was fully attuned to every ripple in his river. He launched powerfully through the flow with terrifying speed, against the current. The young Spinosaurus surfaced, sneezed and roared indignation, but realising the danger, turned to swim strongly upstream; paced by its deadliest enemy, they vanished together forever, becoming one with the story of life on Earth.

Up on the island, Jansen was beside himself. "What the hell was that?"

"A distraction!" Heidi was already scrambling over the rocks in the hope of running south towards the jut. The remaining Spinosaurs circled and roared, lunging for one another. The initial tail swipe had taken the second animal by surprise, knocking the breath from its lungs. It regained its feet quickly, shook and came back like a caffeine-crazed psychopath with a score to settle.

The reaction of the first animal had not been calculated, but the second was in no mood for mitigation. It attacked with a viciously quick snap, its teeth biting into the neck of its adversary, who bellowed anew – now hurting at both ends.

Jansen dove to the ground, taking Heidi with him as an enormous tail swished overhead. Furious, she suddenly realised that he had saved her life, but with Heidi this hardly mattered. "Get off me!" she snapped, scrambling to her feet to leave him behind.

Before Jansen regained his footing, he had to dive again, this time from under a huge, three-taloned foot. With three-dimensional binocular vision, superb eye-head coordination, sensitivity for pitch-down movements, and a structurally robust snout, Spinosaurus was adept at taking smaller, quick-moving, struggling prey. Having tripped on his second attempt to rise, Jansen was all too aware of falling into that category, even as he was falling to the ground.

Heidi made the ship and found two of her island party waiting at the open hatch. "Where's Winters?" she demanded, breathlessly, noting the woman's absence. "Never mind! Load an incendiary into the launcher – *hurry!*"

The men complied.

Heidi ran around to the rear of their ship. Ignoring the huge theropod dinosaurs that encroached dangerously on their position, she fired the launcher. The rocket flamed out of the stovepipe barrel and exploded less than fifteen metres away. Heidi called for another, before bothering to take stock.

The Spinosaurs roared in tandem. Shocked by the sudden conflagration, they broke from one another to back away from the fire. Their own blood streaked each animal's neck and face, while each other's dripped from their teeth and claws. A second eruption from the rocket launcher backed them off still further.

The largest of the pair snapped at the other, more out of fear of fire than fury of battle.

"Ben, *run!*" Heidi shouted, hoarse from the smoking incendiaries.

Jansen did not need telling twice. Springing from behind a rock barely big enough to hide his form, he ran for his life.

Having no warning, Winters had been trapped on the opposite side of the island since the fight began. Seeing her opportunity, she dashed from behind a small outcrop. As she ran out, her luck ran out first. The larger and angrier of the two giants made its own escape, crossing her path. They had all noted that a filthy temperament was just one of the Spinosaurus family traits, so it came as no surprise that a foot-long steel dart up the anus did little to improve this natural state. It snapped downwards, separating Winters from the ground like a scythe through grass; the bite so ferocious that her head flew in the direction she had been running. The huge predator slid over the side of the bank, taking her body down into the depths of the river to feed.

The other Spinosaurus splashed into the river at the island's low northern tip, also to vanish.

Jansen slowed to a halt. Seeing Winter's head on the ground, he walked towards it. Lifting it from the dust, he looked into her eyes, unsure whether the mind had already left. "You're with friends," he said gently, just in case.

"What are you doing?" asked a peremptory voice from behind him.

"It's not always certain whether the brain dies immediately from shock or later from lack of oxygen. This may be her last few moments. She should know she is cared for and will be missed."

"Rubbish! Unless she is to begin her new life as a football, I suggest you throw that disgusting thing away. We have completed our task here." With that, Heidi turned and strode back to the ship.

Jansen watched her go, his right eye twitching with just the beginnings of loathing.

AD1558, 60 degrees north, 31 degrees west, 45 degrees chillier

"Adam, you were with the commander and O'Brien when the princess was taken. Do you recognise this guy?" Baines spoke just loudly enough to be heard over the howl of the gale.

Prentice shook his head. "Not seen him before, Captain. Their main man was a lot bigger than this fella – this one looks more like a priest to me."

The sky was almost black as night. Huge flakes billowed as freezing winds buffeted them, the flowing snow exposing the vortex shedding, around their bodies. Baines held her ground as three men approached their position, midway between the castle and the APC.

At her left stood The Sarge, Heath-Rifleson at the ready, with an assault rifle slung around his shoulders for good measure. To her far right was Pte Adam Prentice, similarly armed. Meritus stood to her immediate right, armed with his officer's sidearm. Baines still carried her stun pistol – determined that no one should lose their lives from any actions of the *New World* crew.

The men from the castle, clearly terrified, were indeed of the clerical persuasion. There could be little doubt, hiding as they were behind the large decorative crucifix carried by their leader. Baines' obviously human entourage seemed to elicit some surprise from them, perhaps even offering them a modicum of comfort.

"Are ye devils?" their leader asked tremulously.

"Always with the devils. We could start developing a complex about that," Baines muttered to Meritus, who wore a 'told you so' smile. Turning back to the clerics, she attempted a friendly demeanour, despite having just sent the castle's garrison running for their lives. "Erm, greetings!"

"The woman speaks!" hissed one of the cowled figures standing behind crucifix-man.

Baines frowned. "*I* am in charge here."

"Well actually, we're the same rank and technically, that's my APC behind us," muttered Meritus.

"You want to do this *now?*"

"Sorry. Carry on, Jill. This is going great so far."

Baines rolled her eyes. "We only want to talk with you," she tried again.

"I am Father Robert," said the man holding the cross. "What dost thou want with us?"

"Are you English?" asked Baines.

"I am a borderer!" he bristled.

"Right. And your garrison sent you three out to deal with us, all on your own?"

"God is with us, madam." As if on cue, his followers began to chant in Latin.

The day had been dark and bleak throughout, but natural darkness was also beginning to fall around them now. To Baines' mind, the chanting kind of worked.

"Commander?" Baines spoke into her comm.

"*Go ahead, Captain.*"

The castle's welcoming committee crossed themselves, backing off in shock.

"Give us some light up here, would you?"

"*Yes, Captain. Suggest you look away.*"

The APC's spots came to life, flooding the area with ice-white light.

Father Robert screamed. Falling to the ground, he dropped his cross. Scrabbling around in the snow, his hands grasped the crossbar. He spun it quickly, right-way-up, holding it out like a Hammer film protagonist.

With light on the subject, Baines studied the three terrified souls before her. "You're monks? I thought this was Reformist country?"

Despite his terror, Father Robert was still capable of disdain. "Mention them not!"

"OK," she replied slowly, more to herself. "If you're monks, perhaps a more pressing question would be: why are you working for a known devil-worshipper?"

If anything, Robert looked even more terrified.

Poor sod, thought Baines. *They push him through the door to wave a crucifix, thinking we're... well, who knows what? And he's just as scared of the boss who sent him out here as he is of us. What a life!*

When Robert spoke again, his teeth chattered together, making his words difficult to understand, "M-my l-lord has s-seen the error of his-s w-ways. He is at p-prayer n-now."

"He has." Baines' was not exactly a question, more a flat statement of disbelief. "So, what? He confesses, says a few 'Hail Marys' and you welcome him back into the fold?"

Robert looked at her askance. He was obviously distrustful, but Baines suspected he also was struggling to follow her mode of speech. Then an idea struck her.

"Sir William is at prayer, you say?"

Robert nodded shakily.

"At the chapel?"

He nodded again.

Baines turned to The Sarge and Meritus in turn, giving each man a crafty smile. "We may be able to bring this whole thing to a quick conclusion, gentlemen."

"What did you have in mind, Captain?" asked The Sarge, not taking his eyes from the men before them.

"According to Beckett's historical plans of the castle and complex, the chapel is about four hundred metres west of here. It's stone-built, but will be far less formidable than this pile," she concluded, indicating the masonry edifice before them.

A half-smile twisted The Sarge's lip and he gave a quick nod of understanding. "Shall we take these with us?"

Before she could answer, the deafening, concussive thump of a pair of fifty-calibre machine guns opened up, directly behind them.

Everyone dove to the ground as impact sparks chiselled yet more stone from the castle walls. In the relative still that followed, the howl of the blizzard harmonised with the buzzing of their inner ears.

"Ouch!" said Baines, her own voice sounding muffled.

"Sorry for the surprise, Captain," Gleeson's tinny voice came from her comm speakers. *"Sneaky little baggars have positioned crossbowmen and reassembled one of those little falconet cannons at one of the arrow slits on the... what* is *that, the third floor? Not sure. Anyway, I've made 'em think twice about it, but suggest you get out of there before they get any other ideas."*

"What?" Baines shouted, massaging her ear. "Never mind. We're gonna get out of here, before they get any other ideas. Bring them, gentlemen. They may be able to help us at the chapel."

The three military men grabbed a monk each by the arm and double-timed them back to the rear hatch of their transport. The prisoners quailed as they drew near the steel goliath, having to be dragged the last few metres and literally thrown in the back.

"Good work, Commander," said Baines as she made her way forward. "Keep an eye on these three."

"Lord Maxwell!" spat Father Robert. "Heretic!"

Maxwell snorted. "Ye work for De Soulis and yer casting doubts on *ma* beliefs?"

"You know this little Herbert, sir?" asked The Sarge.

"Oh, aye. He was novice master tae Kelso Abbey. Were ye no', Rabbie? With a predilection for flaying wee bairns with the birch 'til there was nae skin on their wee backs!"

"I disciplined them. The devil must be beaten out of—"

Pte Prentice threw Father Robert down onto a bench, knocking the wind out of him. "Stay there. I'd hate to have to shoot ye," he growled in his broad Yorkshire accent.

"Let's go," ordered Baines.

"Yes, ma'am," replied O'Brien and the armoured transport set off.

Bess alternated between terror and elation when she first heard the thumping boom of heavy machine guns. During her brief contact with the new people, she had heard similar, if smaller weapons. She knew it must be them, and if they were here, there was every chance Sir Nicholas was with them.

After the guns ceased, she heard a monstrous roar. Standing on tiptoe, atop the small wooden chair in her cell, she could just about see out of her tiny vent in the north wall – her only source of light and air.

She could hardly complain; the poor devils in the hole below had not even that much. Strange lights flickered across the landscape. Old earthworks and ramparts cast eerie shadows across the large east-west ditch running north of the castle, separating it from a second plateau further north, which still bore some rotting timber palisading from an outer bailey, long out of use.

The roar grew louder, the light brighter; soon, she had to avert her eyes. Blinking as her vision adjusted, she could see some sort of... *wagon?* It was huge. More weirdly yet, it moved without horses.

Bess was sceptical about the existence of magic, but there was certainly something very wrong about these new people. They seemed honourable enough, but how had they gained such unnatural powers? Could she place her life in their hands? Possibly, but what about her soul?

She pushed those thoughts aside. Keeping body and soul together was her current concern. She must focus and seek out any opportunity to free herself.

The horseless coach trundled noisily below her, leaving in its wake a choking, oily smoke. Draught cut through the windowless slot in the wall like a knife, bringing the smoke in with it. Growing up on stories about Saint George, she began to wonder if they were more than that. Her father had certainly fancied himself as a rightful successor to the man – what would he have made of all this?

With a sudden sinking feeling, she realised that the new people had not stopped at the north-west Douglas Tower, but were continuing west. She heard the crack of musket fire, followed by pings and ricochets as they bounced uselessly from the vehicle's skin. She shook her head. How was any of this possible? Had they forsaken her? Did they even know she was here?

"You have returned victorious, *Enkelin?*" asked Heinrich, in private audience aboard the *Heydrich*.

Heidi nodded. "I have."

"And you're ready to attempt the next phase of your plan?"

"I am. After a shower, a good meal and a night's rest."

"Of course. You have done well, *Enkelin*. Most would have given up on ever accomplishing our goals after such heavy losses and serious setbacks."

She gave him a wintry smile. "Is that pride I hear, *Großvater?*"

He returned her smile. "Perhaps, just for today, you will sit and dine with me, and call me *Opa*."

Eyes wide as a child's, she could hardly believe her ears. "I must freshen up, before I join you... *Opa*." She bowed awkwardly and left.

"Er, Captain?" asked Gleeson. "Didn't you say the main cannon loops were situated on the *west* side of the castle? Something about converting an old entrance to a gun emplacement? That would be the west side that's now behind us, right?"

Baines looked up, startled. "O'Brien, put your foot down!"

The vehicle's rear camera recorded the flash-boom of a large cannon. The only other indications of the shot were the whistle as it passed them, and the cloud of turf and soil that flew into the air a few metres in front of them.

A second shot hit the ground at almost exactly the same spot, speaking volumes for the gunners' precision, if not their accuracy.

"*Jesus!*" screamed O'Brien.

"Blasphemy!" scolded Father Robert.

"Shut your bladdy hole!" shouted Gleeson.

"Hole!" shrieked Baines.

"That's what I said!"

"NO! *HOLE!*"

O'Brien leaned on the left lever, spinning the tracked vehicle to the right. The seated passengers in the rear slid around, while the guards standing over the monks went down like skittles. Everyone felt the dip under the left track, as they skirted the brand new crater in the path connecting castle with chapel.

"That was bladdy close!" bawled Gleeson, unnerved, despite his usual bravado. "Hey, Merito! How good's the armour on these things?"

Meritus was shaking his head. "That was quite a big cannon. I really don't know. They *are* weaker in the rear."

"Fantastic!" Gleeson spat. "Maxwell, Nick – you guys know these things. They seem to have two large cannons this side. How quickly can they reload to take another pop at us?"

Weirdly, neither of the noblemen seemed overly shaken by the near misses. To the warring classes of warring nations, such things were perhaps par for the course.

"Our *skilled* gunners can fire cannon of *quality* once in every hour," vouched Sir Nicholas, proudly. "You shall find neither in these lands, Commander."

Maxwell bridled. "You insult me, sir!"

Sir Nicholas tensed too. "Thou knowst it for a fact, sir!"

Maxwell stood in the rocking vehicle, balling his fists. Incandescent, he bellowed, "Ye dare *thou* me, sir!"

The APC gave a timely lurch over the rough terrain. Maxwell was thrown back into his seat, giving Baines an opportunity to step into the breach. "Thank you, Sir Nicholas. That tallies with what I was taught – about rates of fire, I mean." She held a placating hand towards Maxwell. "Not quality and er... yes, well, thank you. O'Brien, *step on it!*"

"Anyway," Gleeson added into the brittle silence that followed, "we're right on the doorstep to the chapel now. I doubt they'll fire on us again if the big cheese is in there."

"Let's hope not," muttered Baines. "You've seen this guy before – what should I expect? Lord Maxwell, you too – can you give me any guidance I can use, to treat with De Soulis?"

"He's a madman," stated Maxwell, bluntly.

Baines looked to Gleeson.

"I only saw him from a distance," he admitted.

"And?"

"He looked crazier than a dingo in a wedding dress."

"Great..."

Heidi's comm crackled, *"We're ready to open a wormhole, Doctor. Can you confirm everyone is behind the blast shields?"*

She hit reply. "Confirmed. Proceed, Lieutenant Devon."

Armoured plates drew aside, revealing a large focal array in the *Heydrich's* prow. Despite herself, Heidi was curious to see a wormhole open. Normally this process would take place soundlessly, in the vacuum of space.

A whirring began, as a pinprick of blinding starlight appeared to grow within the machine. Mechanical noises and clicks followed as various lenses locked into place within the unit, and then... nothing.

Within their new timber enclosure, Heidi risked a glance from behind her blast shield. Slowly, others did likewise. Before them, they could clearly see the rear wall of the enclosure, but it seemed to shimmer. A miraging effect that bent the light in strange ways, making it feel like they were looking at the logs in the wall from several angles at once.

Slowly, Heidi reached for her comm. "Devon?"

"We have a stable wormhole, ma'am. Our science team are focusing sensors to look for our 'probe' now. Stand by..."

"Understood." She closed the channel and stepped out before the open wormhole, but could feel nothing from it; no heat, no gravity, nor attraction of any kind. It may as well have been a light show. The strange lensing effect reminded her of the lamina flow water fountains, back in her grandfather's Patagonian fortress.

She smiled slyly. *But this is no decoration.* She reached out a hand, to touch the event horizon.

"Don't touch it!" her comm spat to life.

"Is that One?"

A sigh carried through the comm link. *"Yes, Doctor. Do not touch the wormhole while we are focusing our equipment on it."*

"Why?"

"Because it may confuse our results. There is also the possibility that it will draw you in."

That gave her pause, and she stepped back quickly. "How long do you expect your scans to take? I understand we can only power the wormhole for an hour at a time?"

"That's correct, Dr Schultz. We're applying every bit of processing power at our disposal – no one's even allowed to use the coffee

machine at the moment! But it will still take us at least thirty to forty minutes. That's if it works at all."

"That will not leave me much time on the other side."

"Enough time to have a quick look around and leave your marker, so we can pinpoint the exact time and place next time."

"True. My team and I are fully prepared to leave. Let me know the second you have a lock, and..."

"Yes, Doctor?"

Heidi took a deep breath. "If *mein Großvater* still insists on joining our first mission, you had better ask him to make his way here now. We must all be ready."

"Understood. Reid out."

"Who?"

Another sigh through the commlink. "One *out!"*

Commander Coleman and her driver sat in silence for several minutes, thinking. The shock of being stared down by a row of gargantuan flying reptiles had killed their conversation. "They haven't actually made any aggressive moves yet?" she asked, finally.

He shook his head. The huge Ornithocheirus pterosaurs were no longer perched like gargoyles. Once the lorry stopped moving, they quickly lost interest in it and resumed their business. "They're building nests along the spine of the ship," he muttered darkly. "This is not good, ma'am."

"No, indeed. Not for us, at least. However, for them it seems ideal – there's absolutely no way any terrestrial creature big enough to threaten them could get up there. It's not going to be easy to convince them they've made a mistake."

"Shooting a few of them down might get the point across."

"No, Sergeant. This is our home now – we're not going to go about slaughtering everything that crosses our path. It *was* their home first, after all."

"Our ship wasn't, ma'am."

"True, but our ship wasn't actually *our* ship, either, until very recently. I think we need to adjust our thinking if we're to stay here.

We need to find a way to live in harmony with this world. We tried it the other way back in 2112, remember?"

"You make a good point, Commander, but we can't very well expect people to work these fields under the threat from *above*. I doubt our leaders will be so understanding, but as we're trying a new way...?"

"Hmm. Good counterpoint."

"The situation is quite urgent, too."

"You're referring to our irrigation plans, Sarge?"

"Yes, ma'am. The crops were healthy when we arrived. Rainfall seemed plentiful inside the bowl of these mountains, as you might expect, but high summer has changed things. We're close to drought, ma'am."

"I know. We have the pumping equipment working now, aboard the Rescue Pod. I was overseeing the final testing when you called me away. Trouble is, we've got a lot of pipe to lay. That means working in the lake and under the gaze of these monstrous birds."

"Pterosaurs, ma'am – er... so I've been told."

Coleman nodded. She was not offended by the correction; rather, she made a private pact to take a tablet to her quarters and read all she could about the Cretaceous and Tim Norris, too.

"What about fire, ma'am?"

"To scare them away?"

The sergeant shrugged; it was an idea.

"We'd have to be pretty darned careful," Coleman replied as she mulled it over. "One stray spark could take the crop in this heat, and we don't have our pumping system in place to put out any fires."

"Agreed, ma'am, but the longer we leave them to get settled up there, the harder this is going to be. I thought about setting off a few small explosions on the ground, but I'm not sure it would work."

Coleman looked at him with interest. "Why do you say that?"

He gestured through the windscreen at the busy creatures bringing material from the forests to build their nests. "Well, you saw how quickly they lost interest in us when we stopped moving. I'm thinking they don't have long memories. I reckon a few loud bangs would send them packing in a burst of gull call and guano, but they'd soon be back."

"So you're suggesting we keep a few fires going continuously?"

"Yes, ma'am. I read a report that the people from the *New World* used a similar tactic to allow them to finish their earthwork defences. It seemed to work for *them*, so..."

"It could work for us," Coleman muttered thoughtfully. "OK. I've got an idea. This won't be easy, but it should work. Maybe we'll be able to come up with something more permanent for next year – perhaps over the winter, if there is one. However, for now, we'd better get to it. We have a lot of work to do."

The sergeant met her eye. "Don't suppose this will be safe, indoor work?"

Momentarily relapsing to her own recent days as a sergeant, she brightened. "Most of it can be."

"Really?"

"No."

The more she stared at the anomaly, the more it drew her in. Heidi could barely stop herself jumping into the wormhole with abandon. It was all there, in front of her, all of time. Every mystery, everywhere, every when. Intellectually, she knew that without locking onto their destination, it would be suicide, and possibly even then. However, temptation cares not for the detail, only the prize, and it was intoxicating. If they got this right, just a few metres away was a museum in Munich, in the very heart of the Nazi war machine. She would be able to walk a couple of city blocks and stand outside their very headquarters – The Brown House – and maybe, *he* would be there.

Dr Heidi Schultz was not given to bouts of giddy enthusiasm, but this was a *special* day for her, providing irrefutable proof that one man's – or woman's – floor was indeed another man's ceiling.

Her men looked nervous, even Jansen. Her lip quirked to a smile. *I do believe I'm making an old man of him. Poor Ben.* Her grandfather joined them at last. She hardly recognised him in military fatigues, rather than one of his exquisitely cut suits. He was clearly affecting ignorance to her study of him. If she was feeling whatever it was that she was feeling, then what was he experiencing right now? A dream come true? Excitement for the chance to meet an idol? Anticipation of an opportunity? She sighed. No point in asking.

Her mind turned, just for a second, towards Tim Norris. Her brief time with him was the closest she had ever come to family. He was bad for her, had weakened her, she knew it; a narcotic experience that left her wanting more, but she did miss him, and hated herself for it.

She turned back to her grandfather, ironically to find a little peace within. She was who she was, and it was important she remember that.

The wormhole shimmered before her, an elemental force of near infinite power, exuding its own form of addiction. It was time to focus.

When her comm crackled to life, she started. "Go ahead, One."

"We've found the correct time, Doctor. Readings taken twice daily from the moon, triangulated with the original known location of the Spinosaurus aegyptiacus remains in Egypt, now show that the bones have been relocated to Munich – courtesy of Herr Stromer, I would guess. We're now within three decades of target and should have an exact date for your destination in just a few seconds... ah, here it comes. Yes, we've got a lock on November 7th, 1943. As you requested, Doctor, it's a Sunday, so there should be very few, if any, people within the museum."

The date struck Heidi like a smack in the face. Unable to find her voice, she sought out her grandfather, who in turn stared wide-eyed.

"*He* will be there," Heinrich croaked, his voice weak with reverence.

Heidi nodded. Eventually, she managed, "His final yearly speech to the Party, from the Löwenbräukeller in Munich. However, *he* may be there, but Nazi headquarters, The Brown House, will not. It was bombed by the Allies just a few weeks earlier, in October '43. We're too late."

Jansen cleared his throat. "When you say 'he', do you mean—"

Heidi held up her hand to silence him. "One, how long will we have on the other side?"

"Twenty-seven minutes safely, Doctor, but I suggest you don't return a single second later. We'll have a lot of data to go through before we can guarantee a repeat performance. We may never get it going again."

"Understood. One, is Two there with you?"

"Yes, Doctor."

"You have both done well. If this works, your efforts will not go unrewarded. Now, how does the saying go? Keep the porch lights on? We'll return soon. Schultz out."

"Bon voyage, Doctor."

Heidi strode up to the shimmering hole through time. Taking only the merest second to study it close up, she turned to Jansen. "Ben, bring up the rear. Everyone, follow me."

She stepped through.

Two watched and waited for Heidi's team to disappear before drawing her colleague's attention. Despite their air-conditioned environment, the equatorial sun beat down relentlessly on the black-hulled warship, causing Two to wipe perspiration from her brow.

Reid, otherwise known as 'One', leaned over her shoulder, increasing her discomfort as he spoke too close to her ear. "Is that what I think it is? In AD2122? But that's ten years into our own future!"

"I know," the female lab coat agreed, leaning away from the volume. "And this one is not in Germany, either. It is due south, just a few kilometres east of what will one day be El-Shaikh Ebada in Egypt."

The balding man's forehead wrinkled in thought. Almost reverentially, he whispered, "What the hell does it mean?"

"That Heidi shot a lot of dinosaurs?" Two replied, fatuously. Seeing the look of disapproval on One's face, she relented. "Those animals must range further than we have so far observed. I suppose it could mean we have more than one chance at this?" She let go a deep sigh, blowing out her cheeks. "At the moment, all we can do is log the date and co-ordinates, east of El-Shaikh Ebada and see what transpires. We have been tinkering with time and space for months now—"

"To save the lives of our expedition, and quite possibly the human race," One interjected.

Two spun her seat to look him in the eye. "Yes, and we succeeded in that. But an entire world was not enough for Heidi Schultz, was it?"

Mother Sarah worked with Mary Hutchins and the kitchen staff to sort their remaining supplies into appropriate portions. Her comm had barely stopped pinging message alerts since lunchtime. She sighed, taking it out again. This time there was a call incoming.

"Hi, Beck. What can I do for ya?"

"Sarah, it's time. Please meet with me immediately. Captain Baines is in serious danger."

"I hope that's not the case, honey, but if it is, what can *I* do about it?"

"You know what, Sarah. Please."

"I know what you said in your message."

"Messages. I sent more than a dozen!"

Sarah winced. "Yeah, I'm sorry. I've been real busy with our efforts here."

Beck's sigh travelled through the comm. *"If we don't act now, it may be too late. Surely a few food packages can wait?"*

Her voice sounded so beaten and without hope that Sarah could not ignore the plea any more. "Beck, meet me at my quarters. I did a little reading and, well, I may have found something."

"Thank you. I'll be there in two."

Sarah could clearly hear the relief in the younger woman's voice. *Oh, well. If I can at least allay a little fear from one of my flock, that'll be something, I guess.*

"Mary, could you finish packing this one for me please, honey? I've got an urgent call to take care of."

"Of course. Do you need any help?" asked Mary, earnestly.

Sarah gave her arm a grateful squeeze and smiled. "Only God's help."

Space travel, time travel – it was all too much for Lieutenant Devon. He was no scientist. He had read once that space–time was like a vast blanket, stretched taut, with all the planets, stars and any other gravitic heavenly bodies causing it to bowl around them. He could not help thinking of the universe as a giant ballbag, which would at least account for the ache in his tiny corner of it.

Captain Nassaki had dropped a bomb on the bridge of the *Heydrich*. A place Devon still thought of as *his* bridge, he could not help it. Not a physical bomb, of course, that would merely be destructive. Nassaki's was firmly in the realms of meta – which made it potentially disastrous.

After calling the remaining senior staff together, he proposed closing the wormhole permanently and cutting the Schultzes loose. Hopefully forever – but with Heidi you just never knew.

The crew's first reaction had been shock, but not complete shock. In fact, as Aito spoke, the initial consternation transformed into something like 'can-do', or at least a 'could-do', as people weighed their options.

Naturally, there had been a few shouts of treachery, but even those felt more like 'going on record' than sincerity. People in the Schultz organisation learned very quickly to cover the bases – and their backsides. It was that or kiss them goodbye.

Devon had listened to the arguments in silence until the conversation inevitably turned in his direction. Almost everyone left aboard knew that Aito Nassaki was only nominally captain, but perhaps the fact that he was lobbying to abandon his very own support faction to time, added credence to his call? It was certainly a bold move. Should it fail, he would doubtless pay in a most excruciatingly imaginative manner. Perhaps he felt this was his only chance? Either way, the final decision was going to fall squarely upon Devon's shoulders, and he knew it.

"Lieutenant," Aito appealed to him directly. "The Schultzes are among the cruelest, most destructive people of our time. And now they want to build a bridge with Nazi Germany to rejuvenate their plans?" He turned to take in the whole room. "You know, if we keep letting those guys try to take over the world, one time they might just succeed. And they'll only *need* to do it once! We have the chance here and now, to make sure that the destructive future we know, never happens!

"We have just a few minutes before they return. This really is for the sake of our whole planet, not just the human race. OK, so if you don't care about that, then at least think about yourselves – imagine the lives we could make here. A whole world and no one to share it with! No one we have to fight, for our piece of it!"

He returned his attention to Devon. "Lieutenant, you have the last word."

Devon straightened. *Wow! That was an ominous phrase to dig out and dust off, for so many reasons – did he use it on purpose?*

He cleared his throat. "Things didn't work out too well for the last *Last Word*, did they? What you're asking is for us to betray the very architects of this project, without whom we wouldn't even be here."

"They've served their purpose," Aito jumped in before Devon could travel too far down that road. "It's time for new thinking and a new start. Surely you must see that?"

Still Devon was paralysed with indecision, without even really knowing why. Aito's claims made sense. He enjoyed weapons play as much as the next man, but the Schultzes really were evil, he knew that. Maybe, if they risked rolling the dice once more with the Nazis, it would indeed become a world few would wish to see – yet still he hesitated. "Devil's advocate: what if we need them? Has anyone considered that?"

"No one's doubting their vast intelligence and ingenuity, lieutenant," replied Aito. "Or even their courage, come to that. But we're hardly a ship of fools here."

Devon wondered if that were true. Just about their every act in recent months had been outrageous to the point of insanity. He raised a questioning eyebrow. "OK, second devil's advocate: can we actually succeed with this? Will the ship actually *allow* us to shut them down? Has anyone considered that? The old man was able to take back control, simply by getting his hands on a library tablet!"

Aito smiled. "I know. I permitted it."

The looks of shock on everyone's faces caused his grin to climb still higher. "I knew he would ask for information, when the timing was right for him, of course. I set it up so that I could clone his device. I have his codes now."

A gentle susurration of surprise gusted about the bridge.

"His ability to leave us dead in the water whenever he chose had to be taken away, for all our sakes." Aito took a small, theatrical bow. "Impressed? And everyone thought my brother got all the brains!"

Devon stroked his chin as he considered Captain Nassaki – was he indeed the killer of Sergeant Haig on the moon? Had he just given away the reason behind the murder, or part of it? He would have to find the answer when they had more time, but he would get that answer; he was determined. Getting to his feet, he said, "OK. Are we all in agreement? Right. Let's do it."

While there was a general round of shrugs and nods, the white-coated, balding man wrung his hands. Without waiting for his lead, his female counterpart gave an emphatic yes.

"Very well," Devon continued, with a calmness he hardly felt. "What now, Captain Nassaki?"

Aito gave a single nod to the scientists. "Shut it down."

The balding man continued to wring his hands, so the female shoved him unceremoniously out of the way. After typing a few commands, her terminal died.

"What is it?" asked Devon.

"Power has been cut to this terminal. I'll try over here." She repeated the operation, only to see that station fail too. She turned to Aito. "We may need those codes – Captain?"

Aito pulled a tablet from the sling that supported his wounded arm and linked it with an unaffected terminal. "Try this one, Doctor. It should work now."

She sat and began typing. The workstation did not lose power this time, but instead spat out an error message. She cancelled her request and keyed it all again.

"What do you have, Doctor?" asked Devon.

"The wormhole won't disconnect."

"Theories?"

"I don't know, Lieutenant. I don't think there is anything wrong with our equipment. Captain Nassaki's codes got us around the block. This is something else."

Devon and Aito exchanged a glance. "Something else?" asked Aito.

"I can't explain it – it should simply have closed down, as it was designed to do."

"Can you disconnect the wormhole drive?" asked Devon. "Cut power to the whole section, if you need to."

"Agreed," said Aito. "Do what you have to, Doctor."

She turned away from her console, ashen. "You don't understand, gentlemen. The drive *is* disconnected. Wherever the vast power required to maintain a stable wormhole is coming from, it's not this ship!"

This time Devon and Aito exchanged looks of great concern. Devon leaned over the scientist's shoulder. "Did the travellers arrive at the other end?"

"We received a short radio burst with confirmation," she replied. "After that nothing, but they *are* there. It worked. Therefore, I can only deduce that the power source is geothermal."

"Geothermal?" asked Devon, not sure if he'd heard correctly.

"Yes, we expressed concerns about opening a wormhole through the planet to Heinrich Schultz," she explained. "To little effect, I might add. The wormhole's path travels through our planet between Egypt and Germany – or where they will one day be – in a direct secant line. The distance is less than three thousand kilometres yet cuts well into the Earth's mantle, possibly even as deep as the outer core – we have not calculated exactly. It passes through temperatures of up to 3,700 degrees Celsius, at extreme pressure. Wormholes are believed to exist outside our space–time, but we don't fully understand them – or their susceptibility to external influence. For all we know, such extreme heat and power may even bleed cross-dimensionally. What I *can* say with confidence is that this energy has largely run our planet for four and a half *billion* years, and still has plenty to give. Compared with that, running our wormhole is like using a nuclear power plant to light a torch."

"OK, OK, back up," said Devon, trying to regain his bearings. "So long story short, we've sent them to Nazi headquarters, but we can't stop them coming back? How much damage could they do there?"

She shrugged. "The tide of the war was turning against the Nazis by that point. The eastern front had been a fiasco, Italy had surrendered, and the Allies were massing for a major offensive from the west. I suppose you could say they were in a weakened state – some might say hopeless, but they were still dangerous. Hitler was determined to take as much of the rest of the world with him as possible, destroying Germany in the process."

"I'm no historian, so what would you say was their biggest problem at that point?" he pressed.

"Largely one of supply and resources. The allies were simply outstripping Hitler's ability to make the weapons, tanks, aircraft and matériel his forces needed, many times over. He also had a penchant for replacing his most capable officers whenever they tried to shorten supply lines or regroup."

"OK," Devon answered slowly. "So, if someone – say, of obvious aristocratic dignity and authority – came up with a plan to turn the tide, offered them vastly superior technology and a world of near infinite natural resource, how might that change things for them?"

The whitecoat opened her mouth but failed to utter any sound, so Devon turned to Aito, who was shaking his head as if lost in a personal nightmare. He locked gazes with Devon. "I don't know what to do," he murmured. "I don't know what to do!"

Scottish Borders AD1558

The armoured personnel carrier straddled a narrow earth bridge that crossed a pair of defensive ditches around the chapel site. "This guy likes his privacy," muttered O'Brien.

"Actually, these ditches may have belonged to an older manor," replied Baines. "There are other suggestive earthworks and foundations just west of here."

"You've done your homework, ma'am."

"Aye," interjected Maxwell. "Makes me wonder what else ye ken."

"About what?" asked Baines.

"Me, for a start."

Baines smiled. "That's what I like about you, David."

"Oh, aye?"

"Yeah. Others may think you incredibly self-centred, but you don't let that bother you."

He laughed raucously; even Sir Nicholas cracked a grudging smile for the first time, but they were all shaken into silence as the APC crashed through metre-high stone walls, enclosing the De Soulis family chapel and graveyard. Baines winced, remembering Douglas' warning. He was still the senior captain, but she knew he would never expect her to put the safety of a building above that of a life – any life – and as they were here to rescue a girl who would one day become one of England's greatest monarchs... well, she would do what she could.

"I've got them on infrared, Captain," O'Brien reported. "Two people inside. If it's De Soulis, he has someone with him."

"Probably a bodyguard," Baines thought aloud. "The man has enemies, I hear."

"If I use the fifty-cals, I can easily shred the door, Captain," offered Gleeson. "But according to our scans, one of them is standing nearby. If he steps the wrong way, he'll be turned into a jam jigsaw puzzle."

"We could try talking him out, instead of *taking* him out," Baines postulated.

"That might be a chapel, but those are arrow slits along the side walls, Captain," stated The Sarge. "You'd better be *very* convincing."

"Hmm, point," agreed Baines.

"No worries, mate." Gleeson got out of his seat, heading to the rear of the vehicle. "I didn't say I *couldn't* get you in there. It's just that the fifties will keep on chewing, right through the opposite wall!"

He opened a locker to remove a hand-held rocket launcher. "This beauty, on the other hand, loaded with a door-buster, should just take the doors – it'll probably stun them too. Ya see? It's all good, mate!"

Baines had misgivings, but followed him out of the rear hatch. Gleeson took a quick look around the corner of the vehicle and jumped back as an arrow flew past his ear. "Looks like The Sarge was right as usual, Cap."

"I've learned to trust him about such things," she agreed.

Gleeson grinned. "Stay back!" He rolled across the ground to come up in a crouch behind a gravestone. A second arrow hit the stone. *This guy is good*, he thought. Giving the archer no time to reload, he leaned out from his cover and fired.

The lock evaporated. So did the doors and most of the roof.

"What the hell was *that?*" screamed Baines.

Gleeson had the grace to look guilty.

"You were only supposed to blow the—"

"Don't say it!" He held up a finger. "This was your idea, Captain."

Baines stuttered to a halt, a hand over her mouth as she gazed, wide-eyed at the destruction. "What happened?" she managed weakly.

Gleeson tugged at his ear with embarrassment. "I thought I'd loaded a door-buster."

"So what was that...?"

"Erm, a tank-buster, I think. Look, maybe we could...?"

Baines never heard the rest of his plan to save the building, for at that moment the entire western end of the roof collapsed, sending a secondary eruption of sparks and flame soaring skyward.

She held her head in her hands. "James is going to kill me. And we needed De Soulis alive, to trade him for Elizabeth! How are we going to get them to surrender her now?"

Gleeson slapped the barrel of the launcher into the palm of his hand. "I've got a box of these. OK, I packed the *wrong* box, but you can never have too much firepower, Captain."

"You *think?*" she snapped, pointing at the burning, historic building.

She would have berated him further, but the sounds of breaking glass drew their attention back to the chapel. Set within the eastern gable – Baines assumed, behind the altar – there were three beautifully formed, yet unadorned, lancet windows. The breaking glass was the sound of two men diving through them. They were both on fire.

Gleeson immediately dropped the launcher to pull an assault rifle from around his shoulders, and into the ready position.

The first man ran screaming towards them, completely engulfed in flames.

"Oh, my God!" cried Baines. "I'll get the med-kit."

Gleeson shook his head. "Don't worry, Captain. I've got the pain relief he needs, right here." He clicked his weapon onto single shot and fired, hitting the man between the eyes. He fell, silent.

"Commander!"

"Captain, I know a bit about explosion burns. To do anything else would have only been cruel. I'm sorry, but there it is."

They both turned to see the other man unclasp his burning robe and throw it to the ground, where it continued to blaze. He drew a narrow-bladed sword with an elegant handguard. The blade was fully four feet long, matching the stature of its wielder.

"Sir Willam de Soulis?" Baines called.

"Who are ye?" he rasped, furiously.

"This is the illustrious Captain Baines." The words seemed unnatural, almost as if they came from inside their own heads.

"Sarge! Meritus! Get everybody out here," shouted Gleeson, looking around urgently, unable to locate the source of the voice.

Everyone piled out of the APC immediately, weapons at the ready, leaving just O'Brien at the controls with a gunner.

Meritus stood next to Baines, his expression alarmed and questioning.

"Oh, Turkish delight!" grumbled The Sarge, snapping his rifle to.

Following his gaze, Baines watched a man wearing black 22nd century military fatigues step from the flames of the burning church. "Thank you. I find it much easier to get inside those places when they're on fire." His smile was too wide, like human skin stretched over a beartrap.

"Who are you?" Baines asked, tremulously.

"Lieutenant Rotmütze," Meritus breathed in disbelief.

"Captain Tobias Meritus, how nice to see you again. By the way, I go by Robin Redcap these days."

"But how... I mean you were—"

"Killed?" Redcap interrupted Meritus, clearly enjoying the shock on the face of his former commanding officer.

"What's he talking about, Tobias?" demanded Baines.

Meritus was clearly speechless, so Redcap answered for him, "My dear Captain Baines – do you mind if I call you Jill? We're on such intimate terms, after all."

Baines was shaking her head. "I have no idea who you are. We've never met."

"Of course, forgive me, Jill. I've looked in on you so many times over the last few months that I feel like we're old friends – *more* than friends."

Baines stared, agog. "I don't know you," was all she could manage. The bright firelight showed Meritus, shaking his head at the periphery of her vision, muttering something about this being impossible.

With everyone's attention on Redcap and Baines, De Soulis saw his chance and leapt over the low wall of the enclosure. Scrambling up and down the earthworks, he ran for the castle.

The Sarge saw him go. "Prentice, take two and secure that man!"

Redcap glanced uninterestedly to the east, as the soldiers followed De Soulis. Returning his attention to Baines, he pointed to Beck's gift, hidden beneath her shirt and flak jacket. "I feel you still wear that carved stone, Jill. It worked, you know. I could never quite get *inside*. That's all changed now, naturally – or should I say *super*naturally? This place and time has made me more powerful than I could have imagined. Such fear, such suffering."

Redcap closed his eyes, clearly in rapture. Despite leaving the fire behind, he seemed to generate a heat haze around himself, pulsating from within. He chuckled lightly. "You know, I once read a book about 'wellness and empowerment'. I thought it was a load of self-indulgent paff at the time, but now..." he sighed. "You still don't know who I am, do you, Jill? You wound me, but then I suppose my face was obscured to you at the time."

"What the hell are you talking about?" Baines was completely lost.

"Hell?" he chuckled again. "No. Never been there. When I drew your satellite into my ship from the frigid cold of space, the atmosphere froze immediately, icing over the camera lens. You may remember me giving you a blurry smile and a little wave? Of course, that was when you murdered me in cold blood."

Baines' jaw dropped. "No," she breathed, collapsing to her knees as sudden weight pressed her down. With the last of her strength, she shouted, "*No!*"

"Open fire!" bellowed Gleeson.

Bullets and stun bolts flew at Redcap, swiftly joined by the concussive thud of heavy machine guns, from their transport.

Amidst fire and chaos, they heard Redcap's laughter, but no one saw him leave. He was just *gone*.

Slowly, the echoes of gunfire died away down the valley, replaced once more by the moaning wind and crackle of burning timbers.

They grouped in a ring around Baines. Without hesitation, nor even a word, The Sarge ran to their transport for its defibrillator kit. Meritus knelt to check with two fingers on her jugular. He swallowed. Looking up at them, he shook his head.

"*No!*" Gleeson cried, a shout strangulated by grief. Reaching into his jacket for his comm, he screamed above the wind, "I need Doc Flannigan at these coordinates with full medical assistance gear – stat! *What?* I don't care how you do it, and I don't care who bladdy sees it! Just tell Douglas to find anything that flies and get Flannigan here, NOW!"

He threw the radio down in the snow and fell to his knees, cradling Captain Jill Baines' head in his lap. "Jill! *Jill!* Don't do this to me – don't you bladdy do this to me!"

Epilogue

It felt as though her skin were being stretched, just for an instant; all other sensory perception was lost. Heidi stepped out into absolute darkness. Her only clue as to what had just happened was a subdermal tingling sensation, already fading. The wormhole behind her bent light, but cast none of its own, nor did it give away any sign of the hot Cretaceous sun on the other side. Waving her arms carefully, she felt around. Her left hand tapped against a hard surface. Using both hands she found edges... a packing crate?

"Dr Schultz?" queried a male voice behind her.

"Here. I'm trying to find a light sw—" Before she finished the sentence, brilliant white light flashed to life all on its own, illuminating every corner of what was suddenly, very obviously, a storage room.

She frowned in confusion as the others joined her. "*Großvater?*"

Heinrich also took in their surroundings. "Those lights are rather good for 1943, wouldn't you say?"

"You think our scientists were in error?"

"Hard to say from a storage cupboard, *Enkelin*. I suggest we move out, take a look around."

She nodded and, moving to the door, tried the handle. "Locked."

"You don't say?" her grandfather drawled.

Heidi turned back to the door, rolling her eyes, and quickly got to work on the lock. It was a simple mechanism. She could only assume that security was less of a concern this deep in the heart of the building. What was more of a concern, for them at least, was that the lock was of a fairly modern design – at a guess, middle 21st century.

With a sinking feeling, she opened the door a crack, and immediately closed it again.

A flash of concern crossed Heinrich's face. "*Enkelin?*"

"It looks like we have a full house out there. I did not expect a museum to be open on a Sunday in 1943. I also believed this building would be closed to the public for the duration!"

Heinrich stroked his chin thoughtfully. "As did I. How are the people dressed?"

"Not military. We will stand out. Very well," she continued, taking charge once more. "You and you, guard the wormhole. Do not leave this station. Should you be discovered by anyone, do not let them leave. Most certainly do not let them enter the portal.

"Everyone else, leave most of your equipment here. Strip down to basic fatigues and bring only weapons you can conceal."

Jansen, another soldier and even Heinrich himself followed her instructions without comment.

"Ready?" she asked a few moments later. "Right, we go."

They strode from the storage room like they owned the place, drawing few if any stares. Having travelled less than twenty metres, Heidi pulled up short.

"What is it?" Jansen whispered, then he saw them. Mounted across the wall were thirteen huge vertebrae, seven of which protruded long spines of a flattish profile. Much cracked and broken by the elements and millions of years of geological movement, the largest of the spines was still almost as tall as a man.

Heidi pulled out her comm and ran their isotope tracking software. It beeped. "Remarkable. Still at eighty-eight percent strength after ninety-nine million years."

"It *is* one of ours, then?" asked Jansen, marvelling, in spite of himself.

She smiled, shaking her head ruefully. "We did it. We actually did it! Do you see that unusual bone growth, to the base of the largest spine?"

He leaned forward slightly, the better to see, and nodded.

"That looks like a trauma injury to the vertebrae. It is small and almost completely round."

He looked sharply at her. "You don't think...?"

"Our friend from the other day?" She raised an eyebrow, appreciatively. "The one who took Winter's head off? It is possible." She looked down to her comm, checking the results one last time.

"Excuse me, miss. No comms or cameras are allowed in the museum."

The four Nazis turned to glare at the unarmed security guard, who quailed. "Rules, miss," he mumbled.

Heinrich drew himself up to his considerable height and pierced the little man with a grey stare as merciless as the North Sea. "Go away," he drawled in his most aristocratic German.

The man raised a hand instinctually to the peak of his cap and moved along.

"This cannot be 1943," Jansen stated, flatly.

"I disagree," replied Heinrich. "Look over there. Unless this building is stuck in some sort of time warp, this is most certainly the seventh of November 1943."

They all followed his gaze to pick out a large electronic display, scrolling advertisements for coming events throughout 1944.

"We must hurry," Heidi drew them back to their mission. "We must see what we can learn outside. Quickly now."

They left the museum through the main entrance and stepped out into the street.

"This doesn't look anything like what I was expecting," noted Heinrich.

Heidi was forced to agree. "Come, Nazi headquarters used to be just five hundred metres from here. Perhaps it has not been destroyed after all."

"I'm not so sure, *Enkelin*."

"We must be sure."

"We no longer have the time!"

She turned on him. "Go back then, if you are afraid! I will stay!"

"You would risk being stuck here?" Heinrich was genuinely astonished.

"Stuck *here?*" she retorted, incredulous. "Look around you."

"I do not see how this furthers our plans. Clearly Douglas' rabble have damaged our own timeline through some ridiculous act of incompetence. This world looks a hundred years ahead of where it should be and there are far too few people about for a city centre. We must rethink. Perhaps try another, earlier time."

"*Nein, Großvater*. It is nothing short of a miracle that we made it this far. We must see what we can do with what we have."

"And if you fail and are stuck here, *Enkelin?* What then?"

She smiled, a cold, heartless smile. "Then we begin again."

He returned her smile. "In that case, I wish you good fortune. We will keep the door open as long as we can for you."

She nodded, clicking her heels in salute, and they parted.

Jansen insisted on staying with her, so she led him at a fast pace towards *Brienner Straße* and the Brown House, otherwise known as Nazi Headquarters.

They arrived quickly. Although much of the surrounding architecture and technology was of a style familiar to them – perhaps sixty years old in their own timeline – there were no crowds, no queues, no traffic jams, nor hold-ups of any kind. The air was clean and fresh – perhaps not quite as exhilarating as the Cretaceous, where oxygen levels were a little higher than in modern times, but it was a far cry from the world they had grown up in.

The Brown House was indeed still standing, in all its neo-classical glory. In fact, there was no sign of war damage anywhere in the city, as far as they could tell. However, rather than large flags outside bearing the *swastika*, one carried the German national flag, or *Bundesflagge*, while a second bore the name Palais Barlow.

Heidi sat heavily on a bench.

"What do you want to do now?" Jansen asked gently, equal parts sympathy and fear of her reaction.

"We have but one place left to try," she answered quietly. "It is about two kilometres from here, so our return will be impossible."

"I understand, Doctor."

"Very well. We head east, across the River Isar to *Prinzregentenplatz* 16."

"*His* apartment?"

"Indeed."

Heidi did not speak again until they arrived, a little over twenty minutes later.

"There are no signs of war or the Nazi party anywhere, Doctor. What do you expect to find here?"

"I have no idea." She stepped up to the main entrance, noting the building's general state of disrepair. The lock was already broken, so she strode straight in, Jansen right behind her. They made their way up to the second floor[15] and waited a moment outside the apartment, listening at the door.

"I hear nothing," said Jansen.

"Nor I." Without waiting, she kicked the door, crashing the feeble lock open with ease. Drawing her sidearm, she ran into the apartment's living area.

It was well-lit with natural daylight from the bay window. The furniture was old and cheap. There was a half-eaten salad wilting on the side and a painter's easel in the bay itself. Standing next to the easel, clearly shocked by the guns waved in his direction, stood a male

---

[15] Third floor by American convention.

fifty-something. His hair was still mostly dark, worn in a severe cut with a toothbrush moustache.

Heidi gaped. After a pause, she asked, "*Herr* Hitler?"

The man dropped his brush, daubing red paint onto a fading rug as he slowly raised his hands.

"Are you Adolf Hitler?" she demanded more forcefully, in German.

In a deep, rich voice he replied, "Is this about the rent?"

Author's notes:

To everyone working in the field of natural history, dinosaur research, historical research and archaeology, I once again send a massive thank you for your constant inspiration. As always, a few liberties have been taken...

There were several spinosaurids around during the Cretaceous, *Spinosaurus aegyptiacus* being, of course, the most well-known thanks to a very popular film franchise! (To everyone with any knowledge of Tyrannosaurs, I still feel your pain!) In Patagonia, we also met *Oxalaia quilombensis* and *Irritator challengeri*. Some palaeontologists have postulated that *Oxalaia* may actually have been the same species as *Spinosaurus*, despite the thousands of miles and the beginnings of the Atlantic Ocean between them. Others state differences in the skull and snout – even in the density of the bones and probable musculature. Some believe Oxalaia was probably bipedal, like the 'old' *Spinosaurus* from the JPIII film. These animals certainly seem to be the subject of intense debate currently. This story describes them as separate species because they are incredibly exciting creatures to write (or wrong) about. With regards to the true identities and appearances of these wonderful animals – I'm not touching that with a ten-foot pole! Instead, I chicken-heartedly hide under the comfort blanket of 'fiction' – that way I can tell naysayers to get a life, while secretly agreeing with them! On our trip to Cretaceous Britain, we also meet *Sigilmassasaurus brevicollis*, another spinosaurid. Smaller than *Spinosaurus*, this was still a very large predator – as Aito Nassaki had a hand in finding out... (I can hear everyone groaning at that one, sorry). Although discovered in North Africa, I theorise that these creatures 'island-hopped' due to their aquatic nature, eventually finding themselves on the 'tropical' landmass that would one day be Britain (it seems some things *do* change).

Also in Britain, our characters met *Ornithocheirus simus*, a vast flying reptile (pterosaur) further described in my notes in the back of ALLEGIANCE, and discovered in Britain (and possibly Morocco). I refer to the animals that break into Crater Lake Farm to steal Coleman's crops as ankylosaurids. For anyone wishing to find a visual reference, I see them as descendants of *Polacanthus foxii* – a creature living about thirty million years earlier, in that part of the world. Their backs were covered with armoured scales with two rows of horns also running along much of the back and tail. *Polacanthus*, in ancient Greek, means 'many thorns' or 'many prickles', which does paint a picture somewhat. Certain ankylosaurs resembled a cross between a battle tank and a hedgehog, with size favouring the tank. It's easy to imagine them as 'unfazed' by a puny attempt to send them packing with a shovel!

Carcharodontosaurus saharicus gave its name to the family 'Carcharodontosauridae' which also includes South America's mighty *Giganotosaurus carolinii* and *Mapusaurus roseae*. *Carcharodontosaurus* was another *Tyrannosaurus rex* sized predator from North Africa, and was also discovered by Ernst Stromer during his time in Egypt, along with the famous *Spinosaurus aegyptiacus* and another large theropod predator named *Bahariasaurus ingens*. The Allied bombing of the Old Academy, Munich, during spring 1944, destroyed Stromer's finds, along with the type specimen for *Bahariasaurus*. Since then, arguments have been made for its inclusion within the Carcharodontosauridae, Tyrannosauroidea, Ceratosauridae and Megaraptora families! We await more research and more lucky finds to get to the heart of this – maybe someone will put forward an argument for it being a fish? In the meantime, I think that a 12m long, fast, comparatively lightweight killer (approx. 4 tons) could make a nice but deadly addition to this series in the future.

Rugops primus, like South America's *Ekrixinatosaurus*, was an Abelisaurid and a relative of the better known, but much later, *Carnotaurus sastrei*. Thought to be a North African scavenger, *Rugops* lived around the same time as the giant Carcharodontosauridae named above. This chap was probably around 4-6m in length and 500-750kg in weight with a comparatively weak jaw. As if it didn't have enough problems in a land of truly huge and vastly more powerful predators, its vestigial arms would also have been fairly useless, AND its name means 'wrinkle face' – poor sod! However, like its cousin, *Ekrixinatosaurus*, *Rugops* was small enough to follow you through the trees – so you probably wouldn't call him that to his wrinkled face!

I receive quite a few comments from readers who love the way the characters speak with their own accents (and some hate mail on the subject, as well!) Personally, I believe it brings them off the page a little, while often providing some in-built humour, too. However, with the 16th century characters, I've taken a few liberties (once again). Although communication would not have been impossible, anyone who has ever read Shakespeare knows that the dialect can, at times, be very difficult to understand, so much has the English language changed. To that end, I've gone for a 'feel' of antiquity with the English and Scots dialects, trying where possible to remain true to the period but hopefully without making the characters' words undecipherable – I apologise to the purists and once again hide under my comfort blanket of fiction. Here – have a smiley face :o)

As far as I know, Elizabeth Tudor (soon to be Elizabeth I) was not in Northumberland during 1558. Most likely she was still ensconced within Hatfield House in Hertfordshire. However, Mary was often advised to have her half-sister removed from the succession (and the world). Elizabeth's life hung by a thread on several occasions, especially during her youth, when her continued existence was often at the whim of another. Choosing between family or faith would probably be easy for most of us now, but for Mary it must have been the sorest of trials. She had little affection for her sister, as Elizabeth's mother, Anne Boleyn, had supplanted her own mother, Catherine of Aragon, leading to her downfall. Worse, Elizabeth was a healthy, robust, soberly dressed protestant (in her youth) – at a glance, everything the dressy, Catholic queen was not. However, one wonders whether Mary showed a side to her character at odds with her popular nickname 'Bloody Mary', by allowing her half-sister to live against her own interests. Especially at a time when state-sanctioned murder was not uncommon (though it was often known by other names, so as to pass muster according to the standards of Tudor political correctness). Her dilemma over bolstering the Catholic cause for the sake of England and her personal beliefs, or the sparing of her Protestant sister, must have been – to use an appropriate idiom – a heavy cross to bear. This fictional tale sees events altered by the arrival of the *New World*. However, I have tried to ingratiate my story within a semi-realistic framework of events from the period.

Historically, there was more than one Lord de Soulis. Sir William de Soulis (or Soules), the last, was actually Lord of Hermitage Castle in the Scottish Borders between 1318 and 1320. This was during the reign of Robert the Bruce and more than two centuries before the setting for this book. Regardless, I chose to include him because he was an extraordinary, ready-made 'bad guy'. Allegedly, he entered into a deal with Edward II of England to get rid of the Scottish King – he was certainly arrested for treason. However, the *legend* of Sir William de Soulis is probably more interesting than the reality. Either way, he seems to have been an extremely unpleasant fellow, even by medieval standards. Legend has it that William de Soulis was physically a large, powerful man, with prominent canine teeth and a predilection for extreme cruelty. He was almost universally loathed, or so the story goes, and talking of stories, many circulated that he was also a practitioner of the dark arts. His proclivity for taking young children from the countryside around Hermitage Castle and using them in evil rituals seems most unpleasant! Apparently, De Soulis would summon his familiar, one 'Robin Redcap', during his rituals. According to British folklore, a redcap is a type of evil goblin, often tied to ruined castles in the borderlands. These chaps are known for the killing of travellers and local residents alike, so they can refresh the bloodstains on their hats – as the name Redcap suggests. The legend has it that if the bloodstains dry, the redcap dies. Redcaps were reputedly very quick and powerful. This series will always have dinosaurs at its heart, but even from inception, I always wanted to bring the story forward to include the 16th century borderlands and elements of the Hermitage Castle 'horror story'. It seemed natural to write a dark spirit with a powerful attraction towards such a reputation – like the one created when Baines blew up a satellite in a Nazi pilot's face – especially with a creature like De Soulis meddling with things he shouldn't and opening the door. Robin Rotmütze (redcap in German) tied in nicely with the legend of De Soulis and Hermitage Castle, and was too good to miss. Once summoned by De Soulis, the Robin Redcap of legend inspired terror in the lands around Hermitage, committing many atrocities. To escape a redcap, one must quote a passage from the Bible at it, whereupon it loses a tooth. (I wonder if Redcap regains his power if he remembers to put it under his pillow?) Of course, it's easy to mock superstition from the street-lit modern century, but William de Soulis seems to have been as dark as the thing he allegedly conjured. The story has it that in AD1320 he attempted to abduct a young woman belonging to the Armstrong clan. Her father tried to prevent it and De Soulis killed him where he stood. Alexander

Armstrong, Laird of Mangerton, calmed the lynch mob poised to hang De Soulis, advising him to leave while he still could, but leave the girl behind. Alexander Armstrong was the social inferior, and being saved by such a personage clearly hurt De Soulis' pride. Rather than show gratitude, he began to hate Armstrong, eventually inviting him to a feast at Hermitage Castle. Upon Armstrong's arrival, De Soulis stabbed him in the back. As stated, De Soulis really died in the dungeons of Dumbarton Castle, later in AD1320, and after accusations of treason. However, his legend seems to have become entwined with the fate of his ancestor, Sir Ranulf de Soulis, more than a century earlier. I won't give away details of Sir William's future here, as it will be revealed in book 5, REMAINS. I will simply end by saying that the sketchy evidence regarding the 12th and 13th century family seems to sit, at least partially, where history meets legend. However, depraved cruelty, treason and black magic are all recorded. De Soulis did not live in the Tudor age, but he did exist, and his story is so incredible that I just couldn't resist working him into a timeline, so innocently and apologetically screwed up by James Douglas et al.

The Reiver families ruled the Scottish Borders at that time, engaging in cattle rustling, murder and slaving. They were legendarily tough, as were their ponies. The Maxwells really did feud with the Johnstones throughout the period. More of this in book 5, but their stories became the stuff of song, literature, and of course, legend. The name of Natalie Pearson's dog 'Reiver' was inspired by the Reivers, entwined with the Scottish Borders themselves – the original home of the border collie.

Moving forward through our 'real' history, Nazi Headquarters, 'The Brown House' (so named because of the colour of their early uniforms) in Munich, was destroyed by Allied bombing in October of 1943. The museum housing Ernst Stromer's dinosaur fossils discovered in Egypt between 1911-14, 'The Old Academy', was also bombed by the Allies in April of 1944, and was indeed just a short walk from The Brown House.

Hitler really did live for a time at *Prinzregentenplatz* 16. Initially having the rent paid by his publisher, this was still a big step up from the much poorer circumstances he endured during the 1920s. His dream as a youth was to study fine art but he was rejected by the Academy of Fine Arts, Venice, twice. However, he did eke out a meagre living between selling watercolours and general labouring. By 1939 he was in a position to buy *Prinzregentenplatz* 16 outright. However, looking at his early life, it's a little difficult to see the monster he became – the man who killed, or caused the deaths of, almost fifty million people. The *New World*'s landing in the 16th century has clearly created some very worrying ripples in the timeline from the Schultzes', shall we say, unique perspective. The man Heidi moved mountains to track through time, is a struggling artist and vegetarian, a nobody. Can history be forced to repeat itself? Or can she find a way to make things even worse?

I hope you enjoyed this episode of the New World Series, and once again, thank you so very much for reading. Take care, all,

Stephen.

Oh, and by the way "Alright or wha'?" means hello in Wales. Although technically more commonly used in South Wales, rather than Gwynedd in the north, a hundred years from now I postulate there will be less of a linguistic divide. In truth, I just love Jones' (and Gleeson's) penchant for saying irreverent things that are wildly out of context. Within a world of dinosaurs and science/historical fiction (or 'sci-hi-fi' – I'll have to remember that one!) this actually seems to make sense to me.

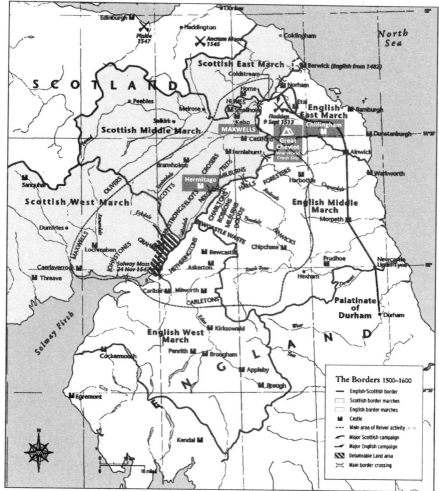

✳ ✳ Including some prominent Reiver family names

The Borders 1500–1600

——	English-Scottish border
▭	Scottish border marches
▭	English border marches
🏰	Castle
- - -	Main area of Reiver activity ✳ ✳
⤴	Major Scottish campaign
⤴	Major English campaign
▨	Debateable Land area
⤬	Main border crossing

Coming soon:

REMAINS

THE NEW WORLD SERIES | BOOK FIVE

Stephen Llewelyn

BOOK 1
DINOSAUR

BOOK 2
REVENGE

BOOK 3
ALLEGIANCE

BOOK 4
REROUTE

BOOK 5
REMAINS

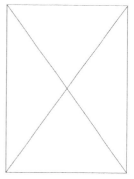

BOOK 6
CURSED

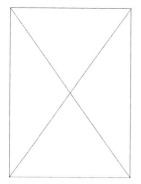

BOOK 7
COLLISION

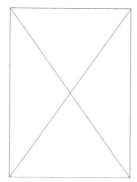

NEWFOUNDLAND

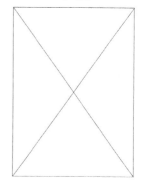

REBIRTH

The
**New
World
Series**

The New World Series

DINOSAUR
audio performed by

CHRIS BARRIE
(Red Dwarf, Tomb Raider)

Printed in Great Britain
by Amazon